He ran a hand through the rough curls at the back of his head. "I have to confess something." His conscience had been tugging at him this whole time. "Only a couple of those library books are mine. Mostly they're my neighbor's. He's house-bound, so I pick up books for him."

Amusement lit up her little heart-shaped face. "Your confession is that you don't read big piles of books, and that you go to the library for your neighbor? I'm crushed. I was thinking there was a secret genius hidden inside that ripped body."

"Maybe I was trying to impress you. We've been dancing around each other all season. Don't you want to see if there's anything to this chemistry?"

Her eyes widened. "*Here?* Are you trying to add public indecency to all those fines?"

"Just a kiss. One kiss. There's nothing indecent about a kiss."

She considered that for a long moment, while a tantalizing tension rose between them. Finally she seemed to make up her mind. She took a step forward, brushing against him.

"Nothing indecent, Solo? I've got news for you."

"What's that?"

"There is if you do it right." And she lifted her mouth to his.

By Jennifer Bernard

Caught by You

A LOVE BETWEEN THE BASES NOVEL

JENNIFER BERNARD

AVONBOOKS

An Imprint of HarperCollinsPublishers

This is a work of fiction. Names, characters, places, and incidents are products of the author's imagination or are used fictitiously and are not to be construed as real. Any resemblance to actual events, locales, organizations, or persons, living or dead, is entirely coincidental.

AVON BOOKS
An Imprint of HarperCollins*Publishers*
195 Broadway
New York, New York 10007

First Avon Books mass market printing: January 2016

Avon Trademark Reg. U.S. Pat. Off. and in Other Countries, Marca Registrada, Hecho en U.S.A.
Avon, Avon Books, and the Avon logo are trademarks of HarperCollins Publishers.
HarperCollins® is a registered trademark of HarperCollins Publishers.

Printed in the U.S.A.

10 9 8 7 6 5 4 3 2 1

Special thanks to Sierra Dean,
Kristina Birch, LizBeth Selvig, my agent
Alexandra Machinist, and the Avon team,
especially Tessa Woodward and
Elle Keck. You're all All-Stars in my book.

This book is dedicated to my sister
Yael, who inspires me in so many
ways, and to my parents, who opened
their minds when it mattered.

Caught by You

Chapter 1

IF DONNA MACINTYRE made a list of people she'd never expect to see at the Kilby Community Library, Mike Solo would be right at the top. He was the popular catcher for the Kilby Catfish, after all, with a grin promising every kind of fun, and the sort of physique built from squatting behind the plate, not carrying a pile of heavy-looking hardback books to the checkout desk.

"Need a hand, Solo?" She slid next to him, propping one hip against the desk. "In case, you know, you're wondering what all these big, thick things are good for." She flicked one of the books; it looked like a serious biography.

Mike, as always, didn't miss a beat. With a flash of his devil-green eyes, he murmured, "I know exactly what big, thick things are good for, but you can demonstrate if you want."

Frank the librarian, nearly dwarfed by Mike's tower of books, choked a little.

Mike raised an eyebrow at Donna. "Look at that, you've gone and upset the librarian, Red. That's bad etiquette."

"I didn't—you—" *He'd* gone right into the gutter, not her. She wanted to protest, but the pink tinge on the librarian's face made her shift gears. "Sorry, Frank. I'll behave." She leaned across the desk. "But you do realize that one of the notorious Kilby Catfish is in our humble library. I just hope the patrons are safe. We all know how crazy those ballplayers can be."

"Now that's just prejudice, plain and simple," Mike announced, looking injured. "I'm a law-abiding citizen here to settle up before I leave town. Frank knows I would never cause any trouble. Unless trouble comes looking," he added, sweeping Donna with a glance that made her skin warm. "I have a few more of these, man. Be right back."

"Thanks, Mike. I'll get started." The librarian reached for the top of the stack. Donna stared, mouth dropping open a bit. Apparently Mike was just as well-known to the staff of the library as to the bartenders at the Roadhouse. Well, well, well.

"Donna, you'd better come with me," Mike added, putting out his hand. "I'm not sure I trust you alone with all those big, thick things."

"Ha . . . ha." The rest of her no-doubt-brilliant comeback evaporated as his big hand enveloped hers in callused strength and heat. She and Mike Solo had been flirting with each other all season, ever since she'd first met him at the Roadhouse. But it had never gone further than that, for various reasons. Her complicated life, for one thing. His Vow of Celibacy, for another. Everyone knew that Solo took a Vow of Celibacy at the start of the season and never broke it.

Hoping her way with words would come back soon, she followed him out of the library into the hot parking lot. It was just so . . . *strange* to see him here, in real life, instead of out on the ball field or partying with the other Catfish. Like one of those "Look, celebrities are just like you" magazine spreads showing movie stars with cups of Starbucks. It made her wonder what else she didn't know about Mike Solo.

He opened the door of a silver Land Rover and reached in for more books, giving her a chance to watch the flexing muscles of his back and a truly spectacular rear end. She averted her eyes before he caught her, fixing her gaze instead on the books he dropped into her arms. On the cover of the top book, the face of Steve Jobs stared back at her. "Do you really read all these books?"

"We have a lot of road trips and I like to keep my brain cells active. I'm a catcher, you know." He extracted himself from the car, burdened with another stack of books.

"So?"

"So, catchers have to be smart. We have to know the game better than just about anyone. Strategy, patterns, human behavior. I have to know what someone's going to do before they even do it. Like you, right now." With a twist of his hip, he closed the door of the Land Rover. It was unfairly sexy, how he did that.

"Me, right now, what?"

"From what I know of Donna MacIntyre, you're going to make a joke. That's your go-to, make a joke. Come on. Tease me, baby. Do that thing you do so well."

She clamped her mouth shut, not wanting to prove him right, though of course he was. Ever since she was little, she'd coped with all the crap in her life by laughing about it. What else could you do?

Lifting her head high, she marched toward the library. Mike caught up with her instantly. "Did I forget to mention I like it?" He leaned down close, so she felt his warm breath on her ear. Shivers raced down her spine. "Don't hide your light for me. Joke away. Bring it on."

"Maybe I'm not in a joking mood. This is a library, after all."

"I keep forgetting that, maybe because I usually see you in a party atmosphere. What brings a wild and crazy girl like you here?"

For a reckless moment, she wanted to tell Mike the truth. The whole story, in revealing detail. But she hadn't even told Sadie, her best friend. Which was all kinds of wrong and had to change, right away. But for now . . .

"Picking out books for the Shark. He's the boy I nanny for."

"Love the nickname."

"Thanks, Priest. I have a knack for nicknames."

"*That's* mine?" The confounded look on his face made her laugh. It was fun getting under Mike's skin.

"Because of the Vow of Celibacy, you know. But don't worry, that's not your only nickname." She winked.

"I shouldn't ask. I really shouldn't. What else?" He shifted his pile of books to one arm and held the door open for her.

She ducked under his arm. "Hottie McCatcher," she told him demurely. "But don't let it go to your head."

"I've got news for you, Red," he whispered, as Frank the librarian put a finger to his lips, urging them to be quiet. "Season's over. The Vow of Celibacy has expired."

Donna's entire body, including her suddenly dry mouth, reacted to that piece of information. With a strangled squeak, she hurried toward the desk.

Mike followed Donna, drinking in the sight of her denim short-shorts and tight T-shirt, which he'd already scoped out as advertising a local zydeco band. Her body curved to a deep indentation at the waist. For about the millionth time, he wondered how it would feel between his hands. Sexy, maddening Donna, with her copper-bright hair and changeable hazel eyes. He knew her face was pretty—heart-shaped and stubborn-chinned, with a damn dimple to boot. But to him it went beyond that. He always found himself caught up in the jokes she cracked, her cheeky attitude, her . . . daring.

After all, the last time he saw her, she'd been standing up for her friend Sadie against the entire Wade clan of bullies. That took guts, and he respected the hell out of her for it.

At the desk, they both unloaded their piles of books. Mike pulled out his wallet and extracted two hundred-dollar bills.

Apparently stunned, Frank dropped one of the overdue books—an account of World War I fighter pilots—on the floor. "Oh, I'm sure it won't be that much." The librarian shook his head nervously. "We're only up to five dollars so far."

"Consider it a donation, then. A little something

extra for keeping all these books out of circulation. Sometimes the season gets away from me."

Donna was looking at him strangely. "You do this a lot?"

"Check out books and forget to return them? Been known to happen. Road trips. Injuries. Team drama." He shrugged. "I try to make up for it. Are we good, Frank?"

"Good, good. Very good."

"Excellent. Maybe I'll see you next season. Hopefully not, of course. Nothing personal." He winked at the librarian, which seemed to unnerve him, as he just kept nodding in response.

He turned to Donna, who had her hands in the back pockets of her shorts. Lord, she was sexy. And fun. The most fun he'd had with a girl in . . . well, definitely since Angela, and maybe ever. And they'd never even kissed.

Yet.

With a lightning-quick calculation—the way he figured things behind the plate—he did the math.

1. The vow was over.
2. Donna was giving him that sassy look.
3. She was wearing that T-shirt that hugged her gorgeous curves.
4. Tomorrow he'd be gone.

"C'mere a second." He took her hand again and pulled her toward the tall, secluded stacks where the biographies were shelved. He'd never seen anyone in this section, and anyway, there were only two other people in the library, including Frank.

"What are you doing?" she hissed. But she followed him willingly. Maybe she'd had the same thought. It took two to create this kind of chemistry, after all.

When they'd reached the deepest part of the stacks, where dust floated in the quiet sunbeams, he stopped, then turned to face her. The sun lit her hair into a fiery cloud. "I'm going back to Chicago tomorrow. But before I go, I'd like to do something."

"Return your library books. I can see that. You probably have some parking fines to pay too. Disorderly conduct, maybe?"

He ran a hand through the rough curls at the back of his head. "I have to confess something." His Catholic-boy conscience had been tugging at him this whole time. "Only a couple of those library books are mine. Mostly they're my neighbor's. He's housebound, so I pick up books for him."

She blinked, her eyes a soft heather green in the filtered sunlight. "Your confession is that you don't read big piles of books, and that you go to the library for your neighbor? What else, do you feed his cat?"

"Only when he forgets."

Amusement lit up her little heart-shaped face. "I'm crushed. I was thinking there was a secret genius hidden inside that ripped body."

She was talking about his body. Looking at it too, her gaze lingering on his chest. That was good. Seize the opportunity.

"Maybe I was trying to impress you. We've been dancing around each other all season. Don't you want to see if there's anything to this chemistry?"

Her eyes widened. "*Here?* Are you trying to add public indecency to all those fines?"

"Just a kiss. One kiss. There's nothing indecent about a kiss."

She tantalizingly considered that for a long moment, while a tension rose between them. He meant what he said; he didn't intend anything beyond a kiss. He was leaving the next day, and one-night stands weren't his style. But Donna had been on his mind for months, and damn it, he wanted one taste of those curvy pink lips before he left Kilby.

Finally she seemed to make up her mind. She took a step forward, brushing against him. A fresh fragrance came with her, like a fern unfurling in the woods. "Nothing indecent, Priest? I've got news for you."

"What's that?"

"There is if you do it right." And she lifted her mouth to his.

As soon as Mike's lips met hers, Donna knew she was in trouble. When he'd said he fed his neighbor's cat, she'd melted inside. Then when he'd mentioned Chicago, something had clicked. If he was leaving, she didn't have to worry about what would happen next. She could have a hot moment with the guy she'd been crushing on for months, end of story. No consequences, no aftermath, no fallout. Just a chance to experience something she'd imagined a thousand times—a kiss from sexy Mike Solo.

But this . . . this was more than she'd bargained for. Firm and skillful, his lips parted hers, their mouths fitting together as if they'd been preparing for this moment all along. One of his big hands came around to the back of her head and cradled it. It made her dizzy, the way he held her, as if she were something precious, something to treasure.

Was this real kissing? Maybe she'd never done it right before. Tingles shot from the back of her mouth all the way to her toes, with a few stops in between as well. Every movement of his tongue sparked a blaze of sensation that made her gasp. As if every kiss in the past had been meaningless, a placeholder for *this* kiss. She pressed against him, losing herself in his scent, his warmth. She wanted to dive inside his big body and nestle inside his heat and strength.

His other hand, the one that wasn't cupping the back of her head, stroked slow fire along the curve of her waist. "God, you feel good," he muttered against her mouth. "Even better than I imagined. And I've been doing a lot of that."

So had she . . . but nothing came close to the reality of his strong thigh pressing between her legs, the panting from deep in his chest, the soft prickle of stubble against her neck as he kissed her shoulder.

God, she was going to melt right here on the library floor. She pulled out of the kiss. "This is crazy. We can't do this here."

His eyes blazed down at her. "No," he rasped. "You're right. Not here. There." He jerked his head toward a door set into the wall at the end of the stacks. Some kind of supply closet? Bookbinding room? Door to another dimension? Did she care?

No, she didn't. Holding hands, they tiptoed to the door, checked to make sure the coast was clear, then ducked inside. Janitor's closet, it turned out, based on the mop bucket she nearly knocked over. Fighting back the giggles, she snuggled back into Mike's arms.

"I knew it would be like this," Mike whispered fiercely, running his big hands under her shirt. Her nipples hardened before he even reached them, just from the thrill of his touch on her stomach. "I knew it ever since I saw you that night at the Roadhouse. I want to see you ignite all the way. Like dynamite. I want you to come, Donna."

An erotic buzz cruised through her system. She opened her mouth to tell him that was highly unlikely—she was too wary with men—but instead she said, "Clothes stay on," the last vestiges of her sanity reminding her that they were in a library. He nodded, and sealed his lips over hers in a deep, mind-drugging kiss. Her knees failed, and she sagged against him. At the same time, he curved his hand over her hip and tugged her closer. Her sex scraped against his thigh and she moaned, the sound buried in their kiss.

Again he manipulated her hip, tilting it just right so he could create friction against her clit, which was pulsing behind her panties and shorts. He clamped his hand over her ass and moved her up and down against his leg. She buried her face in his chest to smother her shocked gasp. *Good Lord.* Each movement made shivers build like thunderclouds, and then, *holy crap*, they hadn't even made flesh-on-flesh contact and she was coming, soaring like a rocket. Pleasure flashed through her in waves. She rode his thigh, the spasms taking her up and away, on and on. Every time she thought it would stop, he shifted something, found a new spot with those powerful thighs, and she blasted off again.

What the ever-loving . . . He hadn't even touched her bare skin. She was still entirely clothed.

"Jesus, Solo," she gasped, stepping back, after

things finally slowed down. "What did you do? How did you do that?"

He shook his head, his face tight, as if he were in pain. Of course. He must be about ready to burst, judging by the bulge straining his jeans. She reached for it, but the rattle of the doorknob had her jumping back.

"Hello? Is someone in there?" Frank the librarian.

Mike clapped his hand over her mouth, which was a good thing because she was about to burst out laughing. It was too ridiculous—busted in the library closet with the Catfish catcher and a mop bucket.

"We have a spare key, young miscreants, so be warned. I *will* notify your parents."

Held tight in Mike's arms, Donna shook with laughter. Her phone buzzed, and she dove into her pocket to silence it. Luckily, the footsteps outside were receding. She glanced at the phone.

Harvey, her ex. Strange. He never called her, why would he? What could he possibly want?

"We better get out of here." Mike, looking very uncomfortable, adjusted his jeans over that still-daunting bulge.

"Anything I can do?"

"Yes. Stop being so sexy and soft and tasty. How am I supposed to recite baseball stats in my head when you're pressed up against me like that?"

And yet when she tried to tug away, he wouldn't let her. "You busy tonight? I want to see you. Tell me I can see you."

Oh, *hell yes*. "I'm all yours, Hottie McCatcher."

That evening, Mike knocked on the door of the address Donna had given him, a tiny guesthouse on the estate of the Shark's parents. He'd spent the rest of his busy last day in Kilby remembering every sizzling moment in that closet. He couldn't wait to spend an entire wild night in a real bed with her. He wanted to see that curvy body naked, feel more of her satiny skin, whisper jokes into her ear . . .

She cracked open the door, and right away, he knew something was wrong. No smile. No color in her face. Her eyes looked swollen. "What happened? Are you okay?"

She looked right through him, as if she'd never seen him before. "Solo. What are you doing here?"

What the hell was going on? "I . . . uh . . . We had plans."

"Sorry. I can't." She tried to shut the door on him, but he held it open. If something was wrong, he wanted to help.

"What's going on, Donna?"

"I just . . . I can't see you. That's all." She pushed a tangle of copper-red hair away from her face, which showed definite traces of tears.

"You don't have to see me. Just close your eyes, let me in, and tell me what's wrong."

She didn't even crack a smile at his admittedly lame joke. "I can't let you in."

Did she mean that metaphorically? It almost sounded that way. "Okay. Let's go for a walk and—"

"This is Texas. We don't walk here. It's too hot."

Well, she had a point there.

"Look, Solo, I'm sorry I didn't call you to cancel. I've had some stuff come up that I have to deal with. If you really want to help, it's better if you leave me alone. Please."

And she closed the door in his face.

What the *hell*. He blinked at the blank wooden barrier between him and Donna. What had just happened? Then she opened it a crack, and he glimpsed the old Donna, the vivid, funny, laughing girl he knew. "I don't think I ever really thanked you for protecting me from the Wades that night at the Roadhouse. You were like . . . some kind of superhero. I know you're going to do great in the majors."

This time when the door closed, a deadbolt slid into place with a firm click.

It stung. Mike had no problem admitting that. He didn't usually get carried away over a girl, at least not since Angela. He didn't lose control in random public places. But Donna . . .

Forget Donna.

He was still repeating that phrase as he got off the plane at O'Hare Airport and strode toward the baggage claim, where his brother, Joey, was picking him up.

Forget Donna. Obviously she didn't want him—well, obviously she did, based on what happened at the library. But it hadn't meant anything to her. She wanted him gone.

Forget Donna. He had other things to worry about—Joey's health being at the top of the list. And then there was his mission to reach the majors and prove everyone wrong, his family, Angela's family, everyone. That required single-minded focus and no distractions. Especially from the sexy redhead who'd blown his mind in Kilby.

Didn't matter. Even if he ended up back in Kilby next season, so would his best friend—the Vow of Celibacy. Beat that, Donna MacIntyre.

Chapter 2

The day before Spring Training

BEHIND THE SCREEN of the confessional at St. Mary Margaret's Holy Church on the South Side of Chicago, Father Kowalski blew his nose. Everyone in town seemed to have the flu. "My son, I will pray for a good season, of course. But a Vow of Celibacy isn't going to win you a call-up to the Friars. You have a better chance of becoming *my* kind of friar."

"That's funny, Father Kowalski." Mike knelt on the cushioned bench, eager to take his vow and get on with the season. He'd spent the winter adding six pounds of solid muscle. He planned to wow them in Arizona, maybe even make the Friars' Opening Day roster. "Don't worry, I never mention my baseball career when I take the vow."

"I heard the Friars just picked up that lefty, Yazmer Perez." Father Kowalski loved to talk baseball and always knew the latest trades and rumors.

"Yup, I heard that too. You know, my brother's waiting outside, and . . ." Wrong thing to say, Mike realized immediately. Father Kowalski also loved gossip.

"How is Joseph?" the priest asked.

Mike shifted on the bench. He couldn't lie; it was a confessional. "Up and down."

The priest aimed another trumpet blast of a sneeze into his handkerchief. "Your father never mentions him."

"That's because he's still gay and my father is . . ." Mike snapped his mouth before he said something inappropriate in a confessional.

"I'm familiar with the situation," the priest said dryly. Of course he was. The melodramatic Solo family was probably in here every other day with their dramas. "How is Joseph's health?"

The kindness in Father Kowalski's voice made Mike blurt out the truth. "He gets a lot of infections. His immune system is shot from the anti-rejection drugs." Five years ago, his brother had contracted E coli while doing research in Africa and the infection had destroyed his kidney. As the only sibling who met all the requirements for living organ donation, and the closest blood match, Mike had immediately donated one of his, but he couldn't do anything to help his brother's shattered immune system.

"I will pray for him," murmured the priest.

"Thank you, Father. Now do you think that we could—"

"How's Angela?"

Angela? Was Father Kowalski trying to torture him? "I don't have a clue, to be honest. But I really should get—"

"I believe she misses you."

Oh, for fu—*no swearing in a confessional.* "Isn't that kind of thing supposed to be confidential?"

"Uh . . . *atchoo.*"

Suspiciously timed sneeze, if you asked Mike. "So, Father, my flight's in a couple of hours and I wonder if we could, um . . ." How, exactly, did you get a priest to move things along?

"Fine, son, fine." Father Kowalski waved for him to proceed, and Mike spoke the familiar words that would cut him off from sex until September, maybe October if he was really lucky. This time, Father Kowalski added a twist. "Unless, of course, you decide to marry before the end of the baseball season."

Mike burst into laughter, the sound carrying out of the confessional into the cavernous shadows of the church. "Nice try, Father. Did my mother put you up to that?" She still hadn't accepted the loss of Angela.

"We'd all like to see you happy again." Father Kowalski made a sign of the cross, and Mike bowed his head. "Speaking only for myself, not for Our Lord, may you have a successful season in all ways."

"Thank you, Father."

Mike strode out of the church before he got roped into any more baseball or dysfunctional family conversation. As always, he felt refreshed and uplifted by taking the vow. It helped him put all his focus onto baseball. Well, nearly all. The image of fiery hair and cream-silk skin crossed his mind. Donna MacIntyre kept stealing into his mind like a pesky base runner.

Outside St. Mary Margaret's, Joey was waiting in his MINI Cooper to drive him to O'Hare. He had Mike's black hair and height, but added a wickedly mobile mouth and dreamy gray eyes to the picture. "Chastity belt all buckled up tight?"

"Ah, sexual frustration, my old friend, it's good to see you." He hopped into the MINI and Joey pulled away from the curb. Even though Mike had gotten him on a weight-lifting program over the winter, his favorite brother was still too thin, his cheekbones jutting out, giving him a monkish appearance. He shouldn't be out, but by tradition he always drove Mike to the airport at the start of the season. Nothing would make him miss that.

"Promise you'll go straight home after this, Joey. Or at least put on a biohazard suit. There's too many germs in this damn city right now."

"Absolutely. I have midterms waiting in my study, along with a bottle of Sam Adams."

"Glad to know you're putting my kidney to good use."

"Actually, I think the kidney might be calling the shots. I never used to want alcohol before the surgery."

Mike chuckled. "My kidney's such a bad influence. Figures."

They hit the Loop, cars streaming past at breakneck speed. Mike soaked it in, since his immediate future held sleepy, slow-moving towns in Arizona and Texas.

"You're going to have a great season, Mike," Joey said in his serious, big-brother voice. "I really think this will be your year. I want you to do me a favor. Focus on baseball and don't worry about me."

Yeah, right. "Get through flu season and we'll talk."

"Look, it's out of our hands. Whatever God intends, that's what will be."

"Sounds like something Dad would say," Mike said bitterly. Their hard-ass, stubborn father still hadn't forgiven Joey for being gay, or Mike for sacrificing his brilliant Navy career for his gay brother.

"Dad isn't wrong about everything," said Joey softly.

"He's wrong about enough." Mike would never regret his choice to give up his kidney. How could he, when he still had his brother around? "Look, never mind Dad. You're going to be fine, so I'm not worried. And you know what—I *am* going to make the bigs this year. Didn't I make a vow back when I gave you the kidney?"

"Do you ever think you might be overdoing it with the vows?"

Mike snorted. "Only if one of them is a wedding vow."

Joey laughed and changed lanes.

"Father Kowalski said Angela misses me." For a moment, he allowed himself to think about her. Angela DiMatteo, the girl he'd loved since second grade, had dumped him when he'd left the Navy. Her ultra-conservative family wouldn't allow her to marry a man who would choose his gay brother over his military career. And no one thought he had a chance of making it in baseball. Just like that, he'd become a nonprospect—a hell of a blow to his pride. It still rankled. He still wanted to prove them all wrong, show them what he was made of.

"Of course she misses you," said Joey. "She's still trapped at home with her parents. You were the only man brave enough to step inside their house. It was some kind of superpower."

"You're no help," Mike grumbled past his smile. He could always, always count on Joey to lift his spirits. Only one other person had a knack for that . . .

Donna MacIntyre.

Would he see her in Kilby? Run into her at the Roadhouse? Would he ever find out why she'd shut him down like that? And why, for the love of St. Mary Margaret, couldn't he get her out of his mind?

Donna surreptitiously wiped a smudge of oatmeal off the sleeve of her navy blazer as she pulled the apartment lease across the desk. *Navy blazer.* Those two words encapsulated her new life in a nutshell. This new Donna never went out, never drank alcohol, never crossed the street against the light, and had a lifestyle suited to a nun.

"Sign here?"

"Yes, right where it says 'sign here,'" the snotty bleached-blond property manager said. Donna ruthlessly suppressed the urge to whip out a put-down. Something like, "Oops, I was blinded by the color of your hair. What do you use on it, Crest Whitestrips?"

But New Donna never, *ever* sassed snippy real estate agents. She clenched her jaw tight and signed the lease.

"Well, congratulations. You're now the proud tenant of a tiny apartment overlooking the sewage plant," purred the blonde.

Sewage plant. *Peachy.* Donna held tight to the keys as she left the real estate office.

Her own apartment. She'd been working toward

this moment ever since the fateful phone call from Harvey that had interrupted her interlude with Mike in the library and shattered her world. "We're going for full custody of Zack," her ex had informed her casually, as if he was ordering a pizza. It sure wasn't casual for Donna. Stunned, reeling, she'd managed to locate a lawyer, Karen Griswold, who had guided her to this point.

First came a new job that offered health benefits. It had nearly broken her heart to leave the Shark and the rest of the Gilbert family, but Ms. Griswold said it was best. Her new position as a blazer-clad receptionist at Dental Miracles offered full benefits and a lot less entertainment. Ms. Griswold insisted that if she wanted to win back custody of Zack, she couldn't live in a guesthouse. She needed her own apartment with suitable space for Zack. She'd done everything else Ms. Griswold suggested—transformed her wardrobe, cut out drinking, eliminated the partying. She'd even pinned a Texas A&M pin on her lapel, since Judge Quinn, who'd be hearing the case, was a rabid college football fan. Whatever Ms. Griswold said to do, she'd do.

Except one thing. Ms. Griswold had advised her not to talk to Harvey alone. But she wanted to give the cooperative approach one more try, so she'd asked him to meet her for coffee before work.

Outside the real estate office, she checked her watch—it had a gorilla face because Zack loved anything related to the jungle. Five minutes late. She hopped into her red Kia, also known as the littlest car in Texas, and drove to a Denny's located in the grungiest part of town, an area where Harvey's new fiancée, Bonita, would never set foot. If Bonita saw them together, she'd freak out.

Surprise, Harvey was already seated in a booth, slouched over a plate of onion rings. He used to be late for everything, but Bonita sure had whipped him into shape. In the old days, he'd worn black leather and chains and called himself Harley, after his motorcycle. Now he wore a suede jacket over a vintage Cuban shirt, his butterscotch hair in a tousled hipster cut.

She slid into the booth opposite him. "Hey, Harv. Thanks for coming."

"Bonita would kill me if she knew," he muttered, dipping an onion ring into tartar sauce.

"About me or about that plate of deep-fried junk?"

"Both," he admitted.

Bonita Wade Castillo equaled "bitchy control freak," as far as Donna could tell.

"Harvey, listen. We can work this out. We're grown-ups now. It doesn't help Zack if we're fighting with each other."

Harvey glanced up, dark blue eyes meeting hers, then sliding away, as if he was too lazy to maintain eye contact. "You know me. Not a fighter, never have been."

That might be part of the problem. Once Bonita set her mind to something, she was a freight train. Harvey probably couldn't stop her if he wanted to. But it was worth a try. "We're Zack's parents, Harvey. You and me. We need to do the right thing for him. That's our job."

That's why she'd agreed to let Harvey's parents, the Hannigans, raise Zack until she could get her life together. It had seemed like the best thing for him at the time. But now . . . now . . .

"Would it be so bad if we took him, Donna?" Harvey asked. "Bonita would be an awesome mom. She just knows stuff, you know? How to do things right. The way they should be."

Donna absorbed that blow in the deepest part of her soul, the part that doubted herself even more than others doubted her. "You're saying I don't?"

"Aw, come on, Donna. Look at yourself. You mess around, you make everything into a joke."

"Maybe some things, but *not this*. Not Zack." She took a sip of the Coke the waitress had set down in front of her. "You know how hard I've been working to get my act together."

"I know you have a lame-ass new wardrobe." He snickered. "What are you, a flight attendant?"

"Dental receptionist. And before that, I was a nanny. Know why I was a nanny? So I could learn everything I needed to know to be a good mother. And so I could save up for a decent place. And so I could buy every child psychology book in creation. I have boxes of them, Harv. And I've read them all. Everything I've been doing for the last four years has been for Zack."

"Oh yeah? How 'bout that brawl at the Roadhouse? When you got up on the bar and yelled at the Wade boys. Got all the Catfish players in trouble."

"That was last year! I don't even know why people are still talking about that." She gritted her teeth. *Stay on track*. "Harvey, do I have to remind you that you didn't want me to have Zack? You dumped me as soon as you saw that freaking plus sign on the test."

"I was young when you got knocked up. I didn't know shit about babies." Harvey shrugged. "Zack's a lot more fun than he used to be. I wouldn't mind having him around."

Wouldn't mind having him around. Donna felt everything slipping away, the slick seat under her butt, the table in front of her, the entire Denny's sliding out from under her. "This is wrong, Harvey. Zack belongs with me. Your parents agree, or at least they did before you suddenly decided you want him. I mean, until Bonita did."

"Don't know about that. They're pretty stoked at how Bonita's shaped me up. She could do the same with Zack."

"You think Zack needs shaping up?"

"He's a pretty good kid, but Bonita could make him even better. Why don't you just step back and let her do her thing?"

Make Zack even better? Did Harvey know his own son? Did he appreciate him? To her, Zack was perfect, a gonzo little goofball who loved to make people laugh. He had the funniest little dances, shaking his skinny little butt around, pulling goofy expressions. Of course he had fits of temper and didn't always do what he was told and had to wear pull-ups at night in case he wet the bed. But he was only four, after all.

What would Bonita want to change about Zack? Would she turn him into a stick-up-the-ass like her? While Harvey tinkered with his motorcycle and ignored him?

No. She couldn't let Bonita and Harvey take Zack. Every instinct, body and soul, told her that.

"Mellow out, Donna. You can still see him. Bonita said she wouldn't mind as long as you're responsible."

Oohhh no, she didn't. "Bonita doesn't get a say," she said through clenched teeth. "Not yet. You aren't even married yet. Not until June."

"Three months, baby. Then we take Zack."

Harvey stood up and tossed down money for his food—not enough to cover her Coke, of course. "You better get used to it, Donna. Bonita knows how to get things the way she wants them. And she's got a lot of clout in this town on her mother's side. Her mom's a Wade cousin, you know. You really do not want to get in her way."

And he slouched away with that low-slung stride she used to see as sexy. *Never again.*

Donna had a few minutes before she had to leave for work, so she stayed in the booth, sucking down her Coke and wiping away angry tears. Of course Bonita would have the entire Wade clan in her corner, while she had no one. Her father hadn't cared about anything involving her since her mother left, and she had a pact with Carrie, her stepmother, that involved two days' warning before face-to-face contact.

Sadie knew about Zack—finally—but most of her friends didn't. And Sadie was in San Diego now with Caleb Hart, the former pitcher for the Catfish, now a member of the Friars starting rotation.

Catfish. Mike Solo.

There he was again, popping into her thoughts without invitation. She still dreamed about making out with him in the library. But New Donna had to stay far, far away from sexy ballplayers. She'd read in the *Kilby Press-Herald* that Mike was back with the Catfish for spring training and doing great. He was considered a top prospect to be called up to the Friars. Good. The sooner he got called up, the less risk of running into him. And she couldn't afford to run into Mike Solo. He was much too tempting—she didn't trust herself around him.

Anyway, given the rude way she'd slammed the door in his face that night, he'd probably written her off and forgotten the whole thing. Just the way she had.

Or would, any day now.

Chapter 3

Opening Day

Texas in springtime had to be one of God's gifts to the world, Mike thought as he strolled into Catfish Stadium. He inhaled the sweet fragrance of roses mingled with the ever-present smell of roasting hot dogs. The sun hadn't yet reached that ferocious glare it would acquire later in the season. It beamed merrily from a cheerful blue sky, a pleasant companion rather than an instrument of torture.

It was good to be back in Kilby, even if it was still Triple A, where nobody knew your name.

Trevor Stark stood at his locker, tall and ice blond, a badass Viking angel with tattoos snaking under his sleeves. Although Trevor was an outstanding player, every time he got close to getting "the Call," he managed to screw things up.

"What's the word on the Roadhouse?" Trevor asked him. "Did they lift the ban yet?"

The Kilby Roadhouse hadn't been too happy about the Catfish versus Wade family brawl last season.

Although Mike hadn't liked him much until then, Trevor had been a champ during the incident.

"Yes, but I heard they might have a new ban just for you."

Trevor narrowed his eyes. "What are you talking about?"

"To give the rest of us a chance, you know?" Trevor Stark's reputation as a troublemaking heart-breaker had spread through every clubhouse in the land.

"A chance to be my wingman, maybe. If you can handle it."

"Check it, y'all," said Dwight Conner, strolling past with his gym bag. "Did you hear the league is trying to make Crush Taylor sell the team?"

"They can try." Mike shrugged as he stashed his cleats inside his locker. "Crush does what he wants. You've been to his parties, right?"

They all went quiet for a moment, soaking in the memory of Crush Taylor's epic all-star all-nighters.

Dwight gestured to the TV mounted in the upper corner of the clubhouse. "Hear about our new phenom?"

Mike looked at the monitor. The infamous Yazmer Perez, a young, fast-talking lefty of indeterminate ethnicity, was speaking to a reporter after the college baseball championships. He'd seen the clip before; everyone had. In it, Yazmer Perez said publicly the kind of thing most players kept to themselves. "The club-house, that's club plus house, get what I'm saying? It's *our house*. Ain't no way a homo reporter needs to come into my house and stick a mic in my face. That shit is phallic, know what I mean? Invasion of personal space. The homos need to go home-o, know what I mean."

The Catfish players shook their heads with varying degrees of bemusement. "Someone better assign a fulltime PR guy to that kid," said Dwight. "When's he getting here?"

"Tonight," said Jim Leiberman as he carefully arranged the gear in his locker. The shortstop—nicknamed Bieberman due to his resemblance to Justin Bieber, and to drive him crazy—was OCD about his gear. If you wanted to mess with him, you moved his extra T-shirt one inch to the left. "Yazmer was supposed be Double A, but he had a 1.23 ERA over eight games in spring training with the Red Sox. Three walks, twenty-six strikeouts, gave up one triple, two doubles . . ." Drowning out the analytical shortstop's recitation, Dwight turned up the volume on the TV.

The reporter now faced the camera. "A spokesman for the Friars said that Yazmer's quote had been taken out of context. He also added that the sexual orientation of members of the media is a private matter, and that the organization disavows Perez's viewpoint."

Duke Ellington, the bulldoglike manager of the Catfish, came on next. "Yazmer Perez is a helluva pitcher, and we're excited to have him join the Catfish. We're confident that Mike Solo and Yaz will make a dynamite battery. Mike'll show him the ropes around here. We're looking forward to a great season."

Mike shoved the rest of his gear into his locker. Sure, he'd show that asshole some fucking ropes.

Like a gag, for starters. "Awesome. Mike Solo, baby-sitter to the spoiled and stupid."

"Stupid? Don't think so. The dude knows how to get press attention." Trevor was still gazing up at the monitor. "Might be a nice break for me."

Oh, the ego of the super-talented baseball player. Mike rolled his eyes, grabbed his glove and favorite bat, and headed for the door, only to run into Crush Taylor and his Armani sunglasses.

"Solo. Got a minute?"

"Sure, boss."

His mind racing, he followed Crush into Duke's office. What could the legendary pitcher and team owner have to say to him?

"I think I've figured you out, Solo," Crush announced, sinking into a chair and propping his boots on Duke's desk. "You have what I call a Superhero Complex, not uncommon in young studs like you. That's why you joined the Navy. You were going to save the world, weren't you?"

What the hell? "What . . . why are you . . . don't you have better things to think about? Like what to wear to the ESPN Holy Shit, He's Still Alive Awards?"

Crush shoved his shades onto the top of his head and squinted at Mike. "Funny. I'm trying to give you a tip here. Want to cut down on the attitude?"

"Sorry."

"So there you are, saving the world, and your brother gets sick. So you give him one of your kidneys, which means leaving your Navy career behind."

"It's a required body part, according to the Navy."

"Wouldn't be top of my list, no offense to the Navy. Then . . . instead of choosing a nice single-kidney appropriate career like, say, male modeling or Porsche salesman, you choose baseball."

"I was on the Navy baseball team. I was freaking good."

"You were the best player they had. They miss you *and* your left kidney." Crush unscrewed the lid of his silver flask and drank. "But I'm not done. Not only did you choose to pursue a professional baseball career, which is very rare, by the way. I can't think of any active players who have donated a kidney. Scrotum, maybe."

Mike picked up his bat and addressed it. "Kill me now," he implored it. "Please, I beg you."

Crush continued with a sort of gleeful relentlessness. "You also chose the most physically demanding position on the field. Especially for a guy with one kidney."

"I wear my chest protector."

"Were you wearing your chest protector when you planted yourself in front of that girl at the Roadhouse?"

"Wha . . . that was last season! I came away with a few bruises."

"It could have been disaster. What if I tell the Friars that their best catching prospect is playing Russian roulette with his health?"

Mike felt the blood drain from his face. "I wasn't gambling with my health, Crush. The surgery was four years ago. I'm completely healed."

"I see you put on some muscle in the off season."

"Yes, sir."

"It's not going to help."

"*What?*" Mike glared at the team owner. What was the man getting at? "Why the hell not?"

"You're good with a bat, but that's not your strength. Calling games and working the pitchers, that's what you do best. You have a gift for getting pitchers to trust you, and giving them confidence. That's your forte, and it'll take you far. If baseball was fair, you'd be in San Diego right now."

Finally it clicked. "Yazmer."

"Yazmer," Crush agreed. "He's the reason you're still in Kilby. Good news, he's your ticket out too. You get me?"

"I think so. Get that loudmouth asshole ready for the bigs, and I get to go too."

"Think of it as an initiation rite. Like getting a tattoo on your ass or drinking an entire bottle of absinthe while screwing three supermodels. That was for your ears only, by the way." Crush tipped the flask at him. "He's got skills, but also a pacing problem. He talks fast, but he pitches slower than snail mail. I think he likes being out on the mound too much. Forgets he has a job to do. He's so slow the umps are thinking about actually enforcing the twelve-second rule. Think you can school him on his pacing?"

Why Yazmer? *Why, of all players?* Mike had dealt with all sorts of crap in baseball. But blatant homophobes were tough for him. "Sure," he said, trying to muster some enthusiasm.

"Should be no problem for a superhero like you."

Mike had a bad feeling about this. More than any acquired baseball skill, he relied on his most important weapon, something he told no one about. His intuition. Gut instinct. That inner voice that he'd learned never to ignore. It guided him in life and behind home plate. Right now it was ringing all kinds of alarm bells.

Crush swung himself out of the chair and unfurled his lanky, rumpled frame. "I wouldn't bet against you, my friend. I saw you in that bar fight last season. You know how to handle yourself. By the way, who was the girl? The redhead up on the bar? The one who made you forget all about that missing kidney?"

"Her name's Donna. She's a friend of Sadie Merritt, Caleb's girl."

"Quite the knockout."

Fiercely protective all of a sudden, Mike growled, "Stay away from her."

Crush dropped his sunglasses back into place. "Oh, she's not for me. I have my eye on someone else. Besides, I saw the sparks. Just about set the Roadhouse on fire. I'm never wrong about these things."

The Catfish won their home opener over the Round Rock Express. Mike went one for three—not bad, when he was still getting into the groove of the season. He guided Dan Farrio to a five-strikeout six-hitter, but he missed Caleb Hart, with whom he worked so smoothly they practically read each other's minds.

When they weren't on the field or batting, the players spent the bulk of their time ogling Angeline, the new promotions girl. She had a long blond ponytail that bounced against her boobs when it came time for "Show Your Team Spirit."

"Let's hear it, Catfish fans! Meow like a kitty cat!"

A chorus of "Meows" filtered around the stadium.

"Swim like a fish!" She pinched her nose shut and shimmied like an eel.

"Put it together, what do you get? The Catfish!"

"*The Catfish*," yelled the crowd.

In the dugout, Mike turned to Dwight Conner and "meowed," scratching his nails down his bulging upper arm.

"Get your hands off me," the big guy muttered, his gaze fixed on Angeline.

"You don't think it's a little lame? Meow like a kitty cat?"

"What?" Apparently hypnotized by her ponytail, Dwight popped some peanuts into his mouth.

Mike sighed. For some reason, Angeline left him cold. Maybe the problem was that her name was like Angela's. Or maybe it was the color of her hair.

Not red.

Forget Donna.

After the game, Duke introduced Yazmer Perez around the clubhouse. Yazmer, the key to Mike's future, apparently. The dude was even cockier than he appeared on camera. He barely took notice of his new teammates, focusing instead on his Bluetooth and his smartphone.

"What is he, texting?" Mike whispered to Trevor Stark.

"He might be tweeting. He's big on Twitter."

Like a spy satellite picking up a signal, Yazmer perked up at the word "Twitter." "Twitter, yo. Gotta connect. I'm @TheYaz, that's capital 'Y,' little 'a,' little 'z.' Thinkin' of changing it up, peoples. Show off my creativity. Thinkin' of 'Y to the power of Z.'"

His fast-talking style made Mike a little dizzy. "What does all of that mean?"

Yazmer stared him down, then turned his liquid gaze back to Duke. "This the chico supposed to Friar me up? Prehistoric, man. Don't know the interwebz, don't know nothin'."

Mike couldn't think of a damn word to say to that. Fuck, if his career depended on this guy, he was doomed. He'd have to come up with some kind of plan to bond with the Yaz. In the meantime . . . He turned to Trevor. "Roadhouse?"

"Hell to the Y-e-s. That's a capital 'Y,' little 'e,' little—"

"Shut the fuck up."

As Mike walked into the Kilby Roadhouse, with its sawdust-covered floors and red chili pepper lights strung along the walls, he couldn't help scanning the crowd for red hair and laughing hazel eyes.

He'd first met Donna MacIntyre at the Roadhouse. She'd been funny and sexy, and she made him laugh, especially when he told her about the Vow of Celibacy.

"As a public service, you should be less attractive," she'd told him. "Get a mullet. Or wear those shiny, baggy sweats. And a wife-beater. It's only fair, if you're going to be off-limits."

"Sorry, you lost me at attractive. After that all I heard was blah-blah-blah."

They'd spent the rest of the night bantering and sparring. Honestly, it was almost as good as sex.

Tonight, there was no sign of Donna. Maybe she was with the Shark. Maybe she had a new boyfriend. *Forget Donna.*

But the Roadhouse wasn't as fun without her. He ordered a club soda and leaned against the long, scuffed bar, possibly at the very spot where she'd perched that fateful night of the brawl. She had guts, Donna did. How many girls would stand up for a friend against a clan of inbred, spoiled frat boys?

"You come back for more bruises, Catfish?" A drawling voice made him turn. Right on cue, one of the Wades—he couldn't remember which one— stared him down, shoulders hunched, jaw thrust forward. The classic bully pose.

"Just toasting the new season. Go Kilby." He lifted his club soda, not taking his eyes off the Wade. Didn't trust him for a second.

The guy didn't move. "Got a tip for you, Solo. Play good."

"Well, since there's nothing I appreciate more than a well-worded piece of advice, here's to you." He toasted again, and finally the dude shambled away.

"What the Jeter was that all about?" Bieberman appeared at his elbow, gripping a Lone Star.

"Did you just say, 'What the Jeter'?"

"Catchy, right? I'm trying to make it a new thing people say. 'What the Jeter is wrong with you? What the Jeter did you do with the milk?' That sort of thing. A tribute to Derek Jeter, the best shortstop of all time. I'm working it into everyday conversation to see if it spreads."

"You should put it on Twitter." Mike looked around at the milling crowd. Denim jackets and cowboy boots, short skirts and long legs, plenty of lip gloss and teased hair, glimpses of cleavage, earrings dangling against bare skin, pretty girls flipping their hair, laughing, teasing, sexy, cute . . .

And not Donna.

He drained his club soda. "Mañana," he said to the other Catfish, who stared after him with expressions of shock and betrayal. He never left the party early. *Too bad*. The Roadhouse without Donna was like a game without a hit. A dinner without steak. A shower without water.

It just wasn't worth the bother.

He strode out of the Roadhouse into the still-warm night. Up above, stars bedazzled the blue-velvet sky. The Wade kid had it right. Play well, get out of town. That was the plan. Definitely, for sure, *forget Donna*.

Unless, of course, she was standing right in front of him.

"Donna?"

He blinked, but she didn't disappear. On his way to the stadium for batting practice, he'd stopped at the Dunkin' Donuts for coffee and a cruller. Now his coffee steamed, forgotten, in his left hand while he drank in the sight of Donna MacIntyre. She stood next to a miniscule red Kia in the drive-through, a little brown bag in one hand and a Big Gulp of coffee in the other.

She looked . . . different.

"You are Donna, right? Donna MacIntyre?"

She rolled her eyes with a Lord-help-us expression that confirmed her identity. "Solo. How've you been?"

"Great. What are you wearing?" It looked horrible, whatever it was. Boxy, boring blue, below the knee. Its only benefit was that it showed off her calves. Unfortunately, they were covered in beige panty hose. "Did you just come from Salvation Army band practice?"

"That's an extremely inappropriate comment."

Yeah, it was, but he was rattled. "Sorry. I'm a little traumatized. Are you on a Mormon mission or something? What did you do to your hair?"

The state of her hair made him want to cry. All the curls had been flat-ironed out of it; he knew the process because his sisters used it on their curly black mops. The color hadn't changed, thank the saints, but she wore a headband that hid most of the glorious red. A headband! And her hair was short too. She'd chopped it to shoulder-length. All that wild, beautiful hair, sitting on a salon floor somewhere.

"Wait, let me guess. You're on your way to an encyclopedia convention."

Looking extremely annoyed, she brushed past him. He caught the scent of fresh woodlands. At least that hadn't changed. As she peered into the Kia, he followed her gaze and saw a sleeping kid strapped into a car seat in the back. The window was halfway open, giving the child plenty of air. He had red hair and his mouth lolled open.

"Is that the Shark?"

For the first time, she looked kindly at him. "You remember about the Shark?"

"Of course. You're a nanny for a Shark. Hard to forget that. Or the rest of it." He raised one eyebrow suggestively, but she ignored his double entendre. His suspicion grew that something was wrong in Donna's world. In the old days, she never let a chance to flirt pass her by.

"I'm not a nanny anymore," she told him, circling

around to the driver's side. "I'm a receptionist at a dentist's office. You should come by sometime. We're famous for our root canals."

Cradling her coffee and paper bag against her chest, she put her key into the lock on the driver's side door. Damn. She was about to drive away, and he didn't know when he'd see her again.

"You know, I could use a good teeth cleaning. They look kind of green up on the Jumbotron. Where's your office?"

"Oh. Where? It's, um, at the corner of Twelfth and Forget I Said Anything."

"Ouch. Now there's the Donna I remember."

She fumbled with the lock. "Well, forget her."

"I tried that. It wasn't any fun."

She glanced up at him, her eyes narrowed, and a *zing* shot between them. For the first time since he'd gotten back to Kilby, Mike felt completely happy with life. He bounded around the car and lifted her coffee out of her way. "There, is that easier?"

"You don't have to help me. I'm fine. Don't you have some balls to play with?"

"Ouch again. I think our Donna's back in business." He squinted at her. "Are you wearing a football pin? Now you're just breaking my heart."

"Welcome to Texas," she said, all sassy. "Where football is king, and baseball is the nerdy neighbor boy your mom makes you play with."

"Them's fighting words, Donna MacIntyre. You can't just say something like that and not give me a chance to prove how superior baseball is in every possible way."

She turned the key in the lock and swung open the

door. He stepped back to avoid getting a crotch full of South Korean automotive metal. In the car seat, the child's legs twitched, and a low wail began.

"Gotta go," said Donna, suddenly in a big hurry. "Nice running into you and all. Have a good season."

"Mama!!!" the boy cried. Mike could see it was a boy now. A boy with bright red hair the exact color of Donna's.

"Shhh, sweetie. It's okay. I'm here, and I got you some milk." She stuck a straw in the cup and handed it to him.

Abruptly, the crying stopped. Donna shot Mike a complicated look—he detected regret, warning, pleading, and probably a few more layers—then closed the door.

He watched her drive away, speculation running rampant. So Donna had a kid. She'd never mentioned any such person. Neither had Caleb or Sadie. Not that it was his business.

Except . . . well, he kind of wanted to make it his business. How many dental offices could there be in Kilby, Texas?

Chapter 4

THAT WOULD TEACH Donna to splurge on a Bavarian cream donut. Just her luck to run into Mike Solo after an overnight with Zack. Mike was even more tempting than the pastry. Sweet Lord above, he looked good. The same devilish green eyes, the same grin. His black hair was cropped closer to his head and he seemed to have gained a few lines in his face. Grooves along his mouth, hollows under his cheekbones, that sort of thing. He might have added some new muscles too. A little something in the shoulders, some extra bulging in the thighs.

Oh sweet heaven, he was one-hundred percent trouble.

She pulled out of the drive-through. "Drink your milk, Zack-a-doodle," she told Zack over her shoulder. "I got you some donut holes too." She fumbled in the paper bag for a nugget of donut and handed it to him.

"Where's the hole?" Zack turned it over and over, so puzzled she had to laugh.

"Good question, kiddo. Hey, while you were

sleeping I heard on the radio that the zoo is getting a new tiger. A white tiger. Let's go see him as soon as he gets here, huh?"

"Yeah!!"

While Zack turned his straw into a pair of fangs and made faces in the mirror, she drove toward the Hannigans' house, her thoughts drifting back to Mike Solo. In his loose blue cambric shirt over a white tee and jeans, he'd looked casual and fit and so yummy she wanted to lick him.

No licking. No, Donna, no, no, no.

Ms. Griswold had been adamant about that. "Pretend you're a nun. I'm serious. No guys. No parties. You're a little angel who was taken advantage of four years ago. You've turned your life around and want only one thing."

A big penis, her devil side wanted to say. Instead, she smiled meekly. "All I want is my son."

"Exactly. All you want is your son. Don't forget it."

"Of course I won't forget it. It's true. But why do I have to act like a virgin saint to get Zack back?"

"Virgin saint. I like that. We can work with that. Here's the thing, Donna." Her lawyer steepled her fingers and clicked her orange-lacquered nails against each other. "You're the mother, so you have a built-in advantage with the family court system."

"That's good, right?"

"Yes, *however*. It also means you're a target. If the other side decides to play ugly, they have enough material to rip you into confetti-size shreds. Your history of partying. That brawl at the Roadhouse. The fact that you had to be hospitalized when you were pregnant. They'll try to turn you into the Lindsay Lohan of Kilby, Texas. Oh." She held up a finger. "Make sure you wear underwear at all times."

The devil inside Donna rebelled. "Is edible underwear okay?"

"This is serious, Donna. No more jokes. You don't joke about bombs at an airport, do you? Same idea. Don't joke about edible underwear when you're trying to win custody of your son."

"Yes, ma'am," she'd said meekly.

Outside the Hannigans', she unfastened Zack from his car seat and sent him down the walkway toward the waiting Mrs. Hannigan, who no longer smiled at her as kindly as she used to. The struggle over Zack was taking its toll, and she hated that.

"Love you, Zack-a-roonie," she called after him, as he did one of his crazy little dances down the pathway toward Mrs. H. He loved it when she made up plays on his name, but even her inventive brain was starting to run out.

Only three minutes late—a miracle considering how hard it was to leave Zack—she took her post behind the receptionist desk of the Dental Miracles office. She fixed her gaze on an anatomically correct diagram of an abscessed tooth. If that didn't distract her from thoughts of Mike Solo, she didn't know what would. *Bacteria entering the bloodstream. Inflammation. Antibiotics.*

"I need to make an appointment," came a warm, low, laughing voice. Her head shot up.

Mike Solo.

"What are you doing here?" she hissed, looking around the office as if they'd been caught doing something illicit.

"Oh, nothing. Just looking for an unlocked closet." He winked. Heat flashed across her nerve endings.

"Inappropriate. I'm working here. What are you, stalking me?"

"Excuse me? I'm here to make an appointment," he said virtuously. "Hi," he said to one of the patients on the waiting room couch. "I'm Mike Solo of the Kilby Catfish. How are you doing?"

"Leave the patients alone. What do you want?"

"As I've been saying for the last few minutes, I'd like to make an appointment, if that's the kind of thing you do here."

"Of course we make appointments." Donna flipped open the big calendar. "What do you want? Teeth cleaning, you said? X-rays? A good spanking?"

Even though she said that last one in a much lower voice, he still caught it. Of course. Mike never missed the joke. "Now you're talking. But no. None of that. I was thinking of a private appointment. You and me. Catch up on old times. Fill in some of the blanks in each other's lives."

"Not interested."

"Liar."

"Go away, Mike. This is a bad idea."

"Why? What's the big deal? You know that Sadie and Caleb are going to get married one of these days. And we'll both be in the wedding. We're going to see each other, so wouldn't it be smart to get all that awkwardness out of the way?"

"What awkwardness?"

He raised his voice to a level more easily heard throughout the office. "Do you really want me to rehash everything that happened at Kilby Community Library? Not that I mind, because it's one of my favorite memories. Then again, I'm a guy, and we don't get embarrassed about that stuff. I'm thinking more of you. Girls can be funny about that kind of thing, as if it weren't perfectly natural and—"

She stopped him, hissing through gritted teeth. "Fine. We'll make an appointment. When are you free? I know you have a busy schedule of Catfish games and stupid pranks. Wait, aren't you going on the road soon?"

"Checking the team schedule, are you?"

"No," she snapped. "Just wishful thinking."

At his wounded expression, she wondered if she was being kind of a jerk. Mike Solo hadn't done anything to her except run into her at Dunkin' Donuts. It wasn't his fault he was like catnip wrapped in the body of a Greek god. Not his fault she'd been fantasizing about him since that damn closet. And before.

"How's tonight?"

"I have a game tonight. Afterwards?"

"I go to bed at nine."

"*Nine?*"

His incredulous look made her laugh. "Some things have changed in my life."

"Fine, you tell me, what's the next available opening in your schedule? Can you take a coffee break right now?"

"Is that the quickest way to get rid of you?"

"For now, yes."

"Fine." After asking Ricki, the billing clerk, to fill

in for her, she led Mike into the break room, with its distinctive scent of scorched coffee adhering to the bottom of the carafe no one ever cleaned. He filled the small space magnificently, his black curls nearly brushing the ceiling. Or maybe that was just her imagination inflating him to godlike proportions.

Her stomach fluttered with lust. Damn. Better to head this off before she got even hornier for him. "Remember how I said some things have changed in my life?"

"Yeah. That was about a minute ago. I can remember a lot further back than that." He swept her with a heavy-lidded look. She put up a hand, blocking his view of her. "This is one of the things. No more men."

"Oh? Batting for the home team now?"

"What? No. No women either. No sex of any kind. I'm turning over a new leaf."

His eyes narrowed a bit, the green darkening to the color of shadows in a forest. "Does this have something to do with the boy in your car? He's yours, right?"

"Yes. He's mine." She couldn't help the pride in her voice. "Zack is my son. He's four. And yes, I'm turning over a new leaf for him." She wasn't really interested in sharing more details than that. He'd probably walk away now and leave her alone. The connection between her and Mike was based on sexual chemistry, and now that sex was off the table, Mike would disappear off the radar. Especially now that he knew about Zack. What hotshot baseball player wanted to get involved with the mother of a four-year-old when no sex was on the horizon?

"Bring him to a game," Mike said, digging in his pocket and pulling out a small folded schedule, on which he scrawled his number. "My dad took me to my first Cubs game around that age. Pick whichever date works for you and give me a call. I'll leave tickets for you."

"But—I just told you. No sex."

"Perfect. Have you forgotten my vow?" He gave her a cheeky wink. Oh, *snap*! She *had* forgotten the vow. "You're perfectly safe with me, my little ice princess."

"I'm not an—"

"Hey, can I call you Frozen? *Let it go . . . let it go . . .*"

With huge, earnest eyes, he flung one arm in an operatic gesture, the most ridiculous Disney princess ever, and she couldn't stop her giggles from bubbling over.

Safe with him? Yeah, right.

After Mike left, she texted Sadie.

Guess who I just saw?

Santa Claus? Again?

Mike Solo. And he saw Z.

So? You should tell him everything. He's a good guy.

She selected for the emoticons for "cat" and "fish," and added a frowny face.

Sadie sent back a string of hearts, flowers, smiley faces, and champagne corks. She was engaged to a former Catfish, after all. She ended with a little animated icon of two people hugging over and over again.

Donna tucked her phone away, smiling to herself. Thank God the Dark Ages of their friendship were over.

Sadie had been Donna's best friend since fifth

grade, but in their senior year of high school, Sadie had started dating the high school quarterback, Hamilton Wade, while Donna had fallen for Harvey. Since Donna couldn't stand the Wades and Sadie couldn't stand Harvey, they'd stopped communicating. While Sadie had gone to college and earned an honors degree, Donna had partied, smoked, gone a little wild, and eventually . . . gotten pregnant.

Total cliché. Like she couldn't have seen that coming. Some pharmaceutical company had some serious explaining to do.

In her second trimester, the worst sickness in the world had grabbed hold of her. It had a medical term—hyperemesis gravidarum, literally meaning excessive vomiting during pregnancy. In her case, really, really, absurdly excessive. After a few weeks of that, Carrie, her stepmom, had kicked her out of the house because of the constant smell.

Sadie was still at college, so Donna had gone to Harvey's, even though he'd broken up with her. She wanted to find her own place, but throwing up all the time made apartment hunting impossible. Not only that, but her case of hyperemesis came with severe depression—completely unlike her usual bubbly personality. Harvey bundled her onto his bike and dumped her back home. Finally, her father had sent her off to her mother in Los Angeles, which he'd sworn he'd never do, even during her wildest high school rebellions.

Road-tripping backup singers didn't normally make the best caretakers, but her mom had done the best she could, eventually checking Donna into a hospital where doctors had put her on an IV and prescribed anti-anxiety, anti-depressant, and anti-nausea meds.

When the baby had finally arrived, Donna had been in such an overmedicated state that she could barely form words, let alone make plans. The baby's future had been decided for her, and when she finally came out of her dark depression, her baby boy, Zack, was with Harvey's parents. The Hannigans were a well-off, conservative, churchgoing couple. They paid for all her medical expenses and offered to raise Zack in their stately Tudor-style home in the best neighborhood in Kilby.

Donna wanted to object to the arrangement, but she was so weak, so exhausted, so depleted that everyone ignored her doubts. Her mother, her father, her stepmother, Harvey, everyone kept telling her it was for the best, that Zack would have the most promising future this way, that she should move on with her life, she was still young, blah-blah-blah. It felt as if she were trying to fight an avalanche.

And the worst was that everything they said was true. How could she raise Zack when she had no job, no place of her own, and worst of all, no clue about children? The Hannigans could offer Zack so much more than she could.

Recovering on the couch at her mother's Los Angeles condo, she'd sipped coconut water—chock full of electrolytes—watered the neglected spider plants, listened to the drone of leaf blowers outside, and concocted her plan. Simple, really.

Step one: Go back to Kilby.

Step two: Get a job.

Step three: Learn how to be a good mother.

Step four: Get Zack back.

Before she went home, she gathered her energy for one all-important fight, and it worked, though it nearly killed her. The Hannigans agreed to let her see Zack every week. In return they asked her to minimize the gossip by keeping her connection to Zack as quiet as possible. Kilby loved a good juicy scandal, and the best way to keep down the talk was to *not* talk. That's why she hadn't dared to tell Sadie, especially when Sadie was dating Hamilton Wade. The Wade family couldn't be trusted.

In four years, Donna hadn't missed a single visit with Zack. And she'd finally told Sadie the whole story, which was tough because Sadie was incredibly hurt that she'd kept Zack a secret, but also wonderful because now Donna had someone to confide in.

But tell Mike everything? That was crazy talk. They didn't have that kind of relationship—or any kind, for that matter.

She opened the little schedule he'd given her, with the cartoonish blue whiskered catfish on the front. One game couldn't hurt, could it? Scanning the schedule, she saw that the team would back in town playing the Albuquerque Isotopes on the next day she had Zack. She'd take Zack to the game, buy him some Cracker Jack, and introduce him to America's pastime.

Too bad it wasn't football so she could mention it to Judge Quinn.

Chapter 5

THE CATFISH'S FIRST road trip took them on a swing through Las Vegas, Tucson, and Fresno. Joey and his partner, Jean-Luc, who happened to be in San Francisco for a tech conference, came to the Fresno game. Mike hit his first home run of the year off a shaky rookie pitcher who didn't know that he fed off the fastball, high and away. He'd learn; Mike had no illusions about that.

While in the dugout, Mike studied the rookie intently, his motion, his pitch selection. He often picked up something that could help the Catfish while watching the opposing pitchers.

Dropping onto the bench next to Yazmer, he said, "You got twice the stuff that pitcher has, but he's got one thing nailed. You see how zippy he keeps the pace? Pitch, throw back, pitch. Keeps it snappy. No messing around. Puts the batters on the defensive, doesn't give them time to adjust. It's a great tool."

"I gotz a tool." Yazmer tightened the biceps of his left arm. "Sonic Boom."

"You named your arm?"

"Named itself, man. Named itself." He touched

two fingers to his lips in a kissing gesture. "Sonic B and me. All it takes. All the way to the top."

Mike gave himself a little shake. Talking to Yazmer was like walking through a maze with the fog rolling in. Pitchers and catchers had to communicate, but how was that supposed to happen when they didn't even seem to speak the same language?

"You have a great arm, no doubts there. No offense to Sonic Boom, but there's more to pitching than that. Location, strategy. Pitch to contact, have you heard of that? Like Greg Maddux said, the best inning is three pitches, three grounders. Back to the dugout in minutes."

Yazmer was making more weird gestures, which made no sense until Mike realized that he was carrying on a mimed conversation with an adoring fan draped over the railing.

Mike gave up, and walked over to sit next to Bieberman. Maybe *someone* would listen to his pearls of wisdom.

"If you get on base, steal second." The shortstop had been fretting lately about his "runs created" stat. "This guy gets in a zone and forgets about his base runners."

"Forgets? How do you know? Can you read his mind?"

"Yeah. And I can read yours. You're thinking about that promotions girl back in Kilby, aren't you?"

Bieberman turned red. "She's a goddess."

"Ask her out."

"I think Trevor likes her."

"Trevor doesn't like anyone except himself. Right, Stark?"

At the other end of the bench, Trevor sat with his long legs sprawled before him, his cap nearly covering his eyes, chewing gum in a lazy manner. Mike wasn't fooled. Trevor paid close attention to everything that went on. Then he did his best to mess it up.

"Wrong. I like Angeline," he said now, his jaw clenching and unclenching with his chews.

Bieberman's face fell. "Told you."

"Doesn't matter, dude. Maybe she prefers brilliant little shortstops to asshole sluggers. You should take your shot. All she can say is no."

"I wrote her a poem." Spots of red flashed across Bieberman's cheeks, as if he were coming down with some weird skin condition. "Well, it's more of an epic saga."

"An epic saga?"

"In three parts. Part one is devoted to the first moment I saw her. Part two is our first conversation, when I asked her about the George Costanza promotion. A lot of people say I look like George Costanza. I thought maybe it would give me an edge."

Mike couldn't say anything, he was too afraid of laughing.

"Part three . . . well, part three is more of a fantasy sequence. I've been working on that one every night."

Mike let out a spurt of laughter. He turned it into a violent cough, covering his mouth with his hand. On the field, the rookie pitcher glared at him, as if personally offended that he wasn't paying attention to the game. Next pitch, beautiful curveball for a strike. Take that.

Mike tipped his cap to the pitcher, then turned to Trevor. "Well, Stark? Bet you can't beat that. An epic saga in three parts. What are you doing for the lovely Angeline?"

"Taking her to Hooters."

Bieberman nearly choked on a peanut. Mike shook his head sadly and watched the rookie strike out Ramirez to end the inning. Life just wasn't fair, not when it came to women or baseball.

Still, it was a good game, topped off by dinner with his brother afterward. He met Joey and his longtime partner, Jean-Luc, in the type of restaurant they preferred—white tablecloths and metrosexual bartenders. Joey stood up from the table and opened his arms wide. Mike thumped him on the back, with his usual flood of gratitude that his kidney had been a match for Joey, and that his brother had accepted it. He hadn't want to, at first, knowing how opposed their father was to the donation.

But Joey had always been there for Mike, and the hell if he'd just let his brother die. When he'd threatened to donate his kidney to Goodwill if Joey didn't take it, his brother had finally given in. In Mike's opinion, the planet was the better for his big brother's presence. Joey didn't know what it was to be mean, or cruel. If there was a more compassionate man on earth, Mike had yet to meet him. Being around Joey made everyone feel good about themselves; it was a gift.

As Mike hugged his brother, he felt bones where there had been muscle. He drew back, alarmed. "What's going on? Aren't you following my workout plan?"

"Don't worry." Joey smiled in reassurance. "Bout of stomach flu. My students think I look romantically tragic, so it's not all bad."

"More than the usual number of crushes?"

"Sad to say, yes."

"It's a tragic day when a gay economics professor gets more chicks than a studly baseball player." He shook hands with Jean-Luc, and they all sat down. Jean-Luc, reserved and darkly sophisticated, watched Joey surreptitiously. By profession he was a tech investor, but ever since that first E coli infection, Jean-Luc had appointed himself nurse, caretaker, cook, and physical therapist.

"I don't think you've ever had to worry in that department," said Joey, dryly. "How are you feeling?"

"Home run, that's how."

"Those extra pounds are really paying off, aren't they?"

At this moment, Mike wished he could donate some of his extra muscle to Joey. He was too thin. What would happen if he got sick again? Mike didn't want to think about it. "How's Chicago?"

They spent the rest of the dinner catching up on the new apps Jean-Luc was financing and their plans for a trip to see his family in France, as soon as Joey was well enough to travel. Joey shared what news he'd gotten from Rita and Marie, their sisters back in Chicago. After they'd finished their last bites of extra-rare steak, Joey carefully blotted his mouth and said, "Been thinking. I want you to give Dad a break."

"A break? Hell no. He would have let you die. And he still lectures me about the kidney."

"His beliefs are his beliefs. I don't begrudge him that. If *I* don't, you shouldn't. I'm asking you, please. He's your father. Our father. And hating him doesn't do you any good, my brother."

"It is what it is."

"Well, think about it. It's important to me. It's important to the family. Rita says he still keeps all your stats in a scrapbook. He reads the *Sporting News* and follows all the Friars' transactions."

"I get it, I get it. Change of subject, please." It tore him in two, that his father put all his love and pride into one son, and not the other. "Let's talk about something more pleasant, like Ebola."

"How about the girl you mentioned, the one you met in Keelby?" Jean-Luc spoke with a slight hint of French accent, though he'd lived for many years in the United States.

"How'd you go from Ebola to Donna? Although come to think of it, she did put me under quarantine."

"You'll wear her down," Joey said. "You're irresistible to women. It's the Vow of Celibacy. Women love a challenge."

But Donna wasn't just any woman. She was . . . Donna. Funny, brave, loyal Donna. And she was dealing with something big; his radar told him that. His better judgment told him to give her a wide berth. Another part of him—the protective side he could never silence—wanted to know what was going on, and how he could help.

"Jean-Luc pointed out that you've said more about Donna than about any woman since Angela." Joey raised an eyebrow. "And you don't use the tone of voice you used for Angela."

"What tone of voice?"

Jean-Luc answered. "As if you were tiptoeing through church."

"*What?*"

"Oh yes." Joey gave Jean-Luc a high five. "Nice description, for a French guy."

Mike took a long swallow of wine. So maybe he had been a little tongue-tied around Angela. He'd been so crazy in love with her, so profoundly infatuated. At least those days were over. He hadn't tiptoed once around Donna, but that was most likely because he wasn't in love with her.

Sometimes he wondered if the doctors had taken his heart along with his kidney, because he hadn't come close to falling in love since Angela. Flirtation and sex, sure. Plenty of that, at least during the off-season. Lust, hell yes. Especially around Donna MacIntyre. But love . . . that shit was off-limits. Not happening.

Zack was so excited for his first baseball game that Donna couldn't understand why she'd never taken him before. They got Cracker Jack and a hot dog, and big cups of Sprite. Luckily, he had no interest in the intricacies of the game, since she wasn't exactly well versed in the rules of baseball. She pointed out Mike in his lobsterlike catcher's gear, and said that he was her friend. When a home run cracked off his bat in the third inning, they both jumped up and cheered, and Zack flung his Cracker Jack over a ten-foot radius.

The Catfish organization went out of its way to make the game fun for kids. A blond girl with a microphone kept popping up and announcing new games. "Hey kids! Is your birthday in the month of April? Come on down to the field!"

"Mama! When's my birthday?"

"September, sweetie. Want to come back then so you can go on the field?"

"Yeah!"

"Maybe Mike could take us." Look at her, pretending that she and Mike were such good friends that he'd do anything for her.

"No, just us."

"Fine. Be that way." She popped a peanut into her mouth to hide the salivating inspired by the sight of Mike jogging around the bases. There was something very arousing about watching someone do something so well. Sure, he was incredibly fit and powerful, and he knew how to move his body with complete control and efficiency. But it was more than that. It was the lightning-quick pickoff of someone trying to steal second. It was the way he scrambled to catch a foul ball that fell nearly out of reach in the stands. It was the way he communicated with the pitcher, a young, copper-skinned man who seemed very jittery and nervous. Mike kept going out to the mound to converse with him.

Afterward, they waited at the exit where the players came out. When Mike Solo strolled out, his hair damp from his shower, his eyes lit with the satisfaction of a good game, her heart did a slow twist. Had she ever really gotten over that crush last season?

Mike crouched down and offered his hand to Zack. "You must be Zack. I'm Mike Solo."

Zack peered at his hand. "What's that white stuff?"

Mike spread the fingers of his right hand wide, and Donna couldn't stop the flash of memory of what his hands had felt like roaming her body. "That's some leftover Wite-Out. I paint a line on each finger so the pitcher can see my signals. Sometimes, when I can't find my Wite-Out, I dip my hand in the chalk on the baseline. Guess I should go wash my hands again, huh?"

So fascinated he didn't even make a funny face, Zack stared from Mike's hand to his face, and back again. Donna's gaze strayed to Mike's thighs, so incredibly strong, bulging against his jeans in his crouched position. He must be in phenomenal shape.

"Hey, I have something for you." From his pocket, Mike dug out a baseball and handed it to Zack. "Look, it's got your name on it. From Mike Solo to Zack."

"Say thank you, Zack," Donna reminded him, when her little boy just kept staring at the ball.

"Thank-you-where's-the-lobster?"

"Lobster?" Mike glanced up at Donna.

Donna let out a snort of giggles. "Your catcher thingie that you wear on your chest. He thinks it looks like a lobster. Actually, he thinks it looks like Larry the Lobster from one of his books. He's never seen an actual lobster."

"Well, I think we have our next mission then." He rose to his feet. "There's got to be someplace in this town that serves lobster."

"Oh no. No. No, Mike, we're not going out for lobster."

He shot her an innocent look. "I had in mind something a little different." Ten minutes later they were standing in the foyer of Captain Scrugg's, gazing at the lobsters crawling around the big tank. Zack pressed his face to the glass and made faces at the beady-eyed creatures.

"I figured cheeseburgers after this," Mike said in a low voice. "I don't remember being into seafood much as a kid."

"You don't have to do that, Mike."

"Relax, Mother Superior. I'm hungry. Hitting home runs takes a lot out of a guy."

"That was really exciting. Zack loved it."

"What about you, did you love it?" He said the words close to her ear, so his warm breath tickled her neck.

"Sure, what's not to love about a guy running the bases in tight baseball pants? I liked how you kept going out to talk to the pitcher too. What were you talking about? Exchanging recipes? How he got that pattern shaved into his scalp?"

Mike didn't look as amused as she thought he would. "Not exactly. He was being a dick and I had to straighten him out."

"Really? That sounds juicy. Drama on the baseball field?"

"You have no idea. We have more drama than a freakin' sorority. That was Yazmer, and he thinks he's king of the world. Decent curveball, change-up, fastball starts strong but fades by the fifth inning. He'll never make it to the bigs like that. He needs to start switching up his pitches in the fifth inning, if not earlier. The guys will figure it out and start waiting for the fifth, then walk all over him. Not only that, but he needs to pick up the pace. I've been whipping the ball back to him in 1.5 seconds to get the point across, but do you think he pays attention to me? No, because I'm just some loser who's been catching for the Kilby Catfish too long."

The hint of bitterness in his voice caught her by surprise. "What's too long?"

"It depends." He shook his head, as if flinging off his moment of moodiness. "The Friars have two great catchers on their roster, so they're in no hurry to call me up. I'm the guy they count on to work with superstars like Yazmer, who'll be pitching in San Diego before the ink is dry on his contract. God, does that sound bitter? It's not. I'm not. That's baseball, and I love it. I just don't like Yazmer."

"Me neither," she said instantly. "Mi enemy es su enemy, that's one of my mottos."

He threw his head back and laughed, low and gravelly, like extra-smoky barbecue. "I think I knew that already."

Zack was tugging on her hand. Shockingly, she realized that she'd forgotten where they were, standing at a fish tank in a small-town seafood restaurant in Kilby, Texas. She could have been circling the moon on a spaceship, or sailing a wooden ship across the Caribbean. The only thing penetrating her awareness was the presence of Mike Solo. Cripes, she'd almost forgotten about Zack!

Guiltily, she knelt next to him. "What is it, Zack?"

"Can we take him home with us? He doesn't have anyone to play with." He held up his baseball and rolled it against the tank. "Here, lobster."

Gently, she tugged his hand away from the tank. "We can't take him home, hon. Where would he live, the Hannigans' bathtub?"

"Yes! I can take baths with him!"

Donna tried to imagine Mrs. Hannigan going

along with that, and failed. "I'm going to say that's a no, Zackster."

He muttered something about Bonita, and she blanched. Oh no. Did he have some kind of crazy idea that perfect Bonita would let him get a pet lobster? Nerf football, maybe. Pet lobster, no. "You can ask Bonita. May the force be with you. Hey, are ready for a cheeseburger?"

Mike, of course, had overheard all that. "Who's Bonita?" he asked in a low voice.

"You don't want to know all the complicated family dynamics."

"Yes, I do. I'm curious that way. It's the next best thing to sex."

"Hey, watch it. There's a kid here."

"Fine. Better than baseball." He put the word "baseball" between air quotes and added a wink. "Better than running the bases, if you know what I mean."

"Bonita"—she gave him a severe look—"is Harvey's fiancée. Harvey is Zack's father. Zack lives with Harvey's parents. For now."

After that, she refused to say any more. If that little thumbnail sketch of her life wasn't enough to scare him away, there was plenty more where that came from.

Mike helped Donna strap Zack into his car seat in the back of the red Kia. How that car fit the three of them, he had no idea—call it cozy and intimate. Donna drove him back to Catfish Stadium, where he'd left his car, and he spent the whole drive trying to think of clever ways to get her to go out with him again. She seemed freakishly determined to keep their relationship distant. Was she embarrassed to have a child with someone she wasn't married to?

True, his parents wouldn't be impressed, but he didn't judge things like that. He definitely wanted to know more about this Harvey, and why he hadn't stepped up and married the mother of his child. Must be a weasel. But Donna didn't want to talk about it, and he had to respect her privacy.

As they approached the big concrete structure with the blue Catfish pennants flapping in the wind, Donna looked over her shoulder at Zack. The kid had nodded off on the drive. "Do you mind if we circle the stadium a few times?" she whispered. "He could use a little nap. That game wore him out."

"Sure." Would it be embarrassing to admit he was happy to circle around the stadium in this tiny car, with Donna's hair gleaming in the glow of the dashboard lights and Zack's soft snore rising from the backseat? He wasn't ready to say good-bye to Donna; he still had too many questions. While they were trapped in this car by Zack's need for sleep, why not take advantage?

"So, Donna, I couldn't help noticing that you wore a pantsuit to the game today. A dark blue pantsuit. Very . . . sobering. Like a bucket of ice water over the head."

A dimple appeared in her cheek. "Yes, well . . . there's a lot of blue in my closet lately."

"I still remember what you were wearing when I first met you. Snakeskin pants and a white top. Sexy as freaking hell."

"Hey!"

"He's asleep."

"I don't want any bad words filtering into his unconscious. The last thing I need is him repeating things to his grandparents. Guess who'd get the blame for that?"

"Sorry. I'll watch it. But you're changing the subject. What happened to the Donna I knew way back last season? That crazy, wild chick in the Roadhouse?"

"Look." She glanced in the rearview mirror, checking on Zack. "If you're looking for crazy, wild Donna, forget it. I'm not that person anymore. I'm a mother, I'm a responsible, taxpaying, *football-loving* citizen of Kilby, Texas. I won't take it personally if we say good-bye now and you find someone else to party with."

"That's not what I meant, Donna. It's a pretty radical change, that's all. I'm wondering what's behind it. Seems like you're trying awfully hard to be something you're not."

"How do you know what I am or am not? We never knew each other that well." She yanked the wheel and sent them lurching around the corner, then immediately slowed down and checked on Zack.

"Good point. I didn't even know you had a kid."

"Well, don't take that personally. Even Sadie didn't know."

"Seriously? Your best friend?"

"Believe me, I got enough grief about that from Sadie. She understood, in the end. She's a hundred percent behind me now."

"Maybe you just need to give people a chance, Donna. Maybe I could help. Take Zack to some games. Play catch with him."

"Why?" They were circling around the back entrance of the stadium again; he saw the upper edge of the Jumbotron peeking above the outer walls, blotting out a block of stars. "Why do you want to do that?"

"He's a cool kid. Why wouldn't I?"

"What exactly are you up to, Solo? It's not sex. It's not partying. You'll be off to San Diego, if what they're saying is true. I don't get it. I'm a dull, boring dental receptionist who wears navy-blue suits and granny underpants. I couldn't possibly be your type."

He gave her a long, level, sideways look. "You expect me to believe that?"

"You saw where I work. Why wouldn't you believe me?"

"I believe that part, but nothing you say will convince me you're wearing granny underpants. You want me to believe that, you'll have to show me."

She laughed. Just a little, at first, maybe from shock. Then it grew into a gurgling, rolling belly laugh, open and free and joyous, as if she hadn't really laughed in far too long. "I'm not showing you my panties, Solo."

"Mama?" Zack's sleepy voice interrupted.

She pulled over next to one of the entrance gates. "You should go."

"Maybe I'll call you later."

"Maybe I'll answer, maybe not."

Deciding that a true gentleman let the lady have the last word, he extracted himself from the mini-car and crossed to the sidewalk on the driver's side. He waved to Zack, then dug through his pockets for his keys. As she put the car in gear, Donna rolled down the window and leaned out.

"Red thong," she said in a whisper, then drove away.

Damn. Of course he was going to call her. There had never been any doubt.

Chapter 6

Donna put her chances of withstanding Mike at about sixty-two percent, based on her strong motivation to clean up her act, versus the incredible temptation he represented. The vow definitely helped. She knew he took it seriously. She wasn't afraid of slipping into bed with him. It was the distraction that worried her, and what other people would assume if they saw her with him.

Just to double-check, she called Ms. Griswold and outlined the situation.

"You say he's sexy? That is, most objective observers would consider him such?"

Ms. Griswold was definitely an odd sort of lawyer. "Off the charts."

"But he's known for his Vow of Celibacy? Is this an official vow, witnessed by a member of the clergy?"

"I believe so."

"And you've slept together in the past?"

"No, it never went that far. We didn't even get horizontal."

"There was intimacy?"

Man, she'd hate to be on the witness stand being

interrogated by Ms. Griswold. "Yes. No one knew about it. Although the librarian gave us a funny look when we came out of the closet."

"Is there any chance this could become serious? I'm talking legal here. Marriage contract, pre-nup, that sort of thing."

"Good God, no."

"Too bad. Now that scenario could have some potential." The lawyer let out a huff of disappointment. "Here's the thing. We're talking risk versus benefit here. Risk of misinterpretation if you're seen is high. No one's going to believe that 'vow' crap. This isn't the Middle Ages. On the other hand, the benefit of being with him is low."

"How do you figure that?" From her perspective, she saw plenty of benefit in being with Mike. Being with him felt both new and familiar. She could talk to him as if they'd been friends forever, and yet he made her feel wide awake, as if she didn't want to miss anything.

"If the vow is real, there's no sex, right? Your reputation could be damaged, yet you get no sex to compensate for that."

Donna's head was starting to spin. "Is this serious legal advice or are you pranking me?"

"I don't make the rules here. This is a lose-lose situation. Stay away from him. That's my official recommendation as your lawyer. Now, how's the volunteering at the pet shelter going?"

"Hypocritically. Can't I volunteer at a place closer to my heart? Something with kids or seniors? I'm great with kids and old people. Pet dander makes me sneeze."

"No. Pet shelters are hot right now. Everyone's doing it. Junior League's all over it. Take my advice, that's what I'm here for."

"I'm not exactly Junior League material."

"We're working on that, aren't we? Now, do you have your outfit for the hearing tomorrow?"

"Sackcloth and ashes, check. Still trying to decide if I should shave my head."

"Mouth, Donna. Watch that mouth."

Oh cripes, it was impossible. The process of de-Donna-fying herself was excruciating. But for Zack, she'd try her best.

The hearing was supposed to set a visitation schedule pending the outcome of the case. The next day, she sat primly, hands folded in her lap, while Ms. Griswold argued for three visits a week to prepare Zack in case he went to live with Donna. Brilliantly, she managed to drop news of Donna's new position at the dental office, her work with abandoned pets, and the football-themed furniture that filled her apartment.

On the other side of the courtroom, Bonita hung on Judge Quinn's every word, taking notes as if she was in class. She wore her long black hair in a high ponytail that somehow managed to look superior. Even when Ms. Griswold spoke, she refused to look at Donna's side of the courtroom, as if it would give her cooties. Harvey looked bored, his legs stretched out in front, crossed at the ankles, arms folded over his chest. Donna wondered what they saw in each other, since they seemed like complete opposites, the overachiever and the slacker. But maybe that was it. Bonita needed someone to boss, and Harvey needed someone to boss him.

After hearing both sides, Judge Quinn ruled that Donna could see Zack two times a week, and set the next hearing for late June.

Bonita shot to her feet. "June twenty-sixth is our wedding date."

"Yes, the court is aware. You are not required to attend the hearing, of course, if it poses an inconvenience. The presence of your representative is enough."

"No, no, that's not what I meant. I meant . . ." She sat down abruptly, tugged by her lawyer. Donna knew what she meant. She wanted the hearing to happen after the wedding. Once they were married, Bonita and Harvey would be a picture-perfect couple. A family court wet dream.

Afterward, in the courthouse hallway, Donna stopped at the water fountain for a drink. As she straightened up, she jerked in surprise; Bonita stood over her, looking down her nose from what seemed like several feet. "Nice try, Donna MacIntyre. I see what you're up to with the new look. But you're not fooling anyone."

"I'm not trying to fool anyone. I just want my kid."

"You've lived in Kilby all your life, do you think anyone's going to forget who you really are?" Bonita radiated complete confidence, as if everything she said was automatically true, just because she said it.

Donna gripped the edge of the water fountain. She'd never felt so short before. "You don't know me."

"Sure I do. You're a party whore and always will be." One slim eyebrow went up, while her disdainful gaze skimmed down Donna's outfit. "And I'm pretty sure I saw that suit on the five-dollar rack at the church bazaar."

Donna's hackles rose, all her good intentions flying out the window. "Well, there's nothing wrong with repurposing someone else's secondhand goods, is there?"

The jab hit home with unfortunate timing; Harvey was just strolling to Bonita's side.

"Hey," he protested, as Bonita went white.

"Do you see what she's like?" Bonita murmured to Harvey, resting her forehead against his shoulder. "She's a bad influence on Zack, honey bear. She's too impulsive, too mouthy. This is why we can't agree to joint custody."

Donna clenched her fists, cursing herself for rising to Bonita's bait. "I apologize," she made herself say. "I didn't mean any offense."

"You have to think before you just blurt things out," Harvey told her in a patronizing tone that made her want to scream. "We have to set a good example for Zack."

"So true," Donna managed, her voice cracking. How had she let Bonita outmaneuver her like that? "That's exactly what I'm trying to do."

"Well, I'll be watching like a hawk. And so will my family." Bonita tilted her sleek head and pinned Donna with a pointed look. "We still talk about that night in the Roadhouse last year. The Wades have long memories."

Apparently everyone in Kilby still talked about that brawl. For cripes' sake, she'd been standing up for a friend! "This isn't the Wades' business. The ruling is up to Judge Quinn."

"And you think *that's* going to win him over?" Bonita gestured at the Texas A&M pin on her collar.

"Like you ever cared about football before. Weren't you hanging out with that Catfish player last year? That's what I heard."

"I wasn't 'hanging out' with a Catfish player. You really shouldn't listen to gossip, Bonita." Lifting her head, Donna brushed past her. "It's bad for your immortal soul."

All things considered, Donna knew without a doubt that seeing Mike again would be criminally stupid. So when he called the next day, as she was painting her toenails a shade of puce that would have made the old Donna ill, she told him flat-out that she couldn't be seen in public with him.

"No problem. I can be your guilty secret. That sounds kind of hot."

Why did his voice have to curl through her insides like warm butterscotch? "It won't be. You're wasting your time."

"Hey, it's my time. I can do what I want with it, at least before batting practice and after the games. What if I just want to talk? Get to know you better?"

Her phone started to slide off her shoulder. She clamped her lower jaw onto it, trying to pin it in place. "There's nothing . . ." The words came out funny, since she couldn't close her mouth without losing her phone. She grabbed it with her right hand, the one that held the nail polish wand. " . . . to know."

"Everything okay over there?"

"Yup." Well, except for the nail polish she'd just gotten on her cheek. Could you put polish remover on your skin? Was that safe?

"Well, Red," Mike was saying, "I don't want to

call you a liar, but that sounds like an untruth to me. Tell me this: How did you meet Zack's father and why aren't you with him?"

"Wow, you really go right for the jugular, don't you?" She rose to her feet to check the damage in the mirror. Yup, a slash of puce right across her cheekbone.

"I believe in swinging for the fences. Going for broke. Sports metaphors of all kinds."

Donna scowled at her reflection. Maybe she should dye her hair puce to match the nail polish. Better yet, dye it maroon and white, Texas A&M colors. "How about going down for the count?"

"Nice one. How about this. I'll tell you one big thing if you tell me one big thing."

"What makes you think I care about your big thing?"

A loaded silence followed. Donna tried not to laugh, tried really hard. She bit her lip until her face turned red, the streak of puce standing out like a scar.

"Now that's just mean, Donna MacIntyre. You don't care about my big thing? You really know how to hurt a man."

She gave in and let out a laugh. It seemed as if she never laughed anymore. Only with Mike. "Fine, I give up. We'll exchange big things."

"Excellent. You first, since I asked first. And I really want to know about Zack, because he seems like a great kid."

The one sure way to her heart was by complimenting Zack. Donna settled herself on the toilet seat and crossed one leg over the other.

"Zack's father is Harvey Hannigan. When I was a

naïve eighteen-year-old, I thought I was in love with him."

"You weren't?"

"To be honest, it was mostly about his Harley, and pissing off my stepmother, and the way his hair kinked at the hairline."

"The old Hairline Kink. Get the girls every time."

"Yeah. I thought it meant he was sensitive and poetic. Like Edward in *Twilight*. Anyway, I got pregnant, and yes, I was on birth control. Sometimes things just happen. He broke up with me right away."

"Why?"

"He didn't want a baby because he was right in the middle of rebuilding his bike. And no, I'm not making that up. He wanted me to get an abortion, but the thing is, as soon as I did the pregnancy test, the name Zack popped into my head. A blue plus sign . . . Zack. That quick. I always knew it was a boy too. Sounds crazy, huh?"

The fumes of the nail polish must be going to her head. She'd never told anyone this, ever.

"I don't think so. I've made lots of decisions based on gut instinct. So obviously you chose to have the baby anyway. Why doesn't Zack live with you?"

She wasn't ready to tell that part of the story. "No way, buster. That's big thing number two. Your turn first. Cough it up, Solo. What deep, dark secret are you hiding from the world?"

"Well . . ." He hesitated for a long moment, long enough that she started to think he was about to weasel out of their bargain. "I had a kidney removed. I donated it. To my brother."

"What?" She paused, her nail polish wand suspended in mid-air.

"I'm a one-kidney wonder. Don't worry, my other organs are still intact."

"Don't make a joke out of this. When did it happen? Are you okay?"

A rumble of laughter rolled across the phone line. "You worried, sweet cheeks? Want to come empty my bedpan?"

"No jokes! Seriously. Are you okay?" An image of Mike taking punches for her at the Kilby Roadhouse flashed through her mind. What if he'd gotten hurt?

"I'm fine. I'm fine. It was four years ago. It's nothing but a scar now."

"Oh, Mike." Tears came to her eyes, which made no sense. Why was she crying over Mike Solo's kidney? Mike, whom she barely knew? But maybe she knew him better than she thought, because it didn't surprise her that he'd donated a kidney to his brother. "Is that kind of surgery risky?"

"You're really concerned." He sounded touched, which made more tears come to her eyes. She jammed the brush back in her bottle of nail polish and swiped the wetness off her cheeks.

"I'm *concerned*," she said sternly, "on behalf of the Kilby Catfish. Isn't it hard to play baseball with only one kidney? Are you going to cause a problem for my hometown team?"

"You don't fool me, Donna MacIntyre. You were crying, weren't you? I heard a tear fall. You were crying because you like me."

"Well, you did stand up for me against the Wades. So there might be a bit of a soft spot going on."

"I'll take it. Bit of a soft spot is better than a hole in the head. Or the gut."

"You really do make a joke out of everything, don't you?"

"You know how that goes, don't you, Ms. Hairline Kink?"

She got up off the toilet seat and stashed all her nail polish supplies in the medicine cabinet, all while cradling the phone against her neck. She'd figured out a long time ago that if you made enough jokes, no one saw you crying. Not that she was crying over Mike. Okay, so maybe she was, a little, because he was a good guy and she *hated* seeing him hurt.

"I should go, One-K."

"I thought my nickname was Priest."

"You got yourself a new one. Congratulations."

"On another topic, where's the best Laundromat in town? It's the craziest thing, but it's hell doing laundry with one kidney."

"You are so full of it."

And yet, before she knew it, she'd agreed to help him do his laundry the next day. After all, how much trouble could you get into doing laundry with a man, no matter how sexy?

"Really? I totally pegged you as a boxers kind of guy." Donna surveyed the pile of laundry Mike had just dumped onto the table at the Suds-o-Rama Laundromat.

"Boxer briefs all the way, babe. We can't all wear red thongs." He winked, an electrifying green flash. "By the way, why do we always end up talking about underwear?"

"Let's change it up and talk about your socks. How many do you have?"

"Well, here's the thing. I don't like doing laundry, and my signing bonus gave me plenty of money to play with. So if I run out of socks, I buy more. They do tend to build up, it's true." His forehead crinkled as he picked up an armful of dirty laundry and dumped it in the washing machine. "Admit it. You're blown away by the glamorous life of the minor league baseball player."

"Absolutely. I'm considering live-tweeting this, by the way."

"I'd be worried, except I know you don't want anyone to know we're hanging out. What made you change your mind about that?" He opened the box of detergent he'd purchased from the vending machine and dumped it in the washing machine.

"I haven't changed my mind. I just don't think anyone's going to see us here. Anyone who cares, that is." The Suds-o-Rama was on the opposite side of town and besides, no one in the Wade family would go near a Laundromat.

"Good. Then you can hang out with me."

"Not for long. I have errands to run."

"Through the wash cycle?"

"Spin, max."

"Fine. That gives us enough time for this." He whipped out an insulated flat container from the very bottom of his duffel bag. As he unzipped it, the most amazing scent rose to her nostrils and mingled with the soapy smell of laundry.

"You brought pizza?"

"Not just any pizza. Tombstone, the best frozen

pizza on the planet. I have a supply shipped to me at the start of each season, then I dole it out like candy at special occasions. Chicago guys and their pizza, you know. I nuked it right before I left the apartment."

She leaned over it, breathing in the tomatoey, savory, mouthwatering scent. "So this is a special occasion? Laundry?"

"Laundry *with you*." He gave her that special smile, the one that tugged a devastating groove into his cheek and made the palms of her hands tingle. "That's special occasion enough for me." He raised his voice so the other patrons could hear. "Anyone here a fan of the Kilby Catfish?"

"Sure, man . . ." "Yep, gonna be a great season . . ." "Nah, football fan here . . ." came a scattering of answers.

"Well, close enough. Pizza's on me, folks. Help yourself to a slice, and think kindly of the Catfish."

He pulled out a package of paper plates, kept a few slices aside for him and Donna, and served out the rest.

"Heard Crush Taylor's looking to sell the team," said a tough old guy in a cowboy hat. "Wants a million dollars."

"Wouldn't be the Catfish without Crush," said a black woman dressed in head-to-toe hot pink. "Kinda got used to all their crazy ways. How many teams bring pizza to the ordinary folks trying to get their washing done? I don't see no New York Yankees here, do you?"

"If I did, we'd have an old-fashioned brawl on our hands," said the first man. Donna and Mike exchanged glances.

"Actually, we're trying to change our reputation. No more partying, no more Roadhouse fights. We're just going to play ball this year, hopefully take it all the way to the championship." When the customers didn't seem impressed, his smile dropped. "What's the matter? You don't want a championship?"

"Like I said," explained the black woman, "we like our Catfish the way they are. It's like your favorite soap opera, except it's all men and they're a treat for the eyes. You too," she added generously. "You ain't bad, but Dwight Conner's my man."

"Good choice," Mike agreed. "Want his number?"

Donna laughed, while Mike and the woman exchanged a fist bump. A warm feeling spread through her as she watched Mike transform a dreary Laundromat in a lousy neighborhood into the only place you wanted to be on a Saturday morning. The only place she wanted to be, anyway. She could spend the rest of the day here, laughing at his quick comebacks and soaking in his wicked smile.

When he slung his arm over her shoulder and pulled her close to his side, it felt so natural and inevitable. Like coming home after a rough winter. It had been so long since she'd simply enjoyed herself in a man's presence. And this wasn't just any man. This was the man whose green eyes and ripped physique had been haunting her thoughts since last September. Now he was here, and he seemed to like her, even though there was no chance of sex.

A helpless smile spread across her face and she allowed herself to relax against him. His body felt so strong and solid. There was no harm in enjoying herself for a tiny moment, right? She and Mike weren't doing anything other than laundry, with a little sexual undercurrent on the side. Throw in some pizza and community outreach, and Crush Taylor would be proud. What harm could there possibly be in this scenario?

Chapter 7

THE LAUNDRY IDEA had been genius. It was such a normal, everyday activity. Well, not for Mike, since he avoided laundry like the plague. He used to tell his sisters laundry made his balls shrink, at which point they'd shriek and tell him how gross he was and somehow end up doing the laundry. During the season, he dumped his laundry at the cleaner's or at the clubhouse. He never did it himself. But it was worth going to a Laundromat to get Donna to finally stop looking at him with that stay-three-feet-away-and-you-won't-get-hurt expression.

Why he was going to all this trouble, he couldn't really say. Except that time passed so quickly with her, as if they were gliding down a sparkling river in a rowboat built for two. And she distracted him. She distracted him from the worry over Joey.

The latest news from Jean-Luc was that Joey had checked into the ER with a 103-degree fever and that he'd lost another three pounds.

"Hey Solo!" Donna snapped her fingers to catch his attention. "Are you reminiscing about your lost kidney?"

"Cute. Very cute." That was another thing. What had possessed him to tell Donna MacIntyre about the surgery? Trying to win pity points? Trying to prove he was more than "Hottie McCatcher"? He hadn't thought about it, he'd just wanted her to know. "Maybe I'm trying to figure out how to get you to stay until it's time for the dryer."

"You sweet talker. How does any woman resist you?" She sparkled at him, those changeable eyes a smoky gray at the moment. Today, thank the sweet Lord, she'd left the panty hose and insurance sales-woman uniform at home, and instead wore cute little madras-print low-riders, Skechers, and a form-fitting sleeveless top that left her freckled shoulders bare. Her body had deep curves to it, the kind a man could lose his mind over, but she didn't dress to emphasize them.

Well, except the first time he'd seen her, at the Roadhouse. And the time he'd taken her and Sadie to Crush's legendary All-Star party. No doubt, Donna could rock a sexy outfit when she wanted to.

"I honestly have no idea. I suppose you'll have to give everyone else pointers."

"Me? I'm such a sucker that you got me to do your laundry when there isn't even the tiniest chance of sex." She shook her hair over her shoulder, tossing him a teasing look. The look of someone who knew she could tease him and not worry about the conse-quences.

He wrapped one of her curls around his index finger and tugged slightly. "Believe me, if we had sex you wouldn't use the word 'tiny.'" Her eyelids flut-tered; a nerve by her mouth jumped. Oh damn. He'd forgotten how quickly they'd both caught fire back at the Kilby Community Library.

"Stop that," she said weakly, casting a glance around the Suds-o-Rama, where everyone else had long since gone back to their towel folding and phone checking.

"Oh, sorry," he said, pulling his hand away so it just happened to skim across the back of her neck. The fine hairs rose up and a shiver traveled across her skin. For the first time, he didn't mind the absence of her long mane of hair.

"What are you up to, Devil?"

"New nickname, huh?" He whispered in her ear, brushing his lips against the complicated whorls. "Better than Priest, that's for sure."

"Oh, you have no chance at Priest anymore." She took a determined step away from him, putting a laundry cart between them. "Not since the library closet."

As if she'd lit a torch to a pile of kindling, he felt heat surge inside him. "You had to mention the closet. You just had to."

"Oh, is that topic off-limits? My bad." She pulled an exaggerated face of apology.

"Do me a favor and let's not talk about it. I'm a visual guy, and that shirt you're wearing really hugs your body, and let's not even talk about that little strip of skin above your shorts."

A glow came into her eyes, a sort of a mischievous, playful light, the kind of expression he remembered from before. She leaned against a washer, a seductive smile playing across her lips. "What's the problem, Solo? It should be perfectly safe to *talk*. The Vow of Celibacy doesn't cover talking, does it?"

"No, but talking leads to—" He shut his mouth with a snap. Right now, talking was leading to hardening. Last thing he needed. Better not to talk.

"What does the vow cover, by the way? Is it just the whole enchilada, so to speak?" She flicked a glance down his body. "What about the à la carte menu?"

He shifted his stance to accommodate his growing erection. *Down, boy. Down.* "We don't really get into details when I take the vow."

"So, for instance, what we did in the closet . . ."

"Not allowed."

"Really?" She purred, trailing a hand across her stomach. Helplessly, he followed it. "Why is that?"

"Because it's a slippery slope."

Her eyes lit in amusement. "Oh, I bet it's very slippery. Wet and slippery and . . ."

That was it. He had to shut her up, now. He pushed the laundry cart aside, and hauled her up against him. "You're trying to kill me, aren't you," he growled into her ear.

"Just trying to get the lay of the land." She batted her eyelashes at him, but they couldn't hide the way her pupils were dilating. The speed with which they got turned on by each other made his head spin.

"Would you stop saying sex words?"

For a moment she seemed to liquefy against him. His blood sang in his veins. The mounds of her breasts pressed against him, the nipples hardening. Oh sweet Lord, what he wouldn't give to push up her little top and fill his hands with her. The memory of how her skin felt rushed through him like a drug. Soft, so soft and silky, as if she spent all day bathing in cream.

"Donna," he breathed. "You're driving me nuts."

"You started it. You whispered in my ear. That's an erogenous zone for me." Her whisper had a husky edge that gave his cock another jolt. With one hand, he maneuvered a cart piled with laundry so it blocked them from view—at least from the waist down. She worked her hands under his T-shirt and ran them up his back. *Oh God in heaven, hallowed be thy name* . . . In his mind, he repeated the words of his vow, but they seemed so far away, almost meaningless, as she nestled her hips against his groin. His erection had grown to mountainous size, which seemed to mesmerize her. She kept moving her hips against him, little undulations that nearly brought tears to his eyes.

He clamped his hands onto her ass, loving the way her curves overflowed his grip, the way they enticed him to misbehave, to crush her against him, spread her out against a washing machine, expose each part of her delicious little body.

Whose stupid idea was the vow, anyway? Would anyone really care if he broke it? Would God smite his baseball career if he strayed? Did he care?

He'd just about decided he didn't when Donna let out a long sigh, and with a last sweet drag of her hands down his back, withdrew them from under his shirt. She even tucked the tail of his shirt into the back of his jeans, as if to block off access to his body.

"You shouldn't be allowed near any woman with ovaries," she said, her face flushed, her eyes filled with desire. "It's just not fair."

"You're not the only one in pain. I'll raise you a pair of blue balls and a hard, throbbing—"

She put a hand on his mouth to shut him up. He took the fleshy heel of her palm between his teeth and nibbled on it. Her eyes hazed over. "If you say one more word I might come right here in the Suds-o-Rama," she hissed.

"No one can see." He wasn't completely sure of that, because he couldn't tear his eyes away from her pink face and moist lips. God, he wanted to kiss her. He could kiss her, right? The vow didn't mention anything about kissing. Maybe he could just lick her bottom lip; yes, that wouldn't do any harm. He slid his tongue across that pillow of flesh, and it was like taking the first lick of an ice cream cone. The flavor of sweetness and wild promise flooded his senses. He parted her lips with his and delicately touched his tongue to the flesh just above the inside of her teeth.

She shivered and let her head tilt farther back. He loved kissing, always had, because he'd been raised a Catholic boy and for many years kissing was the only thing the girls would allow. Now all those hours spent exploring the magic of canoodling coalesced into a timeless golden bubble. This girl. This moment. This eager, warm cave opening for his pleasure. This sweet body rippling with tremors. This slow surrender, both of them falling deeper and deeper into the world they were creating together, a world spun of sensation and trust and desire.

"Mike . . ." she whispered against his lips. "We need to stop."

He felt her mouth moving against his, heard the words, but it took time for them to make their way to his brain. He drew in a deep breath, gathering willpower from the depths of his being, and shifted the kiss from passionate to tender, a slight clinging of her lips to his. "I know," he breathed. "Stopping now. In a second. Okay, now."

They drew apart. Their connection was so strong that breaking it caused a flash, like an electrical short.

No, that wasn't some kind of cosmic short.

It was a camera flash.

He spun around, blocking Donna from view. A tall, striking girl with long black hair waved from behind an expensive digital camera. "Hi there. Don't mind me. You two are awfully photogenic together. Front page material."

Donna jumped back about three feet and hit the laundry cart. Flailing, she wound up on her ass inside the cart, which then rolled against a row of dryers with a thump. She scrambled out. "*Shit*."

"Hmm, swearing as well as making out in a Laundromat? Judge Quinn will be interested to hear about this."

"This is low even for you."

"I warned you." She put the lens cap back on her camera, pulled it off her neck, and stashed it in a zebra-striped cowhide tote bag.

Mike stepped forward. He didn't know who the woman was or what she was up to, but Donna was upset and that's all he needed to know. "Look, miss, that was a private moment you had no business photographing. If you delete that photo right now, we won't have a problem."

"I'm not deleting a thing. I knew she'd slip. A leopard never changes his spots, and Donna MacIntyre is and will always be exactly who she is. Irresponsible and reckless."

Donna turned nearly as red as her hair. "That's not true." Not much of a comeback; she must be really rattled.

"I only know what I see. You're Mike Solo, aren't you? The Catfish player?"

There didn't seem to be any harm in admitting that, so Mike nodded. "If you're thinking of sending this to the press, there's no point. I'm no Trevor Stark. No one cares what I do off the baseball diamond."

"You're right, no one cares what you do. You'll be gone from Kilby before I even bother to learn your middle name. But some people care what *Donna* does, and some of those people are members of the court system." She shouldered her bag, smoothed her hair in a self-satisfied way that grated on Mike's nerves, and glided out of the Suds-o-Rama. The *court system*? For fuck's sake, they hadn't done anything criminal.

"Xavier, my middle name is Xavier," he called after her, because, damn it, sometimes a guy had to get the last word.

Donna, looking stricken, stared after the woman with the camera.

"Who is that?"

"Her name's Bonita. She's my ex's fiancée." He took a step toward her, wanting to offer comfort, but she backed away. "This is bad. Really, really bad. What photos do you think she got? I had my eyes closed, I didn't notice her until we stopped kissing."

"Same here. That's probably all she got, if that's what you're worried about." He still didn't understand. Why wasn't Donna allowed to kiss someone?

"No. She looked too pleased with herself. She must have gotten more. Your hands on my butt, for instance."

The black woman in pink called from across the Laundromat, "She was clicking away for a good long while, there. Surprised y'all didn't notice. Want me to go after her and rip that camera out of her prissy little hands?"

"That's all right," Mike said, when Donna didn't seem capable of responding. "It was just a kiss, and I don't know what all the fuss is about. You all are witnesses we didn't do anything besides kiss."

"Some kiss, though," the woman said, almost wistful. "Made me want to go home and throw my honey right down on the kitchen table."

Donna still hadn't cracked a smile. She looked so lost and scared, which was not usual for her. Fearless Donna with the mane of wild red hair had been replaced with a worried girl with wide eyes and a hunted expression.

He drew her aside, close to the dryer where no one could hear. "We're two consenting adults. And fully clothed. We weren't doing any harm."

To his shock, she burst into tears. "You don't understand. I've ru-ruined everything." She jerked away from him and, quick as a Caleb Hart fastball, bolted out of the Laundromat.

For a frozen moment, he stared after her. What the hell was going on? Did she want to be alone? Was she safe, running while so upset? Should he go after her, whether she wanted him to or not?

"I got your laundry, baby," called the woman in pink. As if he cared about his laundry. There were plenty of other socks in the world. "You go after her. Try another one of those kisses on her. If it don't work, you come try it on me."

Without a second thought, Mike abandoned his laundry. On his way out the door, he veered in the woman's direction and planted a big kiss on her cheek.

"That's a start, baby," she called after him as he burst out the door into the blazing Texas heat.

Visions of revenge danced through Donna's mind, so vivid she barely saw the sidewalk in front of her. She'd catch up to Bonita and smash her stupid camera against a lamppost. Bonita would cry and her perfect makeup would run down her cheeks in streaks of black. She'd barge into the Sunday sermon and lecture the congregation with an extensive PowerPoint presentation on what a nasty person Bonita was. She'd . . . She'd . . . Oh, who was she kidding? Bonita would always win because she was ruthless when it came to getting what she wanted.

"Donna." Mike caught up with her with a hand on her shoulder. Mike Solo, the cause of her current disaster. She rounded on him.

"This is all your fault. You took a *vow*!"

He drew back, frowning. "And I kept it. We kissed, that's all. What's going on here, Donna? I feel like I'm missing a piece of the puzzle."

"I knew I should stay away from you."

He shoved his hands in his pockets, looking miserable. "I'm sorry. Really. I didn't mean to cause a problem for you."

And still he lingered, as if afraid to leave her alone.

He glanced around the neighborhood, which she suddenly saw through his eyes. Broken glass scattered on the uneven concrete beneath a lamppost, a wrecked car resting on rusted rims, still parked at the curb. No one cared enough to tow it away. "You can leave, Solo. I know my way around my own town."

"Sorry, babe. I'm not leaving you like this. If you don't know that much about me by now, you haven't been paying attention."

She knew that. Of course she knew that. He'd stood up to the Wades for her. No one had ever done something like that for her before. Suddenly all her fire evaporated. Who was she kidding? Mike had done nothing wrong. She'd teased him, going on about the closet, taking things in the flirtation direction. She'd wanted to kiss him; she *had* kissed him. She'd wanted more, much more.

She buried her head in her hands, incredulous that she'd screwed things up this much, this quickly. "It's my fault, completely my fault. Bonita was right. I'm impulsive and irresponsible. I'll always be the fuckup. And I wouldn't even mind, because it's kind of fun being the fuckup, but Zack . . ." Her throat closed up with fear. If she lost Zack because she couldn't keep her hands off Mike Solo, she'd hate herself forever.

"Zack what? What does this have to do with Zack?"

"Everything."

Chapter 8

AT FIRST MIKE couldn't completely make sense of the story Donna told. Zack, Harvey, Bonita, the judge, the Wades; it all blended together. Finally he settled her into his Land Rover and told her to stay put while he retrieved his laundry. Then he drove her to the Smoke Pit BBQ. Her blood sugar needed some help, he figured. A giant platter of ribs, fries, and coleslaw ought to do it.

"So you're trying to convince the judge that you've changed and are ready to take custody of Zack?"

"Sort of. I never signed away my parental rights. It was an informal agreement and I've been a consistent part of Zack's life all along, unlike Harvey. So I should be able to take Zack now. That's why Bonita has to do underhanded things like catch me necking with a Catfish. If she can prove that I'm not fit, then she and Harvey could get custody."

"What about the Hannigans? Where do they stand?"

"They're staying out of it, mostly. They're ready to let someone else raise Zack. If I'd just gotten my shit together earlier, before Harvey met Bonita . . ." She shook her head angrily, pushing ribs around on the platter. "Bonita's the one pushing for full custody. Harvey wouldn't mind split custody, or even visitation. He's an easy-come, easy-go sort of guy. If Zack wasn't around for a while, he might wonder what the kid was up to. That's about as far as it goes with Harvey."

Mike could already tell he didn't like Harvey, and he hadn't even met him yet. "Okay, I think I get the picture. But do you really think a kiss is going to make you look unfit?"

"Maybe not. I don't know." Looking wretched, she took a long sip of her iced tea. "It's the Wades, you see," she explained. "Bonita is a second cousin or something. She's just like them. Thinks she rules the world and everything is a competition. The Wades play dirty and they'll do anything to win. I don't think like that. I just want Zack. I don't want to hurt anyone else. But they're all or nothing. Win or go home."

Mike shook his head. He'd think she was exaggerating if he hadn't seen the shit the Wades had pulled with Sadie. "They are a law unto themselves."

Donna poked viciously at the smoky meat on her plate. "They are what they are. And I played right into Bonita's hands. This spare rib is smarter than me."

Mike would give anything to bring back her bright smile. "Listen, Donna. Don't worry about Bonita. I'll pull the vow card if I have to."

"Yeah, that'll make me look even worse. I'll come off as the party whore trying to tempt you into sin."

"You're blowing this out of proportion, Donna. It was one kiss. No one's going to care."

She nodded mechanically, as if all she wanted was for him to stop talking so she could focus on her fear. He leaned across the picnic table and clasped her elbows, one in each hand. If only he could infuse his own confidence into her. "I always saw you as fearless, Donna MacIntyre. Where's the girl who took on Kilby's ruling family and made them look like the asses they are?"

"I'm not fearless." She picked up a forkful of coleslaw, then put it down again. "Okay, maybe most things don't scare me. But I'm terrified of one thing. Losing Zack."

"Donna . . ."

"No! You don't know, Mike. Don't try to tell me everything's going to be okay, or it's not that bad."

He threw up his hands, even though that was exactly what he'd been about to say. "Fine. Have it your way. It's a disaster."

"Are you making fun of me?" She slammed down her fork and leaned over the table, her eyes blazing gold. "I nearly lost Zack once. They almost gave him away behind my back."

"*What?*"

"Oh yes. When I was pregnant I was so sick I wound up in the hospital. Mentally sick, emotionally, everything. Like I was in a black pit with a huge stone on top of me. They had me on all kinds of medication, and I slept a lot, but one day I heard my mother in the hallway, on the phone with someone. They were running through possible homes for Zack. My mom said she couldn't take him because she's on the road so much. Then she said, 'Carrie won't touch the baby with a ten-foot pole.' Carrie's my stepmother.

And *then* she said, 'Donna can't raise him. My girl's a sweetheart, but she wouldn't even know what a bottle is. Unless it says IPA on it, of course.'"

The pain on Donna's face made Mike want to rip something apart.

"May I point out," Donna added, with an attempt at a smile, "I was always more of a Shiner girl. Lone Star on a good day."

"You don't have to joke about this, Donna."

She pressed her lips together, clearly holding back tears. "Laugh so you don't cry, right? Anyway, the next word I heard was 'adoption.' The person on the other end of the line started talking, and I felt like my life was swirling down the drain. I knew if I didn't get myself out of that bed and do something, I'd never see my baby. They'd take him away, give him up for adoption, and I'd never find him."

"What'd you do?"

"I rolled myself out of that hospital bed. I was on an IV drip because I couldn't keep anything down. I felt like some kind of weird pregnant zombie busting out of the grave. I was all sweaty and gross and . . . anyway, you don't need to know all that. As far as you're concerned I was a knockout in my silk negligee and feather boa."

Oh, Donna. Even telling such a painful story, she managed to squeeze in a light touch. His heart ached for her.

"I couldn't even walk right, I was dizzy from all the medication and everything kept swirling around me. Somehow I made it to the hallway where my mother was talking on her cell phone. Next to her was a rolling table with a bunch of plastic-wrapped food trays on it. I grabbed a little packet of plastic silverware, a napkin wrapped around a knife and fork. Then I ran out of energy. I crumpled down in front of my mother, landing half on her feet. I held the silverware up in the air, in my fist, like some revolutionary."

She gripped her fork to demonstrate.

"I said, 'No adoption. I won't sign. I'll swallow this fork first.' And for some reason, my mother believed me. Maybe because it's not often a crazy pregnant girl lies down on your feet. Or maybe because I sounded like myself again after two months of sounding like the Voice of Doom."

"So they canceled the idea of adoption?"

"Yes. That's when the Hannigans stepped in. And I'm grateful. When I think about how close they came to giving Zack away to a total stranger so I'd never even get to see him . . . I mean, what if I hadn't overheard that conversation? What if I'd signed some papers without even reading them, because I was so out of it? Yeah, it scares me to think about losing him, Mike. It scares me to death. I feel like I have this little toehold in his life, and it could get taken away if I make a wrong move." She carefully put down the fork she'd been brandishing. "That's why I shouldn't have made out with you in the Laundromat. Or the library, but at least Bonita wasn't in there hiding with the mop bucket."

"I'm sorry, Donna. I really am. I had no idea about any of this."

"I know. It's not your fault. It's mine. I knew I couldn't trust myself around you." She offered him a smile that landed somewhere between impish and rueful. "You know something? I think the Vow of

Celibacy makes you even more attractive. And I can't believe I just told you that. Or all that other stuff." She expelled a long breath of air.

"I'm glad you did." He thought back on every interaction he'd seen between Donna and Zack. Affectionate, attentive, responsible—he couldn't imagine anyone questioning her fitness as a parent. "I bet the judge will see what I see. Someone who loves her son and wants to take care of him."

A slow flush rose up her face. She looked like she might cry again.

"No one in my family supports me on this. Judges like to hear testimony from family members. But my mother's in Europe right now, my stepmom hates me, and my dad can't be bothered. He keeps telling me I'm worried for nothing. At least, I think that's what he's saying, though it's hard to tell when he only speaks to me from underneath a car. He's a mechanic. If you ever need that Land Rover worked on, we can take it to him. Give me a chance to say hi. God, why can't I stop babbling?"

"Maybe because it's important?"

She gave a few quick nods. "My gut says I could lose Zack. And now I've made things a million times worse. Bonita's going to make it look like all the navy blazers and the good-girl stuff is just an act. Which it is, but not *completely*. I'm not a *bad* girl." She chewed on her bottom lip, reminding him of how it tasted when he'd kissed her in the Suds-o-Rama. "I don't even go out anymore. But who's going to believe me?"

"I can back you up on that. I had to go to the ball-shriveling extent of doing my laundry, just to get you to go out with me. I'll tell any judge that, even though it makes me look a little pathetic, quite frankly."

"Thanks, Solo." Finally, a faint smile made its way back to her face. "That's nice of you."

"Listen, I'll take you home, and you should take a bath, drink a cup of tea, read a book, whatever you like to do to relax."

"Put on Nine Inch Nails and punch holes in the wall?"

"Whatever it takes. And don't spend any more time worrying about this situation. I'll figure out how to handle it."

She shrugged, a hopeless little gesture that made his heart grieve. Donna wasn't used to people helping her; that much was clear. Well, she'd have to get used to it. Because there was no way he'd just stand by while she looked so frightened and sad.

The problem of how to help Donna dominated his thoughts over the next few days, to the detriment of his play at home plate.

They were playing a three-day home stand against the Salt Lake Condors. With a man on second, their slugger hit a long line drive that Dwight Conner chased down in center field. He threw to Leiberman, who executed a perfect throw to home, right in the dirt the way Mike liked it.

And Mike . . . missed it. The runner on second—a guy named Bates, who could have played linebacker in football—was barreling down the third-base line like a tanker truck. Mike got into position, his body firmly planted in front of the plate. He kept his eye on the ball winging toward him, while tracking the progress of the runaway train about to mow him down. And at the last minute, he flinched. He dove for the ball instead of waiting for it to come to him. By the time he caught it, no part of his body was touching home plate and his glove was nowhere near Bates.

Christ Almighty. He was going to hear about that from Duke. Not to mention the way he and Yazmer had been off rhythm all game, conferring after every other batter. Sure enough, as soon as the inning was over—with the Catfish down three runs—Duke collared him in the dugout.

"My ten-year-old niece makes that play, Solo."

"If you're trying to insult me by comparing me to a girl, not cool, Duke."

"I'm comparing you to a ten-year-old. She happens to be female. And tough as a tank, but that runs in the family."

"I'm sure it does."

Duke lowered his voice. "Crush told me about the kidney. I saw you flinch out there. How's it feeling? I gotta ask."

Fucking Crush had ratted him out. "No, you don't. It's not a factor."

"You guarantee that?"

"Absolutely." What if Crush told more people? So far, no one in the media knew he was a one-kidney player. The last thing he needed was reporters crawling all over his personal business, prying into Joey's life. If it were up to him, he'd tell the whole world he had a loving, supportive brother who happened to be gay. But his parents had begged him to keep their personal life private, and he felt compelled to honor that.

"Well, something's up. You and Yaz are a train wreck out there."

"I know, Duke. We have communication issues." That was one way to put it. Another way was that Yazmer paid no attention to anyone but himself.

"Work it out, Solo. Whatever it takes. Group therapy, language lessons, whatever."

"On it, Duke."

He walked to the other end of the dugout, where Yaz sat by himself, his pitching arm tucked in the sleeve of his jacket, head bobbing to a beat only he could hear.

"Yo, Mike-o Solo." Yaz shot him a sideways mocking glance. "Give me a shout next time, I'll cruise my ass home for the play."

"Yeah, right. You wouldn't want to mess with that million-dollar face."

"Right on, baby, right on. I did the math, yo, and my face is worth more than your whole body."

"You might be right about that." Mike sat next to him and held out a packet of sunflower seeds.

"What's this, some kinda peace pipe action? I don't get high with the people tryin' to dictate my ass. Dick-tate." He drew it out with an emphasis on the "dick."

Mike fixed his gaze on the batter's box, where Trevor was at the plate, staring down the Condor pitcher who'd been giving him fits lately. He crouched over the plate like a lion ready to pounce on a rattlesnake.

"It's sunflower seeds, Yaz. Nothing more. And I'm not dictating out there. Just trying to do my job. Control the pace of the game. Share my experience. Like, you don't let Bill Danson anywhere close to a curve-ball because he eats them for breakfast and throws up homers for lunch."

"Not mine. Popped it up, baby, popped it like a soda."

"That's because he has a sore shoulder. I noticed it when he was warming up. You could have gotten a groundout, easy. But you had to get cute."

"Ain't no thing. An out's an out. Gotta be me. I don't do no quick at-bats. I want my time. My time to shine. The Yaz gotta be *the Yaz*. Whoo!" He thumped his chest. "Yo, you gonna sign our petition?"

"What petition?"

"Keep the queers out of our locker room. Keep it clean, baby."

Oh, for fuck's sake. Mike gritted his teeth against the irritation he wanted to unleash. "Yazmer, this is Triple A in Kilby, Texas. We have, like, two reporters in town. Why do you worry about something like that?"

"We gotta set an example." Yazmer popped a piece of gum in his mouth. "Like you, with those In-stagrams. Represent, yo. Consent to represent, keep it de-cent."

"What are you talking about?"

"Hashtag Suds-o-Rama. Hashtag dirty laundry. Hashtag hot chick. Her hands all up in your—"

"All right, all right. Can you give it a rest . . . Whose Instagram?"

"Mine, everyone's. Re-gram, baby. Mik-o Stud-o gettin' his freak on. New respect, brah, new respect." He shoved his shoulder against Mike's.

"Nothing happened, Yazmer. I took a vow. Every-one knows that."

"What I *know* is Instagram don't lie."

Oh hell. He needed to see what Bonita had posted, like *now*. But phones were banned in the dugout. He'd have to wait three more innings to see how bad the photos looked, what they showed. He remembered Donna's hands on his back, under his shirt, and the way she pressed against him . . . so freaking hot. But they'd been fully clothed. How bad could the shots be?

"Get smilin'." Yazmer bumped his shoulder again. "You're a ballplayer. That's a pussy jackpot. One of the perks, yo."

"Anyone ever tell you you're an ass?" Mike said it with as much false good humor as possible.

Yazmer cocked his head to the side. "What'd the Yaz do to you? Besides shake you off like a toxic cloud?"

"I don't have a problem with you, as long as you stick to fastballs and curveballs, and stay away from cameras. I care about baseball. I care about playing my heart out and winning games, not photo ops or freaking Twitter."

Yazmer worked his gum, giving Mike a sideways liquid glance. "Sorry, Prehistoric, I ain't staying away from no cameras. Camera's in my blood. Gotta share this gift with the world. How long you been in Triple A? Take a page out of my playbook. Put yourself on the map. Live big, die hard. That's my motto. Can't touch this. Can't touch this." He jumped to his feet, punching the air.

Mike rolled his eyes, then heard the crowd roar.

Trevor Stark had just hit a monster shot, so high it could knock out a passing bird. Everyone watched it soar and soar, higher and higher, then finally descend toward the stands, well into home run territory, if not even farther, like Catfish record territory.

Stark could sure hit.

He managed to round the bases without any overt gloating, which Mike considered a personal triumph. He kept telling Stark what a dick move that was.

And now, Stark had just saved his ass. The runs Mike had allowed with his home base error were erased, and the Catfish had a one-run lead. When Trevor jogged into the dugout, barely winded, Mike bumped chests with him.

"Way to work the count, buddy."

"And bail you out." Stark winked one crystal-green eye.

"Tryin' to steal my pixels, Stark?"

Mike and Trevor both stared at Yazmer. Sometimes the guy was literally incomprehensible. "What?"

"My pixels. The ones in the headline. They need to say 'Yaz.'"

Trevor scratched the back of his head. "As in, 'Yaz is a fucking asshole'?"

"Don't matter what it says. No big—I'll be top story soon. I got something brewing." Yaz smiled smugly. "Need-to-know basis. Today, you don't need to know."

Mike glanced at Trevor, who looked just as confused as he was. "Whatever, Yaz. I'll tell you what I need to know today. I need to know what pitches you're going to throw. Can we try to keep some open lines of communication on that?"

"Sure, baby."

Ramirez struck out to end the inning, and Mike got busy refastening his gear to get back on the field.

He jogged out to home plate, nodding to the young umpire. Always good to be polite to the umps.

Yazmer took the mound as the first batter, Seth Morton, came to the plate. Mike settled into his crouch and made eye contact with Yaz. He called for a fastball over the plate, because Morton never swung at the first pitch. Never, ever, not once in the history of ever. Yaz shook off the sign. Mike sighed. Arrogant, know-it-all kid. What did he mean by that comment about having "something brewing"? He was such a freaking publicity hound.

Mike gave in and called for the changeup, Yaz's go-to pitch. Yaz went into his windup, planted his foot, and hurled the ball right into the dirt two feet to the right. Mike barely managed to get his glove on it.

Ball one. Gift-wrapped and hand-delivered to Seth Morton of the Salt Lake Condors.

He shook off his irritation and gathered up the ball, tossing it back to Yazmer with no expression. *Gotta work with the guy no matter what an ass he is.*

Donna's face flashed into his mind, her teasing smile as she told him, *Mi enemy es su enemy.* Daring, fierce Donna, willing to transform herself for her kid.

And right then, behind the plate, one of his lightning-quick, intuitive calculations kicked in.

1. Donna loved Zack.
2. Mike had gotten her into this mess.
3. He was a man.
4. A man with an alleged Superhero Complex.

In that moment, he knew exactly how he could help Donna.

Chapter 9

"**H**OW BAD IS IT?" Donna couldn't even look at the photos, which was why Sadie had shown up at the Dental Miracles office and whisked her off to lunch at the Roadhouse. An especially nice surprise because Sadie didn't even live in Kilby anymore. She lived in San Diego with Caleb, but came back often to make sure her mother was handling her absence okay.

"It's not bad at all. No boobage is showing, that's good." Sadie smiled at her, that bright, optimistic smile that didn't fool Donna in the least.

"I'm not worried about that. Does it look like I'm some sort of man-crazy slut who can't keep my hands off the hot baseball player?"

Sadie squinted at her phone. "Well, for sure, no one could blame you. Mike Solo is a great guy, and he's very sexy."

"So that's my excuse? 'Judge Quinn, I plead extreme hotness. No reasonable girl would pass up the chance to make out with Mike Solo.' That's not going to fly, Sadie."

"The photos don't prove anything, Donna. Even if

you slept with him, they don't mean anything. You're single, you're young, why shouldn't you kiss a boy?"

"I don't know. My lawyer has me all stressed out. She called and yelled at me, said if I can't stay away from Mike she'd drop my case."

"Screw her," Sadie said loyally. "We'll find another lawyer."

"You're being so nice about this, after I was so rotten and secretive."

"Would you stop beating yourself up about that? You were trying to respect the Hannigans' wishes. And I was buried in my own drama. You should be mad at me for being so self-centered."

Donna made a face at her friend. "Don't be ridiculous. Why don't we just agree to be mad at the Wades? They actually deserve it. And Bonita, of course. And Harvey, for proposing to Bonita. And Olympus, who designed the camera."

"What about the inventors of Instagram?"

"I don't know how they sleep at night, quite honestly." They smiled at each other. Sadie always made Donna feel better; she was the best friend in the world.

"So what about Mike? Do you two have something going on?"

"No." Donna pressed her lips together. She didn't want to reveal anything more about her and Mike. Something was going on, but she didn't know what. Something different, and . . . significant. But nameless. "We're friends. Between his vow and my new leaf, that's all it's ever going to be."

Sadie looked at her phone, which still displayed the photo of Donna and Mike locked in each other's arms, then back at Donna, her skeptical expression saying it all.

"Okay, okay." Donna gave in. "I find him attractive. I like him. He makes me laugh. There's a lot more to him than I knew at first. And he defended me at the Roadhouse last fall. I've never forgotten that. What can I say? I'm a girl, and when a guy protects me like that, my ovaries start doing the conga. That's all."

"Mm-hm." Sadie, aggravating girl that she was, got a smug expression on her face. "Sounds like trouble to me. Take it from someone so deep in love it would take dynamite to get me out."

"Aww. You deserve it, sweetie." A memory flashed into her mind—the last time she'd seen Caleb and Sadie together, in Sadie's hospital room. He'd been kneeling next to her bed, his tawny head bent over Sadie's dark one. They'd looked completely lost in each other and so beautiful that Donna had teared up. Sadie deserved a wonderful man and a happy future. Donna knew exactly what her friend had gone through before Caleb had come into her life.

That kind of fairy tale wasn't for her, even though part of her longed for it. What would it be like to have a strong, caring, protective man fall passionately in love with her? What would it feel like to bring a man like that to his knees?

As if reading her mind, Sadie said gently, "You deserve it too, Donna. Maybe you don't believe it now, but someday the man of your dreams is going to sweep into your life like a hurricane and you won't know what hit you."

Those prophetic words came back to Donna when she opened the door later that night to find Mike Solo on the front landing. In typical Texas spring fashion, it had gone from shorts to jacket weather in less than a day. A strong wind tousled his hair and sent moonlit clouds skittering across the sky behind him. He hunched his body protectively over a bouquet of lilacs. Their tiny petals shivered with each gust.

"Can I come in?" The wind seemed to snatch his words away, like a gleeful, mischievous imp. "Little windy out here."

"Yeah, sure." She cast a quick glance down her body to make sure she was decent. Sleep shorts and an *Emperor's New Groove* T-shirt. She'd been attempting to balance her checkbook, which had required the comfort of her favorite childhood movie. She gave the lilacs a suspicious glance as she stepped back to let him in. In her experience, flowers were a bad sign. They indicated an apology, which suggested wrongdoing of some kind. Even so, they smelled wonderful, like a hopeful spring dawn. "What's this all about?"

Mike passed a hand across the back of his neck, a nervous gesture she'd never seen from him before. "I . . . uh . . . did something stupid."

"Are you talking about kissing in a Laundromat? I already told you, I don't blame you for that."

"No. It's not that." He inhaled a deep breath, then seemed to remember that he still held a clear plastic cone filled with lavender petals. "Do you mind taking this? You might need something to hit me with."

She didn't take it. "Now you've got me worried, Solo. Spit it out, would you? Are you in trouble with the Catfish? Did Moses come down to smite you with a burning bush because we made out?"

A faint smile finally softened the stern set of his mouth. Unfortunately, that drew her attention to his mouth, and to the rest of him, sexier than ever in black jeans and a Chicago Bulls jacket. He glanced around her apartment, at the posters of Texans player J.J. Watt, the football-shaped beanbag chair, the wastebasket that looked like a football helmet.

"Why does it look like the NFL threw up in here?"

She crossed her arms over her chest. "Because this is Texas and we love football here. And Judge Quinn's a fan and I have to prove I can provide a suitable home environment for Zack."

Mike looked revolted, so she switched the subject back.

"Spit it out, Solo. What's up?"

He squared his shoulders. "Did you know that Bonita uploaded those photos to Instagram and hashtagged the Catfish? A bunch of people saw them."

"Yes, I know. Sadie looked at them for me. She said my hair looked amazing and—"

"I reposted them. And I said you were my fiancée."

"You *what*?"

"People were making Laundromat jokes about dirty laundry and between the sheets and all kinds of crap. I had to do something. So I did that. Now everyone thinks we're engaged. So . . ." He sank onto one knee and held the bouquet toward her. "Donna, will you marry me?"

For one long, frozen moment, Donna dared to believe it was real. Her crazy thoughts from earlier in the day flashed through her mind. *What would it feel like to have a man fall passionately in love with her . . . to bring him to his knees . . .* But this wasn't passion or love. This was some kind of cosmic joke. She snatched the bouquet from his hands and threw it across the room, onto the beanbag chair. The plastic cone slithered off the vinyl and landed upside down on the floor. "Screw you."

For a guy whose fake proposal had just been brutally shot down, Mike didn't look very crushed. "Maybe you should think about it a little more." He held her gaze, his green eyes dark and steady.

"I know what's going on here. You're doing that knight-in-shining-armor thing. Just like at the Roadhouse. Listen to me, Solo. I don't need you to get me out of trouble. I can handle this."

"You've got it wrong, Donna."

"Oh really? Do you always propose to girls after you make out with them?"

"Hardly ever."

"This isn't a joke. And no, I *won't* marry you. Because you're insane and I can't taint my gene pool with any more craziness. It has plenty already."

Something flickered deep in his eyes. Had she hurt his feelings? *Could* she hurt his feelings? Did he have any feelings toward her? "I was thinking that there's a lot of potential here. We get along well. The sparks are there."

Everything he said made it worse. "Shut up, Solo. Just shut up. And get up off your knees." To work off her fury, she whirled around her apartment like a mini-tornado. Get along well? *Get along well?* That's why he was springing this "proposal" on her? "I'd rather marry a horn-toed slug."

"Donna, you're reacting emotionally. Just think about it."

"Oh, I'm not supposed to react emotionally to a *proposal of marriage*?" A proposal was supposed to be romantic and special, one of the most beautiful moments in a girl's life. A *couple's* life. They weren't even a couple!

She marched to the front door and flung it open. "Get out, Solo."

He got to his feet but made no move to leave. "I will. But you're not thinking about the big picture. You're not thinking about Zack."

"What about Zack?"

"Don't you think the judge will look at you differently if you're engaged to be married? To a very well-compensated, up-and-coming baseball player?"

She tasted bile in her throat and ran for the bathroom. Bent over the toilet, she heaved for a moment, but nothing came up. *Get a grip, Donna. Get a grip.*

With the cold porcelain of the tank clamped between her hands, she tried to push all the hurt aside. The problem was that she felt too much for Mike, and he didn't have a clue about it. It wasn't that she was in love with him, but . . . the image of him at the door, his face so gravely serious, that bouquet of lilacs in one big hand . . . oh sweet Lord in heaven. Maybe she had fallen for him. Somehow that pesky crush had developed into a full-on infatuation.

But he didn't know that. And he never would either. She'd keep that reality hidden away until it wasn't reality anymore. She'd cure herself of her crush. Because clearly he didn't feel anything of the sort for her, or he would have mentioned it when he proposed marriage. It was the kind of thing that seemed relevant.

She rose to her feet and stared at her reflection in the mirror. What about Zack? Mike had asked. Yes, what about Zack? She'd do anything for Zack, anything to keep from losing him. *Get Zack back.*

It pissed her off that Mike had a point about the judge, but he did. A single, barely employed twenty-four-year-old suddenly transformed into the fiancée of a solid man with a bright future? Bonita would eat her heart out. For a moment she wavered.

No. No, she couldn't do it. It wasn't fair to Mike. He could have a hundred different girls. He was a hot ballplayer with his whole future ahead of him. Why should he get stuck with her because of one spontaneous make-out session in a Laundromat? Then again, this "engagement" was Mike's idea, so why should she try to protect him?

Most of all, what was best for Zack in this situation?

She splashed water on her face, took in a few deep breaths, then soldiered into the living room. Mike, hands in his pockets, stood at the front window, watching the tops of the cottonwoods whip back and forth in the wind. The square set of his shoulders, his upright posture, the tension in his stance all said one thing: a man doing his duty.

His duty. Again, bile rose to her throat.

Think about Zack.

Mike seemed very far away, but she screwed up her nerve.

"We could fake it," she said into the empty space between them. He turned to face her, his eyes deep and stern.

"Not an option. I can't lie to my family about something like this."

Her former nickname for him, the Priest, flitted across her mind. For a playboy ballplayer, he sure had strict principles.

"Solo, you can't seriously want to marry me. Don't you want to fall in love before you get married?" She made herself ask that question, even though each word pierced her like a thorn. Because she knew the answer she wanted, and she knew it wasn't coming.

"Hell no. I was in love once. I think I'm good."

She laughed. Trust Mike Solo to surprise her like that. "You don't believe in love?"

He seemed to be weighing his words. "I used to believe in love. I was engaged to my high school girlfriend. We stayed together until I left the Navy. She didn't want me to quit the service," he explained vaguely, giving her the impression he was leaving out something important. "We agreed that we didn't share the same values."

She waited for more details, but he set his mouth in a firm line that warned her to back off. Fine. She'd let it go for now, but Mike Solo had no idea how persistent she could be. "So you had a bad experience with love and now you're willing to get married without it. Am I summing this up correctly?"

He gave an impatient gesture, as if all the talk about "love" was an irritation. "I don't believe in the fairy-tale version of love. The 'stars in your eyes, every breath you take' kind. It's all a big illusion designed to sell wedding dresses and honeymoons in Jamaica. Is that stuff more important to you than Zack?"

Ooooh. *Ouch.* Tears prickled the backs of her eyelids, but she shoved her hurt aside. Her feelings weren't important here. Zack was. Besides, hadn't she written off the whole "fairy tale" love stuff ages ago? When Harvey had taken a pass on forming a family with her and Zack?

"You want to be a stepfather? Raise a kid who isn't yours?"

He squared his shoulders. "I think I'd be a damn good stepfather."

Honestly, she couldn't argue with that. She couldn't picture anyone better, except maybe someone who actually lived in Kilby. Then again, maybe it would be an advantage that Mike didn't live here. They'd have a long-distance, come-and-go relationship, not a real marriage. Most of the time, she and Zack would be on their own. She could probably live with that.

"What's in this for you, Solo? I still don't get it."

A strange expression crossed his face, as if he didn't entirely get it either. "I'm going with my gut here. But if you don't want to do this, I can go on Instagram and say it's over. You dumped me. Or I dumped you. Either way."

Yeah, that would probably work. There would be a flurry of talk, which Bonita would gloat over, but it would die down quickly enough. On the other hand, the thought of going before the judge with Mike Solo on her side filled her with a giddy sense of hope. Maybe there was a way to fake it without faking it. "What if we stay engaged until after the hearing?"

"Won't work. Everyone will be too suspicious. If we get engaged, we have to immediately start planning the wedding. Make it real."

A wedding. She felt a little faint and had to grab

the back of her comfy chair to steady herself. "Then we get divorced as soon as possible."

"I won't marry with an eye to getting divorced. I don't agree with my family about a lot of things, but that one's on the list."

She dragged her hands through her hair in frustration. "You can't possibly be thinking that this is the right way to begin a marriage."

"It's not the typical way, that's true. That doesn't mean it wouldn't work. I think we have a lot more going for us than you think. I respect you. I trust you. We have lots of chemistry. I always have a good time with you."

"I have a lot of flaws, Solo. I'm impulsive, I speak before I think, I get into trouble all the time."

"Maybe you need a good man to look out for you." He tucked a hint of a smirk into the corner of his mouth.

She crossed her arms over her chest. "You think it's that simple? March in here and save the day? I have a say in this too."

"Of course you do. You can say no. Or you can say yes." A wicked grin slid across his face. "There might be lots of benefits to a yes, judging by what happened at the Laundromat."

"Let's not go there, please. The point is, I always figured I'd get married to a man I love. And who loves me. It kind of seems like a key ingredient of the whole experience."

Mike's eyes lit up, as if a fuse had suddenly been switched on. "Then the solution is simple. If love is that important to you, all I have to do is make you fall in love with me. Problem solved. So we have a deal?"

"A deal? What deal?"

"We get engaged for real, start planning the wedding, tell our families, tell the judge, all that stuff. But we don't actually say the I do's until I've made you fall in love with me."

She jerked, like a marionette on the end of a string. Fall in love with Mike? She was already halfway there, but clearly he had no idea about that. She certainly wasn't going to clue him in. "What if it never happens? What if I never fall in love with you?"

That devilish smile flashed across his face. "Oh ye of little faith. You should have a little more trust in your man, Donna. What kind of fiancée are you, anyway?"

Her man? Jesus, he was going to kill her with this. He wasn't her man. And yet he'd said the words. *Her man.* What would it feel like to *really* have Mike Solo be her man? *Forget it,* she told herself.

"Um . . . unwilling and resentful?"

"Then you'll fit in with the Solo family just fine." He winked. Suddenly he seemed on top of the world. "I like a good challenge. And I think I'm up for this one. I can be all kinds of charming when I try. Don't bet against me, Red."

"Oh my God. You're completely crazy."

"What are you doing tomorrow night?"

"Why?"

"Because I want to get started. Come to think of it, why wait?"

He strode toward her. A rush of heat swept from her head to her toes as he put his arms around her—so confident, so sure. She wanted to protest, because she was still pissed about this whole thing. The words stalled in her throat as he put his hands on either side of her head and scanned her face as if she were the most beautiful thing in the world. When actually *he* was, with his shadowed green eyes and smile that said, *Come play with me.*

"Don't you dare kiss me, Solo," she whispered. "I'm still thinking about all this."

He stilled, his mouth hovering an inch or so above hers. Electricity pulsed between them, thick and drugging. How easy it would be to rise up on tiptoe and touch her mouth to his. How easy to slide into that mad lust that simmered just below the surface. But her emotions were too chaotic, her thoughts all over the place. If he kissed her, she'd never get them sorted out.

She held his gaze, not giving an inch, until finally he sighed and stepped back. When his warm, rough hands left her face, she felt abandoned, which made absolutely no sense.

"I can tell you're going to be a boatload of trouble as a fiancée," he told her.

"Count on it."

"Oh, I am. I am." With an enigmatic smile, he let himself out the door.

Donna collapsed onto her couch. *Sweep into your life like a hurricane.* Yes, that's exactly how it felt. What the hell just happened? Was she actually kinda sorta engaged?

No. Not in her mind she wasn't. Maybe Mike couldn't lie. But she could. She hated it, but she had practice hiding the truth. After all, she'd hidden Zack's existence from Sadie. Even her current life was sort of a lie. She hated wearing navy blue. Didn't enjoy scheduling root canals one bit. But she'd do anything for Zack.

It would be a piece of cake to pretend that she wasn't already infatuated with Mike. He could knock himself out trying to get her to fall for him. She'd make him work for it. Make him sweat. But he'd *never* get those words from her. Never. And then they could call off the farce with no hard feelings.

Mike's horrible plan was to make her fall in love with him . . . without one word about *him* falling in love with *her*. In fact, he'd ruled out the whole idea of love. And there was no way she wanted to marry someone who didn't love her. Even if she was crazy about him. *Especially* if she was crazy about him.

Chapter 10

DATE NUMBER ONE did not go at all the way Mike planned. Once again, he showed up on Donna's doorstep with a bouquet of flowers—sweetheart roses that perfectly matched the fresh color of her lips. He intended to tell her this, but as soon as she sniffed them, she started sneezing. Not dainty little sneezes either. These were sharp, high-pitched little wheezes, like the bark of a Chihuahua.

"Are you okay?"

"I . . . yes. They're gorgeous. Wow, Mike." She fell into another spasm of sneezes. "I'm definitely in love with you now."

"Ha ha. Are you allergic to roses? You were fine with the lilacs yesterday." He cocked his head, remembering the cone of flowers she'd flung away when he'd proposed.

"It's just . . . *atchoo* . . . certain flowers."

He hesitated, not sure what to do with them. No sense in tossing them anywhere in her apartment; the place was so tiny she'd still smell them. "Hang on. Stay right there. You look amazing, by the way."

That she did, in a sapphire-blue halter-top dress

that showed off her cleavage and a whole lot of her legs. He tore himself away from her and took the steps to the downstairs apartment two at a time. An elderly woman lived there; he'd seen her peeking through her curtains. He knocked on her door and presented the bouquet to her with a grin and a bow. Her face lit up, which filled Mike with the comforting knowledge that at least he'd made *one* lady happy tonight.

Donna was on the landing, watching him with a disgruntled expression. "*Still* not in love with you."

"Not at all?" He gazed up at her, feeling like some sort of Romeo. "Maybe ten percent? Twenty?"

"*Atchoo.*"

Of course Donna MacIntyre would have to make things difficult. Why would he expect anything else?

As he led her onto the outdoor patio of his favorite local Tex-Mex restaurant, La Gallina, she stopped short.

"I don't know if I should do this," she said in a warning tone.

"Do what?"

"Well, I sometimes have a weird reaction to Mexican food."

"Sneezing like a Chihuahua?"

She gave him a narrow-eyed look. "No, nothing like that. You'll see. Or maybe not—it doesn't always happen. It depends on what kind of corn they use. We'll just take our chances, how's that? I just thought I should warn you."

"All right." Mike was starting to think she was playing him, but he shrugged it off and gestured to the hostess, who sat them at a cozy table in the corner behind an old tortilla press. La Gallina was third-generation family-owned, an old ranch house with only about ten tables and lacy curtains on the windows.

"What was it like growing up in Texas?" he asked, after they'd placed their orders for the house specialty, chicken enchiladas with *mole* sauce. "You were best friends with Sadie, right?"

"Since fifth grade. It started out rocky because we both wanted to jump, and we both got stuck turning the ropes instead."

"What?"

"Double Dutch. The jump roping game? We were both obsessed with it. After we got to be friends, we practiced all the time. I think Kilby's a pretty good place to grow up, until you're about fourteen. Then you go a little crazy because you basically know everyone, and they know you. You're sure there must be something more exciting out there, but it's a four-hour drive to Houston, the nearest city. You start going to parties just to experience something different. The something different could be trying beer for the first time, or Gentleman Jack whiskey, or it could be riding on the back of a motorcycle, or streaking across the old lady's lawn next door, or egging the cop car parked outside the Dunkin' Donuts . . . I'm telling you all my flaws, Solo. If you want to back out, do it now."

"Not backing out." Actually, Mike loved listening to Donna talk, no matter what the topic. She was so easy to be with, unlike Angela, who'd always seemed so untouchable, so remote and pure.

Donna was not untouchable. Or remote. Or pure,

unless you counted "pure fun." She was real and unpretentious and she loved to tease.

About halfway through their meal, as Mike was telling her stories from the clubhouse—his problems with Yazmer and Bieberman's quest to add the phrase "what the Jeter" to the English language—her eyelids dropped halfway over her pretty hazel eyes. She ran her tongue over her lips, leaving them pink and glistening. "Mike, I . . . uh . . . I hate to do this, but I think we should go now."

"Go? Why?"

"I warned you about the corn. Certain kinds of corn . . . make me very . . . very . . ." Under the table, with its red-and-white checkered tablecloth, her hand latched on to his thigh. " . . . horny."

"Corn makes you horny?"

"Oh yes." She danced her hand farther up his thigh, making his cock jump to attention. "Extremely. White corn more than yellow corn, and especially if it's GMO and non-organic." She ran her fingers across the crotch of his trousers.

"Donna, *stop that*. We're in a public place." *Again*. "What about Bonita? She could be stalking us with a camera again."

"So? We're engaged, right? Anyway, no one can see us back here."

She traced the contours of his bulging erection. *Oh, fuck*. "Donna, you have to stop. Have you forgotten my vow?"

"But . . . we're engaged, have you forgotten that?"

"Engaged is not married." He captured her hand firmly in his. "And this is still a public place. And I don't think you should have any more tortillas."

She pouted, her bright hazel eyes catching the candlelight, and suddenly he wanted her in his arms, wanted her sweet body curled around his. "Ah, forget it. Let's get out of here," he growled.

"*Yes*. Sorry, but I did warn you. Oh Mike, take me home, you gorgeous man."

He threw a bunch of bills on the table and whisked her out of La Gallina. But when they got home, apparently the effects of the corn had worn off. Donna was yawning and drooping and had no more interest in his crotch. Instead, she stretched out on her couch. "You know what *might* make me fall in love with you? A foot rub."

"A foot rub." Blood was still pounding into his cock. How was he going to manage a foot rub when he wanted to throw her down right here, right now? Too bad. He'd taken a vow. And he was trying to make her fall for him. *Man up, Solo. Rub those feet.* "Okay. I can do that. The PT at the stadium taught me a few tricks."

But his techniques didn't work on Donna. Instead she burst into giggles every time he touched her, giggles that turned into gales of laughter. Apparently her feet were freakishly sensitive. "Never mind the foot rub," he said grimly. "Do I need to throw you in the shower to make you stop laughing?"

"No," she gasped. "Put on a movie. *Frozen* will work."

"*Frozen*? Seriously? I saw it once, I think that was plenty."

"Please."

So they watched *Frozen*, except that fifteen minutes in, she fell asleep draped across him. In that position, he couldn't move without waking her, so he ended up watching the entire movie. By himself.

On their next "date," he had to watch *Frozen* again, since she'd fallen asleep the first time. How many times could a red-blooded, full-grown American male watch those darn princesses? Also, tulips were a completely different kind of flower from roses. So why did his latest bouquet bring back the Chihuahua too?

At this rate, the woman downstairs would be able to open a flower shop.

On their third date, he skipped the flowers and brought take-out Chinese food. It turned out that MSG was just as bad as flower allergens. To distract from her uncontrollable sneezing, she put in the DVD of—what else—*Frozen*.

"If I turn into a Disney princess after this, you get to break the news to Duke," he grumbled.

"*Atchoo!*"

He settled on the couch next to her. By now, they knew exactly how to position themselves when sitting side by side. She liked to curl her feet under her, while he stretched his legs out. She often ended up pressed against his side, perfectly tucked between his arm and his hip. Maybe there was a bright side to the millionth viewing of *Frozen*, he thought. Time to go in for some hand holding.

While the little snowman sang his heart out on the TV, Mike snuck his hand toward Donna's. She seemed oblivious, riveted to the screen, mouthing the words along with Olaf. Seizing the moment, he wrapped his hand around hers, palm to palm.

Bzzzzzzz

The loud drone made him jump two feet into the air. A goddamn noisemaker. In her hand. That little . . .

"*That's it.*" He rolled on top of her, pinning her between his thighs, putting his back to *Frozen*—finally. "You're doing all this on purpose, aren't you? The allergies, the corn, *Frozen*. This is all some sort of master plan."

She blinked at him, innocent as a kitten. "Geez, Solo. I seriously have no idea what the Jeter you're talking about."

A stunned pause, then a snort of laughter rolled out of him. Big waves of mirth followed that one, until he was shaking with them, tears popping into his eyes, his ribs aching. She laughed along with him, her face radiating glee. He laughed until he couldn't anymore, then slumped next to her on the couch.

"You got me. I have to admit. The corn? Nonorganic, GMO . . ."

"I'm not even sure exactly what GMO is," she admitted. "And I've eaten tortillas all my life."

He wiped a tear off his cheek. "You're an imp, you know that? You've been playing me this whole time. So much for my moves. At this rate, I have a better chance of making you *not* fall in love with me."

"Might be a lot less work," she said demurely.

After that, he abandoned his planning method, and simply went along for the ride when he got together with Donna. He asked her lots of questions, listened attentively, and observed. He learned about the pain of her mother's leaving, and how she still idolized the gypsy, world-traveling Lorraine MacIntyre. He heard all about her father, a quiet man who spent most of his time under cars in his shop. He learned about her wild party days; her friendship with Sadie; her spontaneous, warmhearted nature; her dislike of rules and bullies; her deep love for her son. She'd gotten outstanding grades in high school, but hadn't been interested in college. He knew about her knack for mimicry, her way with a quick joke, the fact that she preferred laughter to sadness. Given the choice between being sexy and being funny, she'd pick funny every time.

That didn't make her any less sexy to him, but they were keeping their distance on that front. Strangely, now that they were "engaged," it seemed almost too . . . intimate.

About a week after their "engagement," as Mike headed to the clubhouse to get ready for a bullpen session with Yazmer, Joey called. Mike answered with his traditional greeting. "How's my kidney?"

"What on earth are you doing, Mike? Rita said you're engaged."

Mike winced, feeling funny about his decision for the first time. Joey was like the voice of his conscience. "Yes, although the way things are going, my fiancée might not survive to the wedding. Did you know that some people can't digest chocolate? What kind of life is that?" Donna had played one more prank on him the night before, when he'd brought her a box of Godiva chocolates.

"I'm serious, Mike. What are you up to?"

"You make it sound like getting married is some kind of evil genius plot."

"That's exactly what I'm wondering."

"I promise it's not. I'm really engaged. Mama's

happy. She's willing to overlook the fact that Donna's a non-Catholic unwed mother. Dad isn't. Big surprise."

"Are you in love with her?"

"You know how I feel about that sort of thing."

"Mike." Even over the phone from Chicago, Joey's soft reproach made Mike wince. "Are you really going to let your experience with Angela taint the rest of your life?"

"It is what it is, Joey." Could he help it if Angela had ripped up his heart and left nothing but shredded scraps behind? "Anyway, Donna's about as different from Angela as a girl could be. You'd like her. She's a little spitfire."

"So you like her."

"Of course I like her. She's funny and sort of . . . quirky and fearless. Loyal."

"Loyal," repeated Joey thoughtfully. "So, not the kind of girl who would ditch you because you changed careers."

"Not likely." Not the Donna who had stood up for her friend when no one else had. He tried to imagine Angela climbing up on a bar to defend a friend's reputation—or for any reason—and failed. Then again, Angela didn't drink. Angela was cool, serene, polished. He'd loved her hopelessly ever since he'd sat behind her in second grade and spent the entire school year staring at her long dark braid. He'd been stunned when she let him take her to a dance in seventh grade. Even more shocked when she'd accepted his worshipful proposal when they were nineteen.

In the end, she'd slipped through his grasp, the disdain in her dark eyes gutting him like a trout.

"If she makes you forget about Angela, she has my stamp of approval," Joey said.

"This has nothing to do with what I felt for Angela. That's in a category all its own. This is different. It's the right thing. I made a mess of things for her, and it's my responsibility to fix it. This way she can get her son back, and she really loves him."

"Is that what marriage is to you, responsibility? That doesn't sound very fun."

"Don't worry about that part. Donna and I have lots of fun."

"So maybe you do love her."

Feeling restless, impatient, Mike pulled the phone away from his ear as he tried to maneuver around the door of the clubhouse. Suddenly it swung free and he was staring at Yazmer's cocky face. "I gotta go, Joey. Why don't you just congratulate me and leave it at that?"

"Honestly, I don't know why so many people worry about gays getting married when straight men like you make such a joke of it," Joey grumbled, before hanging up.

Mike clicked off the phone and hoisted the strap of his gym bag higher onto his shoulder. Yazmer was giving him a funny look, as if he'd never really looked closely at Mike before. Had he heard Joey's last comment? Would he put it together that Mike had a gay brother?

Infuriated that he'd even wondered about that for a second—who cared what Yaz thought?—he brushed past the pitcher. "That was my brother," he told him defiantly. "From Chicago."

"Okay." Yaz trailed after him. "Heard you put the ring on the fling."

"What?"

"Two words. Preeee-nup."

"Oh. Yes, I'm engaged."

"Who's the lady in the Solo scenario?" He made a record scratching sound.

A devil's impulse made Mike nearly say, *Actually, Yazmer, it's a guy. Hope you can make the wedding.* He restrained himself. "A girl from here in Kilby. No date's set yet, so you can hold off on the bridal registry."

"Trying to steal my spotlight? It ain't going to work, yo. The Yaz is the Yaz. Everyone wants a piece of me. They can have it too. So long as they slide some silver my way. Plastic too. The Yaz takes plastic."

"All right. I'll see you in the bullpen, Yaz."

"Gonna be late, got my agent calling."

Whatever. It was his session. Mike went to his locker and changed into his workout clothes—sliders, baseball pants, a loose T-shirt, and cleats. He strolled out to the field, where T.J. Gates, Ramirez, and a few others were fielding grounders. The sounds and rhythms of baseball settled into his blood, soothing him. He closed his eyes, absorbing the thud of ball into glove, the crack of bat on ball. Fastball, curveball; he knew the difference from the way they hit the glove. Wild pitch in the dirt. Hard throw to home.

Baseball. He loved this game. When the Navy had released him, baseball had taken him in. He still missed the military life, with its adrenaline and testosterone, but baseball . . . not too shabby either.

He opened his eyes. The bright sun glanced off Ramirez's sunglasses and one of the new rookies' braces. The kid was no more than nineteen, which made Mike feel suddenly ancient. On the far side of the field, Crush leaned against the bullpen fence talking to Mitch, the pitching coach. Crush's ever-present silver flask poked from his back pocket. He turned and, spotting Mike, waved him over.

"Solo," Crush greeted him. "Got a question for you." He glanced at the infielders whipping the ball around the horn, and steered Mike toward the far reaches of right field. "Is something going on with Yaz?"

"Don't ask me. Ask ESPN. I don't understand half the things he says anyway."

"Supposedly he has some big announcement coming, and my gut tells me I'm not going to like it. You're supposed to be getting close to him, working your voodoo catcher magic."

"I'm . . . uh . . . getting there. His pitch count's down. I got him to speed things up, but he went too far."

"I noticed. His last start was an hour and half long. Fans would have felt cheated, if he hadn't spent an extra half hour on the field at the end of the game, demonstrating his dance moves."

"Yeah. He does things big, I'll say that."

"Well, see if you can keep an ear to the ground. I'd appreciate it. Now let's talk about this wedding of yours. Not a big fan of the institution myself, not that you'd know it from my three divorces, but if you're going for it, might as well stretch a double into a triple, so to speak."

"What the Jeter are you talking about?"

Crush paused, blinked, then shook his head as if knocking the phrase from his brain. Mike grinned. Hey, he'd tried.

"The Catfish Wedding of the Decade," Crush said grandly.

"*What?*"

"Let's make a big shebang out of your wedding. It would be good for team-town relations, and you know how sketchy those have been lately."

Mike scowled. "Do you mean good for your campaign to keep the Catfish?"

Crush went on, ignoring, as usual, anything he didn't care to hear. "We'll hold the ceremony right here on the diamond. The invitations could be printed to look like tickets to a game. We'll hand out souvenir baseballs to all the guests. We'll give the *Kilby Press-Herald* an exclusive, they'll eat it up."

Mike tapped his bat against his instep. "I have to talk to Donna about it." Since Donna hadn't—technically—agreed to actually marry him, that should be an interesting conversation.

"Sure, sure. Don't worry about the extra expense. I got it covered. Let your girl pick out the best wedding dress in town. Sweeten the deal a bit." He winked.

Implying that he needed to sweeten the deal? "Thanks for the vote of confidence on that."

"You got it, hot stuff." Crush clapped his shoulder.

Striding toward the dugout, Mike pulled his phone from his gym bag and called Donna. Better give her a heads-up on this. Her machine picked up, her laughing voice saying, "This is Donna's phone. Leave your number and I'll call you back when I actually feel like talking to you."

A slow smile spread across his face. Donna was one of a kind, that was for sure. He lowered his voice to a seductive murmur. "This is your fiancé calling. I know you feel like talking to me, because talking leads to kissing and kissing leads to touching and touching leads to other touching and that other touching, when it's done right, and you know I do it right, leads to 'Oh Mike, don't stop,' and that leads to . . . Anyway, call me back."

He grinned as he hung up. Even leaving a message for Donna was fun.

Chapter 11

LATER THAT NIGHT, Mike opened a Shiner and set it on Donna's coffee table next to a to-go container of baby back ribs from the Smoke Pit BBQ. "Boom," he said triumphantly. "You were drinking a Shiner at the Roadhouse the night of the brawl. And I've personally seen you make a bloody mess of an entire rack of these ribs. So this is a guaranteed allergic reaction–free meal and don't even think about pretending otherwise."

Donna, dressed in loose pajama pants and T-shirt that read, *I solemnly swear that I am up to no good*, eyed the feast happily. "Score one for Solo."

"Damn right. You know what this means. After you've sucked the marrow out of all these, we get to make out for a while."

"How do you figure that?" She was already digging in, a rib in one hand and a beer in the other. Mike tried to imagine Angela eating ribs with this amount of voracious delight, and failed.

"My biggest tool to win your affection is obviously going to be my incredible kissing skills and irresistible physique. You owe me a chance to give it a whirl."

"We already made out, remember?"

"Yeah. I remember." So did his cock, which had been in a semi-aroused state since he walked into her apartment. Which was a little odd, since the profusion of football images was, quite frankly, kind of a turnoff.

"Tell you what. We can make out *after* you tell me about the experience that made you not believe in love anymore." She put her beer bottle to her mouth, shooting him a stern glance over the brown glass.

"Ancient history."

"You said she was your high school sweetheart. If we're going to be engaged, kinda sorta, I need to know. Who broke your heart, Mike Solo?"

He took another Shiner from the six-pack and cracked it open. She had a point. There should be no secrets between them, and why should he hide his history with Angela anyway? "First of all, you're right, she did break my heart, but only because I was too idealistic. I know you'll want to know this, so I'll say it right off the bat. I am no longer in love with her. Period. She shattered all my illusions about women, because I always assumed women were basically goddesses here on earth."

Donna took a big bite of succulent meat. "Only some of us, Solo. Only some of us."

He ignored that. "Her name was Angela DiMatteo and I fell for her in second grade. She was perfect. Her hair ribbon never came undone and her knee socks never fell down. I know, because I would have given my left nut to see her legs."

"You knew her in school?"

"St. Paul's School for Catholic Girls and Boys. She

and her family moved to Chicago from Italy. I spent a month learning how to write, 'Will you be my valentine' in Italian."

"Did she say yes?"

"Eventually, she did. She played hard to get all through elementary school and junior high."

"Then what?"

"We got engaged, I went to the Naval Academy, we saw each other during my breaks. I'd take her for drives and have dinner with her family. Her grandmother used to glare at me and mutter curses in Italian. I didn't care. I just stared at Angela the entire meal. I thought my future was all set. Life with my own private angel. Then my brother got sick, I gave up my kidney, left the Navy, and that was that. She told me her family couldn't accept my decision and she wouldn't cross her family."

Donna had put down her beer and ribs and was staring at him, perplexed. "Accept your decision? I don't understand."

Mike's chest felt tight. He wasn't used to talking about all this. He tried to force some air into his lungs. If she was going to marry him, she deserved to know everything. "Well, it was because of who my brother is. Her family is extremely traditional. My family is conservative too, but the DiMatteos make mine look like hippies."

"Okay, so you both have conservative families." She pulled one leg under her, angling her body toward him. "Are they opposed to life-saving medical intervention?"

"No, no. It's not that." God, he couldn't believe how nervous he was. This brought back memories of when he'd broken the news to Angela and her expression had turned to ice. "Like I said, it's because of my brother."

"Geez, Solo, what's wrong with your brother? My imagination's going wild here. Is he in prison? A serial killer? Drug addict?"

"God, no. Joey's an economics professor at the University of Chicago. Specializing in the economies of third world countries, which is why he was in Africa doing research for his doctorate. That's where he got E coli and didn't get proper treatment in time and . . ." He inhaled a deep breath. "Well, he's gay."

Her expression didn't change. "That's it? He's gay?"

"The DiMatteo family—and my own parents— didn't think I should give up my Navy career for a homosexual. In their mind, he's a sinner."

Slowly, comprehension stole across her face, along with a horror that matched what he'd felt at the time. "Wouldn't it be worse to let your own brother die?"

"That's what I thought. But we're talking about very strict Catholics here, very conservative. I don't know if other Catholics would feel that way, but my family did. And my father is very, very stubborn."

Silently, she toyed with the label on her beer bottle, then drained it in one long gulp. "That's . . . really tough, Mike. How is it with your family now?"

"Awkward. My father won't see Joey, and I get so damn angry about it. Every time his name comes up, it ends in a fight. So we don't talk about him. It breaks my heart."

She squeezed his hand. "You did the right thing, Mike. I'm sorry you had to lose so much because of it. Is Joey okay now?"

"Up and down." His standard answer, but he didn't stop there. "I wish the new kidney fixed everything, but it didn't. He gets every virus within a twenty-mile radius. I worry every time he goes into the hospital because of all the germs there."

Picking up his hand, she nestled it next to her cheek—the sweetest goddamn gesture he'd ever seen. She didn't say things would be okay, or tell him he shouldn't worry. She just offered her sympathy and her soft touch. They sat that way for a while, then Donna let out a chuckle.

"If your family is so traditional, I bet I'm just their type. Don't they put gays and single unwed mothers in the same circle of hell?"

"I'll have to check with Father Kowalski on that one."

"Maybe it's the fun circle," she mused, "where they serve beer and barbecue."

Mike felt the tension in his chest ease. "I hope you get to meet Joey soon. I bet you'd like him."

She clinked her bottle against his. "I know I'd like his kidney."

He chuckled. Just the sort of joke he and Joey liked to make. And her reaction to the news about Joey—pretty much the opposite of Angela's. An odd thought crossed his mind, so odd he had to bury it with a mouthful of smoky, sauce-slathered meat. Was it actually possible that *Donna* was the perfect girl for him? That Angela never had been?

One quiet moment on the couch had done more to make Donna fall in love with Mike than all the flowers in the world. It was a good thing he had no idea how appealing he was when talking about his brother. In her opinion, he was a hero, giving up so much to keep Joey alive. Not just a kidney, but a career, family harmony, and even the love of his life.

That thought gave her a deep stab of pain. Whatever she and Mike had, it was nothing compared to his longtime feelings for his ex-fiancée. Which meant that while she was falling harder for Mike, he was even more out of reach.

Peachy.

"Did you hear what I said?" Mike was poking her in the ribs.

"Ow. No. Yes. Something about Crush Taylor and a wedding?"

"*Our* wedding. He wants to make a big deal out of it. He thinks it would be good for the Catfish's image. You know, local girl snags Catfish superstar."

"Oh Mike. Are you telling me I should dump you for a Catfish superstar? Say, Trevor Stark?" she said, infusing an exaggerated dose of hope into her tone.

"Ha ha. Not funny." He circled her wrists in one strong hand. "You don't belong with that guy. I'd give up another kidney before I let that happen."

His possessiveness gave her a thrill that left her speechless for a second.

"Think about it," Mike continued. "A big wedding would be good PR for you. Picture a big spread in the *Kilby Press-Herald*, you and me testing wedding cakes and bridal veils. 'Local Girl Catches Groom at Catfish Stadium.' I bet Harvey and Bonita won't get that kind of attention. And the judge might be impressed with a big down-home baseball wedding."

Oh *cripes*. Everything Mike said made sense.

Bonita would eat her heart out if Donna made the papers with her wedding plans. More importantly, Judge Quinn would look at her very differently. But an *actual wedding* . . . suddenly it was all too real.

"When? When is he thinking?"

"He didn't say. It's up to us, but I'm guessing he'd want it to be pretty soon. He needs some good publicity after the betting scandal last year, and the brawl at the Roadhouse."

She winced. That brawl was going to haunt her forever. She felt responsible for that crazy episode, but did that mean she owed Crush a wedding? "Mike, are you sure you want to do this? It will be a lot harder to back out of being married if we make a big splash like that."

"I don't want to back out. Do you want to back out?"

"I'm not even *in* yet!"

"According to Instagram you are. And Twitter, and Facebook. And the checkout lady at Kroger's."

Groaning, she buried her head in her hands. "What have we done?"

He stroked her back in firm circles that made her skin tingle. "Look, take some time to think about it. You don't have to decide right away. We can talk about it tomorrow."

"I can't. I have Zack tomorrow."

"What kind of a fiancé would I be if I didn't want to spend time with Zack? That's the whole point of this engagement. I need to get to know him better, and he needs to know me. It's very important to me."

How did Mike do that? How did he sneak past her defenses without even trying?

And now she wanted to kiss him. She wanted to

move her lips over the handsome planes of his face, tug on the black curls at the nape of his neck. The look on her face must have given her away, because he turned toward her and moved his big body over hers. She sighed, ready to slide against him, open for him, drink him in. His scent surrounded her, smoky barbecue and soap. All her senses screamed for contact, for closeness, for skin against bare skin. But her brain sent her another message. *Warning, warning. Get in too deep, there'll be no getting out.*

She scrambled away from him, toward the arm of the couch. "Let me see your scar. From the kidney operation."

He stilled, his green eyes deep as a forest. "Why?"

"I just want to see it, that's all." She'd use anything for a distraction right now.

Slowly he sat back, then drew up his shirt. She'd felt the hardness of his chest a couple of times now, but she'd never seen it bare. He was magnificent, his musculature defined, powerful, intimidating. He had the body of a soldier, a gladiator, a superhero. Below the ridges of his abdominal muscles, a little to the right of his navel, a darker line, about five inches, traced across his skin.

"Does it hurt?"

"No. There used to be some numbness, but it's all normal now. Actually . . ." He hesitated.

"What?" She couldn't stop staring at the scar. That one line of tissue had changed Mike's entire life. It was like a dividing line. On one side, the life he'd planned and hoped for. On the other, the life he had.

"It's the one baseball superstition I have. More of a ritual, really. Before I go up to bat, I always put my hand on my lower belly, here where the scar is. I can't feel it through my uniform, but I know it's there, and it . . . I don't know, it does something for me. Reminds me of Joey, maybe. Of everything that matters to me."

Emotion welled up, clogging her throat. Feelings for this beautiful man, whose heart would never be hers, threatened to overwhelm her.

"Want to touch it?" he asked her softly.

She grabbed on to the opening as if it were a lifeline. *Make a joke, make a joke.* Her go-to. "I just had a flashback to Reggie Dean behind the gym in sixth grade. Thanks a lot, Solo."

Laughing, he dropped his shirt, covering the incredible terrain of ridges and slopes. "Do I need to beat Reggie up?"

"I took care of that myself, thank you very much. I'm short but I'm feisty."

He settled next to her, his body so warm and hard and tempting. Maybe it was time to give in on the making-out issue, after all. Her lust for him was getting out of hand.

"I almost forgot," he said. "Are you free on Saturday? I got us tickets to Crush's fund-raiser event. Figured it would be a good chance to make a statement."

"A statement?"

"An introduction to Mike and Donna. Otherwise known as . . . 'Madonna.' Nah, that doesn't work."

She scrunched up her face. " 'Dike'?"

They both laughed. "Even worse. Never mind, we'll just stick with Mike and Donna. Donna and Mike."

Mike and Donna. It really did have a ring to it. Oh cripes, how was she going to keep herself out of trouble with this thing with Mike? Was it even possible?

Chapter 12

CRUSH TAYLOR WOULD always be famous in the baseball world for his iconic pitching career. In recent years his legend had extended to the parties he threw at his home, Bullpen Ranch. Mostly these parties were opportunities for him to party with the Catfish and other members of the sports world, with the door always open to any interested females. But once a year he hosted a party for the Kilby community, with the purpose of raising money for a designated worthy cause. The Kilby Burn Center, the new library, and the Special Olympics had all been beneficiaries.

This year, the selected cause was kidney disease.

That was thanks to Mike, who had told Crush that choosing the Kidney Research Foundation would go a long way toward convincing him and Donna to agree to his proposed Catfish Wedding of the Decade.

Maybe he should have picked liver research, thought Mike as he watched Crush pour himself a hefty glass of bourbon at the bar near the massive stone fireplace. An early heat wave had forced the partygoers inside, giving everyone a chance to gawk at the spectacular interior. High ceilings with steel trusses soared overhead, angling down to meet incomprehensibly large panes of glass that looked out on spring-green pastures. All the furniture was large and upholstered in suede, cowhide, or nubby oatmeal-colored fabric. Every room had a built-in bar, and ashtrays sat on every surface. Bullpen Ranch was definitely a man's world.

Specifically, Crush's world, judging by the lineup of Cy Young awards and photos of the pitcher posing with people like Catfish Hunter, Nolan Ryan, and Dwight Gooden. Not to mention the many, many women he'd dated and/or married over the years.

It seemed that the entire city of Kilby had paid to attend the event, which included a cash bar, dinner, a silent auction, and a country-swing band called Kissing Cowboys. All the Catfish players had shown up in their nicest outfits, which ranged from Yaz's purple leather tie and patchwork deer hunter cap, to Leiberman's black suit jacket.

"Is that what you wore to your bar mitzvah?" Mike teased him. Not that he had any grounds to mock; he was wearing the same blazer he'd worn to his high school graduation. It strained over his shoulders and didn't quite reach his wrists. Since he'd left the Navy he'd had little use for formal clothes.

"I think that suit looks great on you," Donna told Leiberman, who blushed violently. "You look like a young Cary Grant."

A miniature Cary Grant, maybe, thought Mike with a flash of jealousy. Donna looked incredible. He couldn't stop sneaking glances at her. She'd put her hair up in some kind of tousled knotlike arrangement, and wore an off-the-shoulder black dress that made her skin glow like pearls and her eyes glimmer like gold.

She'd wanted to wear her horrible boxy blue jacket, but he'd reminded her that things were different now. They were an engaged couple trying to make a certain impression on the movers and shakers of Kilby. She'd risen to the occasion perfectly, but the problem now was that he couldn't stop touching her. He hadn't let go of her hand once since they'd walked in, except to grip her elbow, or nestle his palm into the small of her back, where he could feel the flexing of each muscle along her spine. The deep curve of her hip tempted him to explore further, but he clamped down on the urge. Something was bothering her; over the past weeks he'd gotten familiar enough with her expressions to know that.

He had to get her alone, find out what was up. Maybe if they could sneak into a closet somewhere . . .

He was scoping out the nearest closed door when a tall couple approached them. The woman was all too familiar. The last time he'd seen her, she'd been aiming a camera at them. Bonita wore a sleek white sheath and sky-high stiletto heels. The tall, sleepy-eyed man with her had to be Harvey. His fringed suede jacket made him look even more uncomfortable than Mike. Bonita's sharp eyes slid from Donna to Mike, then back again.

"Engaged?" Bonita said skeptically. "You expect anyone to believe that?"

In a gesture one finger removed from rude, Donna raised her left hand. All the fingers curled to her palm except the ring finger, which bore a sparkly cubic zirconium ring they'd selected together. Nothing fancy, since she'd refused to accept anything more expensive.

"I guess seeing is believing," chirped Donna.

"That doesn't mean anything. It won't matter to Judge Quinn until you both sign that marriage certificate. In the meantime, I hope you know that everyone's laughing at you."

At the look on Donna's face—as if her pet goldfish had just been devoured—Mike's determination hardened. This woman was too petty to get custody of Zack. And she should not be allowed to lord it over Donna. Donna was worth a million Bonitas. "We'll be sure to fax you a copy as soon as it's official," he told them. "We'd invite you to the wedding, but I'm afraid there isn't room. Too many major leaguers are coming, not to mention members of Sting's band. Of course we have to leave room for Sting himself, just in case."

Bonita's smug sneer evaporated. Mike wanted to do a victory dance, but Donna's fingernails were digging into the inside of his palm. Oops. Wrong move?

"Would you two excuse us?" Donna tugged him away from Bonita and Harvey, who shot a yearning glance toward the bar. Mike couldn't blame him for that.

He followed Donna, who seemed to know exactly where she was going. He remembered that they'd both been here last year for Crush's All-Star party, though the events of that night were pretty fuzzy. After careening through the kitchen, where the catering staff was busy filling trays with little bacon-wrapped scallops, she pushed open the door to a pantry and dragged him inside.

He looked around at dimly lit shelves stocked with bottles of liquor, cans of olives, and jars of mixed nuts. Apparently, Crush followed the Bar Snack Diet.

"Are you hungry? You should have told me. I would have fixed you up a plate," Mike told her.

Donna crossed her arms over her chest and set her jaw. Her usual dimple was nowhere to be seen. The shadowy sheen of her skin in the low light made him want to lick her cheek. "You're not going to joke your way out of this. What are you doing, making up details about a wedding that probably won't ever happen? I mean, *Sting*?"

"I said 'just in case.' Seriously, you never know."

"You're not being *at all* serious. You want serious? How's this? We're never going to get married."

He froze, noticing for the first time that she seemed genuinely upset. "What are you talking about?"

"Mike, I went over and over our last conversation. I've been thinking about everything you said about Angela and your brother and your family."

"So?"

"You're still in love with Angela. How can I marry someone who loves someone else?"

Drawing back, he took in the stubborn cast of her wide mouth, the lips turned down at the corners, quivering just slightly.

"Is that what's been bothering you the last couple of days?"

She lifted her chin. "I wouldn't say it's been bothering me. It's just a piece of information I'm taking into account."

With one short step, he came to her and caught her in his arms, pulling her against his body.

"*Wrong* information. I'm not in love with Angela. How could I be, after seeing who she really was?" Donna's pile of fiery hair held a sweet, faint fragrance, like early spring wildflowers. The curves of her breasts pressed into his chest. "I loved an illusion. An idea of Angela, someone pure and gentle and perfect. I was this rowdy, physical kid, and she was like a Madonna painting. I never knew what was really going on inside her head. She was so quiet, so untouchable. When she broke off our engagement, all those delusions fell away. I don't love her anymore. Not in any romantic way. I swear."

She tilted her head up, leaning back in the circle of his arms. "I'm nothing like that. Nothing."

"So? You're you. Our relationship is nothing like mine and Angela's. It's more real."

"More real? How can you say that? We're pretending to be engaged!"

He took her chin in his hands. "I'm not pretending. I intend to marry you."

She pulled her bottom lip between her teeth, a crease appearing between her eyebrows. "I don't understand you, Mike Solo. Are you saying our relationship is different from yours and Angela's because you have no illusions about me, therefore you wouldn't ever be *dis*illusioned?"

He let out a hoot of laughter, so loud that her eyes went wide with alarm and she reached up a hand to cover his mouth. He grabbed the opportunity to nibble the soft heel of her hand.

Her eyes darkened. It occurred to him that they were once again alone in a tiny, dark room. "See, that's what I like about you, Donna. You always make me laugh, and you say things no one else will say. Our relationship is different because I'm not a naïve kid anymore. I'm a grown man now."

He shifted his body so that one thigh slid between hers, so she could feel the thrust of his erection. It was rock-hard and threatening to burst through his slightly too-tight pants.

"That doesn't prove anything," she whispered fiercely. "I bet you got hard-ons all the time back then too."

He had to laugh, even though his cock, teased by the contact with her shape, pulsed painfully. "See? You know me so well."

"How can I be sure you aren't still pining for her?"

"Hmm. Well, you could give me a chance to prove it by letting me lick the crook of your neck, right here, where it curves into your shoulder." He nestled his face into the body part in question, felt her tendon go taut, then slid his tongue across it. She shivered.

"That doesn't . . ." she said weakly.

"Okay, fine. How about this?" He sank to his knees before her, gripped her hips, and drew her toward him. Burying his face between her thighs, he breathed in her scent through the thin layer of fabric. "Showing is better than telling, anyway." He inched the cloth up her thighs.

"Solo, you're crazy." Her voice held a quiver of laughter, but no hint of objection. He smiled, amazed that he felt so comfortable with this girl who had burst into his life like some kind of fiery-haired comet.

"Crazy for you, babe. I've been thinking about nothing but this since I saw you in that god-awful blue suit."

"I didn't know it was such a turn-on."

"You're a turn-on. Face it. You make me wild, Donna." He ran his tongue up her inner thigh until the soft flesh gave way to the silk of her panties. He inhaled the heady scent of her private, secret self, the Donna no one else got to see. The vulnerable and tender Donna.

Her breath caught, and she shifted her legs apart. He nearly came right then and there. Her willingness to surrender to him went right to his head. She would never hold back, he realized. Never put false barriers between them. Never treat him like he was barely good enough to touch her shoe.

"I want you, Donna MacIntyre. More than you know." He reached a finger inside her panties and touched wetness. "I'd finger-fuck you right here on the floor if the entire city of Kilby wasn't right outside."

A shudder went through her. She dug her hands into his hair. "Maybe this isn't—"

"Are you scared, Donna MacIntyre? We're engaged, remember? No one would blame us for getting a little carried away before the wedding." He wrenched her panties away from her sex, exposing the soft cleft with its wink of moisture. "As long as you can keep from screaming, we should be fine."

"Stop . . . talking . . . about . . . the wedding . . ." she moaned.

"No. I won't. Wedding . . ." He ran his tongue across the curls protecting her sex. "Wedding . . ." He circled his tongue around her clit, used his thumb to spread the moisture across her lips. "Wedding . . ." He hooked one long index finger inside her clinging channel. "Wedding . . ." His breath hot, he spoke against the hardening, warming kernel.

She gasped and said something unintelligible.

So he kept talking. "Next time I'm going to spread you apart on my lap, baby girl. Bend you over my knee and see what your sweet little ass looks like. I'll put you on your hands and knees and fuck you until you can't say your own name. Let you ride me until I'm raw. Until we're both raw. Until we can't say another word because we've screamed it all out." He kept going like that, the dirty words inflaming him. He put a hand on his own cock, which felt as rigid as a lamppost. At the first hint of tremors shaking her body, he whipped his hand away and clamped it on her ass. As convulsions racked her form, he held her steady, locked between his hand on her rear and his mouth on her clit. Warmth flooded his mouth, the soft flutter of her orgasm like a gift.

Lost in the darkness between her thighs, he heard only vaguely her muffled squeaks as she tried to contain her ecstasy. God, what he wouldn't give to take her to a real bed and make love to her with every part of him. Hands, mouth, cock.

Except . . . the vow. He was in new territory here. Did his *intention* to marry Donna, even when she hadn't fully signed on yet, void the vow?

When he finally withdrew his mouth from her, she was limp as a noodle, while he was still the polar opposite. He stood up, dragging his erection against the length of her body. She fisted her hand into the neck of his shirt and twisted it. Molten gold eyes met his. She looked satisfied and fierce at the same time.

"I want you inside me, Solo," she whispered. "You'd better rethink that vow of yours."

He gave a shaky laugh. "I was just thinking the same thing. At this rate, my dick might explode." He remembered what Father Kowalski had said when he took the vow. "I may have a loophole. My priest was looking out for me. He said something like 'unless you decide to get married.' I *have* decided to get married. The way I see it, if you agree to actually have a wedding, then the vow's history."

She shoved him so he bumped against the pantry door. "Are you using sex to coerce me into marriage?"

"Will it work?"

"No!" She cupped his erection and he let out a groan. "Explain to me why we should get married. Besides Zack, I mean. What made you think of it?"

He closed his eyes, feeling her fingers trace the length of his penis. Her stroking was exquisitely torturous. "You're going to think I'm crazy."

"That's not a problem, because I already do." She pressed lightly on the head of his cock, which swelled enthusiastically in response.

"Intuition."

"What?" Through the hazy cloud of his arousal, he could tell that caught her by surprise.

"Gut instinct. I thought of it behind home plate, which is where I do all my best thinking. I have to keep my mind clear and completely focused. I think it's a right brain, left brain thing. I'm so occupied with balls and strikes that my brain is free to come up with genius ideas."

"You thought of us getting married during a baseball game?"

"Yes," he said simply, because he'd reached the point at which communication was a lost cause.

Just then a noise outside the pantry made them both jump to attention. Donna whipped her hand out of Mike's pants and smoothed her dress down. He put a finger to his lips to shush her, then leaned his shoulder against the door so it would be impossible to open.

The doorknob rattled. A man cursed. "Thought I got this fixed." Crush Taylor. Donna's eyes went wide.

"I'm not going into a dark room with you, Crush," came a frosty female voice. Mayor Wendy Trent. Former Miss Texas, first female mayor of Kilby, and rumored ice queen. Donna mouthed, *OMG* to Mike. "My only goal with this conversation is to give you a heads-up about some information I just received."

"Really?" Crush sounded more skeptical than disappointed. "Your hair says otherwise."

"My hair?"

"All that hair spray usually screams *Touch me and you die*, but this thing you have going on right now says, *Come and get me, cowboy*."

Donna put a hand over her mouth, her face turning red from the effort of not laughing.

"Why don't you have yourself another bourbon and we can discuss your hair hallucinations," the mayor snapped.

Mike's eyes popped wide open, while Donna let out a giggle, which she quickly smothered.

The mayor continued. "You probably know that the Wades have notified the Friars of their interest in purchasing the Catfish."

"The Wades can go fuck themselves."

"Yes, well, they're assembling a strong case to get you removed from the league. Some of your own players have joined them."

Silence. Mike went absolutely still. He hadn't heard anything about players coming forward against the team owner. When Crush spoke again, all playfulness had vanished from his tone. "Who?"

"Actually, it's just one attention-hungry player. And no, I can't tell you who it is. I shouldn't even be telling you this much. But—you know how I feel about the Wades. They should be out of the running based on the gambling scandal last year, but all charges were dropped so it won't play into this decision. Dean Wade is planning a run for mayor. Owning the team could be a big plus for him."

"They can't make me sell my own baseball team," said Crush roughly.

"They can," Mayor Trent assured him. "Which you know very well. Listen, I want to help. This is your last-ditch warning, Taylor. You'd better figure something out, and fast."

Someone called Crush's name, and after a hurried swish of clothing and footsteps, the two disappeared.

"I have a bad feeling about this," Mike whispered. "I'll bet you anything it's Yazmer." A dull headache throbbed at his temples, some kind of hangover-like combination of worry and raging sexual frustration.

"Ugh. If the Wades buy the team, what will happen to you?"

He shrugged. "Not much. My contract is with the Friars. I'd be more worried about Kilby. And you. If the Wades buy the Catfish and Dean Wade gets elected mayor, what would that make Bonita? The mayor's third niece once removed or some shit?"

"They might as well crown her Queen of Kilby," Donna said indignantly. "And hand over Zack while they're at it." She paced around in a little circle, her furious energy lighting up the dim space like a firefly. "Okay, Solo, that's it. Let's get married. And let's do it big. Texas big."

Chapter 13

DONNA TACKED ONE condition onto their engagement. She asked Mike to stop trying to make her fall in love with him. If she looked at it as a purely practical decision, it made sense. She still didn't completely understand Mike's motivations for proposing—gut instinct, really?—but the benefits of Crush's plan trumped all her doubts.

Everything would probably be fine, she kept telling herself. They had fun together, they were hot for each other. He was a rock-solid guy, trustworthy to the nth degree. He was honest. He hadn't tried to convince her he was madly in love with her.

Which she kind of hated, actually. Over the past weeks, in the restless hours before falling asleep, she'd concocted detailed scenarios of Mike declaring his love for her. *Love.* Not a proposal of marriage, not a seduction. Love. The crazy, passionate kind that made you throw everything else to the wind.

That's what she wanted from Mike.

In the meantime, there was Zack to consider, and the Wades and the Catfish and Crush Taylor and Yazmer, and before she knew it, she was meeting Burwell Brown, the reporter for the *Kilby Press-Herald*, to dish about the Catfish Wedding of the Decade.

Burwell did not look happy to be interviewing her at You Bet I Do, the most popular wedding boutique in town—probably because he usually covered state and city politics and other weighty issues. Cascades of lace and tulle surrounded them, as if they were touring the inside of a cream puff. Mannequins aimed blank smiles in random directions. The reporter followed her with a sour expression as she perused the selection of bridal veils.

"I really enjoyed your article about the effects of globalization on the Texas economy," she told him, blinking innocently. She plopped a frothy ivory concoction with a tiara of rosebuds on her head. "More importantly, what kind of veil do you think I should wear?"

He took off his wire-framed glasses and rubbed the ridge of his nose. "Go ahead, rub it in. So. You and Mike Solo. Apparently some people care."

"I'm really sorry you got stuck with this." She laughed at his resigned expression. "How can I make this better for you? What do you need from me?"

"A horse tranquilizer?"

"Funny. I know what you need. An angle. How about this. First Caleb Hart, now Mike Solo. Is there something in the Kilby water that inspires baseball players to fall for hometown girls?"

"No." Burwell shot that one down pretty quick.

"Okay, then. Want to hear how he proposed to me? On one knee, with a bouquet of fresh-picked flowers?" Probably purchased from Kroger, but that detail didn't have to be mentioned.

"Sure, go ahead." With a weary sigh, Burwell Brown started his little pocket recorder. Donna winked at the hovering sales clerk, Amy from two years back in high school. If there was ever a good moment to let her imagination fly, this would be it. They needed to convince everyone that their engagement was real, based on real emotion. *Sell it, girl*, she told herself.

"Well . . . it was one of those stormy nights we had a few weeks ago. I was at home in bed. Half asleep, and already dreaming of Mike. I'd been secretly in love with him for months, but I was sure there was no future for us. He's a baseball player and I'm just an ordinary girl from Kilby. This isn't a romantic comedy, this is real life. Have you ever heard that phrase, 'Build it and they will come'? I think it's from a baseball movie."

"*Field of Dreams*."

"Yes, exactly. I was dreaming of Mike, imagining what it would be like if he threw himself at my feet and told me he was dying of love for me. And then came a knock on the door. The strange thing is, I knew it was him. Destiny works in mysterious ways." She broke off her story. "Make sure to put that quote in, Burwell. People will love that."

"Do you want to write the article yourself? Or maybe I should just go to the romance section at the bookstore?"

"Hey, I'm trying to help you out here, give you something juicy."

"Fine, fine." Despite his grumbles, she could tell he was getting caught up in the story. Who didn't love a good romance?

"I flung open the door," because simply opening it wouldn't be enough, "and sure enough, there he was, all wet from the rain, his thin shirt clinging to his firm muscles, desperate love screaming from every line of his face." Amy gave a dreamy sigh, while Burwell rolled his eyes. "He thrust a bouquet of lilacs at me, the poor flowers drenched from the rain. Then he flung himself to the floor on both knees. 'I must have ye,' he declared." Ooops, she'd added a bit of a Scottish brogue by mistake. She hurried onward before Burwell got suspicious. " 'You've been haunting my dreams ever since I first saw your beautiful face in the third row of the field box section along the first-base line.' " She threw that in because it sounded like a better first meet than the Kilby Roadhouse. " 'Donna, I beg of you. Have mercy on me. Marry me now, or I'll have no more reason to go on.' "

"Really?" Burwell peered over his wire-rimmed glasses. "A call-up to the majors wouldn't do it?"

"What is baseball compared to true love? Make sure you use that quote too. The ladies will love it."

"Are we about done here?"

"Let me just add that it took quite some time to convince me. My heart longed to say yes, but I wanted to make absolutely sure that it was the right decision. For my son."

At that, Burwell looked up sharply. "Did you say 'son'?"

Donna noticed that Amy was leaning in close to hear every word. Too bad. The time for secrecy was over.

"Yes, I have a four-year-old son. Every decision I make is based on what's best for him." As far as she was concerned, this was the most important part. She had to make Mike look like the best potential stepparent any kid ever had. "Mike Solo has a deep love for family. He'd do anything for a family member. When I learned that he donated a kidney to his brother, I knew that my son's well-being would be in good hands if I gave in to my heart's desire and accepted his proposal."

"Kidney?" All of a sudden Burwell looked much more interested in his article. "Can you tell me more about that?"

Oh, *cripes*. Did other people know about the kidney donation? Mike hadn't said that it was a secret, but then again, she'd never heard anyone talk about it. "Um . . . can we skip that part? I'm not sure if it's public knowledge. And I really don't know anything more about it."

"Tell you what. I'll confirm it with Solo before I print it." Burwell looked as though he'd swallowed an entire cream puff.

With a sinking feeling, Donna finished the interview—embellishing as much as she dared. Darn her overactive imagination and inability to think before she blurted things out. What if she'd revealed something Mike didn't want the world to know? As soon as she escaped from You Bet I Do, she called Mike.

"Quick question. Do people know about your kidney?"

"What people?"

"Just . . . people. People in Kilby. People who might read the *Kilby Press-Herald*."

Mike's creative swearwords were all the answer

she needed. She groaned. "I'm sorry, Mike. If Burwell Brown calls you, you can just tell him it was a misunderstanding. That I had it wrong, or I was delusional, or drunk, or anything."

"You know I can't do that. That'll defeat the whole purpose of the interview. Let me think. Just . . . don't say anything for a second."

Blindly, she kept walking toward her Kia, barely noticing the crew working on the utility pole and the new blossoms on the jacaranda trees. If she'd completely ruined things for Mike, she'd have a hard time forgiving herself. He'd put himself out for her—again—and again she'd brought him nothing but trouble.

"What exactly did you tell him?"

"Well, among other things that you can skip over if he puts them in the article, I told him that you donated a kidney to your brother. I didn't say his name, or when it happened, or anything like that. I said it proved you'd do anything for your family."

"Hmm. Well, maybe that's not so bad. Management already knows, but I never told the guys on the team. It won't be a problem if they know. Maybe I'll get a few extra beers out of it, knowing them. Sick bastards."

She blew out a breath of relief. By the lighter tone of his voice, she knew it would be okay. "I'm sorry, Mike. You keep doing things for me and all I do for you is cause trouble."

"I wouldn't say that." His voice acquired a husky edge. "But if you want to make it up to me, I won't say no. Come to the game."

"I'm on my way to work right now. Busy day.

There seems to be a cavity epidemic lately. And everyone wants to ask me about my engagement. By the way, my lawyer wants to send you flowers. Since she usually lectures me on my bad behavior, it's a nice change."

"I've been thinking. I think you should quit that job."

"*What?*"

"I can support you. And that gives you more time to be home with Zack. The judge will appreciate that."

Donna had to lean against a lamppost because the world seemed to be swaying around her. Stay home with Zack? She'd never even pictured that possibility. Her highest hope had been to earn enough to cut back on her hours and get the best possible day care for him. *Stay home?*

For a crazy moment, she wondered if Mike had literally been sent from heaven to improve her life. Then her natural skepticism crept in. "Is this whole thing a big prank? Maybe Hamilton Wade put you up to it, out of revenge?"

"Donna. Come on. How many times do I have to prove that I actually want to be with you?"

A certain three-word phrase might help, but she knew that wasn't coming.

"Come to a game this weekend, Donna. We're having fireworks for Memorial Day, some military tributes. Come early, I'll show you around the stadium. The more we're seen together, the better. Lots of people come to the games. Hundreds. Sometimes thousands."

The thought of watching Mike play baseball again

made her weak in the knees. He was so sexy in his lobster suit. "I wish I could bring Zack again. He's with the Hannigans this weekend."

"I'm sure we can find ways to have fun without him."

They did. As Mike was showing her around the ballpark, he pointed out a closet where the on-staff physical therapist kept her supplies. Since they couldn't pass up a chance to explore another small, claustrophobic space, they slipped into it and locked the door from the inside.

"Terry isn't going to like this. She guards her territory like a junkyard dog," Mike murmured as they slid into each other's arms like seals sliding into the ocean, as if a shared embrace was their natural habitat. As always when Mike touched her, Donna fell into a dreamlike excitement, her senses overwhelmed, the way a fever disorients the brain. She felt Mike's knowing hands find all the spots that drove her crazy, felt liquid spring between her thighs, her nipples tighten. This time, she stopped him.

Mike wouldn't say he loved her, but there was something else he could do.

With a hand on the hard musculature of his chest to fend him off, she threw down her gauntlet. "No more fooling around, Solo. If you really want me, you have to prove it."

He froze, one hand halfway under her shirt, the other on her hip. "Prove it. What are you talking about?"

"Sex, Solo. I'm talking about sex. You know. Make whoopie. Hide the salami. Ride the flagpole. Sex."

"You want to consummate our relationship?"

"If you really must quote my seventh grade health teacher, yes. I want to consummate our relationship." In the light filtering through the edges of the door, she saw the wary look in his eyes. "How else am I going to believe you're serious about this? You said the priest gave you a loophole. Your vow isn't a factor."

"We're not married yet."

"You want to be, right? You said there was a loophole if we agreed to get married. Well, I agreed. So put up or shut up. Fish or cut bait. Isn't there a baseball metaphor that would work here?"

"I don't know. I'm blanking."

"Listen, Solo. I believe you're a good guy. I think you're serious about wanting to help me. You want to rescue me like I'm a damsel in distress and you're the warrior riding in to fight the bad guys. But this is *my life*. My son. I need to know that it's just as real for you."

"And sex would do that?"

"Yes. Because you took a vow, and I know how serious you are about it. If you're serious about getting married, then you'll jump through that loophole and into my pants."

He turned away from her, rubbing the back of his neck. Donna became aware of the smell of Ben-Gay and lemon, medicinal and soothing. Her throat tightened. This was it. She'd called his bluff about the wedding idea. Sex would make it real, and he wasn't ready for it to be real. He'd back out, right now, and the smell of Ben-Gay would make her think of rejection for the rest of her life.

He turned back to her and took her hand. Lifted it to his mouth and kissed it. "After the game. My place. I want to do this right, and I can't perform properly when I'm surrounded by football paraphernalia."

Her jaw fell open. "Seriously?"

"Yes, it messes with my sex drive."

"No, I mean . . . you really want to . . ."

He tugged her hand so she fell against him. A shock went through her, as if they were already in bed, about to make love. "I always wanted to. You ought to know that by now. The vow is such a habit for me. It keeps me out of trouble. It's hard to think about breaking it. But my gut tells me it's the right thing to do, because if I don't, you might never believe I want to marry you."

Every time he said the word "marry," little thrills pirouetted across her skin. "You're right. I probably won't. I'm not perfect, like Angela. I have more flaws than you could ever imagine."

He cradled her face in his palms, the sheer size of his catcher's hands taking her breath away.

"You know something? I once caught a perfect game at the Naval Academy. Matt Durham, right-hander from Florida. I'll never forget it, and I may never catch another perfect game. It was the most stressful goddamn experience of my life. Sweat was pouring off my body, I stank like a locker room. Especially as we got into the later innings. My heart was beating like a drum, every single pitch I called. What if I made the wrong call and ruined his chance for a perfect game? A chance at history? Nope. I don't want perfection. Give me a grind-it-out, back-and-forth, wild and crazy free-for-all any day of the week."

"Are you still talking about baseball?"

"Among other things." Oh that wink, that little flash of the devil. How could any woman resist it? She didn't stand a chance.

"Listen. I want to do something before the game," he told her, running his thumb across her dimple.

"What?"

"Will you trust me?"

"I hate it when people say that."

"This won't hurt a bit, I promise."

"I hate that one even more."

Laughing, he wrapped his arm around her, hugging her close. "It'll be fine. Now let's get out of here."

By then it was time for him to dress for the game, but he still wouldn't let her take her seat. He insisted she wait for him in the shadow of the wide ramp that let onto the field. For a while she watched all the bustle of activity—a microphone set up near home plate, the players filling the dugouts, the crowd filing toward their seats.

Finally, a girl in a blond ponytail and Catfish cap pranced onto the field and grabbed the mic. "I'm Angeline and boy, do I have a treat for you tonight!" She reeled off a hip-hop dance move. "Before we get into our Memorial Day tributes, a little catbird told me we have a certain someone at the ballpark tonight who's about to join the Catfish family. Catcher Mike Solo, come on out and bring that new fiancée of yours with you!"

Suddenly Mike was next to her, his grin lighting up the dim ramp. "Come on, Donna MacIntyre. Let's get famous." He swooped her into his arms and strode onto the field. Green grass punctuated by white lines and grinning baseball players slid across her vision. Red, white, and blue brightened the stands in a Memorial Day bonanza of flags. The crowd went crazy, jumping onto their feet with whistles and cheers. When they reached the microphone, Mike set her down, but he kept her clamped firmly to his side.

He spoke into the mic. "If you're lucky enough to land a Kilby girl, you don't ever want to let her go, know what I mean?"

Whoops and foot stomps rocked the stadium.

"This is Donna MacIntyre, and we're engaged." He had to pause for more raucous cheering. Dazzled, Donna scanned the crowd. She'd never stood in front of so many people before. Was this what it felt like for her mother, singing backup in front of stadiums full of Sting fans? As she scanned the crowd, she spotted a small head of copper-red hair and an exuberant smile—Zack. He jumped up and down, waving at her. On either side of him sat Harvey and Bonita, who looked sour enough to pickle a radish.

The crowd was chanting now. *Donna. Donna.* "Say something," Mike whispered in her ear. "I know you're not shy. Go ahead."

She stepped to the mic, her mind blank. Say what, exactly? As always in moments of stress, she went for the comedy. "Thank you, thank you very much," she drawled in a perfect imitation of Elvis Presley. "How y'all doin' tonight?" The crowd roared in response; Elvis was still big in Kilby.

The blond girl, Angeline, claimed the mic. "So, Donna, how did you meet your sexy ballplayer fiancé?"

Donna sighed inwardly. If only she could turn

back time and meet Mike in a way that made for a better story. "If I say he turned up in my Cracker Jack box, would you believe me?"

"Hear that, ladies? I bet we sell out of Cracker Jack today. Was it love at first sight?"

Geez, the *Kilby Press-Herald* should hire this girl instead of Burwell Brown.

"It definitely was. He's got such a cute butt." She winked over her shoulder at Mike, who grinned broadly. A few female catcalls floated from the crowd.

"Any hot tips about how to catch a baseball player?"

"Um . . . wear a big glove?"

Mike nearly choked, the crowd laughed, and the blonde went speechless.

"When's the wedding, Donna?" someone yelled.

"That's a real good question." Her voice echoed weirdly in the stadium, amplified by the microphone but also deadened by the variety of surfaces. She glanced at Zack, wondering if he understood what they were talking about. Did he even know what "engaged" meant? She hadn't told him about any of this because the court case was so up in the air. Once there was a ruling, hopefully they could all work together to help Zack through the transition.

Bonita was pulling at Zack's shoulder, trying to get him to sit down. He shook her off and waved excitedly at Donna. She waved back, and blew a kiss at him. Bonita shot her a glare, then firmly yanked Zack backward into his seat.

Donna felt the blood drain from her face. Time slowed down, and at the same time sped up, so that even though she was standing on the middle of a baseball diamond on a late May evening, the future rushed at her like a wind tunnel. If Harvey and Bonita had Zack full-time, his life would be full of moments like this. Bonita would always want him to do what she said, *be* what she said. Zack would never get to be his own self, his own goofball, energetic, enthusiastic self.

None of this was about her. It was about *Zack*.

Her best chance to save Zack was to marry Mike Solo—as soon as possible.

With a wide smile masking the deep determination that had seized her, she took the mic, and spoke into it, carefully enunciating every word. "Our wedding will take place on June twenty-fifth."

The day before Harvey and Bonita's wedding.

Chapter 14

"**June twenty-fifth, huh?**" Mike shook his head as he let her into his apartment after the game, which the Catfish had lost thanks to a ninth inning rally by the El Paso Chihuahuas. "That part about blurting things out before you think them through? I'm starting to see what you mean."

She brushed past him and went straight for his refrigerator, hoping to find a Lone Star. Nothing there but several takeout containers that could have dated from any previous decade. "If you're thinking about calling off the engagement, forget it," she said. She showed him the paper she'd picked up on the way over. "Early edition. Practically the entire sports section is devoted to us. Mostly you and your kidney. Oh, also? The Kilby Catfish have a YouTube channel and we're the most viewed clip. I'm really sorry, Mike. We should have decided on the date together."

She debated excavating one of the take-out containers but decided she wanted to live, for Zack if for no other reason.

"No worries. We can throw a wedding together by June twenty-fifth. That's what, nearly a month?

I'm up for the challenge if Crush is, with all those big plans of his." He pulled her in for a hug, which she needed more desperately than he could possibly know. She couldn't stop thinking about that moment in the stands, and how the stakes had suddenly sky-rocketed. "Actually, I'm glad you set the date. It makes things less amorphous."

"Amorphous?"

"Without shape. You know my brother's a professor, right? A few things rubbed off over the years."

With his warmth seeping through her clothing, things didn't seem so bad. "You're just . . . always surprising me, that's all."

"I can definitely say the same for you. Especially after today. By the way, Crush thought you were great. He says you're a natural. Wants you to audition for the part-time promotions girl gig, for when Angeline is busy."

"The what?" She couldn't even focus on what he was saying anymore because his hands were tracing the path of her spine, releasing tension as he went.

"I told him you'd be even better than Angeline, because you're funny and adorable and kind of kooky."

"I'm not koo—ooky." A gasp broke the word into two when he slid his hands to her ass and hauled her against him. An iron rod had developed in his pants. Pleasure formed like crystals in her veins, instant and breathtaking.

"I guess we'll stick with adorable then." He nuzzled her neck with his bristly jaw.

"What's . . ." She gasped at the sensations sparked by the rough stubble against her skin. "What's all this about?"

"This is what happens when you say, 'Prove it.'"

Memory rushed back. The PT supply closet at the stadium earlier in the day. Before the game, before Angeline, before Zack. "I already agreed to get married. That's what the whole June twenty-fifth announcement was all about. You don't have to prove . . . Oh God, that feels good."

He was dropping kisses along her collarbone, every touch sending a wakeup call to her sex.

"Too late. The challenge has been issued. The challenge shall be met. I'm going to take you to bed now."

"Bed sounds good." She gave an exaggerated yawn. Now that Mike was following up on her "prove it" command, nerves fluttered all through her. "It's been a long day and I'm practically dead on my feet."

"You'll be wide awake soon enough." For the second time that day, he scooped her into his arms. With a sigh, she settled against him, soaking in the heat of his skin and the flexing muscles of his abdomen. Magically, her jitters disappeared in a flood of desire.

Carrying her as if she weighed no more than Zack, he walked through the apartment into his bedroom. From what she could see, the entire space held nothing but boxes, a couch, a computer, and a bed.

"You don't do much decorating, do you?"

"Nope. That's a wife's job."

"Well, good." She smiled up at him innocently. "Because I have some extra football stuff that would look great in here. How about a carpet that looks like AstroTurf? Life-size cardboard cutout of John Elway?"

"You, woman, are asking for trouble." He tossed her on the bed, which was practically the size of a football field itself. "No more out of you, Red. This bed is going to be your home for the next little while, so get used to it. Take your clothes off."

His caveman manner sent ripples of excitement through her, but she didn't want him to know that. "Where'd you learn your seduction technique? The Croods?"

"I could have done this instead." He grasped one foot and slid her across the bed to where he still stood, legs spread apart like a curly-haired colossus. Quick as a blink, he whisked her jeans off her body. She hadn't known that it was physically possible for a piece of clothing to disappear that fast.

"How did you . . . Is that some sort of special baseball skill?"

"Take off your shirt," was his only answer. His eyes had gone a smoky dark green. "Please."

"Saying please helps, of course, but you're still kind of bossing me around," she grumbled.

"*Off.*"

Her hands flew to the hem of her top, which had two layers of filmy fabric, one a tomato red, the other a hazy gold. Together they looked sensational and really set off her hair and . . . whoops. The shirt was gone, floating through the quiet air onto the nightstand. This time she'd stripped it off herself, as if hypnotized by the way he was talking. He ate up the sight of her, eyes sweeping across her body until she felt a deep flush come over her. She wasn't shy, and was generally okay with her body, but she'd never been scrutinized this hungrily before.

"You are a dangerous man, Mike Solo." She shivered as he came onto the bed, prowling on hands and knees across the covers like a tiger across the savannah. "It's like you have magic powers."

"That's right. Just call me Magic Mike," he growled.

"Nope. Not until you strip your clothes off."

"Oh, I will. When the time is right. For now, I want to feast on your naked body. Get rid of the underwear."

"Would you stop that?" Her laughing protest only made him lunge at her, teeth bared, to snag the thin elastic at the top of her panties. He gave an inarticulate roar of triumph and dragged the flimsy scrap of rayon down her body. "You know," she said conspiratorially, "those panties only cost me about fifty cents at the Rite-Aid. I'm very thrifty when it comes to shopping. Bet you didn't know that about me. I can probably save you tons of money. Socks, for instance. You tell me how much you spend on socks and I guarantee I can cut it in half."

He put his hands to her underwear and tore them in half. Holy Catfish, that was hot. Good thing she bought such cheap underwear. Her feminine parts launched into an insistent throbbing that made her shift restlessly on the bed.

"From now on," Mike said in that same intense tone of command, "you don't buy your underwear at Rite-Aid. Got it?"

"Um . . . why not?"

"Because you're beautiful and we can afford nice underwear. You can skimp on my socks, but not on anything else."

Hot shivers were racing through her. "You're not the boss of me."

"What did you just say?" He pinned her arms over her head and separated her legs with one big thigh.

"I said, you're not the boss of me," she repeated weakly, her breath coming in unsteady little whooshes.

"No, I'm not the boss of you. I'm just the man who's going to make love to you until you forget who you are. But first, I have a problem."

"What?" Her heartbeat fluttered madly in her throat. His gaze dropped to that pulse point and held. The proof of her arousal in her bared neck.

In a voice thick with desire, he told her, "I've wanted to take you to bed since last June. I want you so bad, there's no way I'm going to last more than a few strokes. So here's what I'm proposing. A quickie, followed by an all-nighter. What do you think?"

She felt her lips quiver into a smile. "Whatever you say, boss."

Oh man. With that permission, Mike let loose of the tight rein he'd been keeping on his libido. He flipped her over so she lay on her stomach, the soft globes of her bottom quivering from the quick movement. Her skin was pale where the sun never touched it, fading into a burnished peach right about where her shorts would end. The contrast made him nearly lose his mind. He shaped the cheeks of her ass, delighting in the fine texture, so silky and vulnerable.

He dragged her ass into the air, putting her on elbows and knees before him. *Condoms.* He had some, somewhere, left over from the time between baseball seasons. Where were they? He couldn't think, she was too beautiful, spread open in front of him like this. His hands brushed over her swelling curves, the deep valley between, and down to the wet, hot cleft below. *Condom, condom.* Where the fuck was it?

"What are you waiting for, Solo?" Donna wiggled her butt back and forth. "You said quickie."

"I'm trying to remember where my condoms are. I'm the guy who took a Vow of Celibacy, remember? I don't usually have to worry about protection."

"Back pocket of my jeans," she said, peeking over her freckled shoulder at him. His hands stilled on her skin. "Don't look like that. I challenged you, remember? And the last thing I need is for another accident to happen. I wanted to make extra sure."

He shook off his momentary hesitation and gave her a little pat on the rear. "Hang on. This'll just take a second."

He found her jeans draped across a box and rummaged for the condom. The thought of Donna carrying around protection had jarred him, because it made him wonder who else she'd had sex with. Which was idiotic, because obviously she'd had a whole life before him. A life that included a baby. Donna was no virgin.

Angela . . . Angela had been a virgin when they first had sex. He'd been her first, and she'd been his first.

He found the condom—not a brand he normally used—and viciously ripped open the package. What was he doing, thinking about Angela? He'd had sex with plenty of women since her. Fun, meaningless sex.

His movements slowed as he withdrew the condom from its foil package. It was a familiar sight. After Angela had dumped him—and after he'd recovered from the surgery—he'd gone on a sex binge, fueled by bitterness and the need to drive her from his mind. That was one of the reasons he'd started taking the vow at the start of the season. Sex was fantastic. He loved sex. But he was on a mission to reach the major leagues, and he didn't want the distraction.

Off-season, he'd done whatever he wanted, with whatever girl was interested. No strings, no drama, no regrets sex. About as shallow as a puddle in a Texas heat wave.

He traced the rim of the condom, readying it to slip on his penis. Donna was different. Obviously, she was different because he planned to marry her. But it was more than that. She touched a part of him that he'd thought beyond reach. He *felt* things for her. And now they were about to have sex, which was great and he was incredibly excited about it . . . but it was serious too. The first time with Angela—a full year after they'd gotten engaged—had been hushed and tentative; it had felt almost sacred. For the first time since his heart had been ripped from his body, he was about to have sex that *meant* something.

He swallowed past the sudden lump in his throat. In a way, this was good-bye to Angela. Good-bye to the death grip she'd put on his heart.

Shaking off the dark thoughts, he rolled the condom onto his erection, which had begun to soften. When he turned back to the bed, it was empty.

Donna had left him. He felt hollow and ridiculous, standing alone with his latex-covered dick pointing at nothing. Hell, he probably deserved to be kicked to the curb, with all his morose thoughts about Angela. He reached down to peel the condom off his penis, when a sound made him look up.

"Dah-*dah*-dah-dah-*dum*." The classic stripper theme. One naked leg peeked from the other side of the doorjamb. "Dah-*dah*-dah-dah-*dum*." She straightened that leg, so the whole limb was exposed, then slithered around the edge of the door. Completely naked, except for his baseball glove, in which her hand was engulfed, shielding her sex. With the other hand and arm, she covered her breasts. Sweet little mounds of flesh plumped above her forearm. A cheeky smile dimpled her mouth. Her hair curled in wild fiery tendrils, just brushing her shoulders. She was adorable and sexy, and his cock went hard as wood.

"That's my glove," he said stupidly. His glove had never been anywhere near a woman's body before. Even from here he could smell the faint scent of oiled leather.

"Yes. Want it back?"

She executed a sexy little twirl. When her back was to him, the riveting sway of her ass gave his cock another infusion of stiffness. Once she was facing him again, she pretended to drop the glove, which gave him a quick flash of her coppery curls.

"Oopsies." She put a bashful hand over her mouth and batted her eyelashes, covering herself again with the glove, which looked like a leather fan. Or a big, thick-fingered hand. His gaze shot to her breasts, which were now exposed, her rosy nipples erotically engorged.

Lust flooded his brain, and all he could think was *Woman . . . want . . . now.* He strode to her, plucked the glove from her hand, lifted her with both hands under her ass, and crowded her against the wall. "Wrap your legs around my waist."

"The bed's right—"

"Too far," he grunted. "Do it."

She did it, and the feel of her soft flesh surrounding him made the mad need pound through his veins. With his last scrap of rational thought, he reached between them to stroke a finger inside her. Wet and warm and velvety heaven. Groaning, he took hold of his cock and poised it at her entrance. She tilted her head against the wall, her eyes half closed, glowing gold. So beautiful, so sparkling and vivid and fiery and . . .

He was inside her. Heat clung to him as he pressed forward, inch by inch, as if claiming his territory. *I belong here*, the crazy thought surfaced. *She belongs to me.* All the way in now, his cock seated completely within her, a sword in its scabbard, a hand in its glove. Exactly where he belonged.

He pulled out so he could plunge in again, feeling the expansion of her passage accommodating his thickness.

"Mike," She sighed, her eyelashes fluttering against her cheeks. "That feels crazy good."

He couldn't answer; he was too immersed in the feel of her, his encased flesh sliding against her slick tissues, her thighs trembling against his hips. He pumped into her, her spine pressed against the wall, her legs tight around him. She might be getting tired holding this position. She didn't spend vast stretches of her life building up her thigh muscles, the way he did.

Another thrust, then another, the pressure building in his spine, the pleasure shorting out his brain. And then . . . the explosion rocked through him, paralyzing him. A groan left his mouth, long and primal, echoing in a distant way, as if it came from someone else.

Euphoria. Release. Happiness. As soon as the spasms stopped, he swung her around and walked her to the bed, then lowered her down. He removed the condom and climbed next to her, cuddling her body next to his.

"You okay?" she whispered.

He nodded. "Give me a minute."

He'd had sex. Broken the vow. He waited for the guilt to swamp him. Instead the image of Donna prancing around naked with his baseball glove flashed into his mind. He relaxed back on the bed and let the laughter roll out of him, free and deep and easy. "You are something else, Donna MacIntyre."

"Thanks. I guess."

He rolled over and skimmed his hand across her belly. The little muscles along her torso quivered. Letting his fingers saunter up the slope of her breast, he realized it wouldn't take him long to be fully hard again. "What made you come up with that glove idea?"

She shrugged. "It seemed like you were getting awfully serious putting that condom on. Thought I'd lighten things up a little."

"You're good at that, aren't you? Lightening things up."

Another shrug. "It's my thing."

He reached her nipple, which stiffened with grati-fying speed. "I'm a little worried what will happen the next time I use that glove."

"Really?" Breathless, she shifted under his touch.

"I'll think of you. And this. Here." He gathered her breast into his hand, the plump warm flesh filling his palm. "And here." Shifting his hand to the thicket of curls between her legs, he squeezed lightly. Her eyelids flickered closed, and without warning, he was completely hard.

"Ready for the second inning?" he whispered as he moved on top of her.

"How many innings are there again?"

"Nine. Unless the score is tied, then we go to extra innings. Longest game in history lasted thirty-three innings. Eleven hours and twenty-five minutes."

"We can break that record."

Chapter 15

Donna CAME BACK to awareness with a start. The sun was slanting through the window blinds, casting long slices of lemony light across the room. She lay on her back, diagonally across the bed, one arm flung sideways, the way Zack always slept, and one leg draped across Mike's thigh. His powerfully muscled thigh, strong enough to bear her weight while he screwed her against the wall.

Holy Sex Marathon. After Mike had broken through his hesitation, they'd made love over and over again. She'd brought only two condoms, so for the "third inning" he'd taken a break and unpacked several boxes to locate his condom stash. After that, nothing held them back from their all-nighter. Sexual satisfaction hummed through her body, along with a slight ache in her private area, which hadn't had much to crow about lately.

She extracted her leg from Mike's thigh and leaned over the bulk of his shoulder to peer at his face. Slack-jawed and deeply asleep, he looked like an innocent choirboy with those black curls tumbling over his forehead. Like an Italian painting she'd seen in an art book at the library. It was only when he opened his eyes, those devil-green eyes, that his mischievous side was revealed. His body sprawled loosely across the bed, magnificent in relaxation, pure masculine perfection. His penis curled against his legs, his heavy balls loose and flaccid under their covering of black curls.

Oh, the things that penis could do. The things it could make her feel, along with his rough, clever hands and greedy tongue.

She shivered and lay back down. The air was still and slightly stuffy, and a hint of sex still tinged the air.

They'd done it. They'd had sex. She'd wanted it, as a way to call his bluff and make sure he was serious about getting married. And because she'd *wanted* it.

Anxiety tightened her throat. Had she pulled her usual routine and acted without thinking things through? She hadn't anticipated *this* feeling, this hopeless, cursed *emotion* nagging at her. Before last night, she'd considered herself to be infatuated with Mike. Now her feelings had shifted. They'd settled into her bones, infiltrated her circulation, like some kind of virus. As if every beat of her heart sent more of it pumping through her body. She loved Mike. Utterly and completely.

Cripes. What had she done? Yes, things were real now. *Too* real. They were going to get married, which meant she'd be tied to someone she was hopelessly in love with—but who didn't love her back. Torture.

He'd had sex with her to prove he wasn't still hung up on Angela. Maybe he wasn't—but that didn't mean he had real feelings for Donna. He'd definitely never mentioned anything like that.

Did it matter?

Mike would get called up sooner or later. He'd leave Kilby. She would stay. She had to stay because of Zack. No way would Harvey or the Hannigans let her leave, and she wouldn't want Zack to be without his extended family anyway. She and Mike would have a long-distance relationship, and everyone knew those didn't work. It would fall apart, they'd end the marriage, and she'd begin the process of rebuilding her peace of mind.

At least she'd have Zack, which made up for everything else.

Mike's phone buzzed from the floor somewhere. One of his arms shot toward it, feeling along the edge of the mattress. Donna rolled out of bed, skipped to the other side, then put the phone in his hand.

"Yeah," he mumbled into it, once he'd plastered it crookedly to his ear. Silence ensued while he listened to whoever had called. Donna took the opportunity to find her own phone and check the time. Six-thirty. She had to be at work at nine. Who would call Mike at six-thirty in the morning?

When she turned back, he was sitting up, rubbing the sleep grains out of his eyes. "Yazmer? That dickhead. Where?" He swung his legs over the side of his bed and strode from the room. Donna couldn't help watching the way his ass muscles flexed with each step. Sweet Lord, he was a sexy, sexy man.

But this wasn't the moment for lust, since clearly something bad was in the works. She untangled the top sheet, which looked as if it had gone through the washer too many times, and wrapped it around her. In the living room, she found Mike bent over a small black-and-white TV that sat on a box in the corner.

"I don't even know if I get any channels," he was saying. "Hang on, let me get to my laptop. Don't hang up."

Donna spotted a laptop on the butcher-block island next to her. Obligingly, she opened it for him and turned it on. Naked, powerful and magnificent, he walked toward her, brushed a kiss across her lips, and leaned over the laptop.

Her lips tingling, she watched as he pulled up Twitter. He searched for @TheYaz, which brought up a profile picture of the pitcher about to kiss a baseball.

Mike scrolled through a series of tweets, in which Yazmer was making some kind of announcement. Slowly, he read aloud. "*Searched my conscience. The dear Lord showed Yaz the way. Crush Taylor gotz to go.*"

Next tweet. "*Tried to get him in on petition to keep locker room sacred. Told me no politics in the clubhouse.*"

Next tweet. "*Want to use my fame to do the Lord's work. Lord told me, Crush Taylor's got to go. Let's make this shit viral. Hashtag CrushIt. RT, baby.*"

He glanced at Donna. "RT? What's RT?"

"Retweet," Donna told him, apparently at the same time his mystery caller did.

"Retweet? This is nuts. Who cares what some rookie pitcher thinks? I gotta go, Caleb. This is too much bullshit first thing in the morning. Catch you later." He tossed his phone onto the butcher-block countertop.

"Retweet?" he repeated to Donna. "What is going on here?"

"You don't spend much time on social media, do you?"

"I post stuff to Instagram now and then. Facebook. I'm just a dude who plays baseball. What am I going to put on Twitter?" He ran a hand through his thick curls, then along his jaw, which was studded with black stubble. He blinked at her. "Donna." He sounded surprised to see her.

"Remember me?" Still clutching the sheet, she gave a little wave.

"Um, yeah. I'm not about to forget a night like that. I just wish the morning hadn't started with this bullshit. I'd rather be under your sheet with you."

He reached for her, but she took a step back. She wasn't quite ready to surrender to the tug of lust that had already sprung up between them. "So Yazmer's starting a campaign against Crush?"

"Yaz wants attention. He needs it like oxygen." He went to one of the boxes occupying the living room and knelt down to rummage through it. After a short search, he pulled out a bath towel. Rising to his feet, he wrapped it around his waist. Donna was a little sad to see him covered up, but at least his torso was still on display, with its rippling muscles and light sprinkling of springy curls.

"He's been passing this petition around to keep gay reporters out of the locker room. It's not like we even have any in this town, as far as I've heard. And how would we even know if they were? What does he want to do, make them wear a big LGBT label on their foreheads? Of course, if it was a hot lesbian reporter he'd be all over it. The dude's a straight-up homophobic hypocrite."

He ran a hand across the back of his neck. Donna was riveted by the way his biceps bunched from the movement. If only Mike wasn't so physically appealing. It just wasn't fair. Even first thing in the morning, after being woken up by a surprise phone call, sleepy-eyed and a little grumpy, he looked beautiful to her.

"Well, I hate to say this, but he's not the only one. We have some close-minded people in this town. When the owner of the Smoke Pit came out as gay, some people boycotted it. But most folks didn't care, so long as they still ran their burger and a beer five-dollar special on Tuesday nights."

A broad grin spread across Mike's face. "I don't know how you do it, but you always make me look on the bright side of things."

"You know my motto. Laugh so you don't cry."

He took a few steps closer and put his hand under her chin, tilting her face up. "I never want you to cry."

She answered solemnly. "Then you have to make a sacred promise to never let me cut up an onion. Those things wreck me."

He laughed, then released her chin and went to check the laptop again. "He just sent out a new tweet. *Don't Can the Catfish. Can the Crush. Hashtag CrushIt. RT, baby.*"

Slamming shut his laptop, he shoved it aside. "How does he even have time for this crap? Last I heard, he was designing a Yazmer action figure and a line of underwear."

"Seriously?"

"Who knows? He talks about a lot of things. You never know what's real. The guy has an imagination almost as big as his ego. We had him pegged all wrong, you know. At the start of the season he was spouting off to the press all the time, and we figured he had no experience dealing with the media. I think we had it backwards. He knows exactly what he's doing. He wants press attention and he'll say all kinds of offensive shit to get it. Anything about gays in sports always gets the reporters going."

"Won't he make the reporters hate him? At least, the gay ones?"

"He doesn't care if they hate him. Any attention is good attention. He'll probably become a hero to the anti-gay crowd."

Finally, the light dawned. She couldn't believe it had taken so long to put the pieces together. "Joey. That's why you're so upset about Yazmer."

"Yeah, my brother's a big part of it." Mike circled around the kitchen sink, pulled a couple of plastic stadium cups from a cupboard, and filled one of them with water. He handed it to her over the island. "Drink up, you need hydration after a night like that."

He winked, giving her a glimpse of the playful, mischievous Mike Solo she was more used to. Not that she didn't like this serious version of Mike as well. She did. Too much.

He filled another glass with water for himself and took a long swallow. "Joey is used to this kind of thing. He'd probably just laugh it off. He has bigger things to worry about, like whether or not his kidneys will hold up. But it drives me crazy. Joey is *Joey*. He's my brother, and one of the best people on this planet, and when I think about Yazmer having a problem with him coming into the locker room, it makes my blood boil. That hypocritical, self-serving, ambitious little snot. He's not fit to breathe the same air as my brother."

His voice vibrated with anger, his eyes blazed deep green, like the sun lighting up a quarry pool. As if embarrassed by his own intensity, he lifted a shoulder, then turned back toward the sink for more water. Donna dragged her gaze away from the sight of the muscles flexing under his tan skin. This man had a knack for taking her breath away.

Which was trouble, big trouble.

She gathered her sheets around her and climbed onto one of the stools at the kitchen island. "So why don't you do something about it?"

"Like what?" He propped his towel-covered rear against the edge of the counter. "Yazmer is the way he is. I've tried to get close to him. They wanted me to help settle him down, show him the ropes. I tried, but all he got from it was a selfie. 'Me and the Kilby catcher. Can he handle the Yaz?' He's like the Kim Kardashian of Triple A."

Donna propped her elbows on the counter and rested her chin in the palm of her hand. "So you can't change Yazmer. There's no point in trying. But there's got to be something else you can do."

He snapped his fingers, eyes gleaming. "I know. I could get up on the bar at the Kilby Roadhouse and give him a piece of my mind. Maybe get another brawl going, since the last one was such a hit."

"Ha ha. I'm serious. He's a baseball player. You're a baseball player. Maybe you should go on TV. Do a PSA or something. Why should he get all the attention?"

"Because he wants it. He's a camera hound. Some

people can't get enough of the camera, but I'm not one of them."

"Well, I think you're very photogenic." She picked up his phone and pretended to snap a photo, aiming at his groin, where the towel clung to the bulge of his privates.

"You'd better delete that," he growled, advancing around the island toward her. "I don't need my junk ending up on Facebook."

She hopped off the stool and backed away from him, still pretending to take snapshots of his body. "How about Twitter, then? Hashtag OMG."

"Hand over my phone or there's going to be trouble, girl." He was only a few strides away from her now. She tripped over the sheet, which had gotten tangled between her feet, and let out a shriek as he lunged for her. Abandoning her covering, she skipped away, so he was left with a handful of bed sheet and a frustrated expression, and she was left completely nude.

He still wore his towel, which was now expanding over a quickly growing hard-on. Spinning around, she aimed his phone at his groin. "Looks like *someone* loves the camera."

"That has nothing to do with the camera," he informed her, wrestling the sheet into a ball, then casting it aside. "That's all you, baby. Might as well sign your name on it."

"With what, my tongue?" She tossed the saucy words over her shoulder just before she slipped into the bedroom and flung her weight against the door. She shouldn't be teasing him like this. She had to get to work soon.

But the door didn't close. Somehow, he managed to get his chest between the door and the jamb, which meant he was able to snake one arm through and tickle her ribs.

She was insanely ticklish, always had been, and immediately shrieked in hysterical reaction.

"My girl's a little ticklish, is she?" He wriggled his fingers under her armpit. She squirmed madly, then gave up and jumped out of reach. The door fell open and he burst into the room, all bulging muscles and black curls. He advanced toward her. "Now I know how to get you back. Tie you up and tickle you until you scream."

"Tickle? Really? Is that the best you can come up with?" She danced across the room, hopscotching around boxes, evading his pursuing hand by inches.

"You little tease." He laughed, low and rich as fresh-brewed coffee. "Are you trying to get me going again?"

"I'm just trying to find my clothes," she said virtuously, having just tripped over a little pile that included her top and torn panties. "What's left of them." Quickly she pulled the top over her head so she was half dressed. The filmy double layer of fabric settled across her chest with a soft prickling of her nipples. The shirt only reached to just below her belly button; she saw his eyes flare with heat. She spotted her jeans on the other side of the bed and took a step in that direction.

"Don't even think about it, Donna. Stop where you are and don't put on another piece of clothing." The deep rumble of his voice, desire percolating through it like black tar, rooted her to the floor. She let him prowl closer while his gaze consumed her body. Excitement blossomed in her belly, liquid heat between her legs.

He stopped about two feet from her. His towel had disappeared during their little chase; he was now entirely nude and completely aroused. His erection jutted toward her, nearly perpendicular to the floor, impressively thick and dusky rose. She swallowed through the sudden extreme tightness in her throat.

You could hang a towel on that thing, she thought with an edge of hysteria.

"Pull your shirt tighter," he ordered.

"What?"

"Pull it tighter across your breasts." His burning gaze was now fastened on her chest. "Your nipples look beautiful like that, poking through that material. I want to see what it looks like tighter."

She put her hands behind her back and bunched the fabric in one hand; the other still held his phone. It pulled tight across her chest, a silky abrasion that made her breath catch. She knew her nipples were swelling larger, she could feel it. Wanting more of the sensation, she arched her back, pressing her breasts against the filmy layers.

"Oh sweet Jesus, you have no idea how hot you look right now. Keep your hands like that." He closed the distance between them and buried one hand between her thighs. The other went to her breasts, somehow managing to span the distance between them.

A spasm shook her. Shocked—was she coming, just like that?—she flinched backward, but he didn't let her get far. He abandoned her breasts and clamped his arm around her back, pressing her against him.

His phone slipped out of her fingers, falling to the floor. The heat of his bare chest burned through her top to her nipples. She gasped as he sank two fingers deep within her, grinding against her clit with the palm of his hand. "Oh . . . oh oh ooh," she cried out in a rising wail. She *was* coming, huge paroxysms pulling her this way and that, flinging her into a world of pure sensation.

She might have even blacked out for a moment, because then she was on her back, the edge of the mattress pressing against her thighs, which were spread wide. Mike stood between them, pulling on another condom. How many was that? And then she gave up thinking as he thrust that powerful spear of flesh right where she wanted it most. Deep inside her, as close to her core as he could get.

She abandoned herself to the wild pleasure. No sense fighting it. She was in deep with Mike, all the way. So deep she had no clue where the exit was.

Chapter 16

LIFE BEFORE MIKE faded into a distant, dull sort of dream. All the elements of her previous reality still existed. She still showed up every morning for work at Dental Miracles. She still made appointments for root canals, showed patients into examination rooms, and took quick trips to the break room to swallow down burnt coffee. She picked Zack up for outings twice a week, and an overnight once a week; Mike came with them as often as he could.

But everything was glazed with the misty sheen of magic that went along with being engaged to a baseball player. The other staff members ate up every line of her interview in the *Kilby Press-Herald*. Someone cut out the article and posted it on the bulletin board in the break room. She kept getting peppered with questions, especially from her young, single coworkers.

"How did you meet him, really? . . . The only guy I ever met at the Roadhouse lived in his van and shot roadkill for breakfast . . . If you ever want to go on a double date, you call me, girl. I'd take Trevor Stark, Dwight Conner, or even that crazy Yazmer. Hell, they're all cute. . . . What do Mike Solo's thighs look like when he ain't wearing that uniform? Mind taking a picture sometime?"

She deflected all the questions with good humor, because she was too happy to be irritated. Not even when she was called in to assist one of the dentists, and instead of handing him dental instruments, she wound up reenacting Mike's proposal, using a box of tissues as a stand-in for the bouquet of lilacs.

She gave some thought to Mike's suggestion that she quit her job, but decided she'd wait until Judge Quinn made his decision. She didn't want to look unreliable or flaky. Given the new timeframe for the wedding, Crush had hired a professional planner who only called Donna for token consultations. The whole thing felt like a dream, with Mike the solid, irresistible anchor to reality.

One day Mike announced that it was time for him to meet her father and stepmother.

"You know, I'd rather get three root canals than have a conversation with my stepmother," Donna told him.

"I have to meet them," Mike insisted. "It's important to me."

"Do you have to be such a boy scout?"

"Take back the 'boy' part," he growled, shifting the conversation from verbal to physical. "And I'm not letting this go, just so you know."

Donna had no wish to take him to the home where she'd been nothing but miserable after her mother left. From the moment Carrie had moved in, they'd clashed. A former army sergeant, Carrie had no patience for a confused, high-energy kid who didn't understand why her mom had moved out, and Donna had done her best to piss Carrie off. She wasn't proud of it, but she couldn't change it now. She still hadn't found a way to get along with Carrie—not that the other woman seemed interested in family harmony. Sometimes Donna thought she got a kick out of their battles.

No, her best chance of getting along with Carrie was in small doses, on neutral territory. So Mike took them all out to dinner at Mama Cat's, generally regarded as the best steakhouse in town.

She'd warned Mike that Carrie had high standards when it came to wardrobe choices (as she'd spent her teen years learning), so he took care to dress in a nice jacket and a white shirt that set off the dark shade of his skin. Donna wanted to wear her own infamous blue blazer, but Mike threatened to throw it in the trash compactor, so she settled for a knee-length cargo skirt and an olive-green blouse with puffy sleeves and a bow at the neck.

He looked her up and down with a horrified expression. "You look like a frickin' boy scout."

"Look, this is your idea. Do you want it to go well, or do you want a re-creation of every morning of my life between the ages of eleven and seventeen?"

"Fine. But as soon as we get back, I'm ripping those clothes off you."

"Deal. You know, sometimes when I see Carrie I play a little drinking game. Every time she insults me I do a shot. But I want to go easy on your kidney, One-K. So we'll skip that little entertainment."

"How about this: For every time she insults you I owe you an orgasm."

"Solo, you don't know what you're promising. It could take weeks for me to collect."

"We've got time, right?" His wicked smile set her aflame, and he wasn't even really trying.

At Mama Cat's, Carrie and Donna's father, known around town as Mac, were already seated at a table by the stone barbecue pit. They each sipped from a Scotch on the rocks, which made Donna's stomach tighten anxiously. Carrie rarely drank, and when she did, nothing held her back from expressing her true feelings about Donna and everything wrong with her.

As soon as their steaks had arrived, Carrie started in on Donna. "Where are the two of you planning to live? There's no chance the Hannigan family will sign off on you leaving Kilby, Donna."

Carrie was a genius at searching out vulnerabilities and an artist when it came to slicing and dicing Donna's self-esteem. How did the woman know that she and Mike hadn't even talked about where to live? Before she could answer, he spoke up.

"Very few ballplayers live permanently in the city where they play. Even if—when—I get called up to San Diego, I'll still need a home base. I don't see why it can't be Kilby."

Donna stared at him. This was news to her. Why had he never mentioned it? He must have seen the shock on her face, because he leaned down and whispered, "I was planning a surprise. A house-hunting surprise."

"*What?*"

"What's that? What's going on?" Carrie blotted her mouth with her napkin, leaving splotches of bright orange lipstick. "Are you two whispering secrets over there?"

"They aren't causing any harm," said Donna's

father uncomfortably. In the early days of Carrie, Mac had tried to intervene when things got ugly, but he'd quickly realized he'd rather be working on a transmission.

"That remains to be seen." Carrie cut into her rib-eye. "I heard the Wades are on the warpath. You didn't make any friends with your disgraceful behavior last summer, Donna."

"The Wades are always going to be the Wades." Donna slathered butter on her baked potato. Comfort food was key in this situation. "What do they have to do with us?"

"They have everything to do with you. To start with, both of you are on their radar ever since that Roadhouse fiasco. Dean's running for mayor, and Roy wants to buy the Catfish. And of course, Bonita is Dean's second cousin by marriage. A real sharp cookie too." The approval in Carrie's voice felt like a complete betrayal. "You figure it out, Donna."

"I'm not worried about the Wades," Mike said calmly, with an air of complete confidence. "We'll take care of our business, they'll take care of theirs. First thing on our list, look for a house."

Carrie's mouth drew tight as she chewed, so thin lines appeared all around it, like shatter lines around a bullet hole. "A house?"

"Yes. A house. Something to live in. I'm tired of short-term leases and cats who belong to someone else and saying good-bye to neighbors I might never see again. I need a home base."

"Don't you have a family somewhere else?"

"Sure. Chicago. But I like it down here. Nice weather. Better for keeping in shape in the off-season.

We need a house with a big yard where I can hit some grounders with Zack." He flashed a smile. "Maybe get a cat. You like cats, don't you, sweetie? You're not allergic, are you?" With a wink, he squeezed her hand under the table. He loved reminding her of the allergies she'd faked.

Donna shook her head, marveling at how smoothly he handled Carrie. How did he do it? How did he play the part of eager husband-to-be with such enthusiasm? To watch him, you'd never guess that his sense of duty was driving him into their marriage. Or some weird flash of intuition behind home plate.

"Well, I just hope you're ready for a big reality check. I wish someone had warned me before I became a parent to someone else's child." Carrie put down her fork and slung the words like little poison darts. "I could write a whole manual on the subject. I'd call it *Pretty Little Liars.*"

Donna gripped her fork tightly, that familiar lost feeling stealing over her. If only her father would say something. She'd spent seven years getting slammed by insults like that and waiting for Mac to stand up for her. Never happened.

Well, she'd just have to stand up for herself, as always. "Did you just call me pretty? That's the nicest thing you ever said to me."

"Now, you know that's not true. Are you trying to prove my point for me?"

Donna opened her mouth to sling back another jab, but nothing came out. Blank. Nada. Not that she couldn't think of something nasty—but, for the first time, she didn't want to. Life was good right now. She had Mike now, his solid presence right there at her shoulder, offering silent support. The pain that had fueled her battles with Carrie . . . poof. Nothing more than a distant echo of it remained. Carrie didn't matter. Zack did, and a fight with Carrie wouldn't help her get Zack back.

Instead of continuing the war of words, she fixed her gaze on her plate. Her steak no longer appealed to her; she just wanted this evening to end. The moment stretched onward, agonizing and endless. Someone guffawed from across the room, someone else dropped silverware on the floor. A warm hand settled into the small of her back.

Mike balled up his napkin and rose to his feet. "Funny thing, I've always heard how friendly and welcoming Texas is. Mostly, it's true. Mostly."

Mike couldn't have picked a better way to get under Carrie's skin. She was a fifth-generation Texan, obsessed with genealogy and pride in her roots. "I didn't mean it to be rude," she said stiffly. "I'm just trying to warn you."

"I think Donna deserves an apology, honey," said Mac softly. "In fact, I'm pretty sure she does. If you won't give it, I will."

Donna's head snapped up. What had gotten into her father? He never defended her. When Carrie didn't say anything—probably still in shock herself—he turned to Donna. "She's sorry, even if she can't say it."

Clearly, no one at the table believed that. Mike pulled out his wallet and extracted some money. It looked like two hundred-dollar bills, but Donna couldn't believe one dinner could cost that much. "This should cover it." After putting the money on the table, he put an arm around Donna and spoke to Mac. "It was nice to meet you, sir." He nodded to Carrie, then steered Donna toward the exit.

As they left, Donna caught her father's eye for one brief moment. He fixed her with a pleading look, as if begging her for something. To forget Carrie's rudeness? Rescue him from her clutches? Whatever it was, she couldn't offer him any help. He'd made his choice, and there was absolutely nothing she could do about it.

As soon as they made it outside, Donna took a deep breath of fresh air. The sky was undergoing a deep violet transformation into night. On a pleasant evening like this, Kilby-ites loved to come to this area, the original downtown. The brick streets and sidewalks had been restored by the city in order to attract more tourists. She had no idea how many tourists came here, but plenty of Kilby families were out enjoying the evening, eating ice cream cones and strolling past the storefronts.

"Want to walk a little? You can show me the sights," Mike said softly.

"Sure. That'll take three minutes. Then we can go make out, right? I'm all hot and bothered from the way you talked to Carrie."

He chuckled, drawing her close to his side, and they wandered down the sidewalk, just like one of the real couples walking hand in hand. "I figured I could call on her Texas pride. She was wearing a Lone Star flag pin and bluebonnet earrings. Is she always nasty like that?"

"Around me she is. I assume she's nicer to other people or she'd be on a rocket heading to outer space by now."

"Why does she have it in for you?"

"Well, I didn't exactly welcome her to the family," Donna admitted. "I loved my mother, and when she left I was pretty upset. Devastated, I guess would be the word. I wanted to go with her, travel the world, you know, but she said no. My dad just kind of went into a shell, like some kind of turtle, hiding under a car at the shop. We had frozen pizza for every meal for like, months. Finally I got burned out on pizza and started looking up recipes for meatloaf and stuff on the Internet. Anything that wasn't pizza."

He took her hand, swinging it between the two of them. "Do you still hate pizza?"

"Yes. It reminds me of that time."

"Damn. You didn't say a word when I brought that Tombstone pizza to the Suds-o-Rama."

"No, because you were so cute, and I didn't want to hurt your feelings." She laughed at him, snuggling into his side. "Anyway, Dad met Carrie when he worked on her Miata. I kept thinking my mom was going to come back, so to me she was basically the Wicked Witch trying to steal my father. I'm not proud of how I acted. Once I mixed some pepper spray into her hand lotion. She had to go to the ER. Another time I pretended I had Ebola. I got fake blood and spewed all over her. I was awful. It's no wonder she hates me."

She tugged him to a stop as they reached the statue of Colonel Kilby and his rearing horse. "Your first Kilby landmark. A bronze statue commissioned by the Wade family on the occasion of the incorporation of Kilby. Do you know how close we came to being named Wade?" She shuddered. "The Wades thought being associated with Colonel Kilby would make the town more respectable, but I've heard rumors that within the family, the town is called Wadeville."

He snorted. "No way."

"Okay, I made that up. See, that's the kind of thing that drives Carrie crazy. She never got onboard with my sense of humor."

"Her loss. It works for me." The smile he directed at her sent warmth gushing straight to her heart. "So your parents split up when you were, what, twelve or so?"

"Eleven. My mom had itchy feet. She always used to tell me that, and I never knew it was a figure of speech. I thought she had athlete's foot or something. She has an awesome voice, and one night the Redneck Diamonds came through town—they're a country band—and she was in the audience, just singing along. One of the band members heard her singing and pulled her up onstage. She left the next day, with them. Never looked back. Well, I mean she sends me postcards and calls and stuff. And I stayed with her in L.A. when I had Zack."

"She abandoned you."

"No, no, I don't see it that way at all. I think she stayed eleven years longer than she wanted to. I'm a lot like her. We both like to joke around and make people laugh. Play the clown."

"What about your dad?"

She rolled her eyes, gave a salute to Colonel Kilby, and headed toward the next landmark. "You saw him. What you see is what you get. I once clocked him at twenty-six hours without saying a single word. His happy place is on his back under a car. It's a freak of nature that I'm related to him in any way. I'm my mother's daughter, one hundred percent."

"I wouldn't say that."

"Fine, I have my dad's red hair. Other than that . . ."

"You stayed. For Zack."

She stopped in her tracks, at the intersection of Twelfth and Main, and stared at him for what seemed like an eternity while his words sank in. Yes, she had stayed, like her father, and completely *unlike* her mother. It didn't matter if Zack was three or twelve or seventeen. She'd stay as long as he needed her. But she'd never looked at herself and her family in that light.

Mike was returning her gaze in a steady, quizzical manner. Her face started to heat, and she wrenched her gaze away before she got too crimson in the face. Why did he have such a good opinion of her? Hadn't he noticed all her many flaws?

Desperately, she waved her arm toward the end of the street, at a squat building surrounded by scaffolding. "Do you want to see the fort?"

"I'm a boy. Of course I want to see the fort. I never knew there was one."

"Well, it was actually a hiding place for a group of bandits during the Mexican-American War. But beggars can't be choosers, so we call it a fort. The city's been working on restoring it. Just in case tourists get bored with the Alamo and want something with zero historical significance and an awesome gift shop."

She showed him the crumbling brick building with arched windows and an old pump-handle well in the courtyard. In the starlight it had a mysterious ambiance, as if ghostly bandits might be lurking in the hedges.

Mike must have felt it too; he gave a shiver and hugged her closer. "Well, it's no Sears Tower or Chicago Mercantile Building. Or Wrigley Field. Or—"

"I see your point. Our historical landmarks suck compared to yours."

"Hey, don't talk about my adopted town that way. I like Kilby. There's plenty of space here, nice people, rocking weather. And there's you." He dipped his head to brush his lips against hers. Tingles danced across her mouth and her lips parted. Just like that, she wanted him.

Perplexed, she tilted her head back and frowned at him. "Where did you come from, Mike Solo? I mean, one minute you were that cute, funny guy I had a secret crush on, the next we're engaged to be married and possibly going house hunting. How does that happen?"

He straightened. "You had a secret crush on me?"

"Yeah, but don't let it go to your head. I've also had crushes on Channing Tatum, the shift manager at Kroger, and my driver's ed teacher, until I found out he wore a rug. And that's just a small sample."

"I get it. I'm nothing special. Just another one of your many crushes. Did those guys do this?" He spun her against his chest and danced her around the empty, starlit courtyard, faster and faster, until she begged him to stop. Then he kissed her, long and deep and hot and hungry.

When he'd kissed her dizzy, he released her, so suddenly she nearly fell backward. He crossed his arms over his chest. "Well?"

"No," she managed. "They didn't do that. You win. I'll tell those other guys to forget all about me. It's going to be especially hard on poor Channing. I don't know what he'll do without me crushing on him, actually."

"He'll live," Mike said, callously. "Now, as for the others, anyone I need to have a talk with? Do I need to march down to Kroger and find that manager? Set the record straight that you're with me now?"

That possessive tone made her melt. Mike was too good to be true. Too endearing, too appealing, too dream-come-true.

But he wasn't a dream come true. He was a mirage. So close, and yet never to be hers. Not really. Not in the way she wanted.

Suddenly furious, Donna shoved a hand against his chest. "Look, Solo, get over yourself. You don't need to act all possessive and jealous. It's not like you're in love with me."

The words fell between them like little bombs. He looked thunderstruck. She instantly wanted to take them back. Why, oh why, did she have to blurt things out in that disastrous way? What now, what now? *Play the clown. Make a joke.* "Wait a second . . . that's it! You *are* in love with me. You have been all along, and this whole thing was a secret plot to lure me into your web of seduction. Admit it, Solo. You looooove me!" She twirled away from him, across the old bricks of the courtyard, and belted out the first song that came to mind—"Love Is an Open Door."

She'd subjected him to *Frozen* enough times that she knew every word. Duplicating the choreography right there in the bandits' courtyard, she ran to the locked door that led into the fort. "Can I say something crazy?" She kept singing, alternating between Anna's lines and Hugh's, as she twirled across to the pump handle, linking her little finger with it when she got to the "jinx" part. "Jinx. Jinx!" She turned a stop sign on the corner into an imaginary cuckoo clock, mimicking Anna's motions as she sang about mental synchronization.

Never in her life had she tried so desperately to clown her way out of a mess.

Finally Mike laughed, her cue to bring her crazy reenactment to an end.

"You should put that on YouTube," he told her, slinging an arm around her shoulders and guiding her away from the courtyard. She grinned, mostly from sheer relief that she'd successfully wiped away the memory of her slip-up.

Because as much as she and Mike enjoyed each other in and out of bed, as great a guy as he was, as many kind and thoughtful things he did for her, she knew the subject of love was completely off the table. It was going to stay that way, forever.

The sooner she accepted that, the better.

Chapter 17

"**O**KAY, ZACK. WHAT have we learned today? How many innings are in a baseball game?"

"Nine!"

"Unless . . . ?"

Zack screwed up his face and sucked on his juice box. "It rains?"

"Well, yes, but also, unless it's tied. Then we go to extra innings. Can you say that?"

"Extra innings!" Exuberantly, he flung his arms into the air, sending a few drops of apple juice against the dugout walls. Mike had gotten special permission to show Zack the inner workings of Catfish Stadium, all part of his campaign to convince the kid of baseball's superiority over every other sport.

Donna had gotten a desperate call from the Gilberts; they were having a cocktail party and needed someone to watch all the guests' kids for two hours. The only person they trusted with their rich friends' children was Donna. Mike had jumped at the chance to spend some time with Zack.

"That's good. High five." They exchanged hand

slaps. "Now, the most important question of all. What's the best sport in the entire world?"

Zack cast him a wicked sidelong glance. "Football!"

Mike groaned and dropped his head to his hands. "You're doing this to torture me, aren't you, kid? You know what, you remind me of someone. A certain redhead who's nothing but trouble."

Trevor Stark came their way, a bat slung over his shoulders. He stood before them, twisting his torso back and forth. "I heard the word 'football.' We got a football fan here?"

"No," said Mike, at the same time that Zack shouted, "Yes!"

"Who's your team, kid? I'm a Lions fan myself."

"Lions? Didn't know you were from Detroit."

"You don't know sh . . . squat about me, Solo." He corrected himself with a quick glance in Zack's direction.

"You got that right. Hey, how 'bout we keep it that way."

"Fine by me. I wish we could make that work both ways. The fact that I know you picked Texas A&M colors for your wedding kinda makes me ill."

Mike couldn't disagree with any part of that statement. The colors were god-awful, but Donna was still trying to impress the judge. And he didn't care for the amount of attention the town was paying to the wedding details. But that was the whole point. The more their wedding was in the spotlight, the better Donna's chances of convincing the judge she was no longer the irresponsible girl who had given up her child to her ex's parents.

Get Zack back. He was totally on board with that mission, and every moment he spent with the kid made him more so. Right now Zack was swinging his legs against the bench, a happy, sticky presence. He seemed unfazed by all the wedding talk, probably because he was too young to understand what any of it meant.

Dwight Conner wandered over, bent down, and did a complicated handshake with Zack. Utterly delighted, the kid grinned from ear to ear, looking so much like Donna that Mike's heart did a slow rotation. "Yo, dude, I heard Bieberman's not feeling so hot today. You gonna play shortstop for us?"

"What's shortstop?"

Mike explained. "The guy who stands between second and third and fields most of the ground balls in a game. You up for it, kiddo?"

"Yeah!"

"All right! See, I knew you were a baseball fan at heart."

"Can I make some touchdowns?"

Mike slapped a hand onto his chest. "You're killing me. Hitting me right where it hurts."

The guys laughed, and Zack grinned up at them. Just like his mother, the little imp.

Trevor caught sight of Angeline, the promotions girl, who had just come onto the field. "I'll catch you guys later. Important business meeting."

"Sure, you go take care of business, bro. Bieberman's probably crying his eyes out in the can."

"Never said he couldn't take his shot," said Trevor arrogantly. "It's a free country."

Dwight shook his head as Trevor loped across the

field. "You know what that guy needs? A little rejection. You can't call yourself a real man until you've gotten your heart crushed to grape jelly."

"Nice image." According to that definition, Mike had qualified as a man four years ago.

At that point, Zack had to go pee, so Mike took him inside the clubhouse, which was empty except for Terry, the irritable physical therapist, who was replenishing the clubhouse's supply of mentholated ointment. Mike gave her a wave and showed Zack to the toilet. The TV was tuned to the channel that would show the Friars' game set to start in the next hour. The two announcers were doing a wrap-up of the day's sports news. Mike leaned against the wall and lazily watched as they discussed the standings. He smiled broadly when they mentioned Caleb Hart's outstanding performance in the first two months of the season.

"He's been rock steady this year. Not the phrase we usually use for Hart, but he's earned it."

"Maybe his time in Kilby made the difference. Crush Taylor, love him or hate him, has a knack with pitchers."

"Tell that to Yazmer Perez." The color announcer chuckled. "He's busy blowing up social media with his CrushIt campaign. Have you ever heard of a player going up against a team owner?"

"That I haven't. It's fascinating to watch, kind of like a clown car wreck. Then again, if you want a crazy news story, you can always count on Kilby."

"That's true, but this story does bring up some hot button issues. Reminds me of the days when the players were upset about women reporters coming into the locker rooms. Same thing, except now we're talking about gay reporters." He turned to the show's guest, a former player for the Red Sox, who could always be counted on to say something controversial. "What's your take, Buck?"

"Well, I gotta hand it to Yaz for having the stones to speak his mind. Everyone's so politically correct these days. So here you have a guy who feels strongly about this issue, and he's a player in the locker room, so it affects him, and he's basically representing other players who don't want to go public about their stance. Agree or not—and I'm not saying one way or the other—my hat's off to Yaz for his honesty."

Honesty. Mike clenched his fists, his entire body going rigid. There wasn't one ounce of honesty in Yaz's body, except the part that said he wanted everyone to pay attention to him. *Honesty.* Did anyone really believe that? Did they believe that Yaz represented the beliefs of other players?

Donna's comment flashed through his mind. *He's a baseball player, you're a baseball player. You should go on TV. Do a PSA or something.*

And then that infallible, impossible-to-ignore inner voice spoke up, loud and clear. *She's right.* Oh bloody hell.

Could he . . . ? Should he . . . ? His family would be mortified. He'd have to get Joey's permission. He wouldn't do anything without Joey's consent, no matter what his freaking intuition told him.

A small hand tugged at his. He looked down to see Zack gazing up at him with wondering eyes. He must have been standing there like a stalagmite for some time. "Did you wash your hands, buddy?"

"Yes. When's Mama coming?"

He checked his watch. Donna was probably on her way by now. "Let's give her a call. I need to get suited up for the game anyway." And he had a bunch of calls to make. If he was seriously going to do what his conscience was telling him, he needed to get busy.

After handing Zack over to Donna and putting on his uniform, Mike barely had time to squeeze in a call to Joey. He picked an out-of-the-way corner of the tunnel that led to the dugout, out of earshot of the players.

"Hey, big brother," he said when his brother's voice came on the line. "Got something important to run past you."

"This is not the best . . ." Joey's voice sounded scratchy and distant. Probably a bad connection, since the clubhouse was notorious for its poor reception.

"You okay? How's my kidney?"

"Processing the aftereffects of a dirty martini." Now that sounded more like Joey.

"Nice. Party it up, bro. Listen, I've been thinking I want to shake things up."

"Didn't you already do that by getting engaged? I want to meet her, Mike. Soon. Send me your travel schedule. I'm not teaching any summer school this year."

That was odd. Joey loved teaching so much that he seized every opportunity to take on extra classes.

"Sure, I'll send it to you tonight. But I'm not talking about Donna. I'm talking about going public."

"What do you mean?"

"Do a PSA or something."

Joey was ominously quiet. "A PSA for what?"

So maybe he hadn't quite thought this through. "Gays?"

Joey laughed, breaking off into a cough.

"Seriously, are you okay, Joey?"

"I'm okay. Honored to be considered someone who needs a PSA. What's going on, Mike?"

Mike filled him in on the situation with Yazmer. Joey didn't say anything for a long time. Background noise filled the gap—a woman's voice, the beeping of a monitor. His heart sank. Joey must be at the hospital, and now Mike was adding to his stress.

"Listen, forget it, Joey. The last thing you need is reporters bugging you, and if I do this, there might be a few. Not as many as Yazmer gets, but the whole point is to go public. So the goal would be to . . . never mind."

"Listen, Mike." Joey cut him off. "I'm fine with it. Just give the family a heads-up, because they won't be happy. But there's something—"

"Solo! Get your ass into the dugout. A kid who called 911 and saved his whole family from a house fire is about to sing the frickin' National Anthem." Duke's voice thundered down the corridor. "And then we have a cat who's going to throw out the first pitch. It's a circus, Solo, you don't want to miss it."

"Coming, Duke." He spoke into the phone again. "What were you about to say, Joey?"

"Call me later. It sounds like you need to go."

"I will. And I'll deal with the family, don't worry about that. Love you, Joey."

"Love you too. Blast it out of the park, my brother."

Mike skidded back to the clubhouse, tossed his phone into his locker, and barely made it on the field in time for the 911 kid.

Yazmer had the start. When he jogged onto the field, noise swelled in the stands. Some applause, some boos, but it didn't seem to matter to Yaz. Noise was noise. He waved cockily, and set his cap on his head at the particular angle he preferred, just within regulation. Mike muttered as he took his position behind the plate. If only he didn't have his damn Father Kowalski ethics, he could mess with Yaz a little. Call a bad game, or just let Yaz call the shots. Tip the batter off to his next pitch. So many ways he could sabotage Yaz. One crap game wouldn't affect Mike's stats, unless he missed a catch, but it would affect Yaz's.

The Reno Aces' batter, Dave Foster, came to the plate. "Heads-up, Solo. I'm aiming straight for that asshole's mouth."

"I didn't hear that," Mike answered with a laugh, before lowering his face mask. Foster stepped into the batter's box, Mike went into his crouch and signaled for a fastball. Yaz shook it off. He called for the curve. No go. He went through all of Yaz's pitches, then finally called time and jogged out to the mound.

"What the fuck?"

"You on the D-L, Schmooz-o Solo?"

Clearly, the man didn't mean disabled list, but Mike hadn't a clue what he did mean. "What are you talking about?"

"D-L. Down-low. Can't trust a catcher that plays it both ways."

Mike stared at him blankly. Finally it clicked.

Plays it both ways. Dave Foster had been spotted in a gay bar once, though he denied he was gay. Mike didn't care one way or the other, but apparently Yaz did. And Mike had been laughing with Foster before his at-bat.

"You miserable little shit, start pitching or get off the mound." He gestured at the stands. "These people didn't come here to watch you exercise your neck muscles shaking me off."

Mitch, the pitching coach, jogged onto the field. "What's up, boys?"

Yaz and Mike were still locked in their stare-down. Yaz smirked. "I want me a different catcher."

"That ain't your fucking decision," said Duke, who had carted his bulk from the dugout. "It's either Mike or that cat that threw out the first pitch. End of story."

"Bozo Solo's a big fail on the get-Yaz-to-the-bigs gig. Different catcher, I'd be King of the Friars by now."

Mike would have given his left nut to be able to punch the smirk right off the pitcher's face.

Yaz went on. "What I hear, that cat'll make the biggies before Solo does."

Mike's gut clenched. Is that what people were saying? He'd been distracted by Donna and all that glorious sex they'd been having. His stats were still good, but he hadn't been obsessively checking the transactions the way he usually did. He didn't know what trades had been made, or what moves the Friars were making. And he'd made so little progress with Yazmer that the guy was requesting a different catcher.

Way to go, Solo.

"Keep this up, neither of you will make it," barked Duke. He had just enough authority to get through to Yaz, whose smug smile dropped.

Bieberman piped up nervously. "I'm allergic to cats. Anyone else allergic to cats?"

Everyone turned to stare at him. "I think that cat might have pooped on the infield grass," he added, shrinking back from the array of intimidating glares. "Can someone . . . maybe . . ."

Mike cut him off. "Yaz and I were just trying to get our signals straight. No need for a summit meeting here. We got this."

"You better," growled Duke. "This is baseball, not middle school. I want to see both of you in my office after the game."

Mike nodded, as did Yaz, with one more resentful look in his direction. With a heavy sigh, he jogged back to home plate, where Foster was chatting with the umpire. "You guys get it all figured out?" Foster asked with a grin. "Bet you can't get called up soon enough, eh, Solo?"

Hell to the yes. But now it was time to put his personal feelings aside and do some work for the Catfish.

"You got that right. When Yaz is in this kind of mood, no one's safe, not the catcher, not anyone. Just a friendly warning." He pulled his face mask down, hiding his grin as Foster eased back from the plate a hair—enough to strike out swinging.

For the rest of the game, Mike worked Yaz's volatile personality, riding the pitcher's quicksilver emotions to produce a six-hit, 4-2 victory. Hopefully someone noticed and gave Mike credit, but Yaz sure wouldn't. He'd do his usual postgame YouTube and Instagram update in Yaz language, all about the brilliance of Yazmer Perez. Hashtag CrushIt.

For the first time, it didn't bother Mike. Because he had a plan to fight back now.

The first time the PSA aired, Mike was in bed with Donna at her tiny apartment with the view of the sewage treatment plant. The production coordinator at Equal Rights in Sports, the group he'd chosen as a vehicle for his message, had given him a list of airtimes. He and Donna surfaced from one of their delirious bouts of sex in time to switch on the TV with only seconds to spare.

"I'm a little nervous," he confessed, rubbing his hand across his chest. "Not used to being in the spotlight."

"Well, you should be. You're just as cute as the ones they always show." Donna's singular loyalty always made him smile.

"Think you're a little biased, what with that secret crush and all?" He couldn't believe she'd handed him such a convenient weapon with which to tease her.

She blushed, as she always did when he mentioned it. "You're never going to forget that, are you?"

"Nope. When did it start? In the closet at the library? Before that?"

"You should worry more about when it ended." She poked him in the ribs. "Which happened pretty much when you opened your mouth."

"What I want to know is, why'd you make me jump through hoops to get you to like me, when you were already there?"

"Shhh! You're up."

Mike sat up against the headboard, one knee bent, the other leg stretched forward. The sound of a ballpark filled the screen, along with his face against the backdrop of a baseball field—not Catfish Stadium, but a field Crush Taylor had installed on his ranch when he first retired.

"Hi, I'm Mike Solo. I've been a baseball player most of my life, but I've been a brother since I was born. My big brother taught me how to skateboard, how to recite the Pledge of Allegiance, and how to stand up to bullies. I've never forgotten any of those lessons, which is why I'm coming forward—with his permission—to say that he also happens to be gay. This should be a private matter, but sadly, for some people it isn't. They want to exclude people like my brother from living their lives and performing their jobs. I think that's unfair and shortsighted. Shouldn't the important thing be how well a person does their job? Not what they do in the privacy of their own homes? That's how I see it, anyway. I'm proud of my brother, and if anyone tried to exclude him, I'd call that a bush league move. I'm baseball player Mike Solo and this has been a message from Equal Rights in Sports."

The music soared, the ERS graphic swirled onto the screen, and it was over. An ad for Rice-A-Roni took the screen, little elbow pastas dancing arm in arm. Mike was afraid to look in Donna's direction.

"We went back and forth on that 'bush league' line," Mike said nervously. "Is it stupid? Did it sound ridiculous? We couldn't think of another baseball saying that sounded right."

Donna threw her arms around him, nearly knocking him sideways off the bed. "Are you kidding? It was awesome. You just told it like it is. And you looked seriously hot. What was that shirt you were wearing?"

"It's an away uniform from one of my high school leagues. No team identification on the front, so it worked. Did it look too tight?"

"No way. It looked hot." Donna's eyes glowed with a golden sheen, her enthusiasm radiating from her like sunbeams. "I'm so proud of you! I was thinking of something like this when you were looking at Yazmer's tweets."

"You're the one who gave me the idea."

"Really? It came out so much better than I even imagined." She raised her hand for a high five. "Touchdown, Mike Solo!"

"What . . . did . . . you . . . say?" Menacingly, he narrowed his eyes at her, then flipped her onto her back. Fighting giggles, she widened her eyes innocently.

"Oopsies. Did I say touchdown? I totally meant . . . goal!"

"Oh, you are seriously asking for it. Try one more time." He stripped the sheet off her and straddled her hips, his cock, completely spent five minutes earlier, stirring with new appreciation for her curvaceous nudity. But now was not the moment for sex; this was a time for ruthless tickling.

"Home run! I meant home run!" She shrieked as he dove in with both hands. "Don't tickle me, I swear you'll make me pee!"

"You'd better not, missy. Say it again! You know what I want to hear!"

"Baseball is the best game in the entire world! Ever! In all of human history!"

"That's more like it." He stopped tickling her, because he knew by now that she was serious about the peeing. And besides, he'd thought of another game that rivaled baseball. "There might be this one particular game with a big advantage over baseball."

And he positioned his hand at the softness between her legs, ready to demonstrate, ignoring the phone calls that were already pouring in.

Chapter 18

MIKE'S PSA CREATED a sensation. It got picked up by the national sports media, which meant lots of free publicity. Everyone wanted to interview him, and every time he spoke, with his charming, mischievous, regular-guy manner, he won new fans—no surprise to Donna. He also won new enemies. He'd gotten a few pieces of hate mail—or at least, hate Facebook posts—and the group that had wanted to get rid of the Kilby Catfish last season suddenly had new life.

"Can the Catfish! We've had enough of the constant scandal and controversy. Isn't it high time the Catfish moved to another location?" read their latest statement in the *Kilby Press-Herald*.

Reporters got to work unearthing all the details of his family history. The fact that he'd been at the Naval Academy, with the eventual goal of becoming a SEAL. The fact that he'd left the Navy when he donated a kidney to his brother. Even the end of his engagement to Angela found its way into the profile *Sports Illustrated* did on him. Most of the coverage was positive, but even so the sudden onslaught of attention was disorienting, especially for Donna.

She'd thought Kilby's interest in the Catfish Wedding of the Decade was over the top, but this was on a whole different level. The next time she brought Zack to a game, there was a photographer waiting near the entrance. After she'd picked up their tickets, she moved toward the turnstile, holding Zack tightly by the hand. The photographer aimed the camera at her face and walked backward while he screamed questions at her.

"What do you think about your fiancé's revelations? What do you think of Yazmer's response? Have you seen his new YouTube video?"

"I haven't seen it," she told him. "You should go interview someone else."

"Why did Mike Solo keep quiet so long about his brother? Was he ashamed?"

"Of course not," she snapped. "It was private. Can you get out of our way, please?" Zack had wrapped both of his arms around her leg, which made it even harder for her to make it to the safety of the stadium.

"If it was private, why is he coming forward now?"

"Because the time was right. Because of that stupid petition Yazmer is circulating. Why are you asking me these things?"

"Are you calling Yazmer stupid?"

Donna glared at the man, who she could barely see behind his camera. Glasses, ruffled brown hair, a weasely appearance. "You rotten creep, did you just twist my words around? For the record, I support Mike, I think Yazmer's a publicity ho—I mean, hound—and I don't have any comment."

By the time she made it inside the turnstile, she was completely flustered. She was absolutely the wrong person to face a nosy reporter. Zack lifted his arms, begging to be picked up. She swung him into her arms and headed for the concession stand where they could buy a gigantic lemonade to share. Mike, already in his light blue Catfish home uniform, came running toward her. The girl inside the ticket booth must have alerted security.

Still holding Zack, she practically fell into his arms. "Oh my God, Mike, that was crazy. I think I totally messed up. I wasn't prepared! He came at me out of nowhere."

"Shhh, shhh. It's okay. Security's on it. They'll try to confiscate the tape."

"I hope they do, because I kind of called Yazmer a ho. I tried to change it to 'hound' but I'm not sure he caught that part."

"Forget about it. I don't want you to worry. This is my battle, and I'll make sure they leave you alone." Enfolded in his arms, she felt a little better.

"Who was that man?" Zack piped up. "He's poopy."

"That's one way to put it, Zack-a-doodle. Let's just say he's not someone we want to hang out with. If we see him again, we'll go somewhere else."

The next day, the headline on the Daily Sports Blog read, "Catfish Catfight! Solo's Sweetie Calls Yaz a 'Ho.'" Donna peered over Mike's shoulder as he read the entire text on her computer.

"Me and my big mouth," she groaned. "Can you just put some duct tape over it for the next month or so?"

"Oh no. I have other plans for your mouth." He gave her a teasing leer, all twinkly eyes and wiggling eyebrows, but she could tell he didn't like the direction the controversy was taking.

"It's turning into a circus, isn't it?"

"Yes, but it's not your fault. Yaz likes circuses. I thought he'd be pissed about the PSA, but he isn't. He gave me a big fist bump. Like we're playing some kind of game for the public's entertainment."

"What should we do?"

"Nothing. Just go about your regular life. If people ask you questions, *don't answer*. I know it's hard. They're tricky. They're experts at getting people to respond. That's their job. Just block them out and do your thing."

"My thing? What's my thing?"

He swiveled the chair and scooped her into his lap. "That thing you do. Breathing. Existing. Smiling. That sort of thing." His kiss drained every last bit of worry out of her. Mike made her feel valuable and important in a way that no one else ever had. Every moment she spent with him made her love him even more, and made the task of disguising those emotions even more difficult.

Good thing she had long practice at hiding her feelings behind a fun-loving, carefree exterior.

The next day, two photographers were lying in wait in the parking lot of Dental Miracles. This time she was prepared. Since silence wasn't her strong suit, she'd concocted another plan.

"Good morning," she chirped to them as she shouldered her purse and hauled her blue-blazer-clad self toward the front door.

"Do you have any comment on what commentators are saying?"

"Thank you so much for asking. I'd like to bring your attention to a new product we're offering. Laser teeth whitening. Works like a dream. Your teeth will look amazing. And since you guys are so awesome, I can even offer you a special deal. One tooth-whitening session and a filling—all for one low price. Sadly, we'll have to leave out the Novocain, but you guys can handle that, right?" Five steps from the door; she'd nearly made it.

"Cute, Donna, very cute. You have a certain reputation in Kilby. You're known as a party girl."

Three steps. "That was in my younger days. I'm a hardworking dental receptionist now, and I'm about to be late for work. If you'd like to speak further about the tooth whitening, let me explain how it works. We strap you into a chair, prop your mouth open, and aim a high-powered beam of light into your mouth. Sure, there's a risk, but all good things come with a price, you know?"

"Is it true you met Mike Solo at a bar? How can you claim you're no longer a party girl when you were involved in a brawl there just last year?"

The door. Right there in front of her. *Open it. Ignore them. Go inside.*

"Is this controversy hard on you, given your history of depression?"

"*What?*"

Luckily, just then Ricki, the billing clerk, hurried up behind her and pushed the door open. "You coming in, Donna?"

Numbly, she nodded and followed Ricki inside.

Shaking, in shock, she slipped into the bathroom and called Karen Griswold, the lawyer. "My hospital records are private, right?"

"Absolutely."

"A photographer just asked me about my history of depression. It happened one time, and it was pregnancy-related! That's not a history, is it?"

"Hmm. Looks like someone's flinging dirt around. Don't say a word to anyone. You hear me? I'll do some digging."

The next time she arrived at the Hannigans' house to pick up Zack, Harvey's Pathfinder was parked outside. Strange, because they usually tried to avoid running into each other during their Zack pickups. It just made everything awkward.

She hurried up the front path, anxious to see Zack. The last time she'd seen him had been at the baseball game where the photographer had accosted them. Not the happiest memory, although Mike had hit his fifth homer of the year and the Catfish had won 5–2.

God, this baseball thing was really taking over her brain.

Rapping on the front door, she noticed that there was no small figure waiting behind the drapes in the living room. Zack must be in his bedroom. Harvey answered the door, then slipped outside to join her on the front walk.

"What are you doing? Where's Zack?"

"He's inside with Bonita. They're making cookies."

"I thought Bonita didn't eat sugar."

"They're using stevia."

Donna made a face. That was one way to make

sure your kid didn't eat too many cookies. "How long are they going to be? This is my time with Zack, and I wanted to take him to see the new white tiger at the zoo. You know how much he loves that stuff."

"Well, see, that's the thing." Harvey shuffled uncomfortably. Under his new Wrangler jeans, he was barefoot. His Western-cut shirt was misaligned by one shell-inlaid button; how had Bonita missed that? "You can't have Zack today."

"What are you talking about?"

"Because of all the controversy over your new boyfriend."

"Fiancé," Donna said automatically.

"Yeah. Makes it even worse."

"The controversy is over the PSA he did, but it has nothing to do with Zack."

A dull flush came and went from Harvey's neck. She wondered what it meant, since Harvey had never been the best at expressing his opinions. "Bonita says it's an unhealthy environment for a four-year-old boy. The judge agreed."

"Unhealthy . . . what do they mean?"

Harvey took her by the elbow and guided her down the front path, away from the house. "Donna, come on. The blogs, the photographers, the headlines. Bonita's upset because you said the word 'ho' in front of Zack."

"Hound! I said, hound!" Weak response, and she knew it. "A hoe is also a garden tool. It's not such a bad word."

"Zack called Bonita a ho when she gave him Cheerios instead of Frosted Flakes."

Donna couldn't hold back a spurt of nervous

laughter. "You know he hates Cheerios. She should know that too."

"This isn't a joke. You turn everything into a joke, but Bonita's serious about this. She didn't want to take it so far, but she believed she had to."

"Oh my God. Is she the one . . . did you tell her about the depression . . ."

The sheepish look that crept across his face told her all she needed to know. "I can't believe you did that," she whispered. "You know it has nothing to do with what's going on now."

"Are you so sure, Donna? What if stress brings it on? Bonita looked it up. Could happen. We both have to think about Zack's best interests."

Zack's best interests. He'd never used that phrase before in his life. Obviously, all of this was coming from Bonita.

Flashes of heat crashed through her body. All the helplessness from that time in the hospital came flooding back. Things slipping away. Decisions taken out of her hands. "You said you'd never talk about it. You swore."

"Things have changed." He wouldn't quite meet her eyes.

"But we agreed." She cast around for something, some weapon. "What if everyone knew you wanted me to get an abortion?"

"Yeah? Are you going to tell the newspapers that part? How would Zack feel if he heard?"

Horrified, she stared at him. "Bonita has this all plotted out, doesn't she? Or have you suddenly developed an evil genius brain? Harvey, this isn't you. I know this isn't you."

A muscle in his cheek twitched; his gaze slid away from hers.

"Why is Bonita so set on getting Zack? Why does it matter so much to her? Just tell me that, so maybe I can understand."

Harvey hunched his shoulders. "All her sisters have kids. She's the only one who doesn't. It's hard on her, being left out. She started bringing Zack around her family and they all think he's great. That's when she got the idea. It's good for Zack, being part of the posse."

The Wade posse? How would that be good?

She picked up his hand and held it in both of hers. "Harvey, listen to me. I get that Bonita wants a family. I know you love her. But look how far she's taking this. Is it in Zack's best interests to be raised by someone who would dig into a person's past medical history and twist it around? Someone who would betray secrets and break promises? Is that the kind of person you really want to be Zack's mother? I might joke around, but I would never do any of those things."

Still, he wouldn't look at her. Tension vibrated between them. A delivery truck drove past, furniture on the way to someone's new home. So hopeful. A puff of diesel exhaust hovered in the air. Donna wanted to stop time right where it was, balanced in a place where she still had a chance to change Harvey's mind.

She saw him waver, saw uncertainty take hold. "Please, Harvey," she whispered. "We need to work together, not shut each other out. You're his father. *You're* the one who should make the decisions, not Bonita."

He pulled his hands away from her. Damn it, she'd overplayed her point.

"It's already done, Donna. The judge issued an emergency ruling."

"*What?*" She actually felt dizzy for a second, as if she might faint.

"They sent the order over to your place but I guess you missed it."

She hadn't been at her own apartment for a couple of days, ever since she'd watched the PSA with Mike. She'd spent last night with him, then gone straight to work, then come here. "You can't do this. Please."

"You have a lawyer, Donna. It's not like you're helpless."

He turned his back on her and loped back to the front door, with his slow, minimal-effort stride.

"What are you going to tell Zack?" Donna called after him. Her heart ached at the thought that her little boy might think she was ignoring him. "Can you at least tell him something . . . not horrible?"

"We'll him you're not feeling well."

"Fine," she choked. It was true, after all, even though she'd never canceled a date with Zack before. She never got sick . . . except for that one time, four years ago, when she couldn't keep anything down and her world went so dark.

In desperate need of a quiet place to get a grip on her emotions, she drove to the Kilby Zoo, where she had planned to bring Zack. Taj, the zoo's new white tiger, had finally arrived. His large enclosure held a cavelike area where he could snooze in privacy. Benches lined the outside of the fence, along with frequent posted warnings not to feed the tiger or put any part of your body through the fence.

She settled onto one of the benches, from which she could just get a glimpse of Taj napping in his cave. The tiger's mighty head lay peacefully on his white paws. His coloring was almost ethereal, a splash of illumination in the darkness of the pen. She watched him for a while, thinking that Zack might find Taj a little boring after all. Weren't tigers supposed to roar and pounce on their prey? What use was a tiger who just napped in the shade?

When she finally felt ready for a coherent conversation, she took out her phone and dialed Ms. Griswold.

"I know," the lawyer said before she could utter a word. "Emergency order. What a backstabbing move. The next time I see Judge Quinn, I'm going to give him a piece of my mind."

"Shouldn't you have been there? How can they do that without my lawyer present?"

"I had a conflict," she said vaguely. "Sorry, doll. You know I care, but you don't pay the bills."

A pro bono charity case didn't rate, apparently, even when her entire life was falling apart. "So they just went ahead and stopped me from seeing my kid? How is that fair?"

"Child's best interests, Donna. I'm sorry." The lawyer was obviously trying to gentle her voice, but succeeded only marginally. "The media attention changed everything. Paparazzi in Kilby—who thought we'd ever see the day? It's kind of a thrill, knowing that the next time I make a statement on your behalf I might end up on YouTube."

"*A thrill?*"

"Sorry. Poor phrasing. What I meant was that the presence of all these photographers has changed the landscape. It gave them an opening to make the case that you're an unfit mother."

Donna's palm was so sweaty she had to grip the phone in both hands to keep it from slipping out. "It's not going to last. It's because of Yazmer and Crush, and I just got caught in the middle of it."

"We can try making that argument, but Mike Solo is a promising ballplayer. From what I've heard, he's likely to be in the public eye for some time. He's also a team leader. He's well-liked and people respect him. With that ability, do you think he's going to avoid the spotlight the rest of his life?"

In the dim recesses of the cave, Taj stirred. He licked one paw with his long tongue, then lumbered to his feet. Donna fixed her gaze on the magnificent creature.

"No, of course not. Why should he? It's part of being a ballplayer. I think it's even in their contract that they have to speak to the media."

"Exactly. So it very likely is not an isolated incident. Mike has a very compelling story, with his military background and his kidney donation. Not only that, he's good-looking and extremely charming. That Vow of Celibacy? Genius. Oh yes, Donna, you've picked yourself a future husband who will continue to be the target of media attention. Good for him, but I'm not sure that was the best move for you, frankly. You might have given Harvey an edge. He can play the stable, normal family card."

Taj sauntered into the enclosure, his feet padding

softly across the turf. A whisper of excitement rippled through the knots of people watching outside the fence. His eyes were pure living gold, and they swept across the crowd with absolute indifference.

"But . . . but . . . you were all *for* the idea of me getting engaged to Mike! You said it was brilliant! The wedding's in a week."

"Did you tell me he had a gay brother? And that he gave that brother his kidney?"

"But . . . but . . ." She seemed to be able to do nothing but splutter. "What difference does it make that he has a gay brother?"

Taj sniffed the air indifferently, as if searching for a good reason to explore. He didn't seem to find one, since he turned, head lowered, and padded back into his cave. She hadn't even taken a picture for Zack, she realized sadly.

"It made no difference, until he went and made that PSA and started making the headlines. Now he's a lightning rod for attention. Judges don't like controversy. They don't like brouhahas. I'm afraid it may come down to a choice. Do you want to marry Mike Solo or do you want to pursue your custody battle for Zack?"

Chapter 19

THAT NIGHT, DONNA made love to Mike with a craving she'd never even imagined before. She felt as if a fever had infiltrated her bloodstream and the only cure was Mike. If she had to walk away from him she needed to soak in as much of him as possible. He didn't seem to have a problem with that, letting her revel in his body, his heat and hardness, forget herself in the electric pleasure they generated.

Finally, he stilled her as she straddled him, her thighs clinging to his hips. "What's wrong?"

"How do you know something's wrong?"

"I read pitchers for a living. You make a nice change of pace. Something's up, I can tell."

She didn't want to talk. She wanted to bone. Screw. Fuck her brains out. She shifted her position, trying to work his penis inside her, but he tightened his grip on her hips. "Talk, Donna. Tell me what's going on."

She dropped her head, knowing she'd cry if she met his eyes. "They won't let me see Zack." The words ripped out of her, a primal whisper of pain. "Because of all the media."

"*What?*" He pulled himself upright, so she was

cradled between his legs. "What are you talking about? Tell me the whole thing."

So she explained it, in all its horrid injustice, taking quick little peeks to see his reaction. Mike's face went grimmer and grimmer, so he looked like a statue with blazing green eyes by the end. He let out a stream of creative curse words.

"So our engagement, which was supposed to help you get Zack back, is now the problem. I'm now *keeping* you from Zack. I'm the reason you can't see him."

"No, no. It's not so much *you* as . . . the spotlight, the controversy, the circus, all that."

"Which I'm in the middle of. Which I caused."

She rolled away from him and pulled a sheet over her. "You didn't cause it," she said miserably. "You just did the right thing. I'm totally behind the PSA, even though I didn't know any of this would happen. If you're going to blame yourself you have to blame me too."

"I'm not blaming anyone. I'm just pointing out that at this moment, I'm the reason you can't see Zack."

"No . . ." She trailed off. What Mike said was true. If she hadn't gotten engaged to Mike, she'd still be up against Harvey and Bonita, but she probably wouldn't be facing a total ban from seeing Zack. "The lawyer says I have to make a choice," she confessed in a faltering voice.

Mike stroked her back, his hands warm through the sheet. "You're saying we have to end our engagement. Call off the wedding."

A sob ripped from her throat, coming out as a pitiful croak. It was what she had decided, but hearing it out loud made her heart crack. "But what if she's wrong . . . I mean, won't it make me look bad? Like I change my mind too much? One minute I'm engaged, the next I'm a single mom again? What if that's bad advice?"

"But you said the emergency order is because of the media crap right now. Because of me."

She nodded miserably.

"The last thing I want to do is prevent you from seeing Zack. That's the whole reason I pushed you into this thing, for Zack. Everything's different now. I'm a liability. I won't ruin things for you, Donna. I won't."

Everything in her wanted to scream that he wasn't ruining things. That he was a blessing in her life, that he gave her strength and joy and comfort. But she couldn't. Because she couldn't lose Zack. She couldn't let Bonita be in charge of Zack's childhood. And that's exactly what would happen if Harvey got custody. If she'd had any doubts before, they were gone. Bonita called all the shots with Harvey.

Mike pulled his body away from hers, out of the tangle of sheets, and swung his legs over the side of the bed. "I'll take the blame. Completely, so it doesn't come back on you. I'll make a public announcement right away. I'll say that I didn't want the media attention to affect the people I care about, so I'm releasing you from our engagement. I'll add some more stuff too, like it's been an honor to be part of your life, and you're the best thing that ever happened to me, and a wonderful person and mother and all that."

With his back was to her, that strong, powerful back, he seemed impossibly distant. She wanted to scream at him. How had he put it? *Some more stuff.* All those nice words were just for show, to impress the public. None of it was real. He'd never pretended there was anything more between them than friend-ship, chemistry, and a desire to help her. She threw her arm across her eyes to hide her tears. The scent of their night of lovemaking, intimate and sweaty, still surrounded her. Outside, the sewage plant rumbled with its nighttime workings.

A soft touch on her chin startled her. Mike was press-ing a kiss to it, then up the curve of her cheek. "It's all true, you goose," he whispered. "Every single word."

Emotion swelled, threatening to swamp her.

"You don't have to say that," she managed. "Whatever we tell the rest of the world, you have to tell me the truth."

"I am." He covered her body with his, his long limbs stretching beyond hers. "It's possible that my Superhero Complex and your act-before-you-think personality might have been a bad combination. And I know I should regret it, because now you'll have to fight to lift that emergency order. But I can't regret everything that's happened between us. I just can't. Donna, I—"

He broke off, leaving her wondering frantically what he'd almost said. That he . . . loved her? Was it possible? A deep panic ripped through her. What if he was on the verge of saying, "I love you," but wouldn't now because they had to break off the en-gagement? She knew him. His instinct would be to protect her from more trouble by walking away.

Desperately, she threw her arms around him and it was like flying into the sunshine. One last ride into bliss. One last drink from the narcotic of sex with Mike. One last dose of her baseball player—and it would have to last her forever. No more Mike—the thought turned her heart into a desert, bleak and empty.

Unless . . . A last-ditch idea flashed into her mind.

Deep in their kiss, she tried to pull away, but couldn't. She pounded her fists on his back to get his attention. Finally he released her, his eyes deep, dark pools of green fire. "What?"

"I have an idea. What if we break off the engagement publicly but keep seeing each other secretly?"

"Huh?"

Mike's brain didn't usually operate this slowly; he must be foggy with lust, which she completely understood.

"As far as the world knows, we're through. We don't appear in public together. We deny that we're involved. We go on with our lives. When it's safe and no one's paying attention, we sneak away and go at it like freaky little bunnies."

"Freaky little bunnies?" He still seemed a bit dazed.

"Or some other metaphor that's maybe not so disturbing."

He rubbed the back of his neck, as if trying to circulate blood back toward his brain. "You're saying . . . sneak around? Hide our relationship?" When she shrugged in carefree agreement, he shook his head. "I don't get it. What exactly would our relationship be?"

"Well, we just go back to the basics. It all started with a flirtation. Remember, from the Roadhouse?"

"Of course I remember."

"Then came the big brawl, when you rode to my rescue. Then we ran into each other at the library. That's when we segued into the kissing and snogging and all that."

"Snogging?"

"Harry Potter fan from way back. After the snogging, we got fake-engaged."

He crossed his arms over his chest, which had the effect of drawing her unwilling eyes to that magnificent part of his body, the dusting of dark curls shading the hard slopes of his pectorals. Seriously, maybe he should be required to put clothes on for this conversation. He was simply too distracting.

"I never considered it fake," he told her.

"I know. You considered it something along the lines of a good deed. A good deed with benefits."

"Now you're just pissing me off." A frown drew creases between his eyebrows. "I swear to you I've never seen you as a good deed with benefits."

Keep it light. Don't show how much he means to you. She waved one hand airily. "Fine, you can use whatever phrasing you like. But it was a good deed and there were benefits. Excellent benefits, if you ask me."

Judging by his stormy expression, Mike didn't seem impressed by this line of conversation. Alarm bells were going off all over the place, but she couldn't seem to stop.

"Sounds like you're making a joke out of this," he said slowly.

The similarity to Harvey's accusation gave her an unwelcome jolt. "No, I'm not. I'm just saying that we've gone about this backwards. You like me, I like you, we like sleeping together, but we never would have gotten engaged if not for Zack. Admit it, Mike. Just admit it!" For some reason, this felt very important. As if everything else would seem like a lie if he didn't agree with that statement.

He narrowed his eyes at her, a tiny muscle flexing in his jaw. "Fine. I admit that. But I was serious about it. I was going to marry you. I wanted to marry you. It wasn't just a so-called good deed. And I thought you were serious about it too."

Serious? How could she have been completely serious about it when he never came close to the topic of love? Which ought to belong in the same sentence as the topic of marriage?

She couldn't bring "love" up. That would be pure disaster.

"I gave an interview to the *Kilby Press-Herald*, didn't I? Would I have done that if I wasn't serious?"

"That's what I'd like to know."

That comment sounded ominous, but she decided to ignore it. She rose onto her knees.

"We're getting off track here. Here's what I'm suggesting. Let's just go back to before everything happened. Before we got engaged. Except that we keep sleeping together, because we've already done that, so why stop now?"

"And no one else will know."

"Exactly. No one else will know."

"What if they find out? Bonita busted us over a kiss."

"We just have to keep it low-key for a while, until all the attention dies down. Until everything is back to normal with Zack."

"So when my family asks me what happened to my fiancée, I say, oops, another broken engagement. But really I'm still secretly boning you?" His eyes glittered with some mysterious emotion she couldn't name.

She scrambled off the bed, planting her feet on the carpet. "I don't know why you're so mad at me. It makes perfect sense. You still get to have sex, but you don't have to go through with something you never really wanted anyway! You ought to be loving this idea."

"And what about my vow?"

"Your vow? It's already . . . It doesn't apply anymore."

He grabbed his shirt, which had gotten tumbled in with her sheets, and yanked it over his head. "You really don't know anything about me, do you?"

"What . . . of course . . ."

"You want me to deceive my family, dishonor my vow, and put your future at risk if anyone finds out. Three things I would never do." He bounded off the bed, located his boxer briefs, and pulled them on.

She watched, horrified, feeling like someone who had thrown a stick of dynamite onto a fire. "You're twisting it all around. That's not what I meant."

"That's what it comes down to. All so I can get some booty. On the down-low, so nobody knows."

"You make it sound so . . ." Dirty. Immoral. Sinful. Wrong. She'd never thought of sex with Mike as any of those things. "You think of me as 'booty'?"

"Of course I don't. That's the whole point. I was going to *marry* you. Give you my name, my support, my life. But you're fine just sneaking around with me. Who do you think you're dealing with here?"

She picked up a pillow and hurled it at him. "You're being crazy, Solo."

With elite-level reaction time, he swatted the pillow aside, then found his jeans and dragged them on. "I thought you knew me better by now, Donna."

The chilly disappointment in his voice made her want to scream. Taking advantage of the fact that his hands were occupied with his pants, she threw her other pillow at his head. He ducked and it knocked over her new lamp, the one with the base shaped like a football.

"You ought to know *me* by now!" she cried. "You ought to know—" She broke off, because the thing he ought to know was the thing she couldn't tell him. That she *loved* him and that's why she wanted to keep seeing him. Because the thought of not seeing him was like death.

While he was able to walk away without blinking an eye.

He righted the lamp. "Starting another brawl, Donna? Great strategy. That ought to really impress the judge." He strode toward the door, all athletic grace and male confidence. Maddening, and so sexy she wanted to rip his head off.

She picked up pillow number three and winged it across the room with all her might. He turned at the last minute and plucked it from the air.

"Wild pitch, babe. One more and the batter walks." He tossed the pillow over his shoulder on his way out the room.

"I hate baseball!" she shouted after him, but heard only an unintelligible answer before the front door slammed shut.

"I hate you," she whispered after him, before collapsing backward onto her bed, which still smelled of his aftershave and essence of Mike. No, she didn't. "I wish I hated you," she added helplessly to the ceiling. Hatred would be so much easier than this bottled-up, invisible, frustrating *love*.

Mike had never been so happy to be going on the road. Tacoma, Colorado Springs, and Salt Lake City? Bring it on. Anywhere but Kilby, Texas, sounded good to him. He showed up fifteen minutes before the scheduled bus departure time to break the big news to Crush in person.

"The wedding's off," he said, poking his head around the frame of the door of Crush's office. "I'm really sorry for the inconvenience. I'll pay for whatever work the planner's already put in."

Crush, who'd been napping, boots propped on his desk, chair tilted back, opened one eye. "I see. She couldn't handle a gay brother-in-law, huh?"

Mike bristled. As furious as he was with Donna, he couldn't let something like that stand. "That's not it. She's the one who told me to go public."

"Hmm. Problems with the pre-nup? She refuse to sign?"

"*What?* No. Nothing like that. Donna's not after money."

Crush uncrossed his legs and spun the chair around to face him. "Must have been the kid then. Can't blame you for not wanting to raise another man's child."

"Christ, no. That wasn't it. Zack's the greatest."

Crush shrugged. "Well. Young love. It's a roller coaster. What are you going to do?"

Young love. What was the man talking about? He wasn't all that young, and love didn't even come into this situation. That thought gave him a weird, sick sensation in the pit of his stomach. As if he'd done something wrong. But he hadn't, had he? Donna had been way off base. Not him.

Crush picked up his iPhone and thumbed through it. Mike decided to give up on this aggravating conversation. "Anyway, just wanted to let you know that you'll probably get some more media attention."

"Lucky me."

"Is . . . uh . . . I mean, I hope I didn't cause any problems with my PSA."

"No. I told you before you shot it. If I'm going down in flames, at least it'll be for a good cause."

"I appreciate that."

"And you know, some days I wonder if it wouldn't be simpler to just let the team go. Let me ask you this, Solo. You've had to make some tough calls in your time. Giving up the kidney. Leaving the Navy."

Oh no. The last thing he wanted was a heart-to-heart with Crush Taylor. "Boss, the bus is going to leave any minute—"

Crush carried on as if he hadn't said anything. "This town has been good to me. Except for that ice queen of a mayor and some ladies who have morality clauses tattooed on their asses."

Nice. "Seriously, the bus—"

"If you had a choice between selling the team to a family you've hated ever since they put your daddy out of business in second grade, or moving the team to another town that meant nothing to you, what would you do?"

"The Wades did that?"

"That's a tiny blip on the radar of what the Wades have accomplished here. You know, people thought I was crazy when I took over this team. The previous owner was going to move it out of Kilby, but even though this town's on the small side, the Catfish get a lot of support here. Sure, I might earn more profit somewhere else. But is profit really that important? The sewage plant makes a nice profit. Maybe I should go run that. Probably less crap to deal with."

With a laugh, he dug out his silver flask and tipped it toward Mike, as if offering him a sip. Mike shook his head no, and Crush took a long swallow. When he was done, he looked at Mike as if he'd just noticed him. "Don't you have a bus to catch? What are you doing here shootin' the shit? The Grizzlies aren't going to beat themselves."

To a glare from the driver, Mike jumped onto the chilly, air-conditioned bus, the last one to claim a seat, which meant . . . oh hell, he was right behind Yazmer. Luckily, the pitcher wore mirrored sunglasses, headphones, and a deer hunter cap tilted over his face. No interaction necessary. He settled into his seat with a sigh of relief. For the length of this road trip, he could put thoughts of Donna on the back burner.

"Hey, Solo," Trevor Stark called from across the aisle, two seats down, as the bus rumbled underway. "Heard you're a free agent now. Romantically speaking."

So much for not thinking about Donna. Sweet Jesus, how had word gotten out that quickly? "Did you really just say 'romantically'? Who are you, Fabio?"

"Fabio wishes he were me. Couple of the guys have been asking about your cute little ex. Just wanted to see if they have the all-clear. If it was me, I wouldn't bother to ask. But some guys have 'morals.'" Trevor air-quoted the word "morals."

"Which guys?"

"What does it matter? You're not with her anymore, right?"

He was saved from answering by a vibration from his phone. Incoming text. He clicked on it. It was from Jean-Luc. *Joey in the ER. Come as soon as you can.*

Chapter 20

CHICAGO IN THE summer. Sticky, muggy heat radiated from buildings and sidewalks. A gray haze hung outside the windows of Chicago General Hospital. Inside, Mike sat at Joey's bedside while Jean-Luc slouched against the wall, looking as worn and weary as a cosmopolitan businessman possibly could.

"How long has this been going on?" Mike still couldn't believe they hadn't called him earlier.

"Don't yell at me, little brother. Doctor's warnings." Joey looked terrible. His skin hung loosely from his neck, its color a pale puce. Dark circles ringed his eyes.

Mike sank into a chair next to his bed. "I should have been here."

"To do what? Watch me die?"

He buried his head in his hands. "You're not going to die."

"I am, Mike. We all are. I'm just going sooner than anticipated."

"No. *No.*" He couldn't bear it. Couldn't stand to hear Joey talking this way.

"Listen to me, Michael Xavier Solo. I'm not interested in making a drama here. I just want to spend some time with you. I don't want recriminations or rendings of clothing. I nearly died four years ago from the E coli. I'm at peace with whatever's coming."

Mike glanced at Jean-Luc, who was staring miserably at his loafers. "What about Jean-Luc? Is he at peace with it?"

"It's harder for him. Don't make it worse," Joey said sharply. "Now come on. I want to hear about you. Something good. Something I can think about while . . . while I lie here."

Something good. Mike's brain was operating about as well as a plateful of fried worms. What was good in his life? "The PSA is getting a lot of attention."

Joey brightened. "So I hear. I've had to decline all requests for comment, but I'm happy it went over well."

"It did."

His mind wandered away from the PSA, toward the conversation with Donna that had inspired it. His brother would love her. He could just imagine him leaning close, peppering her with questions, eyes shining with the delight of meeting someone new and refreshing. And Donna would have teased him the way she did everyone. She would have become his favorite little sister in the time it took her to give him a nickname.

But he and Donna were through. That was never going to happen.

He realized Joey had asked him a question about the Friars and his chances of getting called up. "Duke thinks it's a possibility. Their catcher's got a pulled groin muscle and their reserve catcher's in a massive slump. Hasn't gotten a hit in the past twelve games. It's still early, so they could bring me up to get some games under my belt before things heat up in September."

"So, it could happen. After all your hard work. Everything you sacrificed."

"I didn't sacrifice shit," Mike said fiercely. "Nothing that mattered."

"Angela?" Joey asked softly. "You sacrificed her."

"She made that choice all on her own." He didn't want to talk about Angela. In fact, it made him nervous because she volunteered at this very hospital, accompanying Father Kowalski during some of his end-of-life visits. That was one of the reasons he'd fallen so hard for her, that compassionate, angelic side of her.

"Has Angela ever come to visit you here?" he asked abruptly.

"No. Why? I'm sure she knew she wouldn't be welcome."

"Just wondered why you wouldn't qualify for a dose of her saintly presence."

Jean-Luc spoke from across the room. "I saw her in the cafeteria once. She asked about you, Michael. Asked how you were doing with the team."

"Oh, I'm sure she cares deeply about that. She told me I'd never make the majors."

"*What?*" Joey reacted with more vigor than he had since Mike had arrived. "When was that?"

A nurse tapped on the door, then entered, wheeling a tray with several shrink-wrapped trays of food.

"After she dumped me. One of her reasons was that I couldn't take care of a family if I didn't have a career. I told her my plan to switch to baseball and she laughed. Said that was a kid's dream. Told me to grow up."

"Why, that little piece of . . . of . . . tiramisu." Joey never swore, and never delivered insults. "How dare she?"

The nurse, a brisk, efficient Jamaican woman, was busy taking Joey's vitals. She shot a sharp glance at Mike. "You're getting my patient all revved up, mon. Can't tell if that's a good thing or a bad thing."

"Good," Joey assured her. "Very good. This is my brother, a famous ballplayer. He's about to get called up to the major leagues."

"Unless we're talking about the Cubbies, I'm gonna have to root against him."

"Understood. It's the San Diego Friars," added Mike. "And it's not a sure thing, the call-up. You never know. I could get traded. I could get released. It's baseball. Anything could happen."

The nurse smiled and unloaded the tray of food. "Well good luck to you then. If this man here likes you, then I'll have to make some room for a Friar in my heart. He's a fine man, this here."

"That he is," Mike said tightly, because it was too true. The kind of true that could rip your heart out.

The nurse wheeled the cart from the room. Jean-Luc came to Joey's bedside to inspect the offerings. "Another takeout night," he proclaimed. "Are you in the mood for I Porcini?"

"Perfect." Joey turned to Mike. "I see little point in eating anything unappetizing. At this moment, life is too short for hospital food. And I do believe I just figured something out about you and Angela."

"What?"

"You want to make it to the majors to prove her wrong. In fact, you aren't entirely over Angela." Joey's wry, knowing gaze seemed to penetrate right through to Mike's worst secrets. The memory of his conversation with Donna in Crush's pantry came back to him. She'd said the same thing.

"No. The first part, maybe. I mean, yes, there might have been an 'I'll show her' spoken at some point. Then my natural competitiveness took over, and I want to make it because I want to be the best. The best I can be, anyway." He leaned back in his chair. "The rest is a crock. I'm *over* Angela. I don't think about her anymore."

"You said you stopped believing in love because of her."

"Yes."

"Then I disagree. You aren't completely over her. It's not that you don't believe in love. You're still holding out hope that she'll want you back."

Mike nearly toppled his chair backward out of sheer indignation. "Not a *chance*."

A lively flush flooded Joey's cheeks. "Jean-Luc, back me up here. I'm on to something."

"Certainly, it's true. Beyond a doubt. A man like Mike, with such a loving heart, doesn't simply give up on *l'amour*. He still feels it. Still dreams of it, in his secret self."

"What?" Mike surged to his feet. "You're both out of your gay little minds."

Joey cackled. "We've hit a nerve."

"*Bien sur*," agreed Jean-Luc. He scanned through

a menu on his phone. "Osso buco for you, *mon amour*?"

"And a bottle of cognac."

"You can't have a bottle of cognac. Aren't you on a restricted diet? Shouldn't you be?" Mike protested.

"No, I should not be, and I will not be," Joey declared. "I'm doing this my own way. I will eat what I want, I will be with whom I choose, and I will say what I want. That's how I've lived, and I see no reason to change that now."

Mike burrowed a hand through his hair, feeling completely helpless. What magic words would convince Joey he was going to pull through? Was it even true? He watched his brother and Jean-Luc discuss their order with the meticulous attention of two surgeons planning a heart transplant. When they'd finally made their decision, Joey turned back to Mike.

"So. My brother. There's something I want you to do for me."

"Anything."

"At two o'clock tomorrow, a small group will be gathering in the chapel to discuss end-of-life care. I want you to be there."

"Why?"

"Because it's important to me. Are you going to argue with your big brother?"

"I'm not arguing. Did you hear me argue?"

"I could see you arguing in your head."

"Joey, you know how much I love you, but you can't see into my head."

"You might be surprised. Something happened with Donna, didn't it?"

Mike felt his expression shift. He couldn't maintain a poker face when it came to Donna. His whiplash emotions about her made that impossible. "You're annoying as fuck, you know that?"

"Two o'clock tomorrow."

At two o'clock, Mike stepped into the quiet chapel, with its single stained-glass window featuring a sapphire-blue dove against a backdrop of high-rises, and locked gazes with the last person he wanted to see: Angela. She looked incredible, curse her Italian genes. Her long ebony-black hair was swept into a braid that fell over one slim shoulder. She'd lost weight over the past four years, which made the delicate modeling of her cheekbones even more pronounced, her eyes wider and more mysterious, full of secrets.

Mike shook his head, disgusted with himself. Full of secrets? What was wrong with him? He dragged his gaze away and spotted Father Kowalski in the group. He raised a hand in greeting.

After whispering something to the priest, Angela glided toward him. She wore the kind of loose, figure-hiding dress that used to drive him crazy with wondering. "Hello, Mike."

"Hi, Angela. How are you?"

"I'm well. And you? I'm sorry to hear about your brother."

Mike stiffened. *Sure she was.* "Thank you."

"I mean that sincerely," she added with a spark of spirit. "I have always wished the best for Joey."

"That's so sweet." He smiled with complete insincerity. "So, what's the meeting about? Joey wanted me to stop by. I have no idea why."

A smile touched her lips. "Perhaps he wanted us to cross paths, after all this time."

He frowned uncertainly. She was probably right; why else would Joey have insisted he come to this particular meeting? Did he really believe that Mike still wanted Angela, and set this up as a way to get them back together? "If he weren't on his last kidney, I might have a word with him about that."

An expression of distaste marred the perfection of Angela's face. A very familiar expression. He used to tiptoe around that look, dreading its appearance. He'd forgotten that feeling, as if he was a little boy getting the kitchen floor dirty.

It crossed his mind that Donna would have found that funny. And that she never looked at him with distaste. Even in their most down-and-dirty sexual . . .

Oops. *Chapel*. Angela. Broken engagement.

"Anyway, we're just wrapping up. Would you like to get a cup of coffee in the cafeteria?" Angela was asking him. Just wrapping up, huh? Joey definitely must have planned it this way. After a long hesitation, he agreed, and they left the chapel. It felt completely surreal to be walking beside the woman who had shattered his heart. The woman who had enthralled his horny young imagination for so many years. The woman who'd granted him her virginity once they were engaged, and taken his. Now they were strolling down the hospital corridor as if they were strangers. Punching the elevator button. Watching for the light that would herald the elevator's arrival.

And he felt . . . nothing.

When he'd first asked Angela to a movie, his heart had been racing so fast he'd practically gasped the words. The first time they'd made love, he kept losing his erection out of sheer anxiety. He'd wanted it to be perfect. Since his only experience was with kissing, he'd holed up in his room with *The Joy of Sex* and *How to Bring a Woman to Orgasm Every Single Time*. The first time he unsnapped her bra, his hands had been shaking so hard he punched his own fist. Bruised a knuckle. He'd tried everything in the book, but if she'd experienced an orgasm, she'd kept it to herself.

Instead, she'd smiled serenely and said, "Do you feel better now?"

As if the only purpose of sex was to relieve a guy's blue balls.

The elevator dinged, and the door opened. Great, he had to ride in an empty elevator with Angela. He didn't want to be alone with her.

Why not? He didn't have an answer to that, so he stepped into the elevator. The doors slid shut, enclosing them in uncomfortable silence. Maybe she was waiting for him to start a conversation, since he'd always been the more talkative of the two of them. But she'd invited *him* for coffee, not the other way around. He cleared his throat. "Was there something in particular you wanted to discuss, Angela? I don't have much time." Meaning, he really wanted to get the hell out of there and get back to Joey.

Her eyes lifted to his. The dark, tranquil beauty of them hit him like a punch in the gut. "Well . . . I heard that you are no longer engaged. The ladies, you know, they like to gossip. They like to talk about you now and then."

"You shouldn't listen to gossip." He didn't want to

discuss Donna with her, or his engagement, or really, any aspect of his life.

"So it's not true?"

When he didn't answer, she seemed to come to her own conclusion. "If it's true, and you are free of your engagement, I wanted you to know that my parents have had a change of heart."

"Your parents?"

"And me," she added quickly. "My parents and me. We all think that . . . well, that things might be different if you did become a member of the Friars."

"I don't get it. How would things be different? I'm already a member of the Friars organization. Assigned to a Triple A team, but a member of the Friars. They're the ones who sign my paycheck."

"Yes, and that's exactly it. My family believes it might be a sign, the fact that your team has a religious name, a name they can admire. And that if you did play with them, that is, on the field, with the Friars name on your uniform, and an acceptable contract, that you might be able to be trusted to take care of a family."

Still not understanding, he stared at her blankly. What family was she talking about? An image of goofy Zack giving him a high five flashed into his mind. But Angela didn't even know Zack. She couldn't be talking about him. Then it clicked.

Ohhhhh.

"Are you fucking *serious*?"

She flinched, again with that expression of distaste. Great, he'd offended her with his language, and they'd barely exchanged three sentences. What were they doing? God, these must be the slowest elevators in creation.

"Sorry. I'm used to ballplayers, not sheltered ladies who tap-dance around reality. Let me get this right. Your family would accept me as their son-in-law if I do in fact make it onto the Friars' roster?"

She flushed a deep crimson, like a color from a stained-glass window, fixing her gaze on the doors as the elevator slowed to a stop. "I know how this might sound. I'm not presuming that you want to be with me again. You were very angry with me. But you always used to say I was the only girl you'd ever loved. So I thought, if there was a way we could try again, maybe you would like to know about it."

Finally, the elevator doors slid open, and she slipped into the busy lobby. He followed, torn between wanting to flee this conversation and being riveted by it. It was absurd—surreal—did she even *want* to get back together with him? She hadn't mentioned any sort of emotion along those lines. Then again, she'd always been an enigma to him.

"What about my brother? He's still gay."

"Yes, but . . ." Her gaze slid away from his. "They've agreed to overlook that. They might not go as far as family dinners, but it's still a big step." She gestured toward the sign for the cafeteria, a movement as graceful as a love sonnet. "Shall we?" *That hand.* He remembered how he used to watch her studying in school, registering every turn of a page, every raising of her hand.

"One moment. What about you? In this hypothetical relationship, do we invite Joey and Jean-Luc over for dinner?"

Her wide, serene gaze skimmed across his face briefly. "As you say, it's hypothetical."

"What if we had a son? And that son turned out to be gay? What then?"

Finally, a reaction. One hand went to her stomach, as if protecting her future offspring, and a flash of passion twisted her face. "Obviously, I would pray that wouldn't happen. I pray a lot, Mike. I pray for many things. For instance, I prayed I'd see you again, and that you wouldn't hate me."

Thunderstruck, taking in the obvious tumult she was undergoing, he realized he'd never seen her express this much emotion. He'd always assumed that she'd sailed on with her life like a swan, never wasting another thought on the one-kidney wonder she'd left behind.

"I don't hate you, Angela."

She nodded, a quick flick of her head, and the color faded from her face, the usual creamy serenity returning.

"This is all kind of a surprise . . . to put it mildly . . ."

She stopped him with a slim hand poised between them. How many times had he kissed that wrist, traced every line on her palm, felt the pulse of her delicate veins?

"This isn't some kind of proposal, Mike. I've had four years to think about things, and in some ways I'm a different person. We'd have to start over, learn about each other again. You'd have to win my family over, and you know how much effort that requires."

"Let me ask you something. You're at this hospital a lot, aren't you?"

"Every week or so."

"And yet you've never stopped in to see Joey.

You've known him since we were kids. Why not, Angela? I just want to understand that."

She held her head high, the lines of her neck long and graceful as a statue. "I didn't want to cause any upset to anyone."

"To your parents."

"Or to Joey. I thought he might be angry with me."

Mike shoved his hands in his pockets and nodded. No surprise, knowing Angela. She had always hated conflict. That's why she'd bowed to her parents' wishes and dumped him. Was there anyone in the world who would fit in with the DiMatteos without any friction at all? "I thought you'd already be married by now."

"No. I . . ." She hesitated, something churning behind that serene facade. "My parents have someone they want me to marry, but . . . I'm not sure. He's . . . a little bit older."

He frowned, leaning closer, all his protective instincts screaming. "That sounds medieval, Angela. They can't force you to marry someone you don't want to."

She let out a completely uncharacteristic snort. "No, they can't. But they can manipulate and pressure and smother and pray and—" Breaking off, she put a hand to her mouth, as if she could barely believe she'd let those words out.

Well, well. Was Angela finally seeing the whole picture when it came to her family? Would she finally break free and make her own decisions?

Too late for her and Mike, of course. Much too late. Even though all his old hurt and anger had now been transformed into something more like concern.

Would she be able to stand up to her parents in this situation? For the first time in her life?

Not his problem, he reminded himself. Not his problem. But it felt wrong, not to help her. She'd been so important to him for so many years.

His phone beeped. He scrambled to dig it out of his pocket. Jean-Luc.

Get up here now.

Without so much as a word of explanation to Angela, he spun back toward the elevator. He punched the button, then saw that the button on the tenth floor was lit up. It would take too long for the elevator to reach him. "Stairs?" he yelled wildly to Angela. Silently, she pointed to an alcove across the lobby. He ran for it, elbowing people out of the way as he went.

She didn't follow.

He pounded up the stairs, using every baseball-honed thigh muscle to its maximum capacity. Every wind sprint, every set of squats he'd ever performed, every weight he'd ever lifted bore him up those stairs like a magic carpet. *Second floor, third floor, fourth floor . . . hold on, Joey . . . don't go, Joey . . . I need you . . . please . . . fifth floor . . . open the door . . . where's his room . . . go . . . go. . . .*

By the time he reached Joey's room and flung himself at his bedside, their time together on this earth had run down to its last grains . . . a holding of his hand, a choked "Don't go, Joey," a flutter of a smile, a drift of eyelids, a sobbing Jean-Luc, beeping monitors, a last sweet breath . . .

. . . an exhalation . . .

Chapter 21

WORD SPREAD QUICKLY throughout Kilby that Mike Solo's brother, the one he'd done the PSA about, had passed away. The *Kilby Press-Herald* even ran an obituary that mentioned his academic career, relation to the Catfish, and his work in the Sudan, where he'd acquired the E coli infection that eventually cost him his life. They even ran a picture of him, which Donna pored over, noticing every similarity to Mike and every difference. He looked a lot thinner, more intellectual, but just as good-humored as Mike.

Her heart ached for him. The next time she saw Zack—the emergency order had been lifted once the end of their engagement was announced—they made a card for Mike. Instead of a bunch of words, they drew hearts and gorillas and tigers and flowers. Zack added a baseball at the last minute. "Thinking of you," she wrote at the bottom corner. "Love from Donna and Zack." Zack wrote his own name, which he'd recently learned how to do, then added a strange handlike shape at the end of his name.

"What's that, Zack-ino?"

"Baseball glove."

"Hmm, very good choice. Mike loves baseball."

"It's the greatest game in the world!" Zack jumped up and down on his chair. She gave him a minute, then settled him back down again. "Where is Mike?"

"He's back at home." She wondered when he'd come back to Kilby. Would he have the heart for baseball after losing his brother? But he was under contract. He had to. Probably soon.

"Mike lives here." Zack frowned, puzzled.

"He has another home, where he was born. A place called Chicago. A big city, much bigger than Kilby."

None of that seemed to make sense to Zack. Just as her explanations about why they might not see Mike anymore made no sense. But he was young, and in a year or so he probably wouldn't remember Mike.

She wished she could say the same.

In the wake of the broken engagement, she had to spend some time canceling the cake order, the flower order, the dress order. Sadie, back in Kilby to visit her mother again, came with her to You Bet I Do to return the fabric samples she'd borrowed.

"You know what I feel like?" Donna told her as they entered the frothy white interior of the wedding boutique. "Cinderella after the ball. Like I turned back into a pumpkin."

"Cinderella didn't turn into a pumpkin, silly. Her chariot did."

"Well, my Kia isn't big enough to be a pumpkin."

Sadie slung an arm around her shoulders. "I suppose you have the right hair color to be a pumpkin."

"You're such a good friend."

"I know, right?"

They shared a smile, the kind of smile only two

friends who've seen each other through many disasters can appreciate. Donna handed the samples to Amy, the salesgirl, but Sadie stilled her hand. "Come to think of it, I might hang on to those."

Donna whirled on her. "Sadie! Are you serious?"

Sadie nodded, one of her dazzling, wide grins stealing across her face. "I wasn't sure if it was the best time to tell you."

"Are you kidding?" Donna flung her arms around her friend, then pulled away and jumped up and down like a bunny on a pogo stick. "You're getting married! You're getting married! I'm so excited!" She careened into a lace-draped mannequin, which wobbled precariously. Amy rushed to grab it before it fell.

"Do you mind?" she said snippily. Donna and Sadie ignored her.

"I'm so glad you're happy." Sadie beamed. "I thought it might be hard, with . . ."

"No. Not a chance. I'm so happy I could just scream."

"Please don't," said Amy. "We have customers."

"And you might have another one right now if you play your cards right," Donna pointed out. "Sadie's getting married to a major league pitcher. She's probably going to need a dress."

Sadie confirmed this with a nod, but still Amy looked unconvinced. "You were engaged to a baseball player," she reminded Donna. "Look how that turned out. Those samples might come right on back again."

"Nice vote of confidence. Believe me, nothing is going to keep Caleb and Sadie from getting married. Those two are destiny."

"Fine." Amy sniffed. "Take the samples, but please don't damage any more mannequins. You wouldn't believe how much we pay for those."

Sadie and Donna left the shop and strolled toward Sacred Grounds, the hippie new age coffee shop that had recently opened downtown. The mid-morning sun glowed lethargically behind a haze of overcast. Not so much as a whisper of a breeze stirred the jacarandas that lined the streets. Donna studiously avoided looking at the Colonel Kilby statue and the fort; too many painful memories.

"I have some legal advice for you," Sadie said after they'd gone half a block.

"Am I in trouble? I barely touched that mannequin!"

Sadie laughed. "No, no, it's about the custody fight over Zack. Your lawyer . . . well, she's terrible. So bad that I've been wondering if the Wades are slipping her a little something to give you bad advice. She should have been at that emergency hearing."

"She's pro bono," Donna said defensively. "I pay her what I can, but it's not very much."

"I get that. But this is your child we're talking about. If it's a question of money, don't worry about that. I can help. I have that money from the Wades, and Caleb just signed an endorsement deal for a new avocado-flavored sports drink. Or maybe it's pistachio. I don't know, it's green. Seriously, we talked it over and want to help."

Donna's eyes brimmed with tears. "Oh, Sadie."

"It's not a big deal," Sadie said quickly. "Here's the other thing. Did you know that Judge Quinn is in the Wades' pocket? Mayor Trent gave me a heads-up on that. The Wades have some kind of hold over him. Whenever they want a decision to go their way, they try to get Judge Quinn assigned to the case. Your lawyer never mentioned that, did she? Let alone request a new judge?"

Donna shook her head numbly, looking back at all the times she'd blindly followed Karen Griswold's instructions. "Oh my God. I bet Bonita must have asked the Wades to pull some strings for her. I mean, I'm sure she did. She's related to them, and they hate me anyway. Why wouldn't she pull strings? I would, if I had any strings to pull."

Sadie gave her a one-armed hug. "Well, you do. You have me. And Caleb. We're your strings, and we're here to help. You need a new lawyer, sweetie, and that lawyer needs to file a petition for a new judge."

Tears swelled over the tips of her eyelashes and trickled down her face. "I didn't even tell you about Zack until this year."

"And that was very silly of you. Maybe I could have helped earlier. I understand, Donna. You were afraid to say anything. Fear makes us do all sorts of things. Come on. Let's get a drink."

They walked into Sacred Grounds, where Sadie settled Donna at a table. "Iced mocha?" she asked Donna, who nodded, then busied herself blotting her tears with a recycled paper napkin.

When Sadie came back with her foamy, whipped cream–topped drink, Donna found she had no appetite for it.

"You know, I told Mike I'm only afraid of one thing, and that's losing Zack. I came so close, Donna.

When Harvey told me I couldn't see him, the whole world just went black. Like I couldn't see for fear."

"I'm so sorry, Donna. I just can't believe Harvey would do that." Sadie stirred sugar into a cup of tea.

"I know, he didn't used to be such a devious worm. He's completely under Bonita's spell. Sometimes I think Bonita can't stand the fact that I exist, that Harvey used to be with me. It's like she's trying to erase me from the picture."

"Erase Donna MacIntyre? No chance of that."

"Sadie, I'm so afraid I'll never see Mike again. What if he never comes back to Kilby? What if he quits baseball or stays in Chicago? He was in love with a girl there, someone who broke his heart. He says that's why he's not looking for love."

Sadie pushed the mocha under Donna's nose, so the smell of chocolate filtered into her awareness. "Well, all respect to Mike, and you know I love the guy, but he's an idiot. That's okay. When it comes to love, we all have our idiotic moments. Maybe he wasn't looking for love, but it found him. I know the signs."

Donna drew the paper off her straw, shaking her head sadly. "No. He doesn't love me."

"You love him."

"Of course I love him. I've loved him since . . . oh cripes, I don't know when. Probably from that first night at the Roadhouse, when you met Caleb. Or maybe Crush's party. Or when he stood between me and Jared Wade. I don't know."

"Does he know how you feel?"

"No. I told you, he's not interested in love. The whole engagement was his version of a good deed."

Sadie stirred her mocha with a frown. "Are you so sure, Donna? Mike's a good guy, but I don't see him offering marriage to someone he didn't have feelings for. Maybe he had feelings, but didn't know it."

Donna rolled her eyes. "Trust me, the feelings he *did* have were completely obvious. Not that I was complaining about that part—"

Sadie threw up a hand to stop that line of conversation. "Mike's like a brother. Really don't need the details."

A detail swam to the surface of Donna's memory, of the time they'd broken in the football-shaped beanbag chair, after covering it with a sheet. Naked and spent, Mike had sprawled his long limbs every which way, while he held her across his chest like a child. "Finally found something football's good for," he'd declared with a lazy smile.

The memory of that moment brought it all back— the fun he'd brought her, the unfamiliar security of having a protector—along with a devastating punch of loss.

"Not everyone gets the fairy tale, Sadie."

"Why not?"

"Okay, maybe I had my fairy tale, but I ruined it by running my stupid mouth. I tried to talk him into something he thought was wrong, and he got insulted and stormed off. Then he left town, and now his brother is dead, and I'm sure he's completely wrecked, and he may never come back, and . . ."

She buried her face in her hands, the urge to cry overwhelming her. For a moment she simply sobbed. Whether it was *for* Mike, in sympathy with the grief he must be feeling, or *over* Mike, because he was lost to her, she couldn't say. Sadie stroked her back, made soothing murmurs, and didn't even mention the fact that Donna had knocked over her mocha.

When Donna finally opened her eyes and blinked away the remains of her tears, she saw their little table swimming with brown liquid dotted with white splotches of cream. The fabric samples from You Bet I Do were completely saturated.

"Oopsies."

"Eh." Sadie waved a dismissive hand. "Don't worry. I'll set a trend with my mocha-colored wedding veil. Amy can take all the credit."

When Donna got a call from Crush Taylor asking her to meet him at the stadium, she clocked out early from work. Whatever Crush wanted, it must have something to do with Mike, and that was worth missing a few hours of pay.

It would have been harder to walk into the familiar stadium, which was saturated with memories of Mike, if she hadn't heard that he wasn't due back until after his brother's funeral. Even so, she had to force a smile when she spotted Trevor Stark and Dwight Conner at the other end of the corridor. Oddly enough, they both wore Disney princess costumes. Or something. She wasn't completely sure because they practically ran out of sight.

"It's for the kids at Kilby Community Hospital," explained Crush when she'd settled herself onto a chair before his massive oak desk. "Cheers them up to see big baseball players making asses of themselves. Luckily, that's second nature to some of these guys. Making asses of ourselves, that is."

"I wish I could take a picture for Zack. My little boy," she explained.

"I'm familiar. I have all your press clippings from the world's shortest engagement." He gave her a lazy wink.

"Sorry about that. I know it was supposed to help the Catfish with their image."

He waved her off. "The list of things that are more important than the Catfish image is growing every day. You heard about Mike's brother?"

"Yes. How is Mike?"

He gave her a sharp glance. Usually Crush exuded a dissolute air, as if he was constantly grappling with a hangover. Today his eyes didn't look quite as blood-shot as normal. "So you're not in touch with him?"

"No."

"Do you have a problem with seeing him?"

"No. I mean, he might have a problem seeing me, but I won't know until I see him. If I see him. Do you mind . . . why are you asking?"

"I'd like to hire you."

Her mouth fell open. Of all the things she'd specu-lated about, none had included a job offer. "To do what?" She couldn't even come up with a possibility. "I have two skills, scheduling root canals and babysitting."

He shuddered. "Two things that sound like hell on earth to me." He fingered the cap of his flask, but she noticed that he didn't open it.

"Do some of the players have kids? Do you want me to babysit? Because I don't really do child care anymore. I mean, I love it, but the lawyer told me I need something that has health insurance and . . ."

"I can put you on the staff plan. That's not a

worry. But you wouldn't be babysitting, at least in the traditional sense. Though my players certainly have room for growth in their maturity level. Mike Solo being the rare exception."

"I still don't understand. You want me to babysit the players?"

"No, no. Angeline, our promotions girl, just gave her notice. Actually, she didn't give notice. She just left. Ran off with a RiverCat pitcher, can you imagine? We all thought she was screwing Stark. Bieberman locked himself in the bathroom when he heard the news."

"I still don't . . ."

"We need a new promotions girl. I remembered how well you handled the crowd that day Mike carried you onto the field. Most people would have been flustered, but you made a joke. Answered Angeline's questions just right. I remember thinking what a natural performer you are. Quick-witted and very appealing. Do you have any actors or performers in your family tree?"

"My mother's a backup singer."

"There you go. I think you inherited the performance gene. What do you think?"

"I think I've never done anything like that before and you could probably find a hundred girls who would do it better."

"I don't think so. Someone who knows Kilby, knows the Catfish, has a killer sense of humor, and will drive the Wades crazy the second they see her on the field? I don't think so."

She stared at him for a long moment. "Oh. My. God."

"Yah. The Machiavelli of baseball, that's me." He gave her an unrepentant grin. "Just so you know, I didn't think of this idea. Your illustrious mayor did."

"Mayor Trent?"

"The very one. Says she recommends you highly. Trustworthy, fierce, and funny. Her exact words."

The thought of Crush Taylor and Mayor Trent discussing her gave her a strange sensation. Why would a lowly dental receptionist hold any interest for either of them? And since when did those two do anything other than battle with each other? Hmm. She reminded herself to ask Sadie about that, but turned her attention to Crush's offer. "What does the promotions girl do, exactly?"

"You'll work with our publicity team. Every game has some kind of gimmick going on, and your job will be to emcee it. For instance, tonight we're doing the . . . what is it . . ." He shuffled through the randomly scattered papers on his desk. "Right. We're doing an egg toss sponsored by McGee Poultry Farms. That ought to be a mess. I think they've requested a chicken dance contest too. You'll work with Catfish Bob, the team mascot, who, by the way, no one ever sees out of costume. Lastly, you'll have to wear embarrassingly short shorts and a T-shirt three sizes too small."

At her appalled look, he grinned again. "I'm joking. You'll have to wear Catfish gear, but beyond that it's up to you. Relaxed and fun, that's the goal. Funny is good. You're a hometown girl, and you're mildly famous thanks to your former fiancé, so I think you'll be a draw."

It sounded . . . amazing. And terrifying. "What if

I'm no good? Can I try it out before I quit my other job?"

"Sure. We can do that. But I think you're gonna be hooked. I think you've missed your calling, stuck in that dental office. I think as soon as you take the field and hear the cheers, see all those people watching you, your world is going to light up like you never imagined." He gazed out of his window, which looked out on the baseball diamond, where a few players were hitting fungoes.

Wow. She knew the word "fungoes." When had that happened?

Mike, that's when.

"There might be one more problem," she said slowly. "If Mike Solo doesn't want me around the stadium, I wouldn't feel comfortable taking the job."

"He's fine with it."

A jolt of electricity shot from the crown of her head to the soles of her feet. "How do you know?"

"I asked him. Wouldn't be right to offer a job to a player's ex-fiancée without checking with him first."

"What did he say?"

"He said he'll meet you after recess. I'm not a matchmaker, okay? He had other things on his mind, but he didn't demonstrate any strong opposition to the idea."

Well, that didn't make her feel any better. She chewed on the inside of her cheek. This was an incredible opportunity to try something different. Something that might actually benefit from her personality, instead of getting sabotaged by it. If Mike had a problem with it, then he'd just have to tell her. When he came back. To Kilby. To Catfish Stadium.

But not to her.

Chapter 22

FOR THE FIRST few days after Joey's death, Mike could hardly bear anyone's company but Jean-Luc's. The poor man barely seemed to notice Mike was there. He'd gone behind a thick shell of grief, which left Mike to answer the door when red-eyed students came by with cards and stories of Joey's kindness. Those students, and the need to be there for Jean-Luc, kept him from descending into the black hole that gaped at his feet.

As mourners gathered at the campus chapel for the university's memorial service, everyone from students to staffmembers wanted to hug him and shake his hand. Many of them commented on the PSA. "He played it in class," one student told him. "He was really, really proud of it."

"Is that right?" Mike hadn't realized that Joey felt that way. He should have made a PSA like that earlier, or maybe a public statement. Why hadn't he? With a sharp shock, it came to him—Donna. Knowing Donna had changed him. And the PSA was essentially her idea. And then it had driven her away . . . or he'd driven himself away . . .

He shook himself back to the present moment, since the student was still talking. "He told everyone about his little brother the baseball player. He even gave us an assignment to research the effect of organized sports on the economy of a third world country. He said we'd get extra points if we picked baseball. Joking of course. He was the funniest professor I ever had."

Mike's smile came out more as a grimace. "Can you believe he knew nothing about baseball before I took it up? He studied it the same way he studied national economic policies. I think he grew to love it almost as much as imports and exports." Talking about his brother was difficult, but he tried, for Joey's sake. Joey would want his students to be able to share their memories. He would want his memorial service to be an uplifting occasion, not filled with tears and gloom.

And it was, it truly was, although it seemed to pass in a blur.

When it was Mike's turn to speak, he read from a letter Joey had written him from the Sudan, after he'd contracted E coli.

" 'Getting sick has made me realize how quickly life can change. It's made me determined to live honestly and completely. When I get home, I'm going to come out to the world. Things might be tough for a while, little brother. When I pass on, I want to know I did my best, with as much grace and compassion as possible. If you want to help, hang in there with Dad and Mama, because they won't understand. Keep a big heart and all will be well.' "

Mike couldn't lift his head from the faded piece

of foreign stationery, which he'd kept all these years. "That was Joey. He had no hate in him, only kindness. And I think he lived up to his wish. Grace and compassion—that was my brother."

Accompanied by sniffles and nodding heads, he left the lectern and returned to his seat in the front row between his sobbing sisters and Jean-Luc. The rest of the service was a blur of teachers and favorite students.

Had he fulfilled his brother's desire that he "hang in there" with Dad and Mama? He'd tried. Earlier, at the private burial service, he and his father had exchanged an awkward, stiff-armed hug. Jean-Luc hadn't been invited, but he'd begged Mike to be civil. When Mike had seen Mama's tear-swollen eyes, it hadn't been difficult after all. All the questions burning in his mind had faded away, though they came back now, full force. *Why did you shut him out? Why didn't you visit him in the hospital? Why are you so rigid, so sure you're right?*

That familiar helpless fury made his knuckles go white. He flexed his fingers, spreading his hands out wide on his knees. *Let it go.* You can't change them. Let it go. As if Joey was whispering to him. He stared at his hands, big and wide, the knuckles protruding like little mountains of bone. Catcher's hands, used to blocking wild pitches and capturing throws in the dirt. Used to the force of a 95-mile-an-hour fastball slamming into his glove. Used to tracking a knuckleball on its bumblebee path to the plate. Hard blows were part of his job, but none could be harder than this.

He needed to get back on the field, that's what he needed. Baseball had saved him from the feud with his family after Joey came out. Baseball had saved him when he'd ended his naval career. He always felt right when he was on the diamond. That's where he did his best thinking.

Maybe when he went back to Kilby, he'd figure out how to "hang in there" with his parents.

Besides, Donna was in Kilby. And he needed to thank her for inspiring him to do the PSA. The thought of seeing her again gave him the first glimpse of light in days.

Jean-Luc insisted on driving him to the airport. "You should come to Kilby with me," Mike said as they hurtled down the Loop in his silver Porsche. "Get out of Chicago for a while. Relax with the tumbleweeds and the wacky Catfish."

"You know I never understand baseball. I'm French. I barely understand the purpose of sports. The only reason to visit Keelby is to meet your friend Donna. Joey was very curious about her."

"Well, we had sort of an . . . issue."

"Issue?"

"The kind where she threw pillows at my head and I stormed out half naked. There's a chance I was in the wrong." He told the whole story of their falling out, and when he was done, Jean-Luc was laughing so hard tears shone in his eyes.

"Freaky little bunnies?" He gasped.

"She has a way with words. And pillows."

"I don't think you should be angry with her. All she wanted was to keep seeing you."

"Yes, but sneaking around and lying? Not my style."

"Of course not. Hiding is never easy, but you have to look at her motivation. She loves you. She also loves her son, so things were"—he shrugged—"*compliqué*."

"Loves me? She never said anything like that."

"She was going to marry you, *oui*?"

"Yes, but that was to gain legitimacy in the eyes of the judge. And I had to work hard to talk her into it. I had to try to make her fall—" He snapped his mouth shut. "Oh hell. She said she would only marry someone she was in love with. Then she dropped that requirement, because we decided to make the wedding into a big deal for the sake of the Catfish, to help Crush Taylor out, so I didn't think about that part again."

"I'm finding these events extremely confusing."

"Me too." Mike frowned, watching the high-rises on Lakeshore whip past. It had made sense at the time . . . hadn't it? "We never talked about the 'love' thing after we decided on the Catfish Wedding of the Decade. We just went for it."

"Did you meet her family?"

Mike snorted in disgust. "If you can call them that. They don't appreciate her at all. Her father ignores her and her stepmother treats her like a criminal. I haven't met her mother, because she's always on the road. Donna's so . . . exuberant and fun. But kind too. And very loyal. And she's not afraid to speak up, even though sometimes it gets her into trouble. She's really a great person, in every way. She just needs someone to watch out for her. And someone to . . ."

Oh my God. Of course. Why had it taken so long to see it?

"To what?"

"She needs someone to love her. Almost everyone in her life has abandoned her. Her father, her mother, her old boyfriend." Had he abandoned her too, so stuck on doing things the "right" way that he'd rejected her?

He glowered at the dashboard. Something else had been bothering him, and he might not get another chance to ask.

"Got a question for you. Why did Joey set me up to run into Angela? Did he want us to get back together?"

Jean-Luc, the wind ruffling his hair, shot him an amused sideways look. "He wanted you to either move on *completely* or pursue her again."

"Really? He thought I might pursue her again?"

"That wasn't his first choice, no." He hesitated. "He thought you and Donna were in love."

Mike drummed his fingers on the window, impatiently watching the skyline slide past. Why all this talk of love? He couldn't think about that kind of thing right now. "I just need to get back in uniform. Maybe everything will make sense then."

"If it works, you must tell me. Perhaps I will try baseball. What part should I try to play? Joey always said your part, catcher, was the most difficult."

"First of all, they're called positions, not parts. Second of all, I'd recommend starting with the position of fan in the stands."

"*Oof-ah.*"

"I'm serious. You should try it. When I play, I always feel Joey with me. He loved following baseball, once he saw the beauty of it."

Jean-Luc was quiet the rest of the way to O'Hare.

Just before Mike jumped out at the curb, he said softly, "I know very well how lucky I was with Joey. To love, to be loved, it isn't a snap." He demonstrated with a very French-looking flip of his fingers. "You have Joey's big heart. You are meant to love. A woman, in your case. A very fortunate woman. May you choose well, *mon frère*. Joey always wanted you to be happy. It was his dearest wish."

Mike's dearest wish had been that his brother live. So much for wishes. "Take care of yourself, Jean-Luc."

Catfish Stadium's curving outer walls seemed to greet him with open arms, blue team banners waving brightly. A brisk wind toyed with the gigantic Texas flag at the entrance, ripping it this way and that, occasionally wresting sounds like gunshots from it. Mike dropped his shades over his eyes. He wanted no sympathetic looks, no handshakes, no slaps on the back, no murmurs about the time someone's grandmother died, or their cousin. He wanted to get back on that field, squat behind home plate, and play ball. Get in the zone and stay there until his thighs were screaming and his right hand was numb.

Duke intercepted him at the head of the tunnel that led to the clubhouse and dragged him into the manager's office. Mike crossed his arms over his chest and glared at him. Duke gripped an unlit cigar between his teeth and stared back like a bulldog.

"What?" Mike finally asked.

"You ready to play?"

"Of course," Mike growled. "You don't have to ask that."

"Farrio's pitching today."

"Fine." He didn't care who was pitching. Just let him get out there.

"He's been shaky lately. Lost five miles off his fastball, and his curve looks more like high school batting practice."

"Fine."

"Okay then."

"Okay."

"Also . . ." The manager hesitated, chewed on the end of his cigar, then shrugged. "Eh, don't matter. Go. Stop wasting my time."

Mike scooted out of that office before Duke could slide in some kind of condolence comment. Whatever he was about to say, Mike didn't care. Just give him the ball and . . . rounding the corner, he nearly knocked over a girl in a Catfish cap. He grabbed her before she hit the floor. The familiar feel of sexy, warm curves sent a flash of pleasure through him.

"Hey!" Donna objected in that throaty voice that seemed to have a direct line to his privates. "Oh. Solo, I didn't see you."

"That's because I was around the corner. Law of physics."

"That's not physics. That's geography."

"How is that geography? That's not geography." Smiling—actually smiling—he made a quick visual trip down the landscape of her body, which was clothed in micro-shorts over leggings with swirls of blue and green, a ridiculously tight Catfish T-shirt that didn't quite make it to her belly button, and sneakers. Her red hair flowed in a ponytail through the back of the cap. She looked . . . freaking great. "Why are you dressed like that?"

"Why, do you miss the blue blazer?" She twinkled at him.

"No," he said with automatic revulsion. "I'm just surprised . . . I mean, what are you doing here?"

"I just started working here." She watched him carefully. "I'm the new Angeline. She ran off with a pitcher from Sacramento. Crush is giving me a shot. He said . . . that you didn't mind."

A vague memory returned, Crush yammering on the phone about Donna and some job. "Of course I don't mind," he said gruffly. "You'll be great. What's on tap today?"

"It's . . . uh . . . Seventies Tribute Day. Psychedelic leggings seemed like the way to go."

"Can't disagree with that."

"Mike . . ." Her voice went soft. "I'm so sorry."

He nodded. As he'd expected, her words of sympathy made his throat clog up. But it wasn't the worst feeling, and when she reached out to take his hand, the tight ball in his chest loosened. "I got the card you sent. Thanks." It had been his favorite of all the cards he'd received. He cleared his throat. "What are you doing . . . after? After the game?" he asked her. "Can we talk?"

Her vivid little face shifted, wariness taking the place of warmth. "Sure, Solo, but I have to pick up Zack later."

"You have him back? That's great news." For the second time since he'd seen her, a smile spread across his face.

"Yes. The final hearing is tomorrow. Caleb and Sadie helped me get a new lawyer, and she says we have a good chance, as long as I behave myself."

"No crazy engagements to ballplayers?"

She smiled gently. "I'm doing it all on my own this time."

"Got it. Hey, break a leg out there today. I bet you'll be amazing."

She flashed him a smile as bright as a bunch of spring daffodils. Dimples appeared in both cheeks, her face transforming into a vivid piece of sunshine right before his eyes. Then she skipped down the corridor toward the promotions department, leaving him somewhere between dazed and dazzled. Had Angela ever smiled like that, with her whole being bared to him? Would Angela ever wear psychedelic leggings for a seventies tribute? Had Angela ever thrown herself wholeheartedly into anything?

Angela.

In the clubhouse, he stripped off his street clothes and quickly donned his uniform. He needed to get on the field early to swing the bat a few times. He might be rusty after his week off.

He hadn't seen Angela again since her out-of-left-field . . . proposition? Invitation? He didn't know how to describe it. She'd sent flowers to the memorial service, along with a formal, polite little note. She hadn't attempted to see him before he left, nor had he her.

He jogged onto the field and launched into his pre-game stretching routine, waving to the few players who were already taking practice hits and fielding grounders. The clunk of bat on ball, the casual chatter of the Catfish, the timeless sounds of a baseball field brought him a precious sense of peace. God, it was good to be back. God, he loved baseball.

And if he made the grade, got the call-up to the Friars, he'd have the official go-ahead to pursue Angela once again. If he wanted to. Not that he did. The thought left him cold, or maybe "confused" was a better word. He was still grieving so deeply over his brother that no woman could break through.

Well, maybe one.

We are family . . .

Mike watched Donna dance onto the field to the sounds of Sister Sledge. "How y'all doin', Catfish fans?" she sang into the microphone, her Texas accent more pronounced than usual. "Are you ready to get your seventies groove on? We've got a real fun time comin' up. Who here remembers the seventies? Stand on up if you do."

As some of the older folks in the stands rose to their feet, Donna clapped her hands over her head, leading the crowd in a round of applause. "How about you all come on down here? I got a special surprise for you. Don't be shy, y'all! This is Texas, this is the Catfish, we're here to have some fun."

Donna and her dimples were impossible to resist, and one by one the middle-aged members of the crowd filtered onto the field.

"Now I wasn't around in the seventies, so I had to watch this on YouTube. Y'all let me know if I'm doing it wrong." The classic sound of the hustle blasted over the stadium sound system and in less time that it took to say John Travolta, the whole crew was side-stepping, rolling their hands, and pointing toward the sky in unison. The entire audience was on their feet, stomping and clapping, shouting, "Do the hustle" on cue. Mike had never seen that many people have that much fun at the same time. It was a glorious sight.

Donna in particular shone like a joyful little firefly, a copper-haired beacon of fun. Every time he looked at her—which he couldn't stop doing—a bit of happiness splashed into his soul, overflowing from her, from the crowd, from the moment.

Joey would have loved this.

It wasn't until the National Anthem had been played and the Catfish were taking their places on the field for the top of the first inning that Mike looked around at his teammates and noticed something different.

He saw it first on Dan Farrio, the pitcher. A black armband fastened around his upper arm. Squinting, he saw something else. A piece of rainbow ribbon tied around the armband.

Behind home plate, he froze, then let his gaze travel to first base. Sonny Barnes, the giant, tattooed, bald first baseman, who was so in love with his wife he cried when the Catfish bus rolled away for a road trip, wore one too, right above his elbow. Second baseman, James Manning, whom Mike barely knew—he wore one too. At shortstop, Bieberman's armband seemed extra-large, but maybe that was only in comparison to his smallish stature. At third, T.J. Gates caught his eye and offered a broad grin. He lifted his arm in a gesture of respect, then touched his fist to his heart. Trevor Stark, Dwight Conner, the whole team . . .

They were all wearing armbands for Joey. For him.

A swell of applause rolled through the stadium.

Joey's name was up on the Jumbotron, Joseph Luigi Solo, over a simple black background, the dates of his birth and death, and the words, "Peace be with you."

Oh hell. He was going to lose it. He put his hand to his lower belly, over his surgical scar, the missing piece of him. God help him, he was going to cry, right here in front of three thousand plus fans. Wildly, his gaze flew to the sidelines, his eyes drawn to the bright splash of Donna's hair. Her hands were clasped together under her chin, her eyes misty. When he caught her eye, she seemed to sense his distress, and pulled a goofy, comical face. A sort of freaky little bunny face.

Light flooded the hollow place in his heart. He touched his own hand to his chest, bowed to the crowd, kissed his fist and raised it to heaven, head bowed. *This is for you, Joey. My big brother, forever.*

Chapter 23

AFTER THE EMOTIONAL high point at the start of the game—Donna couldn't help crying, it was so beautiful—things went downhill. Dan Farrio, the starting pitcher, lasted only two innings before Duke pulled him out. His replacement was even worse; he was a rookie who'd just come up from Double A. Mike had to keep going out to the mound to calm him down, and after three innings he got the hook as well.

Donna was busy emceeing the Farrah look-alike contest, which was a huge hit both with the Kilby girls who got to go wild with the curling iron, and the guys who got to appreciate the jumpsuits and tank tops. Whenever things got slow—like when they put the game on pause to bring in yet another pitcher—she and Catfish Bob would do the "bump." Everyone loved that, and the stands turned into a sea of hip bumping. At one point she looked up at the owner's box and caught Crush's eye. He wore a big grin and gave her a vigorous thumbs-up.

Wow. She was actually good at this. It was fun, more fun than she'd ever imagined a job could be.

Sure, the Shark had been fun, but there had also been the constant undercurrent of worry that went with being responsible for a little person's well-being. Here, she felt carefree and light and happy—except when she looked at Mike. The circles under his eyes and the deep lines bracketing his mouth made her heart swell with sympathetic pain. She'd do anything to ease his hurt, anything. But she didn't know if he needed help from her. He'd barely let her say, "I'm so sorry," before cutting her off.

She got it. He wanted to grieve in private, not in the company of a girl he'd offered to marry out of duty.

By the seventh inning, the bullpen was empty. Duke had run out of pitchers; there was only one left. "Yazmer Perez, number 35," intoned the announcer, as if he was introducing any old player, not the most controversial one on the staff. A buzz rippled through the crowd. Donna, who'd been going over the plan for the "birthday parade" with the cameraman, looked up. At first she didn't notice the reason for everyone's whispers. Then she inhaled a sharp breath.

Yazmer wore no black armband. No little rainbow ribbon. As he strutted onto the field, he gave Mike a smug look, as if to say, *What are you going to do about it?*

Mike slowly lowered his face mask and went into his crouch.

That's right, urged Donna silently. *Be the bigger man. Don't let the asshole get to you.*

At first he didn't. Yaz struck out the first Express batter swinging. Mike whipped the ball to the third baseman. It traveled round the horn, binding the players together, ending up back in Yazmer's glove. When the next batter came to the plate, Yaz and Mike seemed to have trouble agreeing on a pitch, and finally Mike shrugged and gave the pitcher no signal at all.

He threw a fastball, which the guy hit, a long line drive into the gap between center and left field. Triple.

Yaz didn't take it well. He stalked off the mound, muttering angrily.

The next batter up, Yaz barely waited until the umpire gave the signal before slinging a gunshot of a pitch just outside the batter's box. Mike lunged for it—if he let it pass, the runner on third would score easily. He smothered it, then got slowly to his feet, clearly feeling a little pain. He took a moment, obviously trying to calm himself, then tossed the ball back to Yaz. As soon as it hit Yaz's glove, he went into the windup for the next pitch.

Donna remembered what Mike had said about getting Yaz to pick up his pace. He seemed to have picked it up, all right. Now he was winging those pitches at about the speed of an overactive pitching machine. He was barely giving Mike a chance to get into his crouch. Almost as if he was trying to grab the spotlight back.

Mike tried to slow him down by taking an extra long time to throw back the ball. The umpire said something that made him nod, then toss the ball back. He set up for the next pitch and started flashing signs. This time, Yaz took his sweet time, stepping off the rubber to call time, then stepping back up, then shaking off Mike's signs. His message was clear even to Donna. *He* controlled the pace of the game, not Mike.

They finally agreed on a pitch, and Mike set up on the outside part of the plate. But the pitch, a fastball, went inside. The batter jumped out of the way as Mike lunged to his left. Then everything got crazy. Mike batted down the ball with his glove, then exploded to his feet, wheeled around, and charged the mound. With a roar Donna could hear from the sidelines, he tackled Yazmer. Yaz responded with a sharp punch to the gut. They toppled to the ground, grappling with each other, raining blows onto each other's backs and ribs and faces.

From someone's radio, Donna heard the announcers going crazy. "This is something you *never* see, two members of the same team coming to blows *during a game*. It's one thing when two teams go at it, but a pitcher and a catcher? There's a lot of bad blood there. Maybe it was just a matter of time before these two took their feud off Instagram and onto the field. Now the home plate ump has thrown them both out of the game, but they aren't going anywhere. Isn't anyone going to stop this?"

Duke and the pitching coach sprinted onto the field and shouted at the rolling pair. The commotion from the crowd created a dull roar in Donna's ears. The Catfish players ran in from all over the field, then hovered at the edges of the two-man brawl. Trevor darted in to pull Mike away, but Mike lifted his head and snarled at him. Whatever he said made Trevor step away and give the other players a "stay back" gesture.

"Looks like the Catfish don't know what to do. In your normal fight between two teams, the unwritten rule is that every single player's gotta come off the bench and join the dogpile. But if it's players from the same team? Whole new ball game, so to speak."

Meanwhile, the Express players poured out of the dugout and stood laughing their asses off at the spectacle of two teammates tearing each other apart.

Why didn't anyone stop them? The umpires were gathered in a knot, yelling at Duke, who yelled back, but didn't make a move toward Mike and Yazmer. Maybe he'd decided it was best to let them fight it out. Maybe he was waiting for the perfect moment. Maybe he didn't want to get an arm snapped off.

There had to be something she could do. She couldn't just stand here and watch Mike, with his missing kidney and his grieving heart, get beaten to a pulp.

Casting around wildly for inspiration, she caught sight of the grounds crew watching the scene from near the dugout. She knew one of the crewmembers because he used to bring his Chevy truck to her dad for repairs. She ran over to him. "I need your help, Ryan."

"For what?"

She tried to sound official and urgent. "Don't ask questions. Just do what I say. Crush Taylor sent me."

Well, surely Crush *would* have sent her, if he'd known the plan that had flashed into her brain. Ryan glanced up at the owner's box, but Crush had disappeared. Probably drinking to the end of his hopes of hanging on to the team, thought Donna. If the Catfish looked bad before, this was beyond embarrassing. She had to stop this, not only for Mike, but for her new boss.

"Okay, Donna, shoot. What do you need?"

Two minutes later, she and Ryan jogged onto the field hauling a hose, firefighter-style. When they were close enough to Mike and Yaz, who were still locked in a cage match, Donna waved her hand to the other grounds worker stationed back at the spigot. He cranked the handle and water spurted from the hose with so much force she lost control of it for a second. It snaked all over the place, spraying Trevor and Duke with water. Trevor threw up his hands to shield himself and Duke started yelling something at her. She couldn't really hear over the blast of the water and the incredible din of the crowd.

The damn hose seemed to be possessed as it flung water at fleeing players and coaches. With all her strength, Donna wrestled it into submission and pointed the stream of water at Mike and Yazmer, who were splayed out on the bare dirt at the base of the pitcher's mound. Water blasted onto them, drenched their uniforms, their hair, their everything, then streamed off their bodies onto the infield grass and the dirt of the mound, which quickly turned to mud.

It was a mess, but it worked. Yaz broke away first, shouting and spluttering. He rolled onto his knees and coughed water out of his mouth. Mike lay on his back, chest heaving, arms thrown over his face. Donna changed the direction of the hose so water streamed onto the grass, then yelled to Trevor.

"Go in there. Don't let them start again."

Trevor took one stride forward, then slipped on the mud and went down hard on his rear. Next came Duke, who got about a yard from Mike before he lost his footing and splashed into a puddle next to him.

The crowd was now roaring with a different sound, one of rollicking laughter. Donna barely heard it through the ringing in her ears. She abandoned the hose and dashed to Mike's side, using the wet grass as a sort of slip-and-slide to reach him. His arm still shielded his face. "Mike, are you hurt?"

"Donna?"

"Yes."

He eased his arm off his face to blink at her. "Did you just nearly drown me?"

"Yes. It seemed like a better alternative than what you were doing."

Duke, wet and furious as a drowning bulldog, scrambled next to them. "You're suspended, Solo. You sonofabitch. You too, Yaz," he called to the pitcher, who was slowly getting to his feet. His soaking wet uniform clung to his body. Donna had to admit he looked pretty darn good. He was a jerk, but he was ripped.

"Photo op to the max," the pitcher said, flexing his biceps. "The Yaz don't usually do wet T-shirt contests."

Mike tensed, but Donna pinned his arm to the ground. "Don't even think about it," she hissed. "Besides, you'd win by a mile."

"Get your asses up off the ground," Duke yelled, though his authority was slightly undercut by the fact that he still couldn't stand without slipping. Trevor stepped over and hauled him up, then steadied him. "Solo, *now*!"

Trevor reached a hand to Mike, who grabbed it and pulled himself upright. He looked bruised, bloodied, drenched, but oddly exhilarated. Donna remembered how he'd looked at the Roadhouse, the warlike gleam in his eyes as he'd taken on the Wades.

"Can someone turn off that goddamn hose?" Duke marched toward it, his cleats making sucking sounds in the wet grass. He gestured toward the head umpire, who gingerly stepped forward.

Water kept pumping onto the field while the grounds worker turned the spigot. Finally it diminished to a trickle. Donna surveyed the damage. Three wet Catfish, a furious manager, and a baseball diamond that looked more like a mud bath.

But hey—the fight was over. Yaz kept showing off his muscles to the crowd, while Mike shook himself off. Duke and the head umpire conferred, testing the wet grass with their feet. The manager of the Express joined them as well, and they bent their heads together in furious discussion.

Oh cripes. With a sudden sinking feeling, Donna realized the inevitable consequence of her brilliant plan. The game would have to be called. No way could they play in a mud slick. It wouldn't be safe. She scanned the other Catfish, who were staring at the mess in disbelief. From the stands, camera lights flashed like fireflies.

Sure enough, Duke soon trotted off the field, beckoning to the announcer. The official word came a few moments later.

"Ladies and gentlemen, we regret to inform you that due to unforeseen circumstances, today's game will be considered a forfeit to the Round Rock Express. The Catfish management would like to extend our sincere apologies and offer all attendees a rain check for a future game of your choice."

The crowd didn't seem too disappointed. After all, it was already the seventh inning, and the Catfish had been on the losing end anyway. And now they were enjoying the sight of two wet and studly ballplayers striding off the field. Girls screamed and whistled, cameras flashed, the "We Are Family" song blasted through the sound system again.

Halfway off the field, Mike looked over his shoulder and caught her eye. He jerked his head toward the stadium in clear, blazing invitation. Her stomach clenched with excitement; she hadn't thought she'd ever see that wicked gleam in his eyes again.

Mike barely lasted the few moments it took to haul Donna into the physical therapist's supply closet. He slammed the door shut, turned the lock, and backed her up against the back wall. "You're nuts," he muttered, putting his hands all over her. "And you make me crazy." He ripped the T-shirt over her head, then filled his hands with her sports bra–covered breasts. She shivered from the contact with his wet hands and returned the favor by dragging his drenched uniform shirt off his chest.

He took a step back and peeled off his uniform pants, so wet they were nearly see-through. "Guess I gave the folks a show, didn't I?"

"Oh yes," she breathed. "But not this good of a show."

He hauled her back against him. Naked and gloriously aroused, he fixed her with an all-consuming, hungry gaze, as if he never wanted to take his hands off her. "God, I missed you. I need you, Donna. Now."

"Yes," she breathed.

"Get naked." The need in his voice clawed at her heart. She stripped off her shorts and leggings. The small room was stuffy from their body heat and the steam rising between them. It made her light-headed, as if none of this was real.

"Turn around, put your hands on the wall." Tight and intense, his voice sounded like a stranger's, but she'd know his touch anywhere. He turned her, placed her hands on the wall, and tugged her hips toward him. She felt the hot brush of his erection against the globes of her ass, the hard press of his body against hers. His hand came around to her front and caught at her curls, fingers parting her and searching until he found the piece of flesh that craved him.

She let out a harsh gasp as he fingered her clit. She'd given up on the possibility of this, never thought she'd experience the intimacy of his flesh against hers again. It was almost too much—having him hot against her, after the misery of losing him.

"Legs apart," he said hoarsely, close to her ear. "Go up on your tiptoes so I can get inside you. I need to be inside you."

"Yes," she moaned, wild for him. She did everything he said, pushing her hand against the wall, opening her legs for him, writhing against the hard shape of him as he bent over her. He ground his palm against her burning sex. "Oh God," she gasped. "I can't . . . I'm going to . . ." She came, big, racking spasms convulsing her body. The orgasm still held her in its grip as he slid into her. A new pleasure sparked hard, and she arched her back to give him more space. Using both hands, he lifted her off the ground. With sheer brute strength, he worked her body over his cock while she palmed the wall for balance. From that angle, he touched a part of her that felt deep and hidden, like a secret spring in a forest, a place so intimate that nothing could be concealed. Not the way he made her shake and tremble. Not the way she whimpered his name, as if she loved him. And then, as he rocked into his own orgasm with a massive groan, words spilled from her lips in soft little murmurs. "I love you. I love you. I love you, Mike."

She didn't think he heard. He seemed entirely primitive, hunched over her body like a beast, claiming her as if she was there only for his pleasure. All the sounds coming from him were grunts and groans, no words at all. She shut her eyes, hoping he hadn't heard . . . and also hoping he had, and that he'd say it back.

But there were no words from Mike. There was nothing but heat and sweat and primal noises, slick flesh and trembles of pleasure. Another long, soft orgasm rolled through her—almost a sympathetic one, as if her body was so in tune with his that she couldn't help coming along with him.

His body relaxed, and he let out a long, hoarse sigh of completion. Gently, with supreme tenderness, he released her and let her feet touch the floor. Stroked her hair, his big hands drawing the strands away from her damp face and gathering them at the base of her neck. She rested her forehead against the wall to catch her breath. *Damn it, Solo*, she mouthed silently. *That wasn't fair.*

He stroked her gently until her body stopped trembling. "You okay?"

"Yeah. You?"

"Yeah. I'm great. Thanks to you. Everything else is crap. I just got suspended and probably have a contusion on my last kidney."

"I'm sorry I got you suspended."

"You didn't, sweet cheeks. That was all me. Donna . . ." He turned her to face him and gathered her into his arms. His green eyes, clear of shadows, smiled down at her. "You really are one fearless chick, you know that? You went and grabbed the hose. That's some kind of mad genius."

"Well, no one was doing anything! They would have stood around and let you kill each other."

"Nah. They tried to stop it but I pulled rank on Trevor. It needed to be done. God, it felt good to let Yaz have it."

She bent down to retrieve her clothes. "I didn't think about the field getting all wet. Duke looked pretty mad. I wonder if Crush will fire me."

"He'd better not. You're the best promotions girl we've ever had. You were amazing. And I'm not just saying that because . . ." He caught himself and left the sentence hanging.

"Because what?" How could he refuse to finish that sentence? Didn't he know he was torturing her?

"Because I'm hot for you." With an exaggerated leer, he snatched her against him. "I could go again, right now. That's what you do to me."

She wrenched herself away and grabbed her tangle of clothes. "Solo, you're as shallow as that puddle on the field. Besides, I thought you had a problem with sneaking around. Aren't you the one who dragged me into this closet?"

"I was an idiot to say those things. I had my head up my ass." He helped her disentangle her bra and shirt.

She yanked on the bra, fastening it before he could assist. "Oh, so now you *do* want to sneak around? You're giving me whiplash."

"No, that's not . . . I just . . . it's been such hell, everything . . . and then I saw you and I felt good for the first time since . . ." Even in the dim light of the closet the heartfelt look in his eyes made her heart clamor. Was it possible he felt what she did . . . even a little?

A sudden rapping on the closet made them both jump. A stern female voice said, "Who's in there? Why is my closet locked? You know what, I don't even want to know. I'm stepping away, and when I get back I want it empty and unlocked. You got that, you horny baseball perv, whoever you are?"

Donna buried her face in Mike's chest to stifle her laughter. His chest quaked under her cheek. Warmth spread through her, and she felt as if the top of her head might float away from the sheer pleasure of being with him again. She loved laughing with Mike. It was maybe her second favorite thing to do with him.

A few footsteps sounded, and then the voice came again. "And if that's Mike Solo in there, you might as well know there's a woman here to see you. Says her name is Angela."

Chapter 24

ANGELA? THE NAME echoed through the tiny closet like a detonation. Angela, here in Kilby? Mike couldn't put the pieces together; it made no sense.

Eyes blazing, Donna stepped away from him. "Angela? Your ex-fiancée?"

"I guess so." He didn't know any other Angelas who might show up out of the blue.

"I thought you never saw her anymore." She was pulling on her clothes with amazing speed considering the tiny space.

"I don't, usually, but she was at the hospital in Chicago."

"Why is she here?"

"I honestly don't know." His thoughts were racing. Some kind of emergency? Family problem? It would have to be something pretty dire to make her fly all the way down to Kilby.

"Solo." Donna, fully dressed now, put a hand to his chest, pinning him to a shelf of towels. "Don't treat me like a fool. She wouldn't be here without a good reason. Give me your best guess as to why she's here. We just had sex in a closet. I think I deserve to know."

He caught her wrist, tugging her to him. "Donna, I didn't invite her here. I didn't know she was coming. All I know is what she said in Chicago."

"Which was?"

Was there any way out of this that didn't involve pissing Donna off? He couldn't think of a single one. "Donna, it doesn't matter. It's over with her."

"Then why is she here?"

"I don't know." He looked around for his clothes, only to find he was standing on them. "But it probably has something to do with her family."

"The family that made her break up with you?"

He bent down to retrieve his clothes. "Yes, well, apparently they've loosened up about that. As long as I make the majors, of course."

"*What?*"

"Yep, that's the DiMatteos for you. It was almost like one of those revenge fantasies I used to have, like, when I'm a big shot in the majors, you'll come begging, that sort of thing."

When he stood up, Donna was pulling away from him, staring at him as if he had three heads. "Revenge fantasy. So . . . getting engaged to me . . . you knew she'd hear about it. Was that part of the whole revenge idea?"

"God no!" He reached for her, but she slipped out of his grasp. "Donna, I swear that never entered my mind."

But she continued on as if she'd barely heard him. "Well anyway, now you're free again, and her parents have loosened up, and she's here and . . ." Tears shimmered in her eyes, but she squared her shoulders. "Good-bye, Mike."

"Donna! Come on, don't do this."

She ducked under his arm and skidded toward the door.

"You'd better go see her, Solo. She's the one you really want, isn't she? She has been all along." With a sound like a sob, she flung open the door.

"Donna! That's not true—"

Light flooded into the room. Still naked, he threw an arm over his eyes, and when his vision recovered from the blast of light, she was gone. Quickly, he pulled on his clothes and ran after her. The pain in her voice ripped at his heart. He couldn't even think about her accusations; all he cared about was finding her. He caught a quick flash of Donna's copper-red hair as she zipped around the corner. He pounded after her and saw her slip out the exit.

Before he could push open the door and follow, someone grabbed his arm. "You're coming with me."

"Duke, I'm in the middle of—"

"You're in the middle of a shitstorm, and the ladies are going to have to wait. The tall brunette left a few minutes ago, said she's staying at the Lone Star Inn. Our own little redhead just drove off. Got any blondes hanging around?"

"No. Duke, this is important."

"And this isn't? You and Yaz?" The thunderous look on Duke's face made Mike's stomach plummet. Duke had already suspended them. Was there more? Maybe there was. He was supposed to build trust with Yazmer, not attack him on the mound. He'd screwed up completely this time, and the Friars probably thought he was an unstable, hair-trigger liability. Bye-bye baseball career.

He groaned and pushed a hand through his hair. "Duke, I know I lost it out there. I'm sorry. If the Friars want to punt me down to single A or something, I get it. But right now I have to go after Donna."

Duke heaved a heavy sigh. "Look, Solo, do you want to get called up or not?"

Mike spun around. "*What?*"

Duke marched down the hall toward his office, and this time Mike followed without protest. "You just ruined the only good moment in a minor league manager's life. Mostly it's all crap, but once in a while we get to do something fun like tell a guy he's being called up. Usually, the guy's pretty happy about that, not running in the opposite direction."

They reached his office, where Duke virtually shoved him through the door. Crush Taylor lounged against the edge of the desk, staring at a photo of Nolan Ryan. He glanced over, tilted his sunglasses down his nose.

"Congratulations, Solo."

Mike felt as if he'd gone on some crazy new roller-coaster ride, one where you get turned upside down and tied to a bungee cord. "I don't understand. I just got suspended. And I deserved it."

"Well, that's debatable." Duke flipped open a box of cigars and offered one to Mike. He shook his head. "Heat of the moment, you know. Extenuating circumstances. Anyway, the Friars are going to honor the suspension, since I also suspended Yazmer. Can't very well let one of you off and not the other."

"What about things with Yazmer? I screwed up about as bad as I could."

"Overall, they like the way you've handled Yaz. His pacing is better and his asshole quotient is holding steady. You're supposed to report to Friar Stadium in four days. That'll give you enough time to wrap things up here. Work out all the issues in your love life. That kind of thing." He winked one bulldog eye. "So . . . where's your excitement? Come on, I need that little tear in my eye I always get when I pass on the good news."

Mike ducked his head, searching every corner of his heart for the triumph he'd always expected to feel at this moment. Nothing. Grief for Joey, worry about Donna, the last remains of anger toward Yazmer. Celebration? No sign of it. What was wrong with him? Why wasn't he jumping up and down? Joey would want him to rejoice. He would want him to savor this moment.

Maybe it was just too soon after returning to the game. "I'm still . . . uh . . . my brother . . ." He trailed off.

Duke gave him an odd little salute. "Nuff said."

Mike stuffed his hands in his back pockets, wishing he could get the hell out of this office. Crush spoke up before he could make his escape. "We're going to miss you around here. I told those bastards in San Diego that they'd be idiots not to move you up. Guys like you don't come along very often."

"Guys like me?" Mike frowned, his gaze straying to the window, where he could make out a sliver of the parking lot, but saw no sign of a red Kia. That's where he wanted to be right now—working things out with Donna.

"Leaders. Guys who don't seek out the spotlight, but when it comes, they stand up for what they believe. On a personal note, I gotta thank you. You made Yazmer look like the ass he is. Hashtag CrushIt is now a complete joke and I can cross it off my list of Things Driving Me to Drink."

"Plenty left there," muttered Duke.

"I heard that. So, Mike Solo, if I manage to hang on to this team, it'll be partly thanks to you. And if the Wades take over, the good news is you'll be off to San Diego."

Mike managed a smile, though that didn't feel like good news, exactly. He'd still care about the future of the Catfish, even if he wasn't part of it. "I hope you keep the team, sir. It's your team. The town likes it as it is. I've been out there talking to people and they like you. If the Wades buy it, it'll just be a trophy to them. They don't have any passion for baseball."

"Thanks." Crush strode forward to shake his hand. "Let me put another little seed in your head. Baseball is a fickle beast. You might have a long and prosperous career, or you might flame out like a moth hitting a zapper."

"Gee, thanks."

"It happens. You can't cry over it. It's baseball. Point is, I can always use a guy like you."

"Um . . . for what?"

"Not sure yet. But you're smart and principled and people like you. You can talk to the press, the players dig you, chicks go crazy for you. That vow turned you into a rock star, and the funny thing is, that's not why you made the vow. I know, I know, I'm a cynical bastard, but you're not, and you never will be. Just keep it in mind, all right?"

He jammed his sunglasses over his eyes, clapped him on the shoulder, and strode out of the office, leaving Mike looking blankly at Duke. "Keep *what* in mind?"

"The hell if I know. When Crush talks, I just nod and plan the next day's lineup. Knock 'em dead in San Diego, Solo. And don't worry about any of the shit back here in Kilby. You did your time, now you can shake the dust off. Bright lights, big city. You'll be up on a billboard before you know it."

"Thanks for everything, Duke. Really appreciate it."

"Hey, nothing to it. Now go find that girl of yours. Or both girls. Not at the same time, unless that's the way you like it."

Mike nearly choked on that image as he left Duke's office. He dialed Donna's number as he made his way back to the clubhouse to change. No answer. She must be really pissed.

The clubhouse was empty. A piece of paper was taped to his locker. "Mike Solo, you just jumped your own pitcher, forfeited a game, got suspended, and got called up! What are you going to do now? ROADHOUSE! Guys want to buy you a beer, bro. See you there. DC."

Dwight Conner. He'd miss the dude. He'd miss all these guys. Jesus, was he really leaving? It didn't seem real. He stripped off his uniform, dumped it in the laundry basket, then walked to the showers. Under a stream of hot water, his thoughts returned to something Donna had said. *Getting engaged to me . . . you knew she'd hear about it.*

Good God, of course he hadn't been thinking about Angela when he made his proposal to Donna.

Angela hadn't even been a blip on his radar. Donna was way off base.

He soaped his chest, the scent of clean skin evoking Donna's presence with almost painful intensity.

She's the one you really want. She has been all along.

Standing there in the shower, he forced himself to consider that accusation. Joey had said something similar, that he'd never really gotten over Angela. Was it true? He never thought about her anymore. But had he let his hurt feelings, his wounded pride, keep him from giving his heart to anyone else? To Donna?

If only he could call Joey. He'd know what to do and say. A pang of grief so deep it felt like a physical entity twisted in his gut. He wrenched the water to cold, sluiced the soap off his body, and slammed off the faucet.

As he was toweling off, something came back to him.

In the closet with Donna, he'd experienced the most intense orgasm of his life. After all the grief and tension of his trip to Chicago, the physical release had been tremendous. So much pleasure had flooded his brain, it was nearly an out-of-body experience. He'd heard Donna's soft words as if from a distance, as if someone else was saying them to some other guy in some other closet. *I love you. I love you.*

She loved him. She'd said so, and he'd been so out of his mind from that orgasm that he hadn't said a word in response. Afterward, she'd acted as if nothing had happened, laughing and teasing as always, until they'd been interrupted. Then she'd lashed out and taken off.

And now Angela was here. Could this be any more effed up?

He dried off and threw on his street clothes. Before he hashed things out with Donna, he needed to find out why Angela was here. And then he needed to figure out what to say to her.

Donna had no time to nurse her broken heart. Her impulsive actions on the baseball field turned her into an instant YouTube sensation. Someone at the game had recorded the crazy scene, uploaded it, and by six-thirty that evening it already had ten thousand views. It seemed that everyone wanted to watch a crazy promotions girl hose down a pair of minor league players. So many calls poured in that she had to turn her phone off. Burwell Brown called from the *Kilby Press-Herald*, requesting a quote for the front page article set to run the next morning. Her old lawyer called, her new lawyer called, even her mother called from New York.

"Sweetie, you're famous! I always knew you took after me," she said in her message. "I can probably get you on one of the entertainment shows if you're interested."

Sadie texted, *Caleb is laughing his ass off. All the Friars think you're awesome and want to meet you. How's Mike doing?*

Now that was something she refused to answer.

Even Crush Taylor texted her, with a permanent job offer and a raise. She didn't answer that either, because she couldn't face the thought of going to the stadium every day, where she'd have to see Mike Solo, the jerk who'd toyed with her emotions and ripped her heart out.

Mike called too, but she refused to listen to those messages. Hey, a girl had to give her broken heart some space. Now that she saw the whole picture with Mike—that if Angela wanted him back, it was just a matter of when—she couldn't bear to hear his voice.

Luckily, the Hannigans had asked her if she would take Zack to dinner while they entertained a business colleague. Nothing gave her comfort like being with Zack. Even when she had to stop him from putting tortilla chips over his eyelids or dipping strings of cheese in his water glass, his goofy, oblivious presence made everything okay.

"I'm sorry things have been kind of crazy lately, Zackster."

"Gramma said I maybe can come live with you."

"Did she?" Hope bloomed like a Texas bluebell in spring. If Mrs. Hannigan had said that, she must think Donna had a good chance of winning custody. "Would you like that?"

He nodded, licking a bit of salsa from his chin. "Can we go get my backa-packa first? And all my animal stuffies?"

"Of course, but nothing's going to happen right away."

"Why not?"

Yeah, why? Why couldn't she just take Zack home with her and tuck him into the little bed she'd painted jungle green? That's where he belonged. "Because it's very important, and important things take time. We have to get them right."

He stared at her blankly, then lifted a sticky chunk of nachos and slurped sour cream off it. Grinning, he waited for her laugh, which she gave him because he was just so darn cute. Then she gently wiped the sour cream off his chin. "Someday we're going to have to get serious about table manners. But you're four, so you can still get away with all kinds of stuff."

"Four! I'm four!" He banged his silverware on the table and waved his legs around.

"That's right, Zacky. Since you're four, you probably understand that I love you tons, right? Like, as much as this whole restaurant, and the whole city, and all of Texas, and the whole universe. Do you know that?"

He grinned, displaying the cache of sour cream he'd collected in his cheek, like a squirrel.

"Ewww!!" She gave an exaggerated shudder, which delighted him all over again.

YouTube didn't matter. Her broken heart didn't matter. Right now, the only thing that mattered was the hearing tomorrow. If she lost her case, her wonderful little boy would be under Bonita's thumb, just like Harvey. She'd crush all the spirit out of him. She wouldn't laugh at his jokes, she'd criticize them, the way Carrie had always criticized Donna. Not with any hint of love, just plain old you're-a-bad-kid judginess.

Her phone beeped. A reminder from her new lawyer to meet in the courthouse lobby at nine. As if she needed a reminder. She'd already taken the day off from both her jobs. For the rest of the night, she was going to ignore the rest of the world. No phone. No YouTube. She'd rehearse her statement, pick the sour cream out of Zack's ears, and *forget Mike Solo*.

Chapter 25

ANGELA HAD BOOKED a room at the Lone Star Inn, an older Victorian-style, three-story establishment with white gingerbread trim and a wide veranda. When she opened the door at his soft knock, she looked like a movie star inviting him in for an at-home interview. Dressed in ivory lounge pants and a scoop-necked cotton T-shirt, with her dark hair loose down her back, she looked more relaxed than he'd ever seen her.

"Mike." She moved forward as if to hug him, but he held back. After a brief, visible adjustment, she offered a smile instead. "I'm so very sorry about Joey. I hope you saw the flowers I sent."

"I did. Thank you." He didn't want to talk to her about Joey. He didn't want to be here. And yet, the magical pull she'd always had over him still existed. As if from a distance, he could see her beauty and calm, mysterious aura, and how it fascinated him. As if there must be something deep and thrilling underneath.

For a moment they stood at her doorway, she inside the room, he in the hallway. "Will you come in? There's something I need to tell you. It's important."

After a momentary struggle, he stepped inside the room, which had a charming, down-home interior with bluebonnet-patterned wallpaper and a patchwork quilt on the bed. The dusty scent of potpourri mingled with Angela's signature lemony body spray. The result made him a little nauseous.

Angela closed the door and gestured him toward an upholstered armchair in the corner of the room. He shook her off; he didn't want to be here long enough to occupy a chair. "I don't have much time. What's up?"

"Do you really hate me so much?" she burst out in a sudden passion, color rising in her cheeks.

"Of course not. I told you I don't hate you. But there's someone I have to go see."

"A girl? The one you were engaged to?"

He tightened his jaw. Talking to Angela about Donna was not on the agenda. "It's personal."

"I heard on the news that you got called up."

"Word travels fast."

"That's not why I came here. I just want to clarify that before we go any further."

"I didn't think that." The Call had just happened, after all. She couldn't possibly have known before leaving Chicago. He walked across to the window, which looked out on a pretty courtyard filled with flowering jacaranda trees. "I admit I'm pretty curious what could be important enough to make you travel so far from your parents."

A quick indrawn breath told him he'd hit a sore spot. He gentled his voice. "Sorry. I didn't mean that the way it sounded."

"No, I deserved that. Believe it or not, I'm not here to talk about us, or my parents, or our history. I'm here for something else."

He turned, propping his shoulder against the window frame, hands shoved in his pockets, bracing himself for . . . he didn't know what. "Shoot."

"No one in your family knows this. *I* shouldn't even know it, but I spend enough time at Chicago General that I learn things here and there. I wasn't sure if I should tell you or not, because it's a patient confidentiality issue. I decided to because this break with your family . . . well, it must be terrible."

He said nothing, waiting, his whole body tight as a drum. Warm air filtered through the screen on the window, carrying the scent of summer.

"After Joey was admitted to the hospital the last time, your father came in. He didn't see Joey, but he saw his doctor. He got his kidney function tested."

Mike frowned at her, this Madonna-like, serene woman gazing at him with wide, dark eyes. He couldn't quite put together the meaning of her words.

"He wanted to donate his kidney to Joey," Angela explained. "He didn't understand that the kidney wasn't the problem anymore, that Joey had an infection. When they told him it wouldn't help, he threw a huge fit. Threatened to sue the hospital. It was quite a scene, which was how I found out about it. They ended up asking him to donate blood, just to pacify him. He kept volunteering more, and more, until finally he was so depleted they checked him in for the night. You know how stubborn your father can be."

Grief stole his breath for a moment. His stubborn, hard-ass father. He must have felt such regret at the end, but he'd never said a word. Did he have a change of heart when it was looking so bad for Joey? When there was nothing anyone could do? No kidneys to save the day? Why hadn't he said anything when Mike was in Chicago? Mike turned back to the courtyard, staring blindly at the blossoms of the jacaranda until they blurred into a wash of lavender. "Did Joey know?" His voice was nothing but a rasp.

"I don't know."

Why hadn't she told Joey? He would have liked to know that his father wanted him to live. His fists clenched compulsively. "You should have told him."

"I'm sorry," she said defensively. "It wasn't my place. And my parents . . . you know how they . . ."

Her parents. Always her parents. Why would they object to a conversation with a dying man? With a sudden flash of clarity, he saw that Angela used the excuse of her parents to avoid anything uncomfortable. She'd done it her whole life. Maybe it wasn't her parents who had forced her—a grown woman—to end their engagement. Maybe she'd made the choice, but had been too cowardly to say so.

He cut her off with a sort of tomahawk gesture. "It doesn't matter. It doesn't matter." He turned to look at her fully, to take in her softness, her passive loveliness. Angela had been petted, adored, and cherished her whole life. Why hadn't it made her stronger? Braver?

Who knew? That wasn't his concern. Softly, quietly, the last vestiges of his adoration for Angela slipped from his heart like evaporating mist.

He rubbed the back of his neck, a little disoriented. "You know . . . Joey always forgave Dad. Knowing this would have made him happy, but for Dad, not for himself."

She offered him a Mona Lisa smile that could mean everything or nothing.

"Thank you for telling me, Angela. I do appreciate it." Time to get out of here, away from the past and into the future.

He moved to walk past her, but she seized his arm. "What about . . . us . . . ?"

Turning to face her, he breathed in her lemony scent, remembering all the times it had made him hard as stone. Now, it did nothing but make him restless. "I thought you came to tell me about my father."

"Well, yes, but . . ." Color washed across her cheekbones. "I can't marry that man, Mike. The one I told you about."

The flash of panic in her eyes clawed at him. At one time, he would have laid down his life to keep that expression off her face. He still felt the pull, the need to shield her, come to her rescue. "You don't have to do anything you don't want, Ang. I promise, it'll be okay. Just say no. Stand up for yourself."

"Yes, Mike. You're right." She twisted her hands together. "See, I can trust you. You and I, it was always so sweet. So perfect, until everything happened."

How could he fix this for her? Maybe he could talk to her parents, or help her move out of the house, or set her up with someone more to her liking. There had to be something he could do. He opened his mouth to offer to speak to her parents, then snapped it shut when he saw what she was doing.

Her hand was at the scoop neck of her loose shirt. She slid it off her shoulder, baring the pale marble of her flesh and a pink bra strap. "You're still the only man I've ever been intimate with, Mike."

He reared back. "What are you doing?"

"Reminding you," she whispered. "Remember how it was?" She slipped off the scrap of lace that was her bra strap.

He flung up his arm to shield his eyes. This was wrong, *wrong*. "Stop it, Angela. I can't."

"You can, Mike." Her wistful voice came closer. "It's okay now. I want you. I'm standing up for myself, and I want you."

He ripped his arm away from his face. She stood before him, bare skin gleaming, inches away and about to come closer. He put his hands out to stop her, then realized that would mean touching her. He didn't *want* to touch her. He didn't want her anywhere near him. All he wanted was . . .

"Don't, Angela," he warned her.

She kept coming forward. "Why not? It's perfect, Mike. Me, the Friars, everything you've wanted."

"No—"

"I know you vowed to make it to the majors to prove something. To me, to my parents. You never forgot us, did you? Now you don't have to." His back hit the door, his head knocking against the wood. Like a rap on the skull, it knocked him back to his senses.

"I'm in love with someone else."

As soon as the words left his mouth, the world shifted, became clear and filled with light.

Angela stopped short. "What did you say?"

"I love someone else." This time, it came out even louder and firmer.

She stepped back, and covered herself back up. "The girl in the news. The one you were engaged to."

"Yes. Donna MacIntyre." As soon as he said her name, her vivid presence seemed to fill the quaint little room. What kind of trouble would he and Donna get up to in a room like this? "Sorry, Angela. I shouldn't even be here right now. I should be with her."

He couldn't save Angela from her parents. That wasn't his job. His job was to get out of this suffocating room and find Donna. Tell her how he really felt about her.

"Then why are you here?" Her face had gone moon-pale.

"I guess I had to see. Had to know for sure." He ran a hand across his face, feeling as if he'd just run a marathon or something. "I'm sorry, Ange. You came all this way, and it took me until this exact moment to know that I love Donna."

She was pulling on a pale pink cardigan, hands trembling, which made him feel terrible. This was probably the first time Angela had ever pushed herself out of her comfort zone, and she'd gotten slapped down. "Is she Catholic?" she asked, surprising him.

"I don't think so." Not that it was any of Angela's business.

"Don't you think you should talk to Father Kowalski before you go any further?"

"Why the hell would I do that?"

He caught Angela's micro-flinch at his use of profanity.

"Because he knows you very well. Almost as well

as I know you. Mike, we've known each other since we were kids. Now you want to just walk away, and for someone like that? She had a child out of wedlock. She gave her baby away, and now she wants him back. What kind of person is that?" The quiet, contemptuous words crawled like chilly fingers up his spine. All of his sympathy for her drained away.

"You haven't met her. How can you judge what kind of person she is?"

"I can't, but I know what kind of person *you* are. You're the kind who rides to the rescue. That's why you would have made such a good SEAL. Are you sure you don't just feel sorry for her because of her situation? Are you sure you *really* love her, and haven't just convinced yourself that you do out of pity?"

Crush Taylor's words rang through Mike's brain. *I've put my finger on what makes you tick. Superhero Complex . . .*

Load of crap, all of it. He was no superhero. He couldn't save Joey. He couldn't fix Donna's situation. He couldn't find a solution for Angela. What he could do . . . simple. He could be true to what was in his heart. Love Donna with all his being. Play his heart out. Stand up for what he believed.

"I don't pity Donna. I respect the hell out of her. She inspires me. I can be myself with her. She's fearless, loyal, brave, trustworthy, funny, quick, and smart. She stands up when other people back down. She turned her life around when no one believed in her." He cocked his head at Angela, with her cool facade and enigmatic smile, Angela who'd never fought for anything in her life. "And I love her, so that's pretty much all there is to know."

He stuck out his hand. "I appreciate you coming all this way, Angela. I'm glad you did. You should do more of this sort of thing. Make your own destiny, don't let your parents do that for you. Good luck to you, and I sincerely wish you the best."

With a stunned expression, as if she could barely believe this was happening, she took his hand. Hers felt cool and lifeless; her touch did nothing for him.

"Good-bye, Angela."

"Good-bye, Mike."

He walked out the door and paused for a deep breath of air free from the cloying scent of rose petals, lemon body spray, and ancient history. Then he broke into a run.

Donna. He had to find Donna.

But Donna, being Donna, just had to make things difficult. She didn't answer any of his phone calls or text messages. He drove past her apartment with the idea of banging on her door—possibly with a bunch of flowers, or better yet, corn tortillas—but the lights were off and her Kia wasn't in its usual spot. He could wait, at least for one night. He knew where to find her. And when he found her, he wouldn't let her go until he told her how much he loved her, how much he'd loved her all along, without understanding that he did.

He swung by the Roadhouse, where the guys were already celebrating his call-up without him.

Dwight Conner bought the first round of Shiners. "Man, did you see the publicity y'all are getting? All this time I been working on my average, squeaking out those extra bases, running down every fly ball fool enough to enter my territory, when all I had to do was get hosed down by a hot chick. Do you think Red would aim that hose at me?"

"Don't ask me. She's a law unto herself, that girl."

Bieberman took a long, mournful swig. "I would have let Angeline hose me down, if she'd ever asked. Or even knew I existed. I think she thought I was an intern."

"Sorry, bro. Her loss." T.J. clapped a hand on his shoulder. "You should do what Solo did—take a vow. Worked for him—he has women fighting over him."

"Does it count if it's not an actual vow? If I'm just celibate because that's the way it worked out?"

"No." Stark signaled for another round. "That just means you're a loser."

Bieberman's face crumpled, and Mike directed a scowl at the big slugger. Did he have to kick the guy when he was down?

"Don't worry about it," Trevor continued. "I'm going to let you follow me around and learn a thing or two."

Though the rest of the crew scoffed loudly, Bieberman brightened. "Awesome possum."

Trevor held up a warning finger. "First thing, don't say 'awesome possum.' Or 'easy peasy,' or anything goofy like that. Don't talk about Deepak Chopra or the statistical likelihood of a curveball hitting the inside corner. Don't jabber on about—"

A brunette with dark skin, a streak of purple in her hair, and a diamond stud in one nostril swiveled her barstool in their direction. "Did someone mention Deepak Chopra? OMG, I love him. Have you seen his new DVD?"

For a spellbound moment, the Catfish all gazed at this vision of beauty, who looked like she'd come to the Roadhouse straight from a yoga class. Mike held his breath. Trevor had been the one to mention Deepak Chopra; the next move was his. Bieberman was blinking rapidly, as if he could barely believe his eyes—or maybe his eyelids were spasming.

With a sigh that held a large dose of regret, Trevor clapped a hand on Bieberman's back and guided him forward. "Hello, gorgeous woman. Meet Jim Leiberman, shortstop, boy genius, and philosopher extraordinaire. Leiberman, meet a beautiful stranger who wants to talk about Deepak Chopra. Now go. Both of you. We have on-base percentages and beer brands to discuss."

"I'll drink to that." Mike raised his bottle and everyone toasted as Leiberman and the brunette began throwing around words like "universal consciousness" and "inner power." "Stark, let me ask you something. Why do you act like an asshole ninety percent of the time, when you're maybe not so bad after all?"

"Maybe?" Trevor's crystal-green eyes glittered, while Dwight Conner propped a brotherly arm on Stark's shoulder.

"A little something you should know about Stark." Conner grinned. "Whatever you think you know about him, think again. The dude's like a master spy. He oughta work for the CIA or something. Always thinking. Always plotting. Not a bad guy to have around if you're in a jam."

Trevor raised an eyebrow, took a swig from his Shiner, but said nothing.

"Huh." Mike eyed him with new respect. "Well, here's to you, Stark. May they keep falling where they ain't." After more clinking of bottles, another question occurred to him. "The armbands. Whose idea was that?"

The guys exchanged glances.

"Why?" T.J. asked. "Were you okay with it?"

"It was cool. Yeah, really cool. I never got to say it because of how the game played out, but yeah. Meant a lot."

T.J. jerked his chin toward Dwight Conner. "All his idea. Came in with the armbands and handed them out before you showed up."

Mike swung toward the outfielder. "You did it?"

"I had a brother who died," Conner explained, his usual smile slipping. "Got in with a bad crowd. DUI. Nothing I could do. I know how it feels, man."

They all shared a moment of silence for Dwight's lost brother. Mike felt the presence of Joey so strongly and sweetly he nearly cried right there in the Roadhouse.

The Catfish might be just temporary teammates who might or might not join him in San Diego someday . . . but at that moment, they felt like brothers.

At nine the next morning, Donna nervously followed her new lawyer, a very sharp black woman named Gloria Gaynor—yes, after the singer, she'd informed Donna—into Judge Quinn's courtroom. The first thing Ms. Gaynor had done was file for a new judge, but no ruling had yet come down on that. In the meantime, the process had been allowed to continue.

Harvey and Bonita sat on the other side of the

aisle, holding hands. *Gag.* Even though they'd decided to postpone their wedding until the court case was settled, obviously they were still working the "stable couple" angle. This made Donna's flash engagement look even worse, of course. Ms. Gaynor had instructed her to talk about Mike as little as possible in the hopes that the judge would forget the whole embarrassing thing had ever happened.

Everyone rose to their feet as Judge Quinn entered. He wore a black robe and a stern expression to go with his iron-gray hair. Early on, Donna had tried a mild joke on him, but had quickly learned the man had no sense of humor, at least when he was on the bench. Amid a general shuffling of feet and scraping of chair legs on the floor, he sat behind the big desk at the front of the courtroom and flipped open his ledger.

"Bailiff?"

The bailiff, a large Hispanic man with a tattoo circling his arm, brought him the docket. Donna's right foot danced with impatience and her stomach did a slow burn. *Just get on with it.* Get Zack back. Get Zack back.

The judge gave a dry little cough and flipped through a few pages of legal documents. "In the matter of Zackary Hannigan, Donna MacIntyre versus Harvey Hannigan, I've unfortunately had to revise my decision due to ever-changing circumstances. This case has garnered more attention than most child custody cases that don't involve a religious or controversial element. Then again, we don't usually have baseball players getting involved, or newspapers writing articles. This has made it more difficult to come to a fair decision."

He fixed Donna with a stern look, but she lifted her chin, refusing to be cowed. Of course she'd try everything possible to win Zack back.

"Although I'm sure the end of your engagement was difficult," the judge said dryly, "I welcomed the relief from the media attention. Finally, I'd be able to assess the situation objectively, as it is, rather than trying to discern the reality through the cloud of gossip. I saw a mother who very much loves her child, and who has taken solid steps to provide a good home. The natural presumption that a child belongs with his mother seemed well-supported. On the other hand, I saw little evidence to back up the father's contention that the mother's past irresponsibility disqualified her from taking her natural place in the child's life. I reviewed testimony provided by the father regarding her hospitalization for depression, and it seemed clear that it was an isolated incident caused by her pregnancy."

Donna cast a sidelong look at Harvey, who toyed with the edge of the table, looking shamefaced. *Ha! You sold me out for nothing, Harv.*

The judge continued. "In addition, the Hannigans have expressed the desire for the boy's parents to take responsibility for his care, now that they're both more mature."

Ms. Gaynor squeezed her hand and the tension in the courtroom rose another degree. Donna's heart leaped into her throat. *This was it.* She was about to get Zack back.

"Then last night I turned on my television to find the very mother whose case I'm about to decide making a national spectacle of herself. Prancing around a baseball field with a hose. Forcing the first forfeit of a game in Catfish history. Consorting with the very same player she was formerly engaged to, the one who created the inappropriate atmosphere that already caused so many problems. And I had to ask myself, can Donna MacIntyre really be trusted to offer Zackary the kind of stable life he's accustomed to? In this case, it's not a question of taking a mother's son away from her, since she hasn't been his principal caretaker. It's a question of whether she can provide a better environment than the one she herself designated as best for him when he was a newborn."

His grim gaze traveled across the faces arrayed before him. Donna knew that hers was frozen. She couldn't move a muscle. If she did, she'd collapse into a ball of dust.

"And so, with a heavy heart, I must rule that Zackary Hannigan remain with his paternal grandparents. All parties will begin a transition period moving toward full custody by Harvey Hannigan. This phase-in will happen over the next year. Donna MacIntyre will retain visitation rights at the discretion of the custodial parent, but is welcome to repetition the court should her circumstances change."

Ms. Gaynor shot to her feet. "Your Honor, if your opinion is based on one incident, surely you should give us a chance to explain that incident."

"That will not be helpful or necessary. My ruling is final. Bailiff, who's next?"

Blood pounded in Donna's ears, a roar that got louder and louder until she couldn't hear, couldn't see, couldn't speak. Things were happening around her, people getting up, shuffling down the aisle, putting papers in briefcases, touching her shoulder, murmuring things in her ear, lifting her to her feet, guiding her forward, but she was barely conscious of any of it.

She'd lost. Lost Zack. Lost everything.

Chapter 26

THE NEXT MORNING Mike tried calling Donna again. No answer. Was she trying to avoid him? That didn't seem like Donna's style. She was much more likely to rip into him. He tried her a few more times throughout the morning while he took care of some business related to his call-up. Talked to his agent, notified his landlord, talked to the travel coordinator at the Friars . . . and called his father, something he hadn't done since their falling out.

"Dad. It's Mike. Just wanted to let you know that I've been called up to the Friars. There's going to be a Solo behind home plate in Friar Stadium. I'm going to send you and Mama tickets, if you want to come."

Pietro Solo might have been an ornery old patriarch, but he was also Italian, which in this case meant a gush of emotion and family pride. When Mike hung up, he had to blink away tears.

Damn, this was getting to be a habit.

By the afternoon, when he still hadn't heard from Donna, he hopped in his car and sped over to her apartment. Her tiny Kia was parked at the curb out front. Home, but not returning his calls. Bad sign.

But he probably deserved that, since he hadn't returned her "I love you" when it counted. He loped to the door and rapped on it.

"Donna! Are you in there? It's me, Mike. I really need to talk to you."

No answer.

"Angela's gone. Will you please listen to me? Give me a chance to explain?"

Still no answer. He pounded on the door.

"I'm not leaving until you talk to me. And that's going to cause a huge problem for the Friars because they want me in San Diego on Thursday. Please, Donna, just open the door."

Finally it swung open. Mike took a shocked step back and nearly stumbled down the staircase.

It was Donna . . . and yet not Donna. No spirit shone from her eyes, no expression animated her face. Her shoulders slumped forward, her head drooped. She looked as if all the life had evaporated out of her—like the inland Salton Sea, where nothing remained but salt. "San Diego?"

"I got the Call."

"Congratulations." But the word was flat, with no joy or even interest behind it. No dimple flashed . . . definitely no hug or kiss.

"What's wrong?"

She turned away. He followed her inside, which seemed to make no difference to her one way or the other. When she reached her couch, she curled onto it like a baby kitten and pulled a woven cotton blanket over her head.

"Nothing." Her muffled voice barely reached him. "Just go away."

"I'm not going anywhere." Carefully, he sat on the edge of the couch. "Not until you tell me what's going on." Something told him this went beyond their relationship. "Is it Zack? Did something happen?" Sudden horror seized him. "Is Zack okay? At least tell me that."

"Zack's—" She couldn't finish the sentence at first. Then, under his patient questioning, the story spilled out in heartbroken bits and pieces. By the end of it, he was pacing around her living room, practically bouncing off the walls, his head about ready to explode. "This is my fault, Donna. I got into it with Yazmer. I got the game forfeited. None of that was your doing. How could the judge make you pay for my fuckup? I'm going to talk to him. I'll take the blame, I'll do whatever it takes."

She inched the blanket down her head, so her forehead and a strand of tangled red peeked through. "Mike Solo to the rescue? I don't think you can fix this."

God, even her voice sounded different. So hopeless. "When's the last time you ate, Donna?"

She dragged the blanket back into place. "Go away."

He crouched down next to her. "Honey, how are you supposed to fight this if you don't keep your energy up?"

"Go away."

"I already said I'm not going anywhere, so you can stop saying that. We have to figure out a strategy. What does your lawyer say? I'll call her right now. What's her number?"

"Mike." She shoved the blankets off her and

scrambled to a sitting position. For the first time, a bit of her old fire came back. "You don't understand anything. I'm not going to fight it. The judge made his decision, and I'm not going to waste everyone's time and money trying to change it."

"But what about Zack?"

She plunged back under the blanket, stuffing it against her ears as if to block him out. But that flash of the old fiery Donna filled him with determination. No way was he going to let her disappear into some kind of pit of despair. He tugged at the blanket. "Come on, Donna. Talk to me. What about Zack?"

When she still said nothing, he rocked her body back and forth with a hand on her shoulder.

"What about Get Zack Back? Have you forgotten about that?"

"What about it?" She cried passionately, yanking the covers off her again. "I was wrong. Zack's better off with them. The judge is right. They're *all* right. I don't deserve to have him. I'm irresponsible, I don't take things seriously, I'm too impulsive, I don't think before I speak, I don't plan things out. What kind of person aims a hose at a baseball field and doesn't think that it *might get wet*?"

A sound escaped him that might have been a laugh, if he hadn't been so caught up in her torrent of words. "The kind of person who was trying to stop a fight—"

She shoved at him. "Don't try to defend me. I don't deserve it. I don't deserve Zack. I'll keep seeing him whenever they let me, but he needs better parents than me. I want what's best for Zack. They were right all along, all of them, and I've been an idiot, thinking I could be a good mom."

"Oh really? Bonita was right? Bonita's better than you? A better mom for Zack?"

Red flashed across her cheeks like a bullfighter's cape. He watched the struggle play across her features, wishing he could help, but knowing it was something she had to work out herself. "Maybe she is," she said eventually in a thin, strained voice. "She's . . . organized."

"Yeah. Very organized. She'll get him to all his appointments on time. Donna, you're talking about Zack here. Fun, bouncy Zack. He's practically a human beach ball. Do you really want Bonita raising him?"

"He'll be with Harvey too."

"Yeah. Harvey. I'm pretty sure Bonita picks his underwear for him and decides how short to trim his nose hairs. Come on, Donna. Get over yourself."

Whoops. In the next second he realized that was the wrong thing to say. "*Get over myself?* That's your big advice?" She kicked out a foot at him. "Get off my couch. Get out of my apartment."

He managed to evade her foot but landed on his ass on the floor. "Donna, I'm sorry, that came out wrong. I didn't mean it the way it sounded."

"I know what you meant." She scrambled off the couch while he struggled to regain his feet. "You meant that I should fight back. Do something. Toughen up."

Using his catcher's thigh muscles to their best advantage, he finally managed to spring to his feet, only to back away before the force of her approach.

"I've had to be tough my whole life, Mike, and look where it's gotten me. I'm done being tough. I'm done fighting. I want to lie on my couch and cry my eyes out the way I deserve."

His back hit the front door of her apartment. "Donna, I used stupid words, but my basic point is, this isn't really about you. It's about Zack. And you know as well as I do that he needs you."

"I don't know that. I thought I did, but I was wrong. Ask my so-called family. Ask anyone in Kilby. They'll all tell you the same thing. Donna MacIntyre is unfit to be a mother."

She elbowed him aside—her strength astonished him—and yanked the door open. "Go away."

"Just listen—"

"*Go away.*"

"Donna—" Somehow he was outside, standing on her landing, and the door was closing in his face. And he hadn't even said what he came to say. "I love you," he managed before the door swung shut.

Slam.

He stood on her landing for a long moment, feeling the heat of embarrassment roll through him in waves. What sort of god-awful moment was that to say something so important?

He should leave. He wasn't helping matters, and he'd just made an utter ass of himself. But he couldn't seem to make his feet move. He needed to be here, near Donna. He needed to convince her how much he loved her . . .

She opened the door a crack. "What did you just say?"

"I love you. I meant it. I want to help you. Be here for you."

An expression of utter desolation twisted her face,

or at least the part of it he could see through the crack in the door. Her eyelids lowered, then lifted again, revealing reddened, hopeless eyes. All her spirit—every speck—had been extinguished. "Horrible timing, Solo. I . . . can't. I just can't. Now leave me alone. Please."

Mike left. He had to. He wanted to tear something apart—anything—and he didn't want it to be something connected to Donna. He drove to the Roadhouse, where a few mid-afternoon drinkers were straggling in. After ordering a Lone Star, he sat on a stool and nursed it for a time. He didn't really want to get drunk; mostly he wanted a fight and was half hoping some obligingly nasty members of the Wade family would drop in.

They didn't. Instead, he passed the time thinking about Donna, her bright spirit, her fierce grief. He thought about Joey, gone from him forever. There was death, and then there was living death, and that's what he'd seen on Donna's face. He thought of Crush's words, and Angela's, and his so-called Superhero Complex. He was no superhero. Nothing he did or could have done would have saved Joey.

But Donna . . . that inner voice was screaming at him loud and clear. There was no way on this earth he was going to stand by and watch Donna disappear from sheer grief. An idea flashed across his mind, then vanished. He needed to think. He needed his comfort zone, the place where he did all his best thinking.

He needed home plate.

He placed a coaster on the bar top, then arranged

four more in a rough approximation of home plate. There, that was better. He conjured the adrenaline of a game, the alertness he experienced when he went into his crouch, the single-minded focus. Donna's whole story rushed back to him.

1. The possibly corrupt judge.
2. The ruthlessness of the Wades.
3. The superhero that he wasn't.
4. The kind of man he really wanted to be.

And there it was. A plan.

He placed a phone call to Crush Taylor and explained what he needed. Crush promised to get back to him.

He gestured to the bartender, whom he recognized from the night of the infamous brawl. "Todd, right? You're a friend of Donna MacIntyre, aren't you?"

"Of course. Went to high school with her." Todd narrowed his eyes suspiciously. "If you're looking for trouble, I can't help you."

"I'm not. I'm looking for her father. Do you know where his shop is?"

"Why?"

"Is it top secret information?" At Todd's frown, he passed a hand over his face. "Sorry, dude. Rough day. I need to talk to him about Donna."

Todd swiped some dirty glasses off the bar and piled them in the dishwasher. "You're probably going to the wrong man. He never seemed like he knew she existed."

"Yeah. I picked up on that. Seriously, I'm not looking to hurt Donna. I want to help her, if she'll let me."

Todd gave him directions to Mac's Automotive Repairs, with one last warning to be good to Donna. Thinking that Donna had a lot more support than she realized, Mike drove to her father's shop. Exactly as she'd described him, Mac was lying on his back on a creeper under a gray Saab. Only his legs, from the knees down, were visible. Mike crouched down and spoke into the dark undercarriage of the Saab.

"Mike Solo here. Just want to let you know that I love Donna and intend to get our wedding back on track, if she'll have me. And also—your daughter's in trouble. She's gotten a raw deal, and we need to do something about it."

One knee bent up, and slowly Mac emerged from underneath the car. "What are you talking about?"

"Righting a wrong."

The older man rubbed his forehead, leaving a streak of grease. To be honest, Mike couldn't see much resemblance between this low-key man and the ball of energy that was Donna. "Might make trouble with my wife."

"Not sure I can help you there."

"Yah. Well . . . just tell me when and where. I'll be there." Mac gave him a little finger salute, then resumed his position on the creeper and slid under the car. Mike had to smile. If that's what passed for a talk in the MacIntyre family, they could learn a few things from the Solos.

On his way out of Mac's shop, Mike got a text from Crush. *Used my in with the mayor to get you a meeting with the judge. Be there in fifteen minutes. He can give you five. Be careful. He's known as a hard-ass and he doesn't suffer fools.*

Five minutes. Jesus, Mary, and Joseph, what could he do in five minutes? Well, it would have to be enough. He remembered very well what Donna had said about Judge Quinn. That the Wades held something over him, something they used to make him do what they wanted. Donna had also mentioned that he was unmarried, with no kids, and no possible way of sympathizing with her situation.

Mike could do that math. He had a feeling he knew where the judge was coming from—or at least close enough to empathize.

He raced into Quinn's chambers with seconds to spare. The judge, gray-haired and immaculate, wearing his black robe like a full-body frown, barely glanced up from the papers he was reviewing. "As I told Mayor Trent, I have very little time, so don't waste it," he greeted Mike in his scratchy, buzz-saw voice.

"Thank you, Judge. I'll get right to the point. I don't know you and you don't know me. But I do know what it's like to keep something secret. In my case, it was my brother. It took me a long time to tell people he was gay. I told myself it was for his sake, and for my parents', and it was. Partly. I had this idea about who I was supposed to be. I had a hard time letting it go, even after I left the Navy. But there was also a side of me that didn't want to deal with crap from the other ballplayers. I didn't want the ribbing, or the behind-my-back whispers, let alone the outright homophobia. So I kept my mouth shut—until I couldn't anymore, and did my PSA for Equal Rights in Sports. The day that PSA first aired was one of the best days of my life. I got more support and more props than I ever imagined in my most crazy optimistic moments. And then, when my brother passed on, my teammates came through. Never expected that. If I hadn't done the PSA, none of it would have happened."

Judge Quinn showed absolutely no expression. Maybe he'd offended the hell out of the man. Who knew? But Donna had already lost Zack—she had nothing more to lose. He checked his watch. Two more minutes.

"All I want to say is this. I don't know what your story is, Judge. I don't care. It's your business. But to protect your secret to the extent of letting the Wades threaten you into doing what they want . . . it's not worth it. Not only is it not worth it, but you could be missing out on something amazing. That's it. That's all I've got. I'll just finish by saying that Donna Mac-Intyre deserves a completely fair hearing, away from the influence of the Wades. And if she didn't get that, you're the only one who can do something about it."

Not a muscle moved on the judge's face. Not a single blink of an eye. Mike inhaled a deep breath, then released it. He gave a little bow of his head, and began backing toward the door. "Thanks for listening, Your Honor."

Had he listened? Had he even heard? It was impossible to tell.

"If I offended you, please don't take it out on Donna. She doesn't even know I'm here."

Finally the judge opened his mouth. "Close the door behind you."

Okay then. Mike hurried out of the chambers, out of the courthouse, past the metal detector and the guards, his heart pounding like a drum the entire time.

It wasn't superhero material, but it was all he had.

Now he could only pray that something had gotten past that judge's poker face. He'd never seen anyone school their expression so thoroughly—and he was used to studying batters and pitchers for tells. After all this was over, maybe he could take Judge Quinn to Las Vegas and clean up at the craps table.

Time was doing something funny. Long hours passed with Donna barely noticing, then things would speed up to hyper-space pace and before she could blink, it would be a different time of day—light instead of dark, or vice versa. The Dental Miracles office called because she'd missed a shift.

"Sick," she told Ricki, since more than one word felt beyond her ability.

"Too sick to call in sick?" Ricki asked skeptically.

"I called." She'd left a message with someone, but she couldn't even remember who. "Sorry."

She called in sick with the Catfish too. When the promotions manager called back, she didn't answer. Someone else would have to hose down the ballplayers from now on. Count her out of that one.

Sadie called. Then she called again. Donna simply didn't have the heart to call her back. She'd be supportive and sympathetic and everything a friend should be, but Donna didn't trust herself not to lose it the way she had with Mike.

Mike. At the thought of him, something stirred in the empty hole where her heart used to live. She could barely look at him while she told him the utter extent of her failure. And then his "get over yourself" . . .

Oh, she just wanted to strangle him. He didn't know. *He didn't know.*

But he said he loved her. He'd said that. Maybe it was some kind of attempt at a wakeup call. A slap in the face. Shock therapy.

I love you. I mean it.

He'd looked like he meant it. He'd looked pale when he said it, completely sober, his eyes vulnerable pools of green. Not a bit of playfulness anywhere, no teasing, no joking. Straight up—*I love you.*

And she'd shut the door on him. She had to. How could she love anyone, how could she *be loved* by anyone, when she'd completely crashed and burned as a human being?

Time passed.

A bowl of Ramen noodle soup was consumed. By her, or at least by the body formerly inhabited by Donna MacIntyre.

The phone rang. She answered by mistake, or maybe on the off chance that it was Mike and he'd tell her that preposterous thing he'd said before, about loving her.

It wasn't Mike. It was her new lawyer.

Before Gloria Gaynor could say a word, Donna hung up and turned her phone off.

She wandered back into the living room and peeled the giant poster of J.J. Watt, the Texans player with the constantly bloodied nose, off the wall. Rolled it up and stashed it behind the football beanbag chair. She went through her entire apartment and removed every stitch of football-themed paraphernalia. Who had she been kidding? No wonder the judge had seen right through her. She added all her navy-blue blazers and boxy pantsuits to the pile. No point in hanging on to those. If she ever went to court again, she'd wear a freaking leopard-print cat suit and six-inch stilettos. Things couldn't turn out any worse, after all.

After that, she hit a road bump of anger and spent some agonized time pacing around the living room, reliving those moments in the courtroom. *Can Donna MacIntyre provide Zackary with a better environment than the one she herself designated as best for her son? . . . It is with a heavy heart that I rule that custody remain with the Hannigans . . . transition period to Harvey Hannigan . . . at the custodial parent's discretion . . .*

She knew what "at the custodial parent's discretion" meant. It meant Bonita holding all the cards, pulling all the strings. Even if Harvey had promised that she'd still get to see Zack, it didn't matter what Harvey said. It only mattered what Bonita said.

She decides how short to trim his nose hairs.

Donna smiled despite herself. Solo sure had a way with words. She dropped onto her couch, to the place where he'd sat, fire in his eyes, telling her to fight for Zack. She could practically feel him there, his big body bent toward hers, worried lines creasing his face.

He cared about her.

He loved her.

The truth sank into her marrow and spread like sunlight. Mike Solo loved her. And she loved him . . . God, she'd loved him for ages, since last season sometime, and the more she knew him, the more she loved him. How could she have pushed him away like that? What was wrong with her?

She sprang to her feet. Phone. She had to find her phone and call him. Tell him she was sorry, so sorry, and that she loved him with every flawed, imperfect corner of her being, and that it wasn't his fault she couldn't be a normal human being. Flying toward the kitchen, she heard a knock on the door. She didn't want to see anyone—only Mike. And it wouldn't be Mike because she'd sent him away.

Her phone was under the table. She crawled toward it, turned it on, and backed out, watching her phone blink to life. A text message flashed. From Mike. *Answer your door!*

She clambered from beneath her kitchen table, ran toward the door, and flung it open. There he was, big as life, beautiful as the wide open sky, a huge grin lighting up his face. With one arm he propped the door open all the way, as if he was worried she'd slam it shut again.

"Listen to me, Donna. You have to come with me. Special hearing. New judge. Quinn recused himself and withdrew his ruling based on the pending request for a new judge. It's just a technicality, but we'll take what we can get. Your lawyer's been trying to call you. We have about twenty minutes to get there."

She gaped at him, trying to make sense of that torrent of words. "New hearing?"

"Yes. New hearing. You have another shot at this, if you want it."

A powerful surge of hope made her sway. Mike steadied her with both hands on her shoulders. Slowly, thoroughly, he studied her, as if seeing every hidden corner of her soul. "It's up to you, Donna. Are you ready to do this?"

Was she ready? All the pieces of her past sifted through her mind like a kaleidoscope. *Her missing mother, her stepmother, her absent dad.* "I pretty much raised myself, you know. And it wasn't enough. I wanted better for Zack."

He waited patiently.

The hospital, her depression, the bright smile of her son.

"I knew I had to work really hard to be what he needed." *The Shark, the little guesthouse, the shelves of child-rearing books.*

Still he waited, not rushing her. He was like a rock, standing before her. Standing with her. A sense of absolute certainty flooded through her. "Yes, I'm ready," she whispered. Then, more loudly, "Let's go."

"Good." A smile curving his lips, he scanned her body, which was swathed in an old T-shirt that sagged to her knees and featured the statement, *Don't feel bad, laundry. Nobody's doing me either.*

"Sorry, babe, you can't wear that."

She looked down, and let out a giggle, half hysterical, half nervous. Could she handle a second chance? Could she manage to not screw this up?

"Come on, my one and only love," Mike crooned. "Pick something to wear and let's boogie."

Chapter 27

MIKE PRACTICALLY THREW her into his Land Rover. A little dazed by the speed at which everything was happening, Donna couldn't stop staring at him. He looked as if he'd swallowed an entire galaxy of stars, while she'd been hanging out in a black hole.

"Did I miss something?" she finally asked him. "Aren't you suspended? How can you be going to the Friars if you're suspended?"

"Sweet cheeks, that was about a hundred years ago. While I was chasing after you, Duke found me. They want me, Yazmer issues and all."

She beamed at him. It felt strange to feel her cheeks stretching in a smile after her descent into misery. "That's fantastic, Mike. You must have been so excited."

"Well, not really. I was worried about you. But I couldn't find you, so I went and saw Angela."

Her smile snapped off her face. "I thought you said she was gone."

"Yes, but it was good that she came, because we're square now. She came to give me something, and now we're even."

"Give you what?"

"Information. She told me that my father tried to donate a kidney to Joey. No one knows, she just happened to find out at the hospital. He's not the coldhearted ass I thought he was. Not completely, anyway."

"That is big news." So Angela had flown to Kilby to bring Mike news that could change his life and reunite him with his family. *Beat that, Donna Mac-Intyre.* "He never told you?"

"Nope. Maybe he didn't want me to know. He's a proud man. Doesn't think he has to explain himself to anyone."

"That was nice of Angela. I mean, to tell you. And come all that way. Of course, there's e-mail and phones and texts and Facebook and Snapchat and—"

He gave her a wicked sidelong glance. "Jealous, Red?"

"What? No, just concerned about her carbon footprint. The amount of fuel it takes to fly to Kilby from Chicago . . . has she no concern for the planet?"

He let out a snort of laughter. "You did hear me, right? When I said I love you."

Heat burned across her face. "I . . . yes . . ."

Grabbing her left hand, he pulled it to his lips, where he could pepper it with kisses. "I can't pull the car over because we might miss your hearing. But I meant it, Donna. I love you. I'm crazy about you. I wish I could have made it more romantic but you did slam the door in my face and my options were limited."

"I'm sorry about that. I was . . ."

"I know. The look on your face . . . it just about

killed me. No sparkle, no life . . . it was like you were gone. My beautiful firecracker Donna, gone. I couldn't stand that. Even if you never want to see me again after this, I had to do something."

That sounded kind of ominous. "Why would I never want to see you again after this? It's just a hearing, right?"

An uneasy expression crossed his face as they pulled into the Kilby Courthouse parking lot. "Just a hearing. Yes."

"Mike? What's going on?"

"I told you. It's another chance to make your case for custody of Zack."

Why would that make him so nervous? Eyeing him suspiciously, she got out of the car and smoothed her knee-length peach seersucker skirt over her thighs. On top she wore an elbow-length cream cotton sweater over a lacy button-down shirt. No blue blazers, no leopard print, but a totally appropriate outfit that suited her style and also took into account how cold the courthouse got when someone forgot to turn down the air-conditioning.

"You have something up your sleeve."

"Can you just . . . *will* you just . . . trust me?" He closed the car door and jingled the keys nervously in one big hand. Even though he towered over her, tough and muscular, a bruise courtesy of Yazmer purpling his cheekbone, what really got her was the uncertainty in his green eyes.

"Mike Solo, I've got big news for you." She marched up to him and grabbed the lapels of his jacket—the same one he'd worn to Crush's fund-raiser, tight across his wide shoulders. "There are very few people in this world I trust—maybe only two—but you are one of them." She pulled his head down and fastened her lips to his. The sensation—such intimate contact after thinking it was over, forever—just about blew the top of her head off. "And I love you. Whatever happens in there, whether I get Zack back or I have to try again in the future, I love you. I love that you made all this happen even though you have plenty going on in your own life. Geez, Mike. Your brother . . . the team . . . the Friars . . . I can't believe you're even here!"

"Well, believe it, baby. Where else would I be? If you need something, I will always be there. Even if all you need is a little . . ." He winked, and made a sound with his cheek that was probably supposed to be dirty, but wound up being terminally cute instead.

"Can we talk about that part later?" She took his hand. "I'm dying of curiosity about what I'm going to see when I walk into that courtroom."

They headed for the courthouse, with its stucco, Spanish-style facade. "Maybe you'll see a closet. With a closed door. And you won't be able to resist."

"Of course I won't. Especially if it contains a mop bucket. Do you know that the scent of bleach water always makes me think of you?"

"In that case, you can look forward to a very clean house in your future."

A shiver shot through her. "Let's not talk about the future yet. I can't think about anything in the future until I know for sure what's happening with Zack."

"Got it." They hurried up the steps and through the metal detector. Donna took a moment to compose herself before pushing open the door to Courtroom 5. She needed to present a mature, poised appearance. The last thing she wanted was to burst in like a slacker student late for an exam.

Inside the room, she skidded to a halt with a gasp that echoed through the courtroom. "Dad?"

Mac, in a battered old leather jacket that must have dated from his wannabe cowboy days, swung around at the sound of her voice.

"*Mom?*" Lorraine MacIntyre sat in the row behind Donna's dad; she put a finger to her lips to shush her.

For a moment, Donna was so confused she wanted to turn and flee. But Mike's solid chest was in the way. She leaned against him, drawing strength from his warmth and the big hand that firmly gripped her shoulder. She whispered to him, "What are they . . ."

"I called them," he rumbled in her ear. "They're here to support you. No need for a heart attack."

"It's not a heart attack, it's more of an out-of-body experience." Her mother—her wild, crazy, gypsy mother—wore an elegant suede jacket with braided trim. She might have borrowed it from some band's wardrobe department, but she pulled it off. Her wild red hair was tucked into a French twist, and she looked at least marginally respectable.

Another face caught her eye. Beth Gilbert. Next to her sat Caleb and Sadie, who was making frantic faces at Donna. The message was clear: *Get a grip on yourself because shit is about to get real.*

"All rise for Judge Galindez," intoned the bailiff.

A Hispanic woman in a black robe, with silver streaks running through her dark hair, entered the courtroom and sat down with a flourish.

"Come on," said Mike. He pulled her toward the front table, where Donna slid in next to Ms. Gaynor just in time to join everyone else as they resumed their seats.

"Cutting it a little close," said the lawyer through gritted teeth.

"Sorry," said Mike, leaning forward from the row behind them. "We had a few things to sort out first. Wardrobe emergency." He winked at Donna.

"Is everyone here?" Ms. Gaynor asked Mike.

"Looks like it. Where's Bonita?"

Donna glanced over at the other side of the courtroom, where Harvey sat next to his lawyer. The Hannigans sat in the next row, right behind him.

"She must be with Zack," whispered Donna, a sick feeling making her stomach sink. Possession was nine-tenths of the law, she'd heard it said. That didn't apply to children, but she knew that courts gave extra weight to stability—to continuing whatever situation the child was in as long as it wasn't harmful.

Judge Galindez rattled through a quick summary of how the hearing had been transferred to her. "I just read through the case history last night. I understand that strong emotions are involved, and that a careful decision is of utmost importance. My impression from the case notes is that most of the argument centered on the character of the mother, Donna MacIntyre." She motioned to Ms. Gaynor. "Let me hear from you first."

Ms. Gaynor rose to her feet. "Thank you, Judge. You are correct in your assessment, which is why we've called a number of witnesses here today. We don't believe the case should have taken that turn, but since it did, mostly in the form of gossip and innuendo, we'd relish the opportunity to hear from some of the people who know Donna best."

"Very well. Call your first witness."

"I'd like to call Beth Gilbert to the stand. My client worked for the Gilbert family taking care of their son for the first eight months of his life. If anyone can speak to her potential as a mother, she can."

The opposing lawyer stood up. "Your Honor, we object to this list of witnesses, which we received only yesterday. We can provide an equally impressive parade of witnesses who will say that Harvey Hannigan is an excellent father."

"The relevance, Your Honor," said Ms. Gaynor, "is that the child's father chose to make my client's past history and character the principal element of the case."

"I'll allow it," said the judge. "Both sides will have ample opportunity to question the witnesses."

Beth Gilbert, looking every bit the wealthy Texas socialite that she was, took the stand, swore on the Holy Bible to tell the truth, and proceeded to describe someone Donna barely recognized. "I'm the first one to tell you that my son Todd is a handful. He never stops moving, and now that he's beginning to talk, he never stops that."

"He's talking?" Donna asked eagerly, leaning forward.

"Yes, he is! In the swing. His first word was 'fast,' at least that's what we think."

The judge banged the gavel. "Can we stay on topic, please?"

"Yes, Judge. I never saw Donna lose her patience

or be anything less than cheerful with Todd. After she left, we had to hire three people to replace her. No one else could handle him full-time the way she did. She's a treasure. All my friends' children love her too. We were crushed when she left."

When it was his turn to cross-examine Beth Gilbert, Harvey's lawyer jumped on that opening. "You said you were crushed when she left, that she left you in the lurch. Is that the action of a responsible caretaker?"

Beth bristled. "She gave us plenty of notice and explained why she was leaving. We couldn't offer her full benefits, which she needed in order to regain custody of her little boy. She's come back to help us out several times since then, even though she now has a new job. She's expressed the desire to remain part of Todd's life even though she's no longer employed by us. We found her actions completely understandable and responsible."

The lawyer quickly wrapped up his cross-examination after that, and Beth stepped out of the witness box. She flashed Donna a thumbs-up as she took her seat a few rows back. Next up was Donna's mother.

"At first I was surprised to get a call from Donna's friend," she said, with that musical voice trained to reach the back of a stadium. "I'm not much of a maternal example, seeing as I ran off on my family about twelve years ago."

Donna cast a look at her father, whose gaze was fixed on his ex-wife as if she were an angel floating back from heaven. Oh my God. *He still loves her*, she realized. No wonder Carrie hated any mention of Lorraine MacIntyre. No wonder Carrie hated *Donna*—a constant reminder of the woman who left. Being married to someone who loved someone else? Nightmare. Exactly what she'd vowed never to do. Exactly why she hadn't wanted to accept Mike's proposal.

And that's what Carrie had been living with. Perhaps for the first moment in her life, she felt empathy for the woman she'd spent her teen years battling.

Her mother was telling a story in that riveting voice, holding the entire courtroom spellbound. She was such a compelling performer, so comfortable in the spotlight, with everyone hanging on her every word. Donna had to smile; she knew how that felt now, thanks to Crush Taylor and the Catfish.

"The doctor diagnosed her with an extreme case of situational depression related to her pregnancy. I was told that her youth and lack of family support were both contributing factors. By the time she came to me, she was so ill I insisted she be hospitalized. They put her on anti-depressants. She took them even though she made me do all kinds of research on the Internet first. She was afraid they'd hurt the baby."

Donna drew in a soft breath. She'd forgotten about that. Even though the doctor had said the medication wouldn't harm the fetus, in her fearful state, she hadn't believed him.

"When the Hannigans and I started talking about what would happen after Donna gave birth, about giving the baby up for adoption, that's when Donna came back to life. She swore up and down that she'd never sign anything like that. And even though she was sick as a dog, weak, barely in her right mind, she was so fierce about it that we believed her."

Donna realized she was holding her breath. She'd never heard her mother talk about all this before. By the time she'd come out of the depression, Lorraine MacIntyre had been back on the road.

"Every one of us, Harvey, Pete and Sue Hannigan, Mac, myself, all of us are only here today because Donna refused to give Zack up for adoption. No one else had any problem with it, in fact, everyone thought it would be best. Everyone except Donna. Even in the worst, most ill moment of her life, Donna refused to let Zack go. She always wanted him. And I believe that everything she's done since then has been with the goal of making a good life for Zack. I'm very proud of my daughter. Very, very proud."

Tears coursed down Donna's face. Hearing the facts of her experience with hyperemesis and depression laid out in a courtroom was like ripping her insides out for all to see. Nearly five years ago, it had happened. Five years that felt like fifteen.

The lawyer on the other side hurled question after question at her mother, but each one gave her mother an opportunity to respond with facts. Facts like "About thirteen percent of pregnant women and new mothers experience depression. Like Donna, most never experience it again. Donna has absolutely no history of ever trying to harm her child, which is the only reason why an episode of depression would ever factor into a custody situation."

Donna's jaw dropped. Her mother had done research? *So* not Lorraine's style. But the opposing lawyer didn't seem to know that. He let her go as well, and as she moved down the aisle with her springy, graceful stride, she gave Donna an intimate smile.

That smile didn't erase the decade's worth of hurt lurking in Donna's heart. But the fact that she'd come here today and stood up for her . . . well, that did a lot.

She heard someone say the name "Mike Solo" and snapped back to attention. The judge was asking Ms. Gaynor a question.

"In the last proceeding, the existence of an engagement to the baseball player Mike Solo was brought up as something that would contribute to Ms. MacIntyre's fitness as a parent. Would you like to call him to the stand?"

Ms. Gaynor glanced over her shoulder at Mike, who sat right behind Donna. The lawyer nodded, as if confirming some sort of agreement, and rose to her feet. "No, Your Honor. This hearing is about Donna MacIntyre only. Mike Solo has a statement for the court, however. May I read it?"

The judge indicated her assent, and Ms. Gaynor read aloud from a piece of paper. "First, I'd like to say that I love Zack and want only the best for him. My testimony can't possibly be unbiased because I also love his mother. I hope to talk her into marrying me, but I'm not sure how that's going to go. I may have messed things up too much."

Whispers stirred the courtroom. Talk about juicy . . . this was going to be all over Kilby by tomorrow. Face heating, Donna kept her eyes fixed on the table in front of her, where a series of old coffee rings in the laminate looked like a drunken Olympics emblem.

The lawyer continued. "Donna doesn't need anyone else to make her a fit parent. She's already that, one hundred percent. If she does allow me back into her life, I vow that I will be the best stepfather I can be. You can ask Father Kowalski back at St. Mary Margaret in Chicago about my record with vows. Or any girl in Kilby, except for the one I intend to marry. Thank you for your time. Signed, Mike Solo of the San Diego Friars."

A ripple of laughter joined the gossipy whispers. Donna fought back a smile. Mike Solo and his vows.

The judge cleared her throat; she seemed to have trouble smothering a laugh as well. The big tattooed bailiff was staring at the ceiling, as if willing himself not to smile. "Well. Thank you for that, Mike Solo. Is there anyone else you'd like to bring to the stand, Ms. Gaynor?"

"I'd like to give Donna MacIntyre a chance to—"

The courtroom door opened and closed with a thump, followed by a whirlwind of whispers and shuffling feet. Donna craned her neck to see over the heads of all the taller people filling the courtroom. Finally a space cleared and there was Bonita.

With Zack.

Donna jumped to her feet, eyes glued to her little boy. Holding Bonita by the hand, he looked bewildered by the crowd of faces before him. On the opposite side of the aisle, Harvey also bolted to his feet.

Zack's face crumpled, but Bonita lifted him onto her hip. She looked as if she were posing for a glamorous-young-mother photo, with a high ponytail and a crisp tailored blouse. On her other shoulder hung a quilted diaper bag, which was ridiculous because Zack didn't need diapers anymore. He wore big boy underpants. She must have grabbed it as some sort of prop.

The judge was banging her gavel through the din. "Who are you, may I ask?"

"I'm Bonita *Wade* Castillo, and I'm engaged to Harvey Hannigan. Since I obviously have a very important role in Zack's life, I thought I ought to be here, not back home babysitting."

Zack started to cry. Bonita shushed him sharply and bounced him on her hip, which just made him sob all the more.

The judge glared at Bonita. "There's a reason why we don't allow minor children in the courtroom without special permission. A four-year old doesn't need to be exposed to the legal process, especially one that involves him. That's what the adults are here for."

"I don't see what the big deal is. I asked Judge Quinn and he said I should come on over. He's supposed to be in charge of this hearing anyway, isn't he?"

Judge Galindez's eyebrows drew together in a scowl. "I'm in charge of this hearing, and I will not allow it to be turned into a circus. Remove the child from the courtroom immediately."

Zack was screaming now, long, frightened sobs that ripped through Donna's heart. She'd strangle Bonita for this. How could she do this to Zack? Finally, she managed to elbow her way past the chairs to reach the end of her row.

"Mama!" Zack cried when he spotted her. "Mama, Mama, Mama!"

In her desperation to get to her son, she didn't see the foot sticking into the aisle. She tripped over it and went airborne for a brief moment. Then she landed splat in the middle of the aisle with a thud.

Cripes. So much for impressing the judge. She

didn't care anymore. All that mattered was getting to Zack. She scrambled to her knees.

Zack kicked his way out of Bonita's grasp, dropped to the floor like a monkey, and hurtled toward her. On her knees on the courtroom floor, she caught him in her arms, her scared, sobbing Zack. He surrounded her with the scent of peanut butter and exuberant boy, his arms tight around her, so tight, as if he never wanted to let go.

Chapter 28

THE SCENE IN the courtroom was utter chaos, but Mike loved every second of it. Bonita's ego had obviously gotten the better of her common sense. Maybe she thought bringing Zack would make her look motherly. If so, that had been a major error in judgment.

Red-faced and clearly furious, Judge Galindez ordered Bonita to remove Zack from the courtroom or be thrown in jail.

"That's outrageous!" Bonita shouted back, pulling out her cell phone. "Do you know who my second cousin once removed is? Did you hear my middle name?"

"No cell phones in my courtroom. Bailiff!"

The tattooed bailiff moved fast for such a big guy. He plucked the cell phone from Bonita's grasp as she kicked him in the shins.

"Don't you touch my cell phone!"

"Get her out of here!" The judge banged her gavel again. Harvey jumped to his feet and scrambled down the aisle to reach Bonita.

"What the hell are you doing?" The whole courtroom could hear his furious whisper.

"Stay out of this, Harvey," she hissed back.

"Are you kidding me? You pushed it too far, babe." With a disgusted shake of his head, Harvey picked her up bodily and handed her to the bailiff.

Mike had never seen a sweeter sight than Bonita being marched out of the room by an officer of the court.

Meanwhile, Zack was still clinging to Donna's neck like a howler monkey. "Judge, can I take him down to the cafeteria?" Donna asked, keeping her arms tight around him.

"You were about to take the witness stand," the judge reminded her.

"I know. But he's so upset." Donna dropped a kiss onto Zack's hair. "He needs me. I have a statement I'd like to make, but I have to take care of Zack first." She lifted her chin, as if preparing herself for the worst. "I'm sorry, Judge."

"We'll take a five minute rec—" the Judge began.

"That won't be necessary." Ms. Gaynor, the lawyer, rose to her feet. "We rest our case. Go, Donna, and take care of your little boy."

On her way down the aisle, Donna met Mike's eyes, her gaze clinging anxiously to his. A deep thrill sank through him that she'd turned to him, that she trusted him. He gave her a reassuring nod and a smile—*everything's going to be okay*.

And it was. He knew it. Could anything top the sight of Zack wrenching himself from Bonita's grasp and running to his mother? Or the image of Donna facing off with the Judge, putting Zack's wellbeing before anything else? Not likely. Even the memory of it made Mike grin. No way could the judge possibly rule against her.

In the end, the judge didn't even have to make the call. After Donna and Zack had slipped out of the courtroom, Harvey shocked everyone and announced that he would not dispute Donna's bid for custody, so long as he was allowed to see Zack at least once a week.

Ms. Gaynor instantly agreed to that on Donna's behalf, since Donna had never resisted Harvey's role in Zack's life. The judge banged her gavel one more time.

And that was how Donna missed the ruling that Mike knew she'd been hungering for since Zack's birth. "Donna MacIntyre is hereby awarded primary custody of Zackary Hannigan. She will work with Harvey Hannigan to formulate a suitable visitation schedule. Case closed."

The courtroom erupted with applause and cheers, as if a Broadway show had just come to a close. It had probably been one of the more entertaining spectacles the sleepy Kilby Courthouse had ever seen. Mike shook Ms. Gaynor's hand, then made his way down the aisle, exchanging hugs with everyone he came across—Mac, Lorraine, Sadie, Caleb.

Beth Gilbert got an especially big hug, one that lifted her off her feet.

"If you ever come to San Diego, be sure to call me ahead of time. Box seats, guaranteed." He extended the same offer to Mac, to the Hannigans, even to Harvey.

"Thanks, man. Listen, no hard feelings, right? I know things got a little out of hand for a while there," Harvey mumbled.

"No hard feelings." Mike shook Harvey's hand.

"If everything goes the way I want it to, I'll be in your life for a long time. So let's keep it cool."

"Cool. Solid. I'm down with that."

Mike clenched Harvey's hand tighter and leaned in close. "One thing. If you or Bonita ever do *anything* that might hurt Donna or Zack again, I will be on your ass like a freaking warrior, you got me?"

Harvey backed away. "Yeah, yeah, dude. Don't sweat it. Bonita and me are through, anyway."

"You are? Then why'd she show up here with Zack?"

"I mean, she doesn't know we're through yet, but we've been having some . . . uh . . . issues. I'm sure you'll hear about it, being a ballplayer." He shifted uncomfortably, shoving his hands in his back pockets. "Water under the bridge, man. Water under the bridge."

Out in the hallway, Caleb explained the mystery. "Sadie's mom got the lowdown. Harvey caught Bonita throwing herself at Trevor Stark at the Roadhouse."

"*What?*"

"Yup. She was there for a friend's bachelorette party. She had a few drinks and Trevor worked his magic, and abracadabra."

"Seriously? That dog."

"You know Stark. The girls go crazy for him, and he isn't one to say no. Anyway, the word is, she was all set to run off with him to major-league-land, but Trevor had her figured out pretty quick. Harvey was mad, but he was ready to take her back. Now it sounds like he's done. He doesn't seem like a bad guy, just . . . meh."

Meh. That about described Harvey. But from now on, Mike would try to think the best of the guy, since he was Zack's dad.

They found Donna in the cafeteria spreading peanut butter on pieces of banana for Zack. When Mike gave her the news, she burst into tears. They all stood around in a sort of awkward group hug, Sadie, Caleb, Mike, and Donna, with Zack staring up at them with a perplexed frown.

"Why Mama cry?"

Donna reached for him, swung him into her arms, and buried her face in his carroty hair. "Sometimes people cry when they're happy. I'm very, very happy right now. I'll explain it to you later. Right now, I feel like celebrating! What should we do, Zack-arillo? Go to the zoo? Feed the ducks? Play hide and seek?"

"Baseball!"

Laughing, Caleb and Mike gave each other high fives, while Sadie rolled her eyes. "They bribed you, didn't they, Zack?"

"Baseball it is," said Donna, grinning. "When's the next game, Mike?"

"There's an afternoon double-header against the Aces, right, Caleb?"

"Got me. All I know is I have to be back in San Diego by tomorrow. What better way to pass the time than at the ballpark? You like peanuts, peanut?" Caleb ruffled Zack's hair.

Zack scrunched up his face. "I'm not a peanut!"

"Well then, do you like Cracker Jack, Cracker Jack?"

"I'm not a Cracker Jack!"

"Do you like big plastic cups of foaming beer—"

Zack's little body convulsed with laughter, while Donna covered his ears. "All right, all right, this could go on for a while. We'll see you at the ballpark. I need to talk to Harvey and the Hannigans. Sadie, do you mind coming with me to hang out with Zack?"

"Love to." Sadie gave Caleb a long, passionate, verging on inappropriate-for-a-courthouse-cafeteria hug before joining them.

After Donna had taken a few steps she turned back and mouthed something to Mike.

It looked an awful lot like, *I love you, Solo.* In his imagination, he embellished that with *and I'll show you just how much the next time I get you alone.*

After the girls and Zack were gone, Caleb slung an arm around Mike's shoulder. "So. I've been meaning to ask you. Best man?"

"You're really doing it, huh?"

"This fall. My little brothers will be the groomsmen, but I want you for best man. You in?"

"Of course. But I might be calling on you first. Fall . . . that's a long time away. At our pace, Donna and I could get engaged and married three times before then."

Caleb chuckled, his steel-blue eyes alight with humor. "You two sure know how to keep things interesting. Are you a hundred-percent sure she wants to marry you? She might want to focus on her new career, you know. She's all over YouTube. I heard she's getting job offers from teams across the United States."

"*What?*"

"She's got that 'it' factor, you know? She walks on

stage . . . or on the field . . . and you can't take your eyes off her."

Sure, Caleb might be his best friend, but right now Mike wanted to punch him in his handsome face. He satisfied himself with a warning snarl.

"Or so I hear," Caleb added quickly. "Haven't seen her in action. I'm just saying, you might want to nail things down with her. A girl like her, funny, smart, tons of fun—"

"You know something, asshole? It's a damn good thing we're in a courthouse right now, or you'd be in serious trouble—"

Caleb grinned. "Dude. I'm one thousand percent in love with Sadie. I'm just saying, you better go get your girl."

Mike did his best to nail things down that very night. With Zack spending one last night at the Hannigans, he had Donna all to himself. Alone. In bed. Naked. At first, all she wanted to do was talk. She stretched her sweet body on top of his and propped her chin on her hands.

"So explain this to me. You told off Judge Quinn? Is he gay? You didn't threaten to out him, did you?"

"No way. No threats. I wouldn't do that. Joey always thought it was crass. I just talked to him. All he did was take back the ruling due to a technicality. Whatever his secret is, it's still safe."

"Okay, so he stepped down from the case, and then you called everyone?"

"Yup. I thought you should know that people love you and you're not alone. It's not always Donna against the world." He shaped the sleek curve of her ass with his hands. "Especially now that you're with me."

She peppered kisses along his jaw. "You're amazing. Why were you so nervous? Did you think I'd be mad?"

"Keep in mind, the last time I saw you, you threw me out of your apartment. And you didn't seem interested in anything I had to say. I didn't know how you'd react, but I had to try something."

Her eyelids flickered. "So . . . at my apartment . . . everything you said . . ."

"I know you were a little out of it, so let me say it again. I love you. I know I told you that I didn't want love. That was pretty much the stupidest moment in my life—and there have been many, let me tell you. I think I was already in love with you, I just didn't know what to do with it. I told myself I was helping you, and that we got along really well, and that I wanted to fuck your brains out. All true, by the way. But not really the point."

"So the whole engagement thing . . . was real?" Her forehead crinkled in a perplexed frown. "I mean, you actually did want to marry me?"

"Well . . . the funny thing is, I think I did. As soon as I saw you again, in that hellacious blue pantsuit, I didn't want to let you go."

She burst out laughing, her sweet breath stirring the hairs on his chest. "The blue pantsuit is what caught your eye?"

"*You* caught my eye. And my heart. And everything else. You're the only woman for me. To me, you're perfect, every part of you. I want you to marry me, Donna. Because I love you, not for any other reason. I want to make a family for Zack. I want us to be together our whole crazy lives."

Her eyes filled with tears. "You really do?"

"I *really* do."

"But . . . what about Angela?" she whispered.

"Angela . . . I don't want to say anything bad about her. She's a good person, but I'm not sure I ever really knew her. I was such a kid when I fell for her. I had a fantasy image of her, it was never real. Maybe I had to grow out of my childhood crush before I could fall in love for real. All good things take time, right?" He gave her a sleepy smile meant to evoke all kinds of time-consuming, sensual activities.

She blinked back her tears, eyes shining. Lifting her torso, she brushed the tips of her breasts against his chest. "How much time are we talking?"

"I have nowhere else to be." He greedily devoured the sight of her pink nipples swelling against the gentle abrasion of his furred chest. "Scratch that. I have to be in San Diego by tomorrow night. Damn it. My suspension's just about over. I wonder if I can start another brawl and get some more time off?"

"Don't even think about it." She cradled his rising cock between her thighs. "Your kidney and I don't want you taking risks like that."

"Honey, when you do that, I can't think about anything." He dropped his head back and groaned with pleasure as she stroked her soft inner thigh along his hardening length.

"I still can't get over everything you did. It's like you waved your magic wand and ta-da! All my problems are gone."

"No. It was you, Donna. I just gave an assist at

the end. But if you really want to talk about magic wands . . ." He thrust his hips up to push against the soft curls covering her sex.

"I definitely do," she purred, making her way down his body with a trail of kisses. "Or maybe there's something else I could do to your magic wand." And then her loving mouth was on him, tasting and savoring every inch of his cock. He twisted his fists into the sheets and gritted his teeth, not wanting to come too soon, to succumb to the incredible feeling of her lips and tongue.

"Wait. You said, 'I do,' Donna. I heard you. It's official, then. We're getting married."

She hummed something against his cock.

"Is that a yes?"

She looked up at him, her eyes full of mischief, and nodded, which had the effect of dragging her lips along his erection in the most maddening way. Trust Donna to do everything her own way. He had absolutely no problem with that, as long as they had things settled. With a huge, contented sigh, he lay back and surrendered to the pleasure.

She brought her hands into the act, feathering light touches along his balls, fisting the base of his cock while her mouth took even more of him inside. *Oh God.*

"Donna, I'm warning you . . ." he ground out. She just smiled and merrily continued with her sensual torture project. Pleasure thundered through his veins, pressure building at the base of his spine. He'd never get enough of Donna. He wanted to do everything to her, over and over again, and then come up with some new things.

Finally he'd had enough. When he was about to burst, he hauled himself into a sitting position and lifted her bodily off him. "I need to be inside you, Donna. I'm begging you."

"Well, if you put it that way. A girl does like to be begged." She grinned as he planted her on to his lap. She spread her knees apart to reveal her sex, open and waiting. With a sense of reverence, he touched her gently, loving how wet her tissues felt, how soft and welcoming. His wisecracking girl had such a soft heart, and it drove everything she did. *She leads with her heart*, he thought. *No wonder she sometimes stumbles into trouble.*

But that was okay. Sometimes you had to make a little trouble if you wanted things to get better. And besides, he'd always be there to make sure the trouble didn't get too bad.

He slipped inside her, his penis finding its way to her core. She sighed, her lips curving happily, her eyes hazing over, gleaming gold. Her clinging, velvety flesh sent stars dancing through his head and he made it official with a silent vow to himself. Him, Donna . . . and trouble. Together through thick and thin.

Chapter 29

OVER THE NEXT few days, Donna sometimes wondered if she'd stumbled into some kind of psychedelic version of her own life, in which everything was painted in neon-bright colors and giant flowers towered over her head. It really was as if Mike Solo had waved his magic wand and made everything better.

Mike flew to San Diego, but not before buying her a plane ticket to come visit. The knowledge that she'd see him again in about a week made everything sparkle, like a field of bluebonnets fresh-washed by a morning rain shower.

She and Harvey met at their old haunt, the glamorous Denny's, to work out the details with respect to Zack.

"Sorry about Bonita," she told him as he slid into the booth. "I mean, you know, I'm sorry if you're hurting." Fine, so she wasn't the most forgiving person on the planet. She could work on that.

He shrugged. "It is what it is. By the end, my parents and me were both tired of her drama. She's already moved on. Says she's going to try to get that baseball player back. If you see him, you might want to warn him."

"Honestly, Trevor Stark can take care of himself. So can Bonita. Are you okay?"

"Yeah, I'm good."

She took a fortifying sip of water. "So. About Zack."

"Wait. I want to say something first. I was going to say it in court but I got a little rattled by all the hoopla."

She pulled her lower lip between her teeth. *Crap.* Was Harvey going to back out of the arrangement? Now that he'd broken up with Bonita, was he going to want to see Zack more?

"I wanted to say this. You are a really, really good mom to Zack. If we were still together, I'd say we should have more kids."

"*Excuse me?*" Was Harvey suggesting they get back together?

"No, no. I didn't mean it like that. I mean, we're not together. So we're not going to have more kids. I get that."

"Good. Because I'm back with Mike Solo, and we're planning to get married. I mean, actually do it this time."

He nodded a few times; she noticed that his hair was already growing out of its hipster cut. "Groovy. That's good. Zack likes Mike. He'll be good. You should have more kids, but with him."

Donna couldn't hold back a smile. A bunch of curly-headed, mischievous kids with Mike—yes, absolutely, without a doubt, she wanted that. The more the merrier. "We're thinking about it."

He rumpled his hair with a swipe of his hand. "The point is, you shouldn't doubt yourself. You're a good mother. Since I'm the dad, I got a front row seat, so you can believe me. Okay?"

A rush of warmth made Donna impulsively touch his hand. "That's pretty sweet of you, Harvey. It really is. Thank you. You're a pretty good dad too, you know."

He certainly could be worse.

Harvey nodded, frowning as though deep in thought. "I guess we're doing okay for two kids in way over their heads."

She smiled at him. "I guess so."

They settled down to business then, and by the time Donna left they had a rough agreement on sharing Zack, and the cute waitress had given Harvey her phone number.

Yeah, Harvey was going to be just fine.

Before she left for San Diego, Donna had more people to see. Her mother had a gig in New York, so Donna drove her to the airport. "Are you really sure you want to stick around in this backwater town?" Lorraine asked as she stood in the security line, her huge, woven travel tote bag slung over her shoulder. "You have real talent, Donna. I saw that YouTube video."

"If you think aiming a hose at some ballplayers takes talent . . ."

"No, no. It's the thinking on your feet, performing to a crowd. It's a real knack, Donna. I could introduce you to some people in show business. It might take a while to find your niche, but you're young and cute."

"No thanks. I'm happy where I am."

"In *Kilby, Texas*?"

"I'm not like you, Mom." Maybe in some respects she was, but not in the most important one. "I need to be here. With Zack. Besides, someone has to keep those Wades in line. And Crush Taylor needs me. He wants to hire me full-time and give me health benefits. Most of the games are at night, so I can be with Zack during the day. Harvey said he'd watch him during some games, and Mrs. Hannigan said the same thing. Crush mentioned possible onsite day care as well. "

Her mother smoothed her bright red hair—its color so close to Donna's—and glanced around the terminal. Already anxious to be gone, Donna realized. "Well, as long as you're happy."

"I'm happier than I ever, ever thought I'd be."

"Invite me to the wedding?"

"God, of course!"

Her father had news too. He and Carrie were going into counseling. Carrie had been furious that he hadn't brought her to the hearing, and had temporarily moved out.

"I'm sorry, Dad."

"Nah. Long time coming." With a wire brush, he scrubbed corrosion out of a valve of some kind. "Things have been sketchy from the start. Didn't help that I hid under a car for about ten years."

"Dad! Was that a joke?"

He shrugged, lifting one eyebrow, and handed her the newly gleaming valve. "Can you put that over there on the bench?"

The scent of motor oil and metal, so nostalgic, accompanied her to the spot he indicated. When she was little, she'd spent a lot of time in this garage with her dad. Maybe she should bring Zack here. She'd never done that, not once. "Dad, would you want to show Zack around the shop sometime? He's a big fan of monkeys, so why not grease monkeys?"

A broad smile creased his face. "Not a bad idea. I'll have to make sure he doesn't swallow a sprocket or something, the way you did when you were his age."

"God, I'd forgotten about that. I always was a bucket of trouble, wasn't I?"

"Nah. You were a bucket of fun. Don't you forget it."

Zack transitioned easily to life in Donna's little apartment, although he had to sleep in her bed with her for the first week. As it turned out, he found the trucks coming and going from the sewage plant almost as fascinating as tigers and gorillas. He stayed glued to the window, counting the parade of vehicles, for hours. Better than TV, apparently. No sooner had he adapted to her place than Mike called with the news that he'd put in a bid on a house.

"*What?*"

"Crush told me about it, and he said I'd better jump before someone beats us to it. It's a big house, right by the river, just down the street from the Gilberts."

"*Seriously?*"

"Can you go check it out? See if it's really what we want? I thought it would be good for Zack, lots of room to run around. It's a nice neighborhood, safe, well, except for the Shark. You don't mind being near the Shark, do you?"

"Of course not! Oh my God, Mike, this is amazing."

"Go see it and call me back. My Realtor said he'd find a way for us to back out if we wanted to."

Donna bundled Zack into her Kia and drove to her old neighborhood. Passing the Gilberts', she caught sight of the little guesthouse where she'd tried to study her way into motherhood. With a little perspective, she had a different take on it. The Shark and Zack had been her best teachers all along. Zack and her own gut instincts. And maybe a few helpful chapters in a couple of books.

The house was perfect. Smaller than the Gilberts', thankfully. The sort of house that might star in a fairy tale, with a gabled roof and a wide terrace leading onto a backyard full of slopes and dips and secret hiding places. Her hands shaking, she called Mike back.

"I love it. Zack loves it. Can we get it? Is it too expensive?"

"Nah. We can handle it. You're going to be a superstar, remember?"

"Right. I keep forgetting. No wait, that's you. Don't you have a game?"

"Yep. Gotta go. Caleb's pitching tonight and we need to talk strategy. You'll be watching?"

"Of course. Well, *I'll* be watching. Zack might be counting garbage trucks."

"I love you, Red."

"I love you too, Solo. I'll see you in two days." She hung up and checked on Zack in the backseat. He was leaning all the way forward, his face pressed to the window.

"Tiger, Mama! Tiger!"

A giant cat with tiger stripes was sauntering past

the "For Sale" sign. It stopped, as if it owned the house and maybe the sidewalk and all the cars too, and licked its right paw.

Zack was absolutely beside himself with excitement. So they were moving into a tiger's territory. Definitely a good sign.

The Hannigans offered to watch Zack while she flew to San Diego two days later. Reuniting with Mike in the inner tunnel of the huge, intimidating Friar Stadium was possibly the most rapturous moment she'd ever experienced. His arms came around her with so much passion and absolute dedication that whatever stray worries she might have had—handsome ball-player alone in the big city—vanished.

"God, I missed you," he groaned. "I can't believe I have a stupid-ass game to play. Why can't we just skip the Cardinals and go straight to my hotel and screw our brains out?"

She laughed against his chest, starbursts of happiness exploding like fireworks in her heart. "Do you need me to hose you down?"

"You know it, baby. Hey, do you want to watch the game in the players' box with the other wives?"

"The *other wives*? I'm not a wife."

"You damn well will be." He dug in the back pocket of his baseball pants, which looked so tight it seemed impossible that anything could fit back there. The ring, when he finally presented it, winked at her with sassy, diamond-studded attitude. *I'm here, I'm gorgeous, get used to me*, it seemed to say.

"Put that on, wife," he growled at her. "Or I'll have to tie you up and put it on for you."

She slipped it on, since when Mike went into commando mode, she'd do anything he said. And because the ring was dazzling. And because she loved him and couldn't wait to marry him. "I get it, Solo. You hit the major leagues and think you can boss me around. Don't forget who wields the hose in this relationship."

He crowded her against the wall. "Wield my hose, baby. I dare you."

Desire flared between them in a sweet, white-hot flash.

"Hey!" A laughing male voice interrupted them. Donna peeked around Mike's torso to see a group of spectacularly fit ballplayers striding past. "Rookie. Get a room."

"Or a broom closet. Something," added another.

"What the Jeter are they thinking?" muttered a third.

No one understood why Mike and Donna burst out laughing. Then again, they had a habit of doing that and absolutely no intention of stopping anytime soon.